U N C H A I N
My Heart
(BASED ON A TRUE STORY...)

L I S A   M O U H I B I A N

For: Jerry West

UNCHAIN

My Heart

Lisa Mashibian

This novel is based on the true story of Bobby Sharp [songwriter for: Ray Charles, Sarah Vaughan, Sammy Davis, Jr., Quincy Jones (producer) and others] and Natasha Miller (a jazz singer).

I want to thank both Bobby and Natasha for their wonderful spirits and for sharing their compelling stories. I hope that their lives, loves and experiences will move and inspire you as well.

CONTENTS

FOREWORD

On July 5, 1961 Ray Charles, his original "little band" and The Raelettes walked into Bell Sound Studios in New York and recorded four songs in one session. Those songs were, "Hit The Road Jack," "The Danger Zone," "But On The Other Hand Baby" and "Unchain My Heart." That is what recording artists and musicians did back in 1961. They called it "Wednesday."

What was interesting about that particular recording session (besides the fact that two of the songs were #1 Billboard Hits and a third was a Top Ten Hit), was that all but one of these songs was published by Ray's own music publishing company, Tangerine Music Corporation. Ray had recently entered into a contractual arrangement with the legendary songwriter Percy Mayfield and this July session was supposed to be all about Percy's songs.

That was true until Ray heard the lyrics to "Unchain My Heart." There was no way that Ray Charles was going to let that song be recorded by somebody else. In many ways "Unchain My Heart" was the story of Ray's life. Ray lived it.

You are holding in your hands the incredible story of the man who wrote the song "Unchain My Heart," Bobby Sharp. Bobby lived it.

The parallels that existed in the life stories of these two men are more than coincidental. The music, the women, the drug use, the accompanying legal problems, it was all there for both of them. If you were in the music business back in the 1950's, this was the world you lived in.

This book will take you through a time period that was paramount to the history of American music. It will also take you through locales like Tin Pan Alley, Destiny Recording Studios, and Harlem. You'll hear names like Joe Cocker, Dick Clark, Sarah Vaughan, Ruth Brown, and Mr. Sammy Davis, Jr.

You will read about the music industry putting out some of its finest records at a time when its business practices were at their worst. The exploitation that occurred in show business was at an all-time high during the 1950's and '60's. Lawyers were only available to the very rich; everybody else was on their own.

And yet, when you reach the last page, you'll probably realize, like I did, that this is not a story about music nor is it a songwriter's story.

This is a story about men, women, husbands, wives, brothers, sisters, mothers, fathers, daughters, and sons. It is a story about family and friends and how you are never alone if you have them. In short, it is a story about life and about how life is not a burden…if you live it.

The life of Bobby Sharp was filled with joy, sadness, anger, love, frustration and all of the other things that fill up all of our lives. I found that it was how Bobby dealt with all of those things that made his journey such a fascinating story.

— Tony Gumina
President, Ray Charles Marketing Group

Put down your head, boy and pray for forgiveness. Your soul lays a gentle sigh upon the pavement. Pumping out its anger. Bleeding for its pain. Put down your head, boy and pray for hunger. For pain. For love. For *life*. For that is what you have been given. And that is what you will receive. Now, in your older years.

PROLOGUE

S HE DIED STANDING UP THAT DAY. The pools of light like blood around her feet. Illuminating the edges. The crowd a dull roar in her ears. A thud to the brain. Her heart beating out the last bits of her tattered past.

She closed her eyes. She opened them again. She looked out from her perch on the stage. A small figure. Dark brown hair cascading down her back. Pale skin reflecting the strobe that surrounded her. She looked to her left. Her knees still weak and slightly wobbly. And there he sat, behind his piano. The light reflecting amber against his dark skin. Gray curls neatly combed upon his head. Slight smile on his lips. Peace. Reassurance. He winks at her. A wink only the two of them can see. And with that wink he pushes her on – and she steps forward, towards the crowd. She leans into them and moves the microphone she has been holding towards her lips and places them gently over it, almost touching it. She opens her eyes. And begins to sing.

A soft, gentle note fills the crowded arena. Softer at first and then growing louder; fuller, filling the arena with that one note, filling it and feeding it. The Arena is silent. As if all are afraid to take a breath; afraid to break the spell of that single note, which hangs on the air and then cascades down upon them. Unintentionally they are roaring and clapping. The silence is broken. The song has begun.

PART I – *Natasha*

So...windswept world — you lay before me now — in all your sturdy glory. And I kneel before you. Once again... Humbly....

CHAPTER ONE

ALAMEDA, CALIFORNIA – *December 24, 2003*

S OMEBODY ONCE SAID that she was a loner. She did not think so. She was only a soul, alone on this planet – unable to trust another.

Others' company was something she "endured" most times. A triteness of conversation that she abhorred. Small minds – always chattering away their thoughts.

But she endured. Because she had to.

It was part of her "job." Part of life. Really.

She shook her head back to reality and continued to pour the coffee into Sy's half empty cup. Black and steamy. Well, no, not black, really.... Actually a muddy gray – you could almost see to the bottom of the cup.

Let's not romanticize this, she thought wryly to herself. She always hated the coffee here. She liked a strong coffee. Something dark and definite. Not this watered down shit they passed off as coffee here at the diner. She had tried making her version a few times – tripling up the amount of coffee and reducing the water by half. She had tasted it – *mmmm...good, dark* – could have been better if she had a better grade of coffee, but it would do.

"Cowboy Coffee," her mother called it when she would make it for them both when she was just ten. "You have a little of your father in you. He *luuuvs* Cowboy Coffee – dark and black with no suga."

Her mother always said sugar that way: *suga* – as if there was no "r". But, no, her customers had not liked it. They complained that it was "too strong."

"Gonna burn my taste buds off with that stuff!" the old geezer spat, smiling at her through his missing front tooth. Sylo gave her a hard time

5

but he loved her...lit up when she walked in the room. *Ah, twenty years ago I would have given her a run for her money,* he thought often to himself. He even said it out loud every now and then.

"Twenty years ago I would have given you a run for your money, missy," wide missing tooth smile spread across his face, blue eyes sparkling. White stubble disappearing beneath the deep cracks of his face; revealing only patches of the coarse, unshaven mass.

*Well, twenty years ago you would have been sixty-five — so I doubt I would have looked twice...*Tasha thought to herself. But she shot him her brightest, wan, half-smile. "You go, Sy.... You're really something, you know?"

Sylo winked, his best wink, the one he had honed over the years. Click-clacked his tongue against the roof of his mouth; threw down his dollar-fifty with flair. Seventy-five cents for the coffee; seventy-five cents for Tasha. (He usually left only a dollar, but today he wished to show his grandiose and manly prowess.) Pulled his hunting cap down low on his forehead and sauntered out of Jake's Coffee Shop & Diner in Alameda, California.

Natasha watched him leave as she wiped the gray-flecked linoleum countertop with long slow strokes. She removed his pie plate and empty coffee cup. *That's okay, Sy, pie's on the house,* she thought as the screen door slammed behind him.

———

The rain landed on the pavement. Wet and wild. Her hair was wet and her clothes were soaked. She stood on the corner — folded newspaper over her drenched hair. Tasha blinked. She blinked again. Small drops flicking from her lashes. She pushed her tongue out and felt the wet drops splash upon it. Splash and disappear — into the folds of her mouth.

She felt the rain on her skin. Raised bumps on her arms; cotton, button-up shirt clinging to her breasts.

Yes, she was wet.

It was Christmas Eve.

Fontana waited at home for her with Brett. The ever-steady Brett. The tree was decorated. They had done that last night. Fontana had strung lights and garland around the edges of her wooden bunk bed. Natasha had attached an extension cord and helped her to plug it in. Fontana liked sleeping between the twinkling lights. "Like stars," she had said dreamily as she closed her eyes last night.

Brett, of course, was worried about Fontana sleeping with all that naked electricity. (Well, he had said: "...sleeping within a possibly charged electrical volt...") Tasha preferred the term *naked electricity*.

And she felt naked standing here on this corner, waiting for her bus. Naked because she was wet, and she knew if she took off her coat and let the rain soak through her blouse, it would be slightly see-through. That the outlines of her body would be clear to each car that passed; to each individual passenger on the bus when it came to a stop. She stuck her tongue out again and felt the rain drops land, then disappear. *Melt* on her tongue. The taste of the rain, sweet and reminiscent of summer.

There was one small package under the tree. A gift from Natasha to Fontana. Fontana had been begging for it since summer. Since her birthday in June. When Tasha had firmly said "No." Yes, she had firmly said: "No, we *cannot* have a puppy." And although she had tried her sternest tone and demeanor, something she hated to do, but felt was "necessary" she hadn't really meant it. No, not really. She had known it at that moment, when the words had left her lips; she had known it as she watched Fontana's face fall; and she had known it while at the pet store a few days later, while putting the deposit down on the full bred Chihuahua. It had taken her six months to pay off the not-yet-born puppy she had purchased.

A stupid buy given their current financial situation. But, hey — she'd had a dog growing up. The wire-haired fox terrier named Grigin she'd had as a kid. The small little dog her mother had beaten after it barked too much; then left out in the heat where it died of a heart attack. The dog she and her brothers had given all of their love and attention to. The dog that for a moment had made her feel so safe. They'd had another dog after that — a Pit Bull Terrier named Mad. He'd passed away naturally as far as she remembered. Not so attached to dogs after that. Didn't particularly love dogs at all....

7

A hard round drop of icy water landed on her forehead and her thoughts moved sharply back to Fontana. Her own life. *But this puppy will be good for Fontana.* Head thrown back once again; ink sky muted by gray clouds; no stars peeking through. *Give her somewhere to put her affections.*

So, wrapped in a small box was a certificate telling Fontana she had the dog of her dreams. An actual puppy with its head poking out of her stocking, hanging on the mantel above a roaring fire would have been ideal. But since they had neither a mantel, nor a roaring fire and since the puppy had not yet been born, Fontana was going to have to make do with a certificate.

"Make do?" Tasha hated it when she used her mother's phrases.

She made a mental note to discontinue this.

———

Bobby Sharp sat in the one easy chair in his living room. A small twig-type tree was strung carefully with tiny multicolored lights; lights which twinkled and reflected off the legs of his worn, black Wurlitzer piano. It was 9:00 p.m. and already his eyes were feeling heavy. The TV was on – the volume muted. He liked to watch the shows without sound – to add the dialogue himself – in his own head fill in the blanks, with his *own* imagination. Christmas shows were on this Christmas Eve, of course. His friend, Albert Hutchins, had invited him over to his house, to have Christmas Eve dinner with he and his family. Albert's daughter, Melba and his son-in-law were coming over with their two kids. A boy and a girl: ages five and seven.

"Family will be good for you! You can't stay home alone on Christmas Eve," Albert had said earlier that afternoon when he stopped by to drop off Bobby's presents.

But Bobby had preferred to be alone. And he was at an age where he found children and loud, unexpected noises slightly irritating. 79. 79 years of life already.

Christmas and New Years to him were a time of reflection. A time to muse about his past. He preferred to be by himself to do this.

PART I – NATASHA

A few opened gifts lay around the chair he sat in. One, a tie from Albert, the other a sweater from Melba. They both had taken it upon themselves to help Bobby to expand his style of dress. *But,* Bobby mused silently to himself, *that would never happen.* He liked his jeans. He liked his short-sleeve plaid shirts. He had many of them. Each one the same, as it should be.

Tomorrow, as he did every Christmas day, he would make a trip down to the Homeless Shelter, opened gifts in hand, and give the tie and the sweater to some deserving gentlemen down there. His golden brown eyes twinkled at that thought. He loved to give. There was a simple joy in it. He would take other gifts as well, small things he had picked up throughout the year: A silver hairbrush set; a shaving kit; a brand new pair of blue wool socks; a red knit cap and a box of cookies shaped liked trees and stars and decorated with green, red and yellow glittery sprinkles. None of his gifts were wrapped. He would put them all in a large brown grocery bag, and once arrived, take out his gifts – including the sweater and tie and hand them out to the deserving. The cast changed every year. He almost never saw the same face twice. And not one of the residents ever knew his name.

He handed his gifts out silently. With a smile and glint in his eye. A nod that said: "Yes, I know…there is no need for words. Just take. And enjoy the moment this gift will give you, for these *moments* are all we have."

Then he would turn, nod silently to the attendant sitting at the front desk, get into his Cadillac Seville and drive back to the small, unobtrusive apartment in the neatly lined nondescript neighborhood he had lived in for the last thirty years.

For the last fifteen years, this had been his Christmas. This had been enough.

This had been all he needed.

He closed his eyes – he drifted off to sleep – the TV blaring to the background of his dreams:

Cold: snowy night; radio blares to the blast of snow against his windshield… song seeps in through tinny speakers…

9

UNCHAIN MY HEART

He leans in; his hand shakes; his cheeks are hollow; cold seeping into him; fingers ragged. He turns the radio up. It blares louder. The DJ's voice over the song. "Our new number one by Ray Charles...."

Bobby coughs.... He pulls his coat collar up over his ears. Wind seeps through the cab; he can see his breath. The snow a white glow beneath the cab — shining through the hole in the floor — right near his foot. He puts the car in gear. He slowly depresses the gas...Cold...cold...too cold....

CHAPTER TWO

NATASHA RAN UP the outdoor flight of stairs to her apartment. She hurriedly put her key in the door, wiggled it, dropped it, picked it up — began to turn the lock — but the doorknob moved on its own, and there is Brett, tall and steady as ever, smiling — smiling with his mouth, eyes questioning, searching...*accusing?* She shakes if off, kisses him on the cheek.

"Hi!" she says breezily. Face reminding, reminding her, of last night... his thumb at the nape of her neck, pressing down so gently, moving slowly along the line of her spine. Slight sweat forming in the hollow of her lower back.

Warm, firm hands down the length of her body. Slight chill; despite her warmth.

Warm body against her. Aching sensation. Union. One.

All these thoughts despite her extreme exhaustion, and she pushes them far to the back of her mind; letting her breast brush against him lightly as she moves into the living room.

She was late, obviously. She should have called. But didn't. Sy had lingered over his coffee and pie. Chatting and chatting with her — regaling her with tales of his youth and fishing prowess. The Christmas's he used to spend with his wife; his unmatched generosity. He had once bought his wife a rabbit fur coat, "Can you 'magine that? An entire coat made from identical rabbits...." Sylo had sniffed from over his pie, steaming mug of coffee in hand.

Sylo had told her how he was planning to buy his wife the matching white rabbit hat, but she had up and died on him.

"Can you 'magine that? She just up and died one morning while making my breakfast. Her back was to me, she had just poured the coffee into my favorite mug – you know the one I told you about with the blue antlers on it – poured the coffee, put in a teaspoon of sugar just the way I like and began to stir, and then, just like that," he grabbed his chest emphatically to make his point, "she grabbed her chest and then her left arm, took a deep choking gasp…" Sylo set down his coffee cup and grabbed his throat to force a choke for added emphasis, "grabbed the edge of the counter and fell to the floor. I watched it all in slow-mo; I watched her go down… nothin' I could do 'bout it."

He went on and on, repeating every single minute detail to her. She didn't have the heart to ask him to stop; to tell him it was Christmas Eve, and her daughter waited (very impatiently Tasha was sure) for her at home. Sy's eyes were hazy and red with memory – his look far away – into the past of a different life. So, she'd let him go on, and instead of leaving at 8:00 p.m., as she usually did, she did not get out of Jake's Diner until 8:45 – missing her designated 8:05 bus and thus, being forced to stand in the rain and wait for the 9:05 bus.

She could have waited inside. But something in the rain that evening enticed her. It was cold. Yes. And wet – obviously. But her tongue ached for sensation. Her breasts ached for sensation. Her body wished for…feeling…of any kind. Even the wet, cold variety.

So she had stood in the rain for twenty minutes. She had taken off her coat and let the rain soak through her blouse. She had secretly wished that a car would pass and see her standing there with her partially see-through blouse and wet hair, with her hands stretched out wide and her head back to catch the rain. But no one passed. It was desolate. And she knew, that in reality, if a car had passed she would have quickly pulled on the coat that she had let drop halfway down her arms, almost to the ground; she would have stood up straight, and pretended she was not doing anything unusual.

She felt guilty when she finally made it home at 9:30 and Brett opened the door with that hungry look in his eyes. Had she subconsciously let Sy ramble on because she wanted a justifiable excuse to have those few, precious moments to herself? That twenty minutes in the rain with no inhibitions?

She tried to relay all this to Brett with a glance, but he ignored her, had turned away, was moving towards Fontana and then turned back toward her and smiled, gesturing with a slight nod of his head towards her daughter –

Who lay, curled up in the overstuffed green, flowered armchair in front of the faux fireplace wall unit Natasha had bought at Home Depot, hugging an old and worn large off-white (it used to be white, but age and wear had yellowed its fur) stuffed bear that she had not had in her arms in four years.

Okay, Natasha thought, *I feel guilty!* She sighed, the sight of her daughter melting her heart as always and went to Fontana and slipped her arms beneath her, cuddling her now gangly form. The warm smell of her sleep eliciting memories of the baby and then small child she once was. It was her cue.

Fontana awoke. "Hi mom…" she said, identical "Tasha" half-smile in place. They peered at each other through different shades of brown eyes – Natasha's soulful and brown as mud and Fontana's light brown with amber flecks to the center sparking back.

"I love you Mom," Fontana said. "I love you too, honey," Tasha replied.

Brett sat on the armchair that Fontana had been sleeping on only an hour ago. "She really *missed* you, tonight, you know." The words trailed after him. Tasha stared back. Silent. Muting her memory.

She tried to say; *wanted* to say: *I know, I know. I was standing in the rain. I let it drench my hair. I threw my coat back. I was free. And crazy. For a moment.*

Can you see?

Do you understand?

But instead she said: "Yes, I *know* I was *late*. You don't have to point it out to *me*." Frustration welling from her chest, she knew it wasn't his fault but her anger was directed at him. She stared at him; waiting. Trying to squelch the swirling pain — was it pain? — or panic? — or both? — The swirling energy she felt beginning in the pit of her stomach — beneath her heart. She felt the fire rise beneath her large brown irises. She pushed it down — deep down into her gut. She pulled herself into — *herself*. A firm fixed motion of containment. She turned back to him and made a conscious attempt to soften her eyes — to remove the fire and let the mute brown settle back in. She looked at Brett. She softened.

"Honey, I know you mean well, but *I am very aware* of when I am late." She quickly put the vision of the rain on her tongue; her body wet and her coat thrown back to the night and the passing cars — out of her head.

Brett stood up from the chair and moved toward her. He reached tentatively for her shoulder. A gesture of comfort. She moved her shoulder away from him, a slight movement that was meant to wound. She took another deep breath, and pulled her calm intelligence around her. She felt his stare, could see his hurt, a quiet unimagined hurt and she felt her body relax a bit. She tried to be light; funny, "Well, at least I'm not off in a bar drinking it up with the guys having a great time and shirking all responsibility...I'm a waitress for God's sake..." She winced internally at this statement.

He looked at her; he could see how tired she was — seemed to be a little more tired than usual. She *did* push herself, hard. And it worried him at times. He wished she'd slow down a bit — not try so hard for everything — be able to settle for the *small* things in life, as he could. But it was his love and belief in her that had compelled him to finance her first little CD; to encourage her to do jazz standards....

She stared back at him, answering silently with her eyes as well.... Yes, they had had that conversation before — many times. About her impatience to perform. Her frustration at having to wait — to do something she hated in order to do something she loved.... The Abyss would always sink in at that thought; the Abyss that sucked her down and said: "You might get *stuck* here. You may be a waitress for the rest of your life." Then the panic would come. The panic that both paralyzed her and pushed her on.

Then calmness. She knew she owed him an explanation. "Listen, honey..." she began, "Sy was there, alone. On Christmas Eve. He was talking about his wife — the one he lost five years ago — remember I told you about that?" She let the silent baring of herself lay between them, let the gravity of the situation sink in.

"Well, he wouldn't stop...telling me all the details of her death. It was sad...I couldn't interrupt him to tell him I had to leave. I felt *bad* for him. I let him talk. It was my Christmas gift to him." The silence drifted down over both of them. Brett moved toward her and wrapped his strong arms around her small shoulders. She let his warmth wash over her, breathed in the smell of his musky cologne. Leaned back against him; leaned *into* him.

Why did any of this even matter at this point? She loved him. It was Christmas Eve. They had presents to exchange. Sex to have. Eggnog to drink and a very early morning tomorrow with Fontana – who would undoubtedly be up at 6:00 a.m. in her excitement to find out what her present was.

Oh God, I hope she's not disappointed with the Certificate, Tasha found herself thinking again. *Stop! You paid for six months on that! She better not be disappointed! I've got to stop having these internal conversations with myself....*

She had noticed that Fontana had placed a medium-sized, nicely wrapped box under the tree for her. She smiled to herself. No doubt Brett had helped Fontana wrap it earlier this evening. She put her arms around his neck and kissed him slowly on the mouth. How could she stay mad at him? What was the point?

———

She opened her eyes, the press of a small face against hers. Nose to nose, Fontana was peering intently into her eyes. Squishing her own eyes together – shutting them tight – then opening them wide. Tasha knew what she was doing, straddled above her like that; she probably had been doing it for five or ten minutes, Tasha guessed. She was "squish-blurring," something the two of them used to do when Fontana was younger; it started at about age five.

Nose to nose they would come close to each other, so close that the image of the other would blur – then they would close eyes at the same time and say "open!" – open them quickly and laugh to discover the face

15

that would appear. The other's face would always change shape. "Like a clown!" Fontana would say, wide missing-tooth grin covering her face, "You look like a clown, Mommy!" They would squish their eyes together, over and over, remaking each other's faces and laughing – nose to nose – connected.

Fontana, now, at nine years old had decided to do this again. It had been a long time – a year maybe, since she had wanted to do something so "childish." (Fontana's word, not Natasha's.)

Silly girl...Tasha thought to herself and rolled over to grab Fontana and bring her back to her; to hug her while she still could, while she still had the opportunity – well really, while she was "given" the opportunity by the Queen, herself.

"Come here Queen Bee..." Tasha said, laughing; and then quietly, the purr in her voice evident: "You come here little one."

That got a glance. A reprimanding glance that said: *Little one? Little One? I played our childish game and you call me Little One???? See if I do that again....*

But by that time Tasha had caught her and was tickling her and they were both laughing and Fontana had dropped her defenses and Tasha forgot about her money problems for a moment – and her dreams of Stardom – and they just *were*. A single moment of mother/daughter unity – each one letting down her defenses. Brett groaned and rolled over. Tasha pulled back. Fontana jumped up and off the bed reflexively. She ran out of the room and yelled to her mother.

"*C'mon Mom*. It's Christmas morning – let's open our presents. *I* got something for *you* that you are *really* going to like. Brett helped me wrap it." This would be her one and only reference to Brett all day. It was a gratuitous reference. A recognition Fontana gave as her Christmas gift to him. She was feeling generous. So she did it. She acknowledged his presence.

Brett and Tasha exchanged a look, and simultaneously rolled out of bed, one off each side; each grabbing and throwing on the nearest available piece of outer clothing. For Tasha, a robe, that had been thrown on the back of the cherry Sack-back Windsor armchair that used to be her grandmother's and now sat next to her bed – meant to be a decorative antique, but in actuality was a clothes holder; and Brett grabbing the sweats he dropped to the floor last night before making love to Tasha.

He pulled them up and over his now hardening erection and remembered...remembered...Tasha – irresistible.... How could he tame her? It was that wild quality that attracted him – drove him crazy and it was the same wild quality he wanted to *tame*. Yes, he wanted to *domesticate* her. Bring her under his control. *Care* for her. But always illusive, she was just beyond his grasp. He had time, he could see – soon – soon – he knew.

Pulling his sweatshirt over his muscled chest, he headed out the bedroom door, through the living room where Tasha and Fontana were already sitting on the ground under the tree and Fontana, with sweaty, sleep-marked hands was eagerly handing Tasha her gift. Brett headed into the kitchen to make the much-needed coffee for him, and thick hot chocolate for Tasha. A treat he knew she indulged in the morning after a show or on any special occasion.

Tasha brushed back a wisp of brown hair that had fallen over her eye and pulled up the edge of the robe that had slipped off of her shoulder, unconscious of him as he passed, totally focused on Fontana. But these gestures, he felt, were secretly for him. Telling him, subtly that she lived only for him. That nights like the one they had spent last night – were *what kept her going*. That his sex, what he had to give her was what drove her on. That he was *feeding* her. He shook his head and passed through the kitchen door and away from sight of Tasha and Fontana.

Natasha never even noticed he had passed – Had actually kind of forgotten about him in her absorption of Fontana. She carefully untied the blue satin ribbon surrounding the box that Fontana had handed her. "Blue ribbon, so you can wear it in your hair too," Fontana explained knowingly. "Who wants to wear red ribbon in their hair? Red ribbon is too bright."

Always the practical one...Tasha thought as she smiled warmly and moved to tie the blue ribbon around her hair in a nice bow on the top – just to be silly.

"No, not like that, *Mom*. Around your ponytail – like you do for work!"

Is this how she sees me? A waitress who pulls her hair into a ponytail for work? What about a beaded gown...For my performances? What about equating me with the singer that I am? How about a microphone? — Well, no that's not fair, Fontana cannot afford a beaded gown, nor a microphone — okay, then how about a tube of bright red lipstick. Equate me with that. Equate me with fire. Equate me with passion. Not blue ribbons for my daily ponytail!" And before Natasha could stop herself she heard her voice: "How 'bout a tube of red lipstick, Hon?" She said it lightly, like a joke, she thought, as she glanced up at Fontana.

And watched, in an instant, Fontana's face fall. She'd thought and planned that blue ribbon. It went perfectly with her present. And it was *practical*. Red lipstick was not practical. She quickly internally determined that her mother was stupid. Thereby erasing her hurt and covering it with anger.

Natasha watched all this flick across the features of the daughter she knew so well and instantly felt regret. She took the blue ribbon off of her head and tied it around her wrist. *Natasha Miller, just keep it to yourself!* she silently admonished her strong and careless tongue. *Just don't talk. Be quiet. Do not speak. It is not worth it. Go on automatic pilot.* Squelch it. *You are hurting people. Again.*

"Oh, Honey, you know I was joking. I *love* my blue ribbon and I am going to wear it *every* day." She kissed Fontana on the cheek and watched her soften, watched some of the anger fall away — watched her look STRAIGHT INTO NATASHA'S SOUL and call her on her lie — silently accepting. And watched her daughter forgive her. Her preternatural wisdom kicking in.

"I can't wait a second longer! I have to know what's in this box!" Natasha said loudly with excitement as she tore off the paper and then the lid, threw the lid to the side and pushed away the pink tissue paper.

Fontana's eyes sparked as she peered over the edge of the box, as if it was *she* that was receiving the present instead of giving it.

Natasha gasped unintentionally, the blue gem in the broach catching her eye.

It was a sapphire broach in the shape of a butterfly. And it was — *real*.

"Fontana, how did you do this, Honey?"

"I *worked* for it," Fontana replied defiantly. "I saw it in the window and I wanted it and I worked for it and now I'm giving it to *you*." She folded her arms across her chest for emphasis.

Just then Brett walked into the living room with two steaming mugs and handed the one with the hot thick chocolate to Natasha. She was desperately craving it at just that moment and she looked at him gratefully, silently thanking him. Brett exchanged a secret glance first with Natasha, and then with Fontana – a glance that Fontana pointedly ignored.

"Yes, she worked for it," Brett said with a wink. "Washing windows and putting away dishes.... And that spotlessly clean room you've been noticing for the past few months. The porch without the leaves on it. Oh...and all those 'A's' she brought home on her tests."

Fontana's head had been bent, carefully examining a small piece of ribbon she continually curled between her thumb and forefinger. But she quickly jerked her head up and gave him a look at that comment. No one or no thing needed to motivate her to get an "A" on a test. That was *hers* and *hers* alone.

Brett smiled. *Ah, I've got her attention*, he thought. He had both of their attentions.

Natasha looked up and into Brett's eyes. Questioning: *How could you afford this? You didn't buy it on credit did you? You know I don't need this stuff...* on and on her mind worked its statements upon him. And he responded without words: *You are worth it. I love you. We'll work it out. We'll be fine. I love you.*

One small tear formed in the corner of Natasha's eye. How could she be so lucky? To have a boyfriend who was so caring, and to have a daughter who was so...so...*special.*

Tasha always knew Fontana was "special." More special than she ever was or would be. Yes, Natasha was classically trained. As a singer and a violinist. She had talent, yes. But her talent, her violin had been forged out of her from need – a life raft that pulled her out of her childhood. And up into the present. But, she felt that was where it stopped: Her talent. She did not have the depth; the inherent wisdom that Fontana had. Precociousness overshadowed by youth – Fontana was an "old soul." Tasha had said this many times. An "old soul." She knew it.

"Oh, Honey.... It is *beautiful*. No one has ever given me such a beautiful gift." Tasha pulled Fontana close to her – out of herself – into her and wrapped her arms around her. Folded Fontana up in her love, and Fontana, for once, let her, snuggling close to her Mom, breathing in her smell; her sensuality. Even at nine Fontana sensed the sensuality of her mother. Even if her mother did not see it.

Brett still stood. Looking down at both of them. Proud of himself and his actions. Pointedly ignoring the fact that he had not been acknowledged by Fontana in all of this. He stood, and beamed down at both of them. *His girls*, he thought to himself.

If Natasha heard him refer to her as "his girl" he knew her temper would flare, so he kept it to himself. But he knew, he had them....

CHAPTER THREE

NEW YEARS EVE. 10:00 p.m. He owned one case of them, and he took only one bottle out, once a year. Another annual ritual.

He kept this case in the back of the small hall closet, hidden behind the coats and one extra set of recently dry-cleaned burgundy drapes; behind the 1972 avocado green Hoover vacuum cleaner and the broom and mop and dustpan. Each dusky green bottle was meticulously cleaned each month to keep off the dust, and they sat, patiently waiting, for just this day. And on the morning of the eve of the New Year he would pull one bottle out, smooth the edges of the olive green and black label and put it into the old cream-colored Frigidare in the small kitchen of his very small apartment. There it would sit to chill until evening.

Dom Perignon 1973. Bobby was now on bottle number 11, of case number two – 23 bottles – 23 years. No alcohol. No drugs. Except for this one night. When he would, at 11:30 p.m., set up his chilled bottle and crystal glass on the small table by his easy chair, turn on the TV, pop the cork, and methodically drink glass after glass until the bottle was empty and the ball had dropped.

Then he would put the empty bottle into Recycling, wash and dry his crystal glass, put it away in the high cupboard to the right of the sink and go to bed.

Another holiday purposely spent alone. Another yearly reflection. Another milestone crossed.

Natasha settled into the comfort of her chair and sipped her tea. The sun had long ago slipped down the sky and it was beginning to snow. She and Fontana and Brett had played tag outside in the cool, brisk air – their new tiny puppy lapping at their heels. Then they'd all come in to a quite filling dinner of roast turkey, mashed potatoes and green beans, which Tasha, if she should say so herself, was quite proud of. Not much of a cook, really, she was just happy the turkey turned out; didn't burn; the mashed potatoes were smooth, everyone had liked it. The puppy had noisily lapped away at the water in his small round plastic white dish; looking eagerly from side to side each moment as if trying to get Fontana's and only Fontana's attention; and then fell with Fontana happy, full and exhausted into her bed, for once sound asleep by 8:30.

Like a Rockwell painting, she thought. *How nice; how odd.* One thing she was *not* was Rockwell, but the moment was noticed. She tried to appreciate these things. The sun had long set and it was just beginning to snow. Strange because it never snowed in Alameda, but an unexpected flurry of white flakes swirled in the air, touched the wet ground and immediately melted. Natasha watched the fragile flakes descend delicately to their death on the pavement outside her window. She inhaled deeply. And reflected on her day.

Brett sat beside her. Arm around her – Content. She let him. She had to. How could she not? He'd been so good to both she and Fontana. She had no right to feel so irritated with him all the time. He was a kind man. A *gentle* man. She was lucky. She exhaled, a long, deep-seated feeling releasing in her sigh, and laid her head back against his shoulder, resting her back against the crook of his arm. Content. Content. On the night of New Year's Eve they are both content.

CHAPTER FOUR

F ONTANA SAT ALONE at the bus stop. It was February and it was cold. The bench was green and dirty and the air was thick with smog and the smell of traffic. Her nine-year-old large, wide eyes dart back and forth furtively across the busy street. Long, medium-blonde hair ("dishwater blonde" she was once told) is held back with a brown barrette and is slightly stringy at the ends. She reaches up absently to smooth the flyaway ends that have come loose and shakes her head, feeling disgusted with the fact that she did not have time to wash it this morning, something she is self-conscious about. Her feet dangle over the edge of that dirty bench, and just hang there. They do not touch the ground. Her off-white shoes are scuffed, but neatly tied in two big bows, bows she took the extra time this morning to tie, her bow-tying ability being one of her main points of pride. One of her pink socks is scrunched down near her ankle and Fontana reaches down absently to pull it up, readjusting the light blue backpack on her shoulders which has bunched up her pink sweater. Fontana did not have time to put her sweater on properly because they were rushed, and so the sleeves are pulled back and it sits, unbuttoned and apart over her blue t-shirt. This bothers her. She fidgets with the edge of her blue denim skirt and looks down the road yet again to see if the bus is coming. Is it late? Or did she miss it? Brett dropped her off this morning because they were late, *again(!)*, Fontana thinks "again" with emphasis to her self. She *hates* being late. She does not like things that are out of order.

*This is a common occurrence…*she thinks, exasperated by the situation. Huge sigh that is not heard; another bus that goes whizzing by that is not hers…. Now she is going to have to catch the second bus, the one that comes twenty-five minutes later and causes her to miss morning recess and to have to run as fast as she can across the empty play yard to her third grade classroom before the tardy bell rings. Mrs. Schinct always stares at her when she runs in; half disciplinary; half — what? pity? Even at the age of nine Fontana is subtly aware of the irony of pity mixed with "discipline." *And the name "Fontana…"* she thinks wryly, her old soul flicking to life. *What in the world was my mother thinking with* that *name? Couldn't she have given me a* sensible *name? Jane or Mandy or Jill, perhaps?* (Her mother hated it when Fontana said "perhaps," so she said "perhaps" as often as possible.)

She craned her neck out and around once again to see if that damn bus was coming down the street yet. *Well, at least Brett left me here alone,* she thought. Something her mother would never do. She, very efficiently and with great aplomb had told him as they'd reached the bus stop that the bus would be there in *just one minute* and her mom would usually just drop her off. "Okay, okay…" he said, a hint of a question in his eyes and then he'd left, just to prove he trusted her she supposed. Her thoughts drifted upon each other as the sun began to beat upon her back. Just another day…and she sighed…and wiped the sleep from her eye with the back of her hand and stared straight ahead. She was tired and slightly cranky and barely noticed the slight figure that was walking slowly towards her.

He is wearing a brown plaid, short-sleeve, button-up-the-front shirt, which has one small pocket on the upper left side. There is a small piece of paper neatly folded and lying inside that pocket, the outlines of which are barely visible through the crisp and neatly pressed material of his shirt. His jeans are freshly pressed and white Adidas tennis shoes peak out from beneath the hem of his pants.

He had noticed her, a little girl alone in the world, long before he had purposely made his way toward that dirty green bench. Something about her compelled him to approach her. Tough exterior that covered a vulnerability that was naked and aching; scuffed shoes and quickly put together outfit, she stared straight ahead. He noticed that each item of her clothing no matter how worn or hastily put on, was neatly pressed. Like himself. A desire for order in a chaotic world. Fontana noticed him then. She tugged absently at her braid and glanced warily at him from the corner of her eye, being careful to keep the carefully manufactured illusion of staring straight ahead in place.

She continued to sit on that bench and watch the cars fly by. One after another, their stream of colors a blur against her half-closed eyes. Red. Blue. Green. Basic colors that she had learned in school. Her mother would never know. That she sat alone at this bus stop and reveled in it so discreetly.

He made his move toward her. A gentle man. Both frail and sprite in his walk. A wink as he approaches. He hovers, for an instant, and then sits down. She looks away. She pretends as if she does not see.

He sits, hands folded neatly in his lap. He looks at her again. Will not stop his gaze. He winks. She looks back. She must. He is no threat, she discerns. He will not harm her, she knows.

He begins to speak. She listens.

"What is it you feel you need? What is it that you are *missing*? Why do you sit here so forlornly?"

She is amused that this older man speaks to her so succinctly, as if she is an adult. He does not mince his words or make them smaller for her. She appreciates this. She replies with her full heart and mind: "I feel alone in this world; solitary; as if there is no other on this planet like me. I have thoughts – big thoughts that I can't tell anyone, because all expect *less* of me than what I can do." She could see he understood precisely what she was saying. He nodded in agreement with her words, as if, he too, had felt and understood her dilemma; the *boredom* of living below her potential. The *boredom* of life; the great *responsibility* she had for others. Especially the one who hovered most dearly in her mind, the one that looked like her, but was older; that seemed so wise at times, yet was filled with a naked innocence that frustrated Fontana.

He nodded again, bidding her to go on, "I am alone. And don't know why, but I don't need to be with others. Is that strange?" She turned to him now, the first time she had looked directly at him and requested his response with her intimate silence.

He spoke, "Yes, I know that in all things you are wondering what it is you should *do* with your life; what it is you should *be*. I see that you are

25

frustrated with all things. But know this: Your life is your own. Your wishes are your *own*. *What you wish to do with your life; you will do.* You are the Master of your own life. All things are within your grasp. All things will be as you ascertain they will be. Do you understand???" His words were hard; firm; like the tight red rubber ball she had held in her fist earlier that morning. And she rolled them around in her mind; again ascertaining the strength that he afforded her. These simple words; said, alone on that green bus stop bench.

He got up then to leave. And left Fontana alone on that dirty bench. Alone and yearning. Filled up – and yearning.

There was a moment, after the man had left, when Fontana stood at the curb, the dirty wind fondling her hair, the barrette coming loose from her braid, her head thrown back, the bus speeding by her. She did not step back onto the curb. She did not move out of the way. She did not wait for it to stop. She did not want to. She felt the ground rumble beneath her as the bus whizzed dangerously close, her body pushed back by the weight of the wind it created. Pushed back and teetering against the curb. The green bench momentarily forgotten. School momentarily forgotten. Her backpack flung upon the sidewalk. Her arms stretched straight out to the sides. *She does not care. She does not care.* The loud, loud honk of the bus horn. The faces peering out at her from the windows high above. Small windows with rows of seats. Faceless half-plastered stupid smiles on round white globes. Unblinking eyes. Gray sky. Gray clouds. Gray heart. Gray bus. Cold, dirty wind mixed with the heat of the exhaust. Deep breath. Exhaust in her lungs, she lets herself fall back, over the curb and onto the sidewalk. Fall straight back and land, bottom first onto the pavement.

No one noticed. She was alone.

CHAPTER FIVE

Natasha stood behind the counter of the coffee shop and hurriedly tied an apron around her waist; checking as unobtrusively as possible to see if Agustus had noticed her, once again, late arrival. But his head hung over the grill as he scraped bacon off and flipped runny eggs. And although it was 8:00 in the morning and cold outside, a slight sweat trickled down the side of his face, edging its way toward last night's growth of stubble. He did not bother to wipe it off. He hated that goddam grill and he willed all of last night's pent up aggression towards it.

Natasha's brown hair was tied with the blue ribbon Fontana had given her for Christmas. The ribbon lay gently at the nape of her neck, the circles under her eyes from last night's show showing against her pale skin. She did not have time to put on makeup, just a swipe of pink lipstick. Slight bulge beneath her t-shirt. She ignored it.

Memory of last night hits her suddenly, a slap to her face. Late, 2:00 a.m., she had staggered in, dead tired, carrying her daughter – which she should not do – Fontana's legs were so long they almost dragged to the floor. But she had felt so sorry for her, Fontana was so tired, she had just curled up and fell asleep in the corner of the makeshift dressing room, her homework lying on her lap, the pencil rolling from the palm of her hand to the dirty carpet. So, Natasha had carried her, to the car, from the car up the two flights of stairs to her apartment, and gently, gently, laid her in her bed. Beneath the covers, shoes pulled off and warm body curled into a small ball, the baby in her still lingering on her cheek; on her closed eyes, in the half-smile that melted on her lips.

Fontana looked so sweet then, Natasha stayed for a moment, hovered over her bed; no sign of the precocious child evident in that sleeping angel. She had absently patted her stomach, then had jerked back, a reflex of fear in her arm. Closed her eyes, turned and softly clicked Fontana's door shut.

Trudging back to the living room she had moved toward Brett, who so obviously waited for her.

There was a click of the bedroom door and he turned his head, jerking up and away from the can of beer in his hand.

He had been staring at the TV since she had come in earlier carrying Fontana – A blank screen with blue and white fuzz. A picture that went off hours ago.

Natasha peeked around the corner, guiltily, checking to see if he had fallen asleep.

"Honey, you were out late tonight. Everything okay?" Brett's said to the empty air, feeling her presence behind the wall. Knowing her scent.

She moved to stand in front of him. He went on, "I worry, you know.... You look *tired*." He glanced at her stomach, she glanced down too.

"I know, I know, but I can't quit the shows." She felt the pull; the tear in both directions, well four directions now, her music, Fontana, Brett and now the little one growing inside of her, she continued, making her choice – "The CD's just starting to take off, I put so much time into it and you put your *money*. Don't want to let you down, lose the chance; let *myself* down. We talked about this. This is something we're doing *together*." She could see the guilt and then the concern in his eyes. The guilt he was beginning to feel for her "working" in her state. The guilt she *let* him feel for "pushing" her. But she *wanted* to be pushed. She moved closer to him. Kissed him on the head.

"You understand, don't you?" Her eyes searched his inquisitively. She cooed to calm dawn the fierce protectiveness she knew lurked deep within him. He tried to ignore the purple shadows that seemed to be darkening every day.

"You know I *understand*," he emphasized the word, "yes, I *understand*, but don't *push* yourself, Tasha, its not worth it." She was stubborn and single-minded and he loved her. But he was not going to let this one go.

She felt her passion flair then. That feeling that *there might not be enough time*. That she must accomplish all she could *now*, while she had her chance. But what chance? She was still singing in tiny clubs and small bars. But, still it was *her chance*, and she was still young.

He got up then, and flicked off the TV, "You 'bout ready for bed? – let's go on in the bedroom then *Honey*!!" He swatted her ass, she jumped, looked back behind her, irritated for a moment. He put his arm around her shoulder, she leaned her head against the broadness of his chest.

He had relaxed – she could feel it – gratefully; perceptively – the relax of the muscles in his thick neck. She ran her fingers through his hair – the movement/gesture relaxing her as well. She sighed, patted her stomach for his benefit – "Bed...can't wait..." voice tired and saying essentially, *No sex for you tonight, mister....* But her body ached in anticipation of sleeping next to him and she smiled. He smiled back, playfully. This willful, strong, beautiful woman that he loved so much; that was carrying his baby. How lucky could he be? He pushed his concerns far to the back of his mind. He wrapped his arm more tightly around her shoulder.

Quiet.

CHAPTER SIX

Did someone once say —
There was a light at the end of a tunnel

That could lead us out of darkness?
And away from temptation?

Did someone once say —
That love would conquer all?

Did someone once say —
There was a small hope at
the end of the rainbow?

A hope
That conquered fear —

If they did —
I could not hear
I could not hear

Lift
Up, up and away
Let my spirit fly
Upon the wind

PART I – NATASHA

Let the sorrows
of today
Be lost beneath
tomorrow's
gentle din

Lift
Up, up and away
Let your spirit
come to mine

No one
will ever know
the love
A heart
can never find —

The last word left her lips. Hovered over the small crowd – then fell silently. A song she had written that morning while working at the coffee shop. Fifteen people in the audience. A bunch of regulars on a Tuesday night that had come to look forward to Natasha's sweet voice as they downed a beer. Ate pretzels. Were taken away for a moment. She bowed her head. Closed her eyes. She knew it was not much. Her small song. But she *felt* it. Wanted to share it. Was grateful to the audience for listening.

A humbleness settled over her each time she sang. It was no contrived act of forced humbleness. No, it was *her* – or rather the lack of her, on stage. She felt that she disappeared when she sang and that she became – nothing – no smaller than a pinpoint. Time removed. Still.

Fontana was behind the stage in the makeshift dressing room. Alone. Forgotten – for a moment. Natasha's moment – of nothing.

The song finished, Natasha took a deep breath and looked around the half-empty room, shaking her head silently to herself. Shaking herself back to reality – to the present. Blank faces staring back at her – wide eyes. The room silent. One man in the front has stopped mid-air – hand to mouth – corner of a pretzel touching his lips. *Staring.* Staring at her.

A hesitant hang in the air and then the clapping – first one; then another and another. All mesmerized by her voice – Natasha does not see this.

She only sees: the blank stares, the silence after she has finished – the moment of hesitation before the obligatory clapping.

I feel so much when I am singing. How can it become dissipated and lost upon the air before even reaching their ears?

They are kind, her regulars. And supportive. And she loves them and has known many for the five years she has been coming to the Stage Coach Inn & Bar. She is kind back. And appreciative. But slightly removed. She has mistaken their awe for indifference.

Deep breath. Exhale. Resolve. She steps off the stage and walks through the tables shaking hands, smiling her slight smile. A hug and kiss here and there. Her remove taken as mystery. Adding to her allure.

She will not show hurt. Nor disappointment. It is not her way.

She walks quickly to the makeshift dressing room behind the stage. It is 11:05 p.m. now, it all took longer than she expected; as usual. She grabs the leftover square green and yellow flyers for Friday's show – flyers she'll set out at Jake's when she gets in tomorrow morning.

Fontana the wise old soul with the learned heart that she is, sits, legs splayed beneath her, pencil drooping from relaxed fingers, math book open in her lap, college ruled notebook slid down her thigh, halfway on her leg and halfway on the floor – head lolling to the left, dark eyelashes a closed fringe upon her cheek. The sight of her child so peacefully asleep on the floor like that brings a pain to her heart. She looks across the room and notices Derk the janitor mopping the floor too slowly in front of her child's sleeping form.

Moment on stage completely forgotten. Singing career forgotten. The muscles in her legs tighten uncontrollably. Ready to leap. *"What are you doing in here????"* Her voice is loud, louder than she had intended – her throat is tight; constricted. He turns to her, now; startled. Smiling. Pleasant.

"Such a pretty girl you have. I have a granddaughter looks just like her. Miss her somethin' crazy. Hardly get to see her much anymore since her mama moved away. Sorry to startle you, ma'am…didn't mean to." Natasha watches him closely. Stares him down; looks deeply at him… But, no…no…he is only an old janitor, doing his job and she is overreacting; *again.* He moves to the other side of the room; out of her way.

She scoops Fontana up, asleep and all. Bends down with her left hand and grabs her school stuff and her backpack. Fumbles with it. Feels a sharp pain on her left side. Almost makes her double over; deep breath, exhale; anger – she ignores it. Moves on.

"Can I help you with that, Ma'am?"

"No, no thank you. I'm fine." She just wants to get out of there; get Fontana home, get her in bed; get in bed *herself*. How selfish of her to keep her out so late. She can't do this anymore, she knows. She is going to have to make a choice: Either leave Fontana with Brett, or stop the late-night shows. But Fontana *likes* to come; *likes* being with her Mom. There seems something so wrong always in leaving her home; not *involving her*. Fontana would not like it, she knew that for sure. She huffed. Turned and stormed, as best she could with a nine-year-old on one hip and a backpack in the other hand, out of the makeshift dressing room.

Derk just stood in the middle of the room. Hands on hips. One hand up for a moment to wave goodbye. He turned to survey the room once more before leaving and noticed that Natasha had left her makeup case. A pretty, light blue ribbon hung off the edge, so he stuffed it neatly inside; gently closed the top of the case and moved it to the side of the counter. Wiped the top of the counter down, left the room and locked it on his way out. He was sure that that frazzled looking young lady would have to come back for it some time.

It was almost midnight by the time Natasha struggled up the stairs once again with Fontana in her arms; feet dangling almost to the ground, precariously balancing her bag and Fontana's backpack on her free arm. She dropped the pack, fumbled in her bag for her keys, cursed herself for forgetting her makeup case, she'll have to go back to the bar tomorrow to pick it up…one more thing to do that she absolutely does not have time for. Doesn't want to put Fontana down, and then resigns herself to waking Brett. So Tasha kicks the door lightly with the toe of her boot, hitting it much harder than she had intended because of the unbalanced weight of Fontana, and her light tap sounds more like a giant thud. Brett has been waiting up again, Natasha knows. He opens the door too quickly and peers around, hair slightly disheveled, looking as if he has just woken from sleep.

33

Fuck! She takes a deep breath. Ignores the searing pain that is once again mounting, a band, starting at her left side and ripping through the center of her slightly distended stomach. Bites her lip. Feels the blood. Likes the taste of the salt. Heaves Fontana higher on her hip, indicates with a nod of her head to Brett that he is allowed to pick up the bags, and carries Fontana into her bedroom. By this time she is so exhausted, she lets Fontana flop on the bed. *She is out...* Natasha thinks. *Oh, the wonderful thing about children and sleep, for the most part when they fall asleep, they stay asleep. Something that disappears after having a child, or perhaps it automatically disappears after the age of twenty-five, who knows? Why am I thinking this? Oh, because I have not had more than six hours sleep in five years. Because I am exhausted. Because I feel bad. Because NO MATTER HOW HARD I TRIED OR HOW GOOD A MOTHER I THINK I AM, I AM ALWAYS FALLING ONE STEP SHORT. Once again, I feel guilty, okay. Okay!* Another, self-talk tirade.

She gently pulled off one of Fontana's shoes, then the other and pulled her grandmother's hand-stitched pink and baby blue quilt high over her – tucking it gently under her pointed chin. It is February and still cold, and she feels a certain safety in the movement. She tucked the edges of the quilt far under and around her. If Fontana was awake, and if she was younger, she would have exclaimed exuberantly: "Like a burrito!" and Natasha would have laughed and touched her nose lightly with her index finger and said "Yup, *my* little burrito and I'm going to eat you up!" But, not tonight. Tonight she kissed her smooth non-furrowed forehead lightly with feverish lips, smoothed her amber blonde hair back on her head and silently padded out of the room, leaving the door slightly ajar. To be close. Protectiveness still lingering deep within her. An instinctive protectiveness that would never leave and sought no provocation.

And the pain, the pain...it is subsiding a bit, thank God. The mixed feelings that have come with this child, she mused. *So different from my pregnancy with Fontana. An elation, certainly. Fear, of course. Not fear of raising the child. No, just a feeling that something is just not quite right.* She shook it off. She would do what was necessary. She was strong. And she'd been through worse. She would be fine. *Think of the practical...think of the practical,* she reminded herself. *And thinking of the practical, I need to get to bed.* She had the morning shift at work tomorrow – which meant a 6:30 a.m. wake-up time. No time to think.

CHAPTER SEVEN

*W*OMEN TALK A LOT, Natasha thought to herself as she cleared the table. There was a table of noisy hens just to the left of her station and their voices were grating on her nerves – if she drank she would liken this to a hangover. Too many late nights piling one on top of each other. And each screech of their high-pitched shrill voices grated on her and sent her neck muscles to tense even more, her shoulders to crunch up closer to her ears. *How do men do it?* she thought. *No wonder they hide in bars until all hours and lose themselves behind the din of TV...it is nerve-wracking!"*

Natasha was not in a good mood this morning, although she should be. She and Brett had had a great night of sex last night – the gymnastics-type sex that a five-month pregnant woman should not be having. Something she was surprised she was capable of, given the pain she was having only moments before he opened the door with that hungry lust in his eyes – Yes. Brett could always get her with sex. That look, the way he would enfold her in his arms, the safety – and then the sex – and her hormones since becoming pregnant had gone wild! Was this normal? This lust for sex *all the time* while a child was growing within her? A strange hormonal reaction to the changes taking place in her body? Brett would take her from behind, afraid, she sensed of crushing her stomach should he lie on top of her, and ever so gently he would make love to her and then hold her and all would be right with the world for a few moments. And he would drift off to sleep and her eyes would close – to sweet nothing – no dreams – just him inside her; holding her. Until morning.

When she would rush out of bed, feigning lateness — well what feigning? They always seemed to be running late — and leave Brett lying, still rumpled and somewhat asleep in their warm bed. Jump in the shower and rush to start her day. Make Fontana's lunch, something preferably healthy, and then hurry out the door, Fontana in tow, the door slamming loudly behind them.

He had asked her to marry him. Asked her with sincere eyes and sincere intent (she had surmised at the time). But, no, this is not something she had wanted. Could not add *marriage* to the sweet, simple confusion of her life at this moment. Did not want to lose the passion that they shared; the *bond*. No. No. Not this time.

She had been married once before, to Fontana's father, once had been enough. A marriage that had disintegrated somehow with the birth of Fontana. Disintegrated upon the dust of their desire. And the pain of the failure of that marriage was not something she was willing to endure again.

No, not so soon.

So Brett stayed. Her *boyfriend*. And this child, this child of love would save them from the terrible tragedy of her past mistake.

From the tragedy of her parents' mistake.

This is how it would stay.

And, thankfully, each and every time he entered her, the pain would subside. Her fears would subside. Her frustrations would subside. Her whole body would relax into him and she would feel *peace. Must have been a muscle spasm,* she thought to herself now as the noisy hens clacked out their conversation.

Because today she felt fine. No pain. Just exhaustion. But no pain. Absently she wiped the top of the counter and stared longingly out the large window at the cloudy and fog-infested sky. "Fog-infested" — she liked that phrase. "Fog-infested" is how she felt inside. As if there was a great fog growing inside of her.

She wiped back the piece of light brown bang that had dropped down over her right eye with the back of her hand and sighed audibly. A craving growing inside of her.

Sy looked up and smiled – finding her sigh alluring – thinking it only for him. She felt his look and moved toward him to pour his coffee. Secret exchange between them: *Women...!* He nods and grins down into his fresh cup of coffee. Tasha – half-smile firmly in place turns her back to him and moves towards the counter to pick up an order of eggs.

———

Bobby carefully puts his key into the front door of his apartment and turns it, gently – listening intently for the soft "click" that always gave him safety. Coffee in hand, he reaches down to grab the newspaper lying on his stoop, rolls it and tucks it under his arm automatically, and then slowly and with great anticipation opens the door to silence – a sound he finds refreshing. He moves over worn carpet toward the small dinette in the mini dining room off the green tile-flecked 70's style mini kitchen and gently lays the Alameda Sun on the table. He slowly takes a sip of coffee from his covered, Styrofoam cup and settles down to read the morning news.

CHAPTER EIGHT

Interestingly he had nothing to say to her. Her boss, Agustus, his head as always bent down over that hot and greasy grill. Another morning at the coffee shop; another morning flipping eggs, frying bacon, flipping pancakes – always gruff; *grunting actually* – Natasha thought to herself. He was *always* here when she arrived – even if she was the first one here to "open up." She had a set of keys, he had given them to her. Christ, it was almost her second home and he expected her to clean up and lock up as if he wasn't there – as if he wasn't going to be there, after she locked the door behind her and locked him in.

He hardly noticed her, really. Tasha – who so took for granted the attention and adoration she elicited from others, noticed, that her boss, Agustus de Santos, did not notice her for the most part.

But he *trusted* her, this she knew. He trusted her and he watched her from the corner of his eye. She could feel his head jerk up if she made a mistake, dropped a fork, felt a plate almost slip from her hands. She would glance towards him; reflexively and his head would jerk up at the same time, gruff smile fixed on his face beneath the growth of last night's beard. *Did he shower this morning?* Tasha couldn't tell.

But behind the gruffness were blue eyes. And they were warm and caring. And, somehow, they made Tasha feel safe.

She could feel his trust in her, even if it was only trust in her ability to do a menial job. *Oh, stop!* She silently reprimanded herself. *This I do well. I will do it well. And he trusts not my ability to do a "menial" job, but* me. *I have the keys. It is a support. A trusting of my essence.* At this thought she silently balked. *A trusting of my "essence?"* Thoughts like these simultaneously attracted and repelled her. For she was one-half practicality; one-half spirit. And she preferred to rely on her practical side. Though her spirit often took over and led her. A war she raged within her on a daily basis.

And, of course, there was a new set of chattering hens sitting in the corner this morning. Two older women in their mid-sixties. Retired – dark lipstick on thin lips fixed in place. Plaid scarf wrapped fashionably around the loudest one's neck. She spoke and her voice carried (*New York?*) high-pitched and grating as always across the coffee shop and to her ears. *Does she feel it necessary to SHOUT to her friend who is only twelve inches away??* Tasha thought sarcastically to herself. The older woman's hands were gesturing wildly – large diamond ring catching the sun as she gesticulated.

"Chemo-therapy is a *hawd* thing, a *hawd* thing.... It doesn't matter how much money you have, what kind of family you come from – its raampunt *everywaar.*" The thin-lipped, lipsticked woman said "rampant" – drawing out the "a" and stating the additional "a" as if it was a "u" – *raaampunt* – with emphasis on the second syllable.

Yes, definitely New York, Tasha thought again.

"It's just *amaaazing.* AMAAAZING with all the drugs we took, all the things we did, that our children turned out as *nawmal* as they did," the woman half-shouted to her friend. This statement grabbed the attention of half the people in the coffee shop. Some looked up, then down quickly. Others continued to stare. It caught Tasha's attention in particular. *Older women with a past. Funny how we think the older have always been old. That they have no past. That they have had no youth. Funny how we assume that the old are boring and have not lived.*

The woman droned on. Tasha turned her back to her and tried to tune her out. Sy did not come in this morning. No one to exchange a wink with.

Strange, Tasha thought to herself. *Sy always came in. He never missed a day.*

Tasha was glad she worked the morning-shift today. She looked forward to 3:00 p.m. and glanced edgily at the clock on the wall above the coffee maker – 2:30 – half an hour more. She planned it out in her mind now as she slowly wiped the counter in even, round, swirling circles: She would get off; rush to pick up Fontana – so she wouldn't have to take the bus home alone. Then they would go into the studio – the small studio Tasha's friend, Josh, let her use when he was not in it – Fontana could do her homework, and Tasha (who had stashed her violin in the coat closet of the diner) could practice her violin and write and tinker around with the recording equipment – maybe record something simple – her vocals over a looped drum beat with a simple violin over it. Well, maybe two hours would not be enough time for that – but she could do *something* and Fontana would be with her and Fontana was her inspiration – the thought of it caused excitement to well within her – the excitement – could it be lust? – that made her feel she either wanted to have sex or make music. She always chose music and then Fontana – or well, equally.... Her mind was drifting and the loud words were echoing across the coffee shop again, edging their way into her revelry.

"Suzy said to me, all her friends who had *Baaahmitsvaaas*" (the bejeweled and be-lipsticked woman elongating the words "bar mitzvah" into one long, drawn out word with lots of vowels, in her now even louder New York accent – the momentum of her conversation having built upon itself and escalating with excitement). "All felt the same way, they all felt *ovawelmed*. The cawsins, the people, the guest lists. I'll help ha – It's neva too late for a good *pawty*...." Hands with red fingernails still gesticulating wildly, large diamond glinting loudly in the sun.

Natasha sighed audibly. No one heard her.

———

Fontana sat in her chair at her desk in her fourth grade classroom staring straight ahead. She pushed her glasses back up her nose with her index finger – a pointed gesture of annoyance and listened to Mrs. Schinct drone on and on. Math. It was Fontana's favorite subject, but Mrs. Schinct moved too slowly – consequently Fontana wore the same bored and absent stare on her face that every other student in the room wore except for Jimmy Yesmine. He had a small head and large glasses and black, badly cut hair. His eyes were bright and eager and he raised his hand in earnest at each and every question Mrs. Schinct asked. *"Oh, oh, oh!"* He would try to suppress his shouts of enthusiasm, the back of his upper arm being held up by the hand on his other arm in some sort of misguided salute to mathematics.

Mrs. Schinct ignored him most of the time – looking expectantly around the room for other volunteers and then, looking pointedly at Fontana, who most definitely did not have her hand up – staring straight into her eyes; Fontana staring straight back. No hesitation in her stare – her eyes saying: *I will not answer. I am not Jimmy....* Mrs. Schinct looked at Jimmy's outstretched hand again in exasperation, and then called on Claire, the shy girl sitting in the very last seat in the fifth row.

Claire, of course, has no idea what the answer is, but her budding beauty forgives her lack of mathematical prowess and every eye of every boy in the room lingers on her blonde hair and delicate features even after Fontana finally speaks up and says (loudly):

"The answer is 13. 28 divided by 2 minus 1 equals 13." She had figured this out in her head long ago and makes her statement with the annoyance she feels deep in her heart and soul. Annoyance, first of all, at her teacher for making this *so damned easy.* Secondly, at Jimmy, for embarrassing her, by being as smart as her, but acting like such an idiot. Thirdly, at the class, for *not* knowing the answer, and fourthly, and most importantly, at Claire – because all the boys have just now turned away from her, and she is blushing fiercely and she will probably get an "A" without hardly trying or even *knowing* the answers, just because some, or more likely, *more than one* boy will help her, her teacher will take pity on her vulnerability – *and that is just the way life is for Claire.*

Claire was always dressed perfectly. And she always wore *dresses* and ribbons in her hair. And her hair was always perfectly combed and her skin shone – like someone very caring had scrubbed her down just that morning. And on top of it all she wore *patent leather shoes.* With never a scuff. Fontana had to admit to herself that she was jealous of Claire's neatness. Of the cleanliness of her clothes and the way they were perfectly put together. The perfectionist in Fontana ached for this kind of clothes-order in her own wardrobe – although she would never, *ever* wear dresses. It would interfere with her tree climbing. And monkey bar swinging.

Claire in her shy and unassuming way had attempted to speak to Fontana a couple of times on the playground. Once, when Fontana was swinging on the monkey bars, Claire had stood below her looking up admiringly – and when Fontana had dropped down, landing with a thump on the tanbark and then had knelt down quickly to pull up her pink socks, Claire had come up to her hesitantly and asked if Fontana would teach *her* to swing on the monkey bars.

"You can't do it," Fontana immediately replied authoritatively; quickly – before she could stop herself, before she had even thought about it – "*You're* wearing a *dress*." She emphasized the word "dress" as if it were something disgusting; as if she were saying: *You're wearing a piece of slimy mold.* Claire's eyes got wide, then teary and then she turned on her small patent leather heel and ran away.

Fontana immediately felt bad. She half-heartedly wished that she could stop herself from saying things – things that would just pop out of her mouth. But, of course, the other part of her prided herself on her witty commentary. But, deep down, she had to admit that something about Claire at that moment was partially likeable and Fontana felt slightly bad for slighting her when Claire had reached out. She kicked the ankle of her left foot with her right, a habit she had when she was reprimanding herself. *Well, maybe she'll try again...*Fontana thought while walking back after lunch.

Fontana and Claire locked eyes now from across the classroom – Fontana from seat one, row three and Claire from the last seat in row five. Claire felt Fontana's eyes on her reddened face. She felt Fontana's strength and relished the comfort that Fontana had reached out to her in her embarrassed shame at not knowing the answer to the math question. A simple one, obviously, that Fontana knew instantly – Claire could tell. And Claire knew it too – it sat murky in the back of her mind, behind the fear that prevented her from speaking in public situations. Claire was thankful to Fontana for "saving" her that way. She wished the last boy in the room that was still staring at her would turn back around. When they stared, it made her uncomfortable. She did not know how to protect herself from their stares. Their advances. She flicked her blue eyes down, toward her math book – pretending to study the page and felt relieved, the hotness in her cheeks beginning to subside.

———

Bobby had fallen asleep on the couch in his small apartment. The warm afternoon sun fell on his face, memories of a tragic past playing themselves upon his features. Sun illuminating the silent memories that carved those features, now in restful state; the two deep lines around his mouth; the etched smile lines around his eyes. The slight twitch of his right eye. As if he is being slapped or hit. His body involuntarily jerks as he sleeps. The sun warms him. Hazy memory upon his dreams:

Young man in his youth.

Sleep takes him back there easily. If only it could be released, but it sticks to him; a living ghost.

> *A small apartment. Shooting up. A young girl passed out on his bed...won't move, won't move...how does he wake her up?? He tries to move her; she is leaden; heavy. The panic; the inability to move. The drug taking effect. Blissful, blissful sleep. Morning comes. Light on his face. Unwanted. He is more alert. He tries to wake the girl again. Still she will not move.*
>
> *Dragging...dragging...her to the door. Feet dragging, he has his hands hooked under her arms. She is cold. He is sweating. RINGING...RINGING...Panic...the ringing will not stop. A voice from behind the door; it is muffled...but the ringing...it is in his ears; it is everywhere.... Police pounding on his door. Cold metal bars. Alone, in that prison cell, waiting....The ringing will not stop.*

The ringing of the telephone jolts him out of sleep. He twitches; rubs his eyes. Gets up, heads to the phone, fumbles with it, answers it methodically. "Hello?" He didn't receive many calls, who could it be?

"Excuse me sir, is this, uh, B. Sharp?"

"Who may I ask is calling?"

"This is Care You All Carpet Cleaning and we are running a special on carpet cleaning this month, the month of February only, and we would like to extend our special offer to you, as a preferred customer who has used our services before." The faceless voice on the other end of the line is flat and without feeling.

"Preferred customer? I've never used a carpet cleaning service. I clean the carpets myself. How did you get my number?" Bobby, clearly becoming agitated, but always polite, was not happy with the caller. And more than that, it disturbed him that someone he did not know had his number. Although his number was listed, he did not like strangers calling him. He hung up the phone and turned his back to the table.

CHAPTER NINE

She was alone, and she didn't know why. The alley was dark and she was running, running down the deep tunnel. She saw no light in front of her — only darkness. A darkness that she was moving towards with wooden legs. As if swimming in mud — slow motion — but running — ever so slowly.

The figure was chasing her and she had to get away from it. It was a large lumbering figure and she could not see its face — but, she knew if it reached her she would be dead.

What did it have in its hand? A knife? Something sharp, she could tell. And it glinted momentarily as it caught the quick light of a moon that only moments ago did not exist.

She felt hot breath upon her neck, felt a hand slip around her waist. Felt the darkness of it as it brought her close to it. She sank back into it — she felt the pain, a knife to her side.

Natasha woke up suddenly — the scream caught in her throat.

"You were moaning, Tasha — Are you okay?" Brett's hand had slipped around her expanded waist during sleep — he was holding her gently, rocking her, his breath upon her neck — attempting to soothe her.

She reflexively moved away — rolling away from him — grabbing her extended belly — the pain searing through her side. Seven months pregnant and these pains — they came so suddenly. Almost too much to bear.

She'd spoken to her doctor about it, but after an unscheduled sonogram and a forming baby that looked healthy and happy, Doctor Simpkin had declared both mother and child "good to go," and told Natasha that it was probably just "growing pains" on her part – a pulled sciatic nerve, perhaps or her hips expanding as the baby grew.

"By the way, have you thought about a name for the little fellow?" the kindly doctor had inquired, warmth and humor shining from bespeckled, watery blue eyes.

"No, no, we were thinking of 'Baron,' but, of course, Brett would like the child named after him," Natasha replied, attempting to hide her agitation at the thought.

The doctor smiled easily back. He secretly felt that much of the physical pain she was feeling was stress related. "Mom," Doctor Simpkin cleared his throat, "*Natasha*, a few deep breathing techniques could help you, maybe you should take a few minutes to lie down in the afternoon."

"Why? Why? Is there something wrong? Something you're not telling me?" Natasha said, alarm rising in her eyes, her normally low, soft voice, rising two octaves.

"No, no, of course not," Doctor Simpkin reassured her. This is why he was decidedly low-key about his verbal observations to his patients. Most of his pregnant patients were highly sensitized, easily alarmed and his words of caution or an undue test or remark could be misconstrued and create a stressful situation for both mother and child. "No, no, Natasha, of course not," he repeated again for emphasis, "you and the baby are *perfectly healthy*, believe me." He looked straight into her eyes, sincerely, willing the panic to leave her. He watched it subside, watched the irises of her large, brown eyes contract back down, cease to dilate. Watched her catch her breath, release it, force herself to breathe. Yes, she had been holding her breath. She consciously released this.

"*You'll both be fine.* Believe me. You, young lady, just need to get a little rest. Don't push yourself so hard. There will be time for everything. You're still *young*...." Doctor Simpkin let the word "young" trail off – He'd had patients like Natasha before – young, determined women who seemed to think they could "do it all." Perfectionists with high expectations of themselves. Fed by a society and media that made it all look so easy, so *doable*. And these frustrated and exhausted girls – well not *girls* he reprimanded himself

PART I - NATASHA

— *women*, really — Women in their twenties and thirties pushing themselves past their own human limits. Juggling jobs, family and in Natasha's case a budding music career as well — in a misguided attempt at female independence — but more than that, and in Natasha's case especially, he sensed a determination that refused to be thwarted.

Yes, she needed rest. He noticed again the light purple shadows under her eyes, the pale porcelain skin, a little too pale, he thought. Yes, just rest, that was all. He patted her gently on the shoulder, instructed her to get dressed and walked out of the examining room, softly clicking the door shut behind him. Natasha was left sitting, alone on the examining table — inner legs still wet and sticky from the gel he had put on his finger before examining her — "This may be a little cold," he said.

Yes, cold, in more ways than one. She searched the room now for a tissue — spied one on the counter next to the sink, grabbed it, wiped herself off hurriedly. *Just like a bad case of sex; all the wet, none of the fun....* She shook her head, laughing at her little private joke and the fact that she had just a teeny bit of humor left in her large and bloated body, patted her stomach, "C'mon little guy let's get out of here," she said out loud to the room, "seems we're both *just fine*, good to hear, now I have nothing to worry about." She laughed again, somewhat forced, yet somewhat relieved, as she pulled on her jeans and white t-shirt (she had just graduated to those oh-so-lovely jeans with the pleated stretchy panel of a slightly lighter color in front — it was thrilling...) grabbed her purse and hurried out the door.

Was there a moment when she thought the doctor was telling the truth? No. Inherently she felt that there was a problem, and as she made the slow drive home, winding past the large maple and oak trees that lined the back streets she was taking to her apartment she mused at the doctor's reproachful words, "Absolutely nothing to worry about, Natasha." "Get some rest, Natasha...." She saw the disapproval in his eyes and it pissed her off. She felt he was condescending towards her, but more than that and perhaps it was wishful thinking, she had to admit, she *trusted* him. She trusted the warmth in his eyes. His gentle manner. The caring with which he approached her.

Yes, maybe wishful thinking, she thought again. She inherently felt that there was *something* wrong, she just could not put her finger on what it was. The baby moved, that was for sure, not as much as Fontana had – Fontana was a firecracker from the moment Natasha first felt the tiniest stir in about her third month. And from then on in Fontana became more and more active. Until, finally, in the ninth month Natasha could absolutely NOT WAIT to get her little girl out of her and into the world. There was a true excitement that had built with Fontana before she was born. A connection that she knew her baby daughter felt as well before the birth. An unspoken understanding; a contentment. An argument and compatibility. Natasha laughed to herself as she drove the partly shaded winding streets in her new used Volvo. A purchase she had diligently saved for and most recently acquired. She loved the spring and the budding flowers and green on the trees. Spring and fall, her two favorite times of year. Spring, rebirth, fall, a quiet laziness and change of color that meant sleep; a rest. A moment of chill before the spring. Winter: Quiet, dark reflection. A stillness. Spring brought summer and summer was full of light. Always the seasons excited her. Even if it was only the seasons in Northern California. A slight cold in the evenings. A heavy fog at certain times of the year. A strange and unusual snow every thirty years or so, like the one they had so unusually, over the Christmas break. Natasha saw this as a sign. A sign that something wonderful was going to happen. She could feel it; she knew it.

So, she took a deep breath and put her fears to rest. She chose to believe the kindhearted doctor who judged her for working too hard. He just did not understand. He was older, from a different generation, he, she could sense, felt that all pregnant women should be home, with their feet up, perhaps getting up just in time to make dinner for their hard working, bossy and adoring husbands. Yes, he had a very unrealistic and archaic view of the modern world. A view and an expectation and a slight disapproval that did not fit with modern times, *or reality for that matter,* Natasha thought to herself. She laughed again slightly. A laugh that startled her.

She realized she had laughed more today alone than she had in a long time. She needed to do more of that.

Yes, this baby was different. Perhaps because he was a boy. His moves were slow, lazy; and at seven months, wherein Fontana had been practically tumbling in her stomach, Baron, (or whatever they were going to call him, Brett? Ugh! – She didn't want to have a "Junior" running around – well they'd get to that when they got to that – hopefully without an argument...). Tasha hated to argue with Brett and avoided confrontation whenever possible; but she was getting more and more short with him. So she tried to keep their conversations short and to the point. They had their differences, yes. He was really into his workouts and his fitness instruction. She liked that about him: his *physicality*, she focused on that and decided to again attribute her increasing irritation with him to severe hormonal fluctuations due to pregnancy and give herself a break – she was allowed to be cranky, right? It was *de rigueur* for pregnant women or so she heard. But she was not usually cranky. Removed, yes. But cranky, no, that was not her style. Anyway, Baron, Brett, she decided to call her little guy B.B. to herself until they decided, he would end up with both names anyway, the fight would be which one would come first.

Little B.B. moved slowly, like a fish in molasses. A little arm or leg moving just a bit, and yes, ever so *slowly*. Every now and then his little rear would, over the course of hours, make it's tiny way a few inches across her belly. Then stop. Oh, she hoped he wasn't going to be fat. Fat and lazy. *Oh, what a terrible thought, Natasha!* She laughed again to herself. Everything was going to be all right. She would be *all right*. The baby would be all right. The doctor was right. She was tired. Maybe she would take just the tiniest of naps when she got home. She had left work early today in order to go to her doctor's appointment, she had not even offered to come back after the appointment was done, as she usually would. And Agustus had not asked her to. He just looked up, grunted out "Uh-huh, see you tomorrow," and let her leave. She watched him watching her as she hurriedly left the coffee shop.

She loved the coffee shop in her own twisted way. It's long, oblong windows framed in wood on the small side street. The short bus ride to get into that part of town hadn't even bothered her. She had kind of liked it, she reminisced now that she had a car. Yes – another one of her "escapes." She would use the time on the bus to write out lyrics, or poems, or to sketch out melodies in her head. She carried with her a microcassette recorder and was always humming new melodies and chord progressions into it. She didn't care if the other people on the bus thought she was crazy…she was in her own world and so happy, she would lose track of time, sometimes almost missing her stop, she would have to jump up, grab her things run to the doors before they closed on her, almost tripping down the large metal steps that led to the pavement, lined with dirt. Just a short walk from the bus stop to the Diner. Just down the street on the corner, really. She was sure Agustus could see her slightly distant figure, were he to go to the window. And she had a feeling he was standing there waiting for her as she approached – a shadowy figure that would quickly disappear as she neared. A figment of her very fertile imagination, most likely.

They had an easy relationship, she and her boss, and she ignored his strange and secretive behavior. None of her business, really. And she knew inherently that he only wished for her safety. This is all she saw.

She did not feel the intense longing that accompanied those extended stares. She did not notice the shiver that ran down his arm to his spine when he handed her her check with "a little extra somethin' for you and the kid…."

She was not afraid of him. Although others in the coffee shop were. Agustus did not think that anyone knew that he kept that large, black case in the broom closet. But Trish, the other waitress usually on shift with her had seen him stashing it there early one morning, "sneaking it in," she had told Tasha. Her blue eye shadow moving and flitting as she raised her plucked and lined brows.

"Well, just go in there and look and see what it is," Natasha had said matter-of-factly. Exasperated as always with small talk. She did not see what the big deal was, he was the boss and if he wanted to keep a case in the closet and fill it with marshmallows or cash, she didn't really care.

"*I'm* not looking in *there!*" Trish replied, between large chomps of her purple chewing gum, one hand resting on her jutted hip. "What if he *sees* me?" Her blue eyes widened then narrowed, years of small intrigue etched upon the tiny, pinched features.

"So he sees you," Tasha replied. "So what?" She looked intently at Trish and willed her with all her might to stop chomping her gum, but Trish continued, unheeded.

"I don't trust that man. He's my boss, but I just don't trust him." Trish's tone was hushed; conspiratorial, a quick sideways flick of her sky-shadowed eyes to the hot and steamy kitchen.

Natasha stared at Trish, exasperated by the magnitude of her small talk. She had a radio interview tomorrow on the jazz station KCSM-FM in San Francisco and it was all she could think about. They were going to mention her new CD – the one Brett had suggested she do, well *insisted*, really and then helped her to fund; a recording of a few of her songs that they had done back in the summer...a few standards and a couple she wrote herself and together they had sent it out and now it was getting some airplay. *Jazz...what was I thinking? It certainly has not made the music road any easier.* But she loved it. And one thing she vowed was to always be true to herself, and her heart. Her mind worked itself around itself, her thoughts racing...only one ear half-cocked to Trish's lamentations.

Agustus' head was down as always, bent over that open grill, a slight sweat trickling from his temple along the left side of his face towards his chin. Natasha tried not to notice this aspect of him. And she tried not to wonder where the sweat went when it trickled *all the way down.* Did it fall onto one of the burgers? Into the fries? On the fried eggs? Into the bacon? No one would notice, Natasha thought. The food at Jake's Diner was definitely not high-end. Although, she thought, with a slight pride, the coffee *is* the best it can be. She took a great responsibility and pride in her coffee customers. More than one had commented on the rich depth of her brew. Now that she had finally perfected it. She instinctively looked down the counter to where Sy usually sat; but his stool still stood empty. She shook her head.

No, Agustus was not dangerous and Trish just had too much time on her hands.

Agustus, of course, although he never raised his head, heard the entire exchange, even though Trish's voice had been pointedly hushed. But a hushed voice is the greatest allure and Agustus had very good hearing, even after his very noisy nights. He was actually surprised he had any hearing left at all. But his ear, his instincts, his savior, perked up and he resolved to watch Trish and wait for her first mistake and then fire her. He held no loyalties and she could not be trusted. Agustus had a very definite set of standards that he expected of others. A silent, rigid, interior criteria that he measured others, and his employees against. It was a "code of conduct" if you will and he adhered to it adamantly. He disliked gossip. He disliked gaudy makeup. He disliked skirts that were too short. These were some of his criteria for women. And Trish had today alone, failed two of his minor criteria; gossip and gaudy makeup. The rest of his list he dared not even think about. And as for men, well, Agustus was not in the habit of keeping company with men, except at night, and his night-time expeditions were wholly different from his time spent in the day and so required a completely different set of criteria which he refused to let himself think about during the day, when he was working.

But, Natasha, Natasha...she had something special. An allure he wished to indulge; but knew he never would. A fierce protectiveness that came over him when she walked in the room. A silentness that muted him. He swallowed his words when she was near. He broke into a sweat. He never wanted her to leave. He *admired* her dedication to her music. Her dedication to her daughter. Her dedication to *herself* and who she was and how she would never, ever compromise herself; her keen intelligence; her ideals. He admired the way she took pride in her work at the Diner, even though he knew she hated it. She never behaved as if it was "beneath" her. Never. And she made a damned good cup of coffee – though these things he would never tell her. She was what he wished he could be openly. But, no, he had settled for the monotony and security of owning the Diner. And his secret night escapes. He did not have the courage to be out in the open like Natasha. His curse. His love. His quiet restraint. He glared again at Trish. No, not much longer with *her* around.

———

Agustus walked down the dark, damp Alameda alley. San Francisco had been wet and the night cold. The fog bringing haze to all he saw. It was 2:45 a.m. The bar had closed at 2:00. He had been asked to leave; although he'd wanted to linger; squeeze out one more drop of joy. He'd done good tonight. The guys had loved him. He gripped the worn case hard in his clenched fist; brought it up to his chest; cradled it closely for a moment; as if protecting it from the wet. His private joy. No one was to know. His secret.

CHAPTER TEN

BOBBY SHARP DRIVES DOWN the tree-lined street in his new Cadillac. And although he does not need much, does not *want* much, really, he allows himself this one new luxury every few years. He inhales the scent of new leather, one of his favorite smells, and adjusts the knob on his radio, turning it up just a little bit. The muffled voices of conversation waft past his ears. Pleasant background static. He likes the voices on jazz radio; they do not shout. This agrees with him. He listens more intently. A woman is being interviewed. A woman with a very soft and sincere voice, slightly husky, but clear. And well spoken. *Astute!* he thinks to himself. Something in this voice draws him to her. She feels familiar. And smart. He likes listening, as if this voice is an old friend. One he has known forever. But she is young, he can tell.

The announcer announces a break from the interview and a nice "song interlude by Natasha Miller," and her song fills his ears, his car; the leather on the dash soaking her up. He breathes in again; deeper and turns up the knob just a tad more. He pulls over to the side of the road and stops the car, gently clicking the engine off; the purr of the caddie humming to a stop.

That voice...something about it...a haunted and familiar quality that continues to pull and draw him in inexplicably. *It soothes his soul.* An attraction; excitement...how to put his finger on it?...a thing he has not felt since...since.... *Harlem. Writing.*

Turn upon his insides. Virtue lost; virtue gained. All hinged upon *his* songs. All given up. *No more temptation.*

But her voice has struck him; a thimble upon the prick of his heart. Pangs seeping from his gut; seeping and replaced by ice calm. He pulls his cell phone from his pocket and dials the jazz station, punching in the numbers as the announcer states them. He confirms with the cool sounding woman that answers the phone that the singer's name is Natasha Miller, and calls information for her number. Strangely, she is listed. *A single, young girl, listed in the phone book? Odd and brazen in this day and age*...Bobby thinks to himself as he pulls a pencil out of the glove box and scribbles her name and number on the back of the yellowed folded letter he keeps in his pocket. The numbers are light; seemingly temporary but dark enough to read: 510/555-4422. *510 area code? Alameda.* He is compelled. He must not ignore it.

He carefully folds the paper back up and puts it neatly back into his upper shirt pocket.

A slow, methodical drive home.

Parks the car at the curb. Makes his way to the front door of his small place, turns the lock, insistent "click" of safety; steps inside, pulls out the folded piece of paper that has been sitting obediently in his pocket, unfolds it gently and deliberately; squints at the faint numbers written on the back of the handwritten letter and carefully dials the numbers.

555-4422, no area code is necessary. He likes the familiarity of this. He inhales and waits for it to ring. One, two, three, four – fifth ring...

"Hello?" gruff, male voice grates his ears through the receiver. "Hello?? *Hello?*" More urgent and annoyed.

This was unexpected. Bobby imagined her alone – not *with* someone. The voice startles him. He hangs up.

———

Once again on the playground Fontana thought she saw Claire staring at her. She was alone. Standing in the middle of the blacktop. Her hands folded across her chest. Her perfectly pink slightly full bottom lip jutted out in a tiny pout. Her long, brown lashes flicked down quickly when she noticed Fontana staring back at her.

Fontana jumped down off the monkey bars and landed with her usual thump onto the tanbark. She fell, ever so slightly onto her knees, something she did somewhat on purpose to prove to herself her invulnerability, straightened up purposely after having bent down to brush the small pieces of light brown tanbark pressed into her knees. Fontana wore blue, flowered shorts and a pink sweater. Her own combination on this slightly spring day. Not warm enough for short-sleeves yet, shouldn't even be wearing shorts, but shorts, with a sweater. It was Fontana's compromise with herself. And her mother, well her mother, pretty much trusted her to pick out her own clothes. She would help her to dress, sometimes, but her mother felt that Fontana's expression of herself should be her own — and this suited Fontana just fine.

Yes, Claire had been staring at her, unabashedly, for Claire. Who was usually shy and withdrawn. This shyness was often mistaken for cute coyness by others, *especially boys,* Fontana snorted to herself. But she was beginning to discover that Claire was not coy, just shy and she felt a strange protectiveness of Claire even though she did not even know her. Fontana continued to stare at the well-groomed fair-haired girl standing alone in the blue dress and purposefully strode towards her. Keeping eye contact the whole time. This bold movement set Claire off. It made her nervous. But she did not move. She just continued to stand in the middle of the playground and tried her best to meet Fontana's steady gaze as she strode toward her. After all, it had been *Claire* who had summoned Fontana with her entire will, and Fontana had *noticed.* This made Claire happy. She felt no one noticed her. She did not know that she garnered attention. She had been used to this undo attention all her life, and felt more victimized then adored. She did not know how to handle the constant stares and often felt that it was because *there was something wrong with her.* She tried constantly and in vain to fix herself, but the more she tried, the more she would clam up when called upon, or blush or blunder. The more she tried, the more she would *clam up.*

Claire was actually quite intelligent. No one could see this, though, but Fontana had begun to sense it, with the sixth sense that she had been born with, took for granted and honed since her birth. So, Fontana strode straight towards Claire and when she reached her she stuck out her hand, like a boy would do, and said, "Hi, I'm Fontana, you probably know that since we have been in class together for most of the year…anyway, I notice that you don't have any friends, so I can be your friend…If you want to. I will show you how to do tricks on the monkey bars…I'm pretty good. Remember you asked me before?" Fontana was slightly surprised at herself for doubting that Claire would remember her, and she shouldn't have made that slight about "not having any friends," but for all of her adored state, it really did seem to Fontana at that moment that Claire did *not* have any friends. Fontana had never noticed that before. Fontana, of course, did not *need* any friends. She chose whom she wished to associate with. She always had, and as she found most people her age boring and beneath her, she often chose her books, and was thus a straight "A" student, which she, of course, was very proud of.

Claire just stared at her. Her big blue eyes blinked their long brown lashes slowly. She did not speak. Just looked straight into Fontana's eyes.

Fontana was crushed, then angry. She did not like rejection. But she was sure that Claire had been *calling* her. Strange to say it, but she *felt* it. And her "feelings" were always right. She stepped her left foot back, quickly, her temper getting the best of her before she could stop it. She had wasted her time with this one. Why did she even try *anyway??* She began to spin around, to leave, to go back to the tanbark and the monkey bars and her thoughts where it was safe and she was happy and she did not have to worry about stupid girls in blue dresses that made her feel bad for them. She began to spin around when she heard,

"Wait!" A cough, "Wait, Fontana, wait, don't go…I, I, I, I stammer sometimes. I am slow, don't go." The urgency in her almost new friend's voice commanded Fontana. She stopped before she could fully spin around on her tennis-shoed heel. She had forgotten to pull up her blue knee-socks, she suddenly remembered, and she hurriedly bent down to pull them up. The new neatness of her socks bringing her comfort. She stood back up. She looked at Claire. Claire was very neat.

"Nice to meet you, Claire," she said as the lunch bell rang loudly, suddenly and insistently. They both ran to the classroom, their hearts light and touching only for a moment; then separating again as they each took their seats in Mrs. Schinct's domain. Fontana in the first seat of the third row and Claire in the last seat of the fifth row. The quiet comfort of their almost new friendship drifting between them silently across the room.

———

She cried alone in the living room. Her head in her hands. Large, wet tears rolled slowly down her oval, porcelain face. No one was home. She was relieved at this and let the tears slip, unheeded and drip down off of her chin. The pain stabbed again at her side and she was fully physically relieved when it finally subsided.

Brett was still at work – thank God. He'd been called in to teach a last minute aerobics' class this afternoon – one he had not been scheduled to teach. *Good for him,* Natasha thought, *Let him burn off a little of that aggression I've been feeling lately.* Fitness instructor – in great shape – it was his body she had been attracted to, and his steady evenness. She did not wish to rock this with her own internal instability. Her need for something *more.* The feeling she felt welling up from within her. The fear. Doubt. *About what?* she silently mused to herself. *Everything was fine.* But she felt a remove from him that frightened her. A remove that had been growing with the baby. A remove she refused to face. She didn't like it. And she did not like the silent instability it created between them and within her. She needed smooth, even, *easy.* Even though, she herself was not always smooth, even, easy – though the world would never know so. She kept her outer facade smoothly in place.

Fontana clearly did not like Brett. Natasha could still not figure out *why.* Brett had been kind and fair to Fontana. He'd never raised his voice or challenged her – perhaps that's what she had needed – someone to "challenge" her – perhaps that is what *both* of them had needed.

No, no, no! Natasha sobbed to herself – two and a half years together and she was pregnant and he was *good* to her and *this is all going to work damn it!* she muttered to herself between choked-back sobs.

It was unlike Natasha to cry. She considered herself pretty tough and looked with horror upon sniveling whiney women who burst into tears at the drop of a hat.

She lifted her head from her hands to notice the clock on the wall reading 3:15 p.m. – Fontana would be getting home soon. Natasha had told her strong-willed daughter that she would have to take the school bus home alone today, as she had the interview at the jazz station and then her doctor's appointment, and had received a reprimanding glance that said: *Again, you're not doing your part – I'm only ten – You're lucky I'm so mature....* Then the resignation and then, something that always came as such a surprise to Natasha, a conscious caring, almost maternal and protective, of Natasha and the baby within her; Fontana's unborn brother. It was as if, even pre-birth, Fontana was already assuming the role of "big sister." And taking it *very* seriously.

Her strange and mysterious daughter. Just the thought of her and then the latent, lingering thought of her own mother kicked Natasha out of her momentary personal weakness – a lapse she never allowed herself.

"Enough!" she said resolutely out loud to the empty room. "Enough Natasha Miller – you have things to do." Natasha had discovered long ago that if she kept busy any lingering negative feelings from her past were tempered and action – of any kind – propelled her through her *present* to fulfill her *future* destiny.

She jumped up, to the best of her bloated ability and waddled to the bathroom, her left hand moving instinctively to cover the sharp pain ebbing and beginning to subside on her left side.

She went into the bathroom and turned on the faucet for cold and forcefully splashed the icy droplets onto her face. *Once, twice, three, four, five, six, seven, eight, nine, ten* – she counted the splashes – the fixed rigidity and monotony of her actions giving her solace. Refreshing.

She examined herself in the mirror – face a little pale with small red flush spots from the chill of the water fading from the center of her cheeks. The requisite blue under her eyes – easily covered up with concealer for shows – dark brown hair straight and flowing just past her shoulders and almost down her back. Red eyes still a little puffy – *I'll get ice; slap it on; ignore it.* She did not want Fontana to see that she had been crying when she got home. It was important to Natasha that she be strong for her daughter.

Strong. And available.

I know! I'll bake cookies! That thought perked her up and the thought of Fontana coming home to a house filled with the warm scent of freshly baking chocolate chip cookies made her smile. She padded to the small kitchen in her fluffy green-socked feet and pulled a roll of store-bought and premade slice and bake Toll House Cookie Dough from the fridge.

She felt so *motherly.* She liked it. Just as she was peeling the plastic paper off of the roll the phone rang. "Shit!" The knife slipped off the plastic, caught the side of her pinky, cut it slightly, small drop of blood dripping to the cutting board. She shook her finger grabbed a paper towel, reached for the phone.

"Hello?" Her voice was slightly agitated. "Hello?" she said again, most insistently, cradling the phone beneath her chin and neck, wrapping the paper towel tighter around her little finger. Ready to hang up. *Those damn telemarketers!* she thought to herself for the millionth time.

"Is this Natasha Miller?" The small voice on the other end said.

"Yes." Emphatically; definitely; but something kept her holding on.

"Hi, I'm Bobby Sharp and I heard you on the radio recently...."

CHAPTER ELEVEN

"*A AAAGGGHHHH!*" The scream was far away and around her. Was it from her? Wildly she looked from side to side; slice of pain to her left side intensifying, splitting her in two. "*Aaaaaaagggghhhh!* Dear God! *What is happening???*" The words spilled from her – still, dry whispers beneath cold sweat. There was not this much pain; this much haziness with the birth of Fontana. Loins splitting; stomach ripe and bursting – but the baby was not moving. It sat a lump within her, a stone lodged within her belly. An eight-and-a-half pound stone that was without movement. A weight that she had carried within her and now refused to leave.

The last three months of her pregnancy had been difficult, the searing pain on her left side coming and going in relation to the amount of stress she put on herself, or so that is what she had told herself, and Natasha had forced herself, finally, against her own strong will and independence to take it easy and allow Brett to baby her a bit. She sat in the evenings with her feet up and even took the last two weeks off of work and then quit. She really had no choice. She was too tired. It was as if the baby were sucking every last drop of her will to live and energy from her tired body. She had gained weight too. A lot more than with Fontana and this extra weight and the ever-so-slow movements of her lazy child had affected her own quick and vital movements. They were both slow; sluggish. And she had despondently resigned herself to her new lethargic and rotund disposition.

The last two weeks of her pregnancy were the hardest. Hard to just *be home*. She tried to write, tried to sing; but it was as if the baby had wrapped itself around her vocal cords; her voice escaping choked and thin. So she stopped. Brett was happy, though. Happier than she had seen him in a while. After his actions only a month and a half earlier. Something she tried to push away even now, while lying on the operating table in the delivery room, bright white lights glaring from overhead. Consciousness floating in and out. Memories coming and receding.

A dream; yes it was a dream, she thought. That last month and a half before the contractions. The silent exchanges she and Brett would have. Did he sense her feelings? No, he did not approve of her staying out late in her advanced state. But he never said anything. Just looked concerned until that one night when she came waddling up the stairs, seven-and-a-half month swell leading the way after a show at Jake's. She had finally given in and left Fontana home with him that night. With the pain in her side and her increased bulk, she just couldn't risk the late-night temptation to carry Fontana up the stairs should she fall asleep. And although she had been pregnant and not feeling so vivacious, her show had gone well. She had received a standing ovation and stayed long after it was over to talk and sign CDs — allowing herself to revel in the warmth and affection of long-time customers who'd come repeatedly to see her and now were somewhat like family to her. Watching Fontana grow up. Watching Natasha grow up. Watching this current pregnancy. She went through these things with them. She felt comforted by them.

So she had stayed late. And tiredly made her way up the stairs at almost 2:00 a.m. to find Brett sullen and staring at the television set. She was surprised to see him up. Usually he was fast asleep by the time she came in, especially if it was late like this. But he had waited up and he definitely had something to say.

"It's not good for the baby." It was a short, curt statement. She ignored it. She couldn't stop doing shows. He knew it. She knew it. She moved away; moved past him; stepped silently down the hallway to the bathroom, the sweet relief of her pee taking away the sting of his direct remark.

She heard the guest room door click behind him then, right before she flushed. And she made her way into their bedroom. Alone. She would sleep alone. *No guilt!* She silently screamed to herself. But she felt an aching that he was not near her; an aching mixed with relief - and she rolled over in bed; long nightgown twisting over her bulk. Alone. She heard a slight snore from the room next door. Yes, Brett asleep. She closed her eyes; weary.

CHAPTER TWELVE

"*J*UST SHOW ME YOU LOVE ME, *Tasha*. Just show me you love me! You can stay all night out at clubs with people *you don't even know*. With people that don't even care about you…while you are carrying *my child*. But you can't even kiss me with pure pleasure when you get home. I know what you're thinking. I know you don't really love me. I know NOTHING COMES BEFORE YOUR MUSIC. I know I am second. But it can't be that way anymore. You are going to have *my* child. And I now have *some* say in what you do with *your body* and *your time*!" His face was red; inflated with anger. He stared at her and balled his fists by his sides.

Natasha looked back at Brett, coffee mug in hand, anger apparent in her eyes. She moved back away from him; stared straight at him. And then she spoke; her words low and forcefully stinging the space between them. "No one tells me what to do with my body or my time! You are sorely mistaken, mister if you think that you are in charge of me!" Her quick temper flashing to lash him. Tongue slapping out her words before thinking. Eyes blazing deep brown. "*You do not own me! You never will!*" There, it was said. And she was immediately sorry.

She was out of breath and huffing considerably now. And had backed away as far as she could and was standing, fists clenched with her back against the wall, and somehow, somehow, as she spoke he had approached her and was against her. Pushing his body against her extended belly, trying to love her, but she pushed him away. "Stop it! I'm just not in the mood!"

But he continued to press against her; to try to hold her; comfort her as he had been able to do in the past. But it was too forceful; it was not the same and suddenly she grabbed her side; doubled over; "Oh, God! Not again, oh God! Oh God! Why won't this pain stop?" She slid down the back of the kitchen wall slowly; holding her coffee cup out; about to drop it; Brett grabbed the cup quickly from her hand, balanced it in his right hand and used his left to support her as she slid.

"You okay, Tasha? Everything okay Tasha?" He didn't know what to do and through his words she had slid down the white kitchen wall to the linoleum speckled floor and just sat there. No more anger, tears blazing through the pain.

"We've got to get you to a doctor, Tasha, this just isn't right."

"No, no, just give it a moment, let me be. Just let me catch my breath."

"Tasha, I'm so sorry. I didn't mean to hurt you. You know I love you. I'm *sorry*...there's just *so much going on*.... I'm not sure...I'm not sure if you *love* me." There, he had said it. Tears filled his eyes. Anguish she had never seen. She reached for him. Both arms out, he bent down to cradle her; hold her. He helped her up. They stood against each other in the kitchen's morning light. Silent exchange; leaning into each other. Silent apologies.

Great emotion leads to real clarification, doesn't it? Natasha's hard mind flicked to life as she leaned against him. Fear gone. Clarity – clear. She saw them for what they were at that moment. Two scared parents-to-be struggling with a love that may not still be if it were not for the baby. She pushed it from her mind. Stood fully up. Shook it off. Moved forward. His hand on the back of her arm; leading her to the small chair at the kitchen table.

"AAAAAAAGGGGGGHHHHHHH!" She heard it again, waking from her dream state, that primal cry that came from outside of her, yet from deep within. The stone that refused to move down from her belly through the birth canal. She saw Brett's face hovering above her own. Concern streaked his handsome features. Was that a tear in the corner of his eye? Or was he just tired from the endless hours they had spent together while she was in labor.

Brett, the model of a "husband" during the whole ordeal. Stroking her forehead when the contractions came; fetching her cool cloths when needed; following every instruction that was given him by a doctor or nurse. *The past forgotten…the past forgotten….* Sitting, concerned beside her bed, in the birthing room as she went through the contractions. Breathing with her. *"Wooo! Wooo! Wooo!"* Natasha had not taken any prenatal birthing classes. She had done that with Fontana when she was younger and found it to be a complete waste of time. You feel a contraction; you push. Breathing is breathing. Breathing in little "Ah, ah, ah, ah's" or whatever it was they advocated was a stupid distraction. But Brett had been there, attentive and caring.

As if nothing had happened. Nothing at all.

She had envisioned: friendship; caring; a nice light interaction. Independence. Freedom. But, no this is not what it had been. It had been hard; slow; full of pain; contradictions. She and Brett hardly spoke toward the end, his warmth turned to stony silence; their exchanges short and curt. Their friendship; their love…just fizzled. Did she ever really love him? She searched her mind through the haze to try to find the cause of it all – it was her, her, she knew….

No, nothing had gone as she had planned…no…nothing at all.

And now, here they were, stark-gray operating room. Natasha's eyes flicked wildly left to right; ceiling; up; down. Something was wrong. *So wrong.* There were too many doctors. *They must have given me something…* she thought woozily through hazy kitchen memory. An incident and clarity she had willed to forget but in some strange way had brought her peace. She had known at that moment that she was free. She did not know how. She just knew.

"Aaaaaaaaagggghhhhh!" The pain overtook her again. The same searing pain that went from her left side – a band through her belly; a knife ripping through tight jelly. Still no movement. Her baby was still. "Come on little one, wake up!" Natasha cried internally to her son. "Move, now! I love you, *come out!*"

Their relationship while he was inside her had been a fragile one. He was strong and big. And sluggish. And she loved him and she wanted to meet him. But that nagging sense, that *nagging sense*, that she had tried to ignore had made it difficult to find the same connection that that she had had with Fontana.

Come on little B.B.! I LOVE YOU!! She screamed with her whole soul while she willed her body to push out the little guy.

"Push, honey! Good, good, you're doing great…" Brett said between choked sobs.

Why is he crying? Natasha thought to herself. She glanced wildly from doctor to doctor. *Doctor to Doctor!* A surgeon, her obstetrician. "What's going on?" she cried. "What's *wrong*? Why am I in the operating room? I thought I could deliver in the birthing room. Why have you wheeled me in *here*? Why don't I remember getting here? *What is the matter?*"

Blackness.

CHAPTER THIRTEEN

S HE WAS ALIVE. She blinked her eyes and looked around the room. Lights still glaring.

Blink. Blink.

Pain.

Blink.

Moan. Her voice was far away. Somewhere else. Not her own.

Some other woman who lay there – bleeding.

She pushed, again, *hard*. The baby slipped out. No cry. No sound forced from its mouth. Slightly blue. No wiggling toes and arms. Beautiful in its stillness.

Brett does not cut the umbilical cord – he lets the doctor do it; watching as the nurse silently holds the long cord and the doctor clips. One snip. And it is over. No one speaks. Doctor Simpkin looks at Brett sympathetically; eyes moist. *Fond of her,* Brett thinks, noticing it all – all moving slow motion – he reaches for the baby automatically; watches his hands. He had been holding a small white and blue hospital blanket and did not even realize it. *How did I get this? Who handed it to me?* Random thoughts again. No meaning, really.

Tenderly he wraps the small, still bundle in the warm hospital blanket and cradles his son gently in his arms, stroking its smooth and still cheek. The tiny blue body in his arms...cradling...cradling.

Standing at the foot of the operating table, he looks down at Natasha, lying inert on the cold steel and covered by a thin white sheet. He watches the blood drip down from between her spread legs and onto the linoleum floor; shiny crimson against glaring white. He thinks how someone is

going to have to clean this up. Her calves are still resting in the metal stir-
rups covered by half moons of plastic cushion; she looks asleep.

Commotion; clamoring heard only through cotton fog: Hospital moni-
tors beeping emphatically, signaling that Natasha is dangerously close to death.
Brett standing silently on the fringes; doctors and nurses buzzing around her,
ignoring his still, large presence; doctor barking out orders: "Get me two cc's
of adrenaline, quick, her heartbeat has slowed to thirty beats a minute."

"Her blood pressure is fifty over thirty, doctor."

"Her blood pressure is dropping too rapidly. Stat! *Stat!*" The authoritative voice slices through the sterile air.

Not real. It moves in slow motion; fades away –

———

He knew the sun slid down the sky and that it was dusk. He had been
inside these hospital walls for a full thirty-six hours. He had not seen sunlight; had hardly slept. He sat in the hospital cafeteria alone. Staring into
the muddy brown of his weak coffee. Two doctors with trays filled with
food passed him, joking congenially – Brett watched – hang-dogged, as
they disappeared around the corner and into the Doctor's Private Lounge
as it was labeled so clearly on the heavy blue door.

He gulped one long gulp of his coffee. He did not feel the caffeine. He
only felt the brown liquid, slightly warm, slide down his throat and into
his stomach. Felt the warmness there as it sat in that empty space.

He had not had much food since yesterday.

He had almost lost her, and even now it was iffy. Nothing mattered.

He did not crave food. He did not even want the coffee – but he wanted something to *stimulate* him, to take away the deadness he felt stretching
through his muscled limbs. Muscles that ached and throbbed from hours
of tension. Physical tension he had not even known he was feeling. He was
sorer now than after any workout. A soreness that melded with the dead
heaviness he felt each time he tried to lift an arm or a leg.

And a dull thud of a heart. A stone that beat sullenly within his breast.
With all the rest – of the non-feelings.

He knew he had lost her – lost them both – and even though she had clutched his hand direly before again passing out, whispering, "Our love…our baby…." He knew she was lost. And he was certain, though he held no proof – for words should speak only for themselves and not be taken at face value – that by "our love" she meant the love they had created together: the child. The dead child.

Memory flashed as white light behind lightening guilt.

Natasha's back sliding down the kitchen wall. Her big belly heaving against his. It was all so quick; their argument; the pain; the slide. *Had he caused it???* Guilt ate at him now. A guilt he could not ignore. Did he have a right to demand her love? Even though she had been carrying his child? No.

He had not physically hurt her, no. But his jealousy had been raging. A feeling he had not felt before. He had stopped himself. He had left no marks on her skin. He had let her go.

Staring into the depths of his coffee cup, sitting alone in this cafeteria, he wished he could call on Religion now to guide and comfort him. But no, what little Protestant upbringing he had been given growing up had promptly been replaced in his life by the ecstasy of working out when he moved from Missouri to Northern California. A high that far surpassed the spiritual "high" of his youth.

He had noticed Natasha right away in his aerobics' class. He remembered this now as he stared into his murky coffee. She – struggling to keep up. He could tell she did not work out enough – not by her figure – her figure was great. Long and lean and slightly curvy; her dark brown hair tied back by a bright pink ribbon. A novel sight amongst the hard-core exercisers around her: Women in their twenties and thirties that approached their exercise and his class with the mentality of pre-servicemen in boot camp. Hard-edged from years of sought out and welcomed torture. Toned bodies the badge they wore for their dedication. Early wrinkles etching their way around glossed mouths and expertly lined eyes – lines born from lack of fat and lack of sleep – their early mornings spent working out instead of sleeping before work.

Brett's critical eye took in all of this every morning – then he reprimanded himself for his criticalness and reminded himself of his inborn

Christian heart. And then, one morning he had noticed Natasha and her unaware purity; and her inability to follow his class precisely so contrasted with the experts around her and drew to him a sense of protectiveness over her he had not felt before.

He had approached her after class.

He had been tender. He *had* protected her.

Until that night.

Until now.

He should have been more adamant about her pushing herself so hard. He should have *insisted* that she quit work earlier and *just stay home.* He should have *cared for her more.* Gone with her to her shows. Gone to the doctor with her more. He *should of, should of, should of....*

And he feared, no – he *knew,* and he shook his head vehemently – trying to drown his thoughts; his knowledge; in the last of the muddy coffee which stared back so still and dull. Black memories. *Accusing* him.

He slammed his brown cafeteria mug down on the Formica table and it hit with an unexpected thud. A man and woman lost deep in whispering conversation suddenly looked up and over at Brett, startled by his sudden display of emotion. A tear in the woman's eye – quickly wiped away by the pinkie of her left hand. *Someone else who lost someone? Did he care?*

He stared straight ahead, lost in his own thoughts. Not ready to go home yet. One more visit to Natasha's hospital room before going home. He took a deep breath and got up from the table and made his way out of the bright cafeteria, ignoring the clock on the wall above the exit that read: 2:45 a.m.

———

So then, he put his head down in his hands and he cried. His broad shoulders shaking uncontrollably with the weight of his sobs. He was alone in the apartment now. Natasha was still in the hospital. Two days of fighting for her life. Kidney and liver failure. *How did this happen? How did they not catch this? How did it come to this??* Brett could not believe it. He could not believe that their lives had changed so drastically. So *instantly.*

CHAPTER FOURTEEN

THERE WAS A SMALL KNOCK on the bedroom door and Natasha lifted her swollen head from the silk pillow. *What time is it?* she thought wearily, watching hazy sunlight stream in from half-open blinds. Still her mind was fuzzy and her body weak. Thin, white arms lying limply at her sides. Sweat from the previous night dried and matted in her hair. The high fever finally broken and after a week in the hospital she had been released to go home.

Brett had carried her up the stairs. So tender and attentive he had been; cradling her lovingly in his arms – how could she ever have doubted him? In her haze, she mentally doubted her doubt.

He had stood by her bed, day and night, during the difficult ordeal in the hospital after the loss of their baby and her severe near fatal toxemia. How long the baby had been dead inside of her the doctors at this point were not even sure. A week? A day? An hour? It was hard for them to tell, they had told her. She had not witnessed Brett tenderly holding the dead child in his arms. Near death herself, she had passed out from the pain and complications. She did not even see the child. And no one had the heart to show him to her. But Brett had been there afterwards, in her recovery room as she floated in and out of consciousness, either sitting beside her lovingly stroking her outstretched hand, or her forehead; or she would notice him through orange haze sitting, head lolling to the side as if he were fighting sleep, in the small blue chair across the room from her bed.

Did he ever actually really sleep? she had wondered in her stupefied state.

PART I – NATASHA

She saw Fontana once, through the filmy gauze of her disease. Standing hesitantly at the back of the room with Trish. Her light brown eyes flecked wide with fear; amber receding. Her usually aggressive, cross-armed stance released. Arms hung motionless at her sides. Vulnerability naked and aching. All this Natasha saw quickly and instinctively; the thick fog of medication pressing her deep into the hospital bed.

And then Trish had taken Fontana's small hand in her own and Fontana had *allowed* this. Supple in her lack of retribution. And Trish Wilcox had led Fontana out of the room and Fontana went willingly. Mute. Silent. No accusatory words behind her gaze. All as if in a dream.

Natasha's eyes fluttered back shut. *So heavy…so heavy…. So* tired.

She opened her eyes to the warmth of her own bedroom now and saw Fontana peeking around the door.

"Don't you have school today, Honey?" Natasha choked out – voice hoarse and throat dry – still – from the intubation tube that had been used to keep her breathing steadily and keep fluids out of her lungs. She swallowed, forcibly feeling the scratchiness – the lump of pain still there.

Why don't they pad those stupid things? she thought characteristically to herself, thinking of the hard-edged plastic tube that was shoved so unceremoniously down her unsuspecting throat. *Just sharp plastic edges – shoved down your throat – how archaic.*

Momentary flash of vitality flushed through her mind and then disintegrated behind the weariness within her.

Natasha cleared her throat again willing strength into her voice for her daughter.

"Honey?" Fontana had edged herself next to Natasha's bed. Natasha hadn't even noticed. Fontana had moved imperceptibly and now stood peering with great maternal authority over her mother.

Natasha cleared her throat yet again, a weak exhale of air – attempting to clear the cobwebs from her throat, her mind, her body. She spoke; willing all of her maternal energy into her vocal chords – attempting to convey a mother's security – a sense of safety to Fontana.

"Honey, be a doll and get me a glass of water, would you?" A squeak; an attempt at normalcy urging her voice. But panic rose within her as the words escaped. *This is not normal*, her logical mind rang out. *I am not normal!* Fire rang within her — she shut her eyes tight to hide the fear that rose behind them. She opened them after several moments, Fontana had already left the room. Quietly stepping across the small apartment in her tennis-shoed feet to fulfill her mother's request. She heard the telephone ringing from far away.

Fontana had not spoken a word; had only conveyed a sense of wisdom and security to her ailing mother. *How can a ten-year-old make* me *feel more secure? It's supposed to be the* other *way around,* Natasha thought, exhausted. Just then Fontana reappeared with the water, handed it silently to her mother with round, watchful eyes. "Mom, it's grandma on the phone."

Natasha struggled to sit up. Fontana reached towards her, pulling her arm in an attempt to help her; watching Natasha begin to sweat again with the effort of her movement. She watched the color drain from her mother's face. She said nothing, but only arranged the large feather pillow behind her mother's head, fumbling with the size of it and the weight of Natasha's adult body. Natasha reached to her left and picked up the receiver. "Hello?"

She held the receiver close to her ear. The high muted voice strained at the other end of the line and Natasha visibly tensed. "I'm...I'm...all right.... I just need to get better...just tired...so tired...." Fontana cocked her head to hear. Natasha sat up straight, a slight strength moving through her, she reached over and brushed a lock of hair from Fontana's forehead. Ignored the bit of perspiration beginning to form on her own. "No, no, it's all right...." She cleared her throat. "It's over now. Over." She glanced over at her daughter, not wanting to say too much. "I just need to get better...I'm, I'm still weak...." She gripped the receiver tightly — knuckles shining blue beneath thin skin. Fingers becoming numb. She sucked in a short breath — ice-blue calm descending.

"Sure, mom, whatever you want.... Listen, I've gotta go...." She could not acknowledge the words *I love you.* She hung up; laid her head back on the soft pillow. Closed her eyes.

Fontana picked the glass up from the nightstand where she had set it and handed it again to her mother. Natasha drank greedily at first, a raw heated thirst coursing through her, then willed herself to slow down. To show dignity and resolve and moderation to this child, even in her current state.

The loss of her baby hit her again – a slap to the face; the reality of it a thud; a weight; an anchor upon her ankles dragging her down. She felt the tears threatening to come; the constriction of her throat; the pain in her belly; an empty hollow pain made of nothing. She pulled Fontana close. Half in an attempt to hide her weakness from her daughter; half in love and thankfulness for this child – the one she *did* have. Gratefulness and grieving mixed together, Natasha finally allowed herself to cry, large choking sobs; holding her daughter; Fontana succumbing to her mother's affections. Supplication in receipt of her mother's misery. Still; quiet. She still did not speak.

CHAPTER FIFTEEN

T HE SUN STREAKED BUTTERCUP LIGHT through still half-closed blinds; dust illuminated and floating around them. Dust Natasha did not know existed. Dust she had ignored over the past few weeks. She and Fontana were in her bedroom slowly getting dressed for the funeral. The mundane routineness of it all giving Natasha welcome solace.

*Aiden...*Natasha thought, *I will only refer to him as "Aiden" — not "the baby" — as if it is an inanimate object, but* Aiden. *My child. The child that gave his life for me.*

She could think about it now. Only two weeks had passed, but she could think about it now. *Aiden*, a name she and Brett had both agreed on. A *neutral* name. And by naming him, and seeing him, she was finally able to slightly quell the dull thud of muted anxiety that had continued to rise in her gut.

Natasha gently rolled up one white sock and leaned over to help Fontana put it on her foot, a gesture Fontana allowed; having begun to revel in her mother's affection. And as she slipped the black patent leather shoe on Fontana's foot, she spoke impulsively, "You don't have to see the baby put in the ground, honey." The statement was firm; definite...a resolve within.

Fontana stopped moving then; perfectly still; staring straight into her mother's eyes; hesitation for a second and then the resolute stomp of her one shoed foot; a yank from Natasha's palm. "I *need* to go! I need to see my baby brother put to rest." Natasha pulled away. Quiet. Folding back into herself. Staring mutely at Fontana, unable to speak. Unable to think of anything to say in response. Staring. Back.

For the truth was, she, herself secretly did not want to go. She did not want to see her dead baby again. It had been a routine viewing at the morgue while making all the arrangements and it was almost more than she could bear. She wanted to put it out of her mind; her heart; and move on. But the dull, lifeless feeling in her own limbs would not leave her. She could not shake her fatigue. Her utter inability to *feel*. Anything. And she had not sung a note in over a month. She did not have the will to. She did not even care. It had left her. The fire she had held so close to her breast. It had left her. All will had left her. But these things she must never let Fontana see. These feelings she must continue to keep secret. She smiled. Over-brightly. She cleared her throat, still feeling the scratch of the tube deep within.

Mustering courage for her defiant daughter who, unlike herself, so insisted on this closure – she grabbed Fontana's hand firmly, and with a bright, mute smile on her face she led her out of the bedroom. Like two schoolgirls clad in black and on their way to a party they swung their arms and did not speak. Hands clasped tight; they moved towards the living room, and Brett, who sat patiently waiting.

The drive to the funeral home was long. And although it was only ten miles away, the unnatural and eerie silence in the car stretched out the mute minutes. Fontana did not attempt to speak, nor to even make one witty wise remark. She had not spoken much since Natasha's return from the hospital. Only observed.

Natasha sat still, staring straight ahead as they passed endless telephone poles and street signs. The lump and bile rising in her throat; apprehension filling her abandoned gut. She laid her head back gently against the cool leather of the car's headrest and exhaled silently as Brett drove slowly; mechanically down the winding roads toward the cemetery.

He straightened his back. Gripped the wheel tighter; muscles rippling beneath his funeral attire. Jacket, tie, pressed button-up-the-front cotton starched shirt. Things he normally did not wear.

I must be strong for Natasha, he repeated in his mind over and over again – a mantra he had made his prayer. *I must be strong for Natasha....* But she was so withdrawn. So silent. They had hardly touched since the baby died. Had not made love.

He parked the car in the lot and waited for the "girls," as he had come to think of them, to get out of the car. He still called them "the girls"; *his girls.* A longing; a pang, ran through his chest. *His girls.* He choked back a sob; refusing to cry. Once was enough.

I must be strong for Natasha....

He stepped behind Natasha as her foot landed on the pavement, steering her firmly by the elbow; afraid to touch her more. She seemed so fragile to him. Fragile and hollow. It was a part of her he had not seen before and it scared him. He said nothing.

"Thanks, Honey." She looked to him, grateful for his calm assurance.

"Of course." The reply was stiff. No emotion. Numb.

Natasha tripped then, unintentionally, as she stepped up the curb to the sidewalk and she clutched him; letting his assurance sink into her; steady her. He reached around her back and pulled her close. Fontana continued to hold tightly to her mother's hand. She looked up at Brett, smiled, looked away. Unexpectedly happy at his presence at this particular moment.

They entered the wide double doors of the church.

"Oh my God," Natasha exclaimed under her breath as she looked out and over the filled church. Pew after pew filled with people, something she did not expect. People from the community; from the Stage Coach, from the Diner. "What are all these people doing here?" She turned to Brett. He surveyed the room.

*Deserving of you, of course...*he thought to himself characteristically. But how could she know how special she was? How could she know how guilty he felt for not taking better care of her; for *pushing* her. Is that what he did? Push her too hard? Again the guilt assaulted him; again he pushed it away.

And that's the great thing about Tasha, he thought as he slowly continued to take in the scene at the church, *her complete unawareness of her power.* The calm authority she applies to everything. The way she gives others the ability to pursue their own dreams because of her quiet pursuit of hers. The strength she has always held; yet now has disappeared and been replaced by what? – this fragile and hollow woman who clung to him and he did not know. Had he ever told her this? Had he been good enough to her? Had he given her *enough?* These questions rambled through his mind now as he tried to concentrate on the present, a present he did not want to face.

No, he had to answer honestly, *he did not know.* All he knew was that he *loved* her. With his whole heart he loved her, an ache that rested now in his limbs and would not go away. And he knew she was gone – going – to some strange dark place that he could not journey to.

He continued to glance around the church as they slowly walked up the long, burgundy-carpeted aisle toward the alter with its tiny open coffin, seeing a few close friends: his workout partner Daryn; Jan and Don from down the street. Agustus from the coffee shop; Trish – an ever-steady presence as always and an unexpected source of friendship and support. He turned to Natasha, she nodded back silently.

The precariousness of life washed over them both simultaneously and they silently and gratefully thanked God in their own individual ways for the gift of these unexpected friendships. Natasha noticed with slight humor that Trish's blue eye shadow was tactfully toned down in submission to the dire circumstances and she was grateful and humored by the uniqueness of Trish. For this also, had been a gift.

She reached the casket hesitantly. Flowers draped over its tiny edges; the lid open for viewing. Off-white silk against the small cherry wood coffin soft and inviting. *Like cotton under the Nativity,* Brett thought, catching himself.

They had both thought they would have to take out a small loan for a proper burial. They had even started the proceedings, but Natasha's friends at the coffee shop and at The Stage Coach had taken up a collection and raised enough money for the funeral, even leaving enough left over for Natasha and Fontana to do with what they wished. "A little something to cheer you up!" Al, the owner of The Stage Coach had said cheerfully as he handed Natasha the white unmarked envelope stuffed with bills.

Natasha had been amazed. Amazed at the kindness of this little community she lived in. Amazed that so many people recognized her; cared for her. Cared at all. She had always felt so alone, even when doing the benefit events she so enjoyed; the things that took her away from herself; the things for no pay; the things Brett would get mad about: "You are not in a position to volunteer your time at this point," he would say sternly, "you can volunteer your time when you are *successful*, when you have made it...." He had said it with emphasis, but without anger. Was this her payback? Was this how they knew her? That is not why she had done it, but what a welcome respite this unexpected gesture had offered her at that moment.

So, she and Brett had splurged and chosen the cherry wood casket with the off-white silk interior. She peeked over the edge. The casket was tiny. The baby even tinier inside; laid out like a prince – he looked beautiful and rosy and Natasha gasped audibly aloud to herself, her hand reflexively flying to her neck. The tears threatening to well yet again. *He is almost ethereal in his stillness*, she thought, instinctively picking him up and wrapping him lovingly in the small white blanket they had brought, as if he were still alive. As if she would take him home after this dreadful thing was over. As if it was all – all right. Normal. A normal family. Holding their new baby.

She held her child for the first and last time.

Fontana pulled her small Kodak camera from the pink purse dangling from her shoulder. She stepped back a few paces from Brett and Natasha and with methodic intensity she carefully focused and then snapped her picture. The picture she had been wanting since the day her mother had returned from the hospital without her baby brother. The picture she would keep in memory of him.

Love welled in Natasha's eyes. The overwhelming feeling of it expanding her heart; her solar plexus, overtaking her anxiety; her misery. Her emptiness. Love for her daughter; for her lost son. And she realized, yet again, as it sank into her and fed her emptiness; the inherent wisdom of children. The path that each of her children had led her down. She realized her daughter's insistence on saying goodbye to her baby brother, had helped her to do the same. To finally find closure. To say goodbye. And release him.

PART II – *Bobby*

And so the words she said were still undone — as worlds unfurled beneath a sun — that hung so low, then disappeared...and it was all without fear....

CHAPTER SIXTEEN

HARLEM, NEW YORK – *1959:*

HE SAT WITH HER in his room. He didn't know where to go or what to do. She was lying there on his bed. Was she dead? He couldn't tell. He didn't want to know. His mind was racing; he was high; but sinking. How old was she? 17? 18? 19?

He didn't want to look at her. She'd been there for hours.

Curse the day he had let that aunt into his life; into his apartment. "I've got some.... You want some?" she'd said, flashing the stash she had, quickly pulling it out from within the secret folds of her small black clutch. "We just need a place to do it.... I've got nowhere to do it...can we go to your apartment? You live alone, right?" She glanced furtively from left to right. He noticed the sweat beginning to form on her upper lip.

Bobby hesitated. Something about her was rubbing him the wrong way. He'd met her on the corner. Isn't that strange? To meet a woman of her caliber on the corner? She was well-dressed. Well put together. She wore a brown felt hat with a touch of fur at the corner and Bobby had imagined her in church on Sunday wearing that hat with matching caramel leather gloves.

She had a little boy with her, maybe five years old, it was hard for Bobby to tell. He was small. And quiet. The Girl wasn't with her that time. He had never met the Girl before.

Yes, the first time he had met her – "the Aunt" as he now referred to her in his mind – well, the first time he met her, she was with the small boy and she was standing on the corner and she was buying drugs, just like him. They had struck up a conversation. She had seemed nice. Safe. They had a mutual bond. The baggie of heroin she held discreetly in her hand. He knew he would see her again. He liked her then. She was older, in her mid-thirties, like Bobby. But she seemed and behaved older even still. Bobby had about him a "young" way. A youthfulness that belied his mid-thirties actual age. And this woman. This "older" woman was a safety to him in a strange and complex way. A mother complex? He hadn't cared at that point.

Because now this "safe" woman; this older woman, had come into his apartment with her niece and given him the drugs he so craved. Ah, the sweet relief. Not a high anymore. Just relief. Relief from the shaking and sweating and the runny nose and the nausea. Now he felt normal. But still he wanted more. She had left a little more for him when she had rushed out.

"I gotta go," she'd said. Just like that. And she'd left her niece passed out on the bed. He looked at her again. Her arm was flung out to the left. A small dribble of spit oozed from the side of her mouth. He reached toward her. He poked her. Nothing. She did not move. Not one iota.

And it had happened *instantly*. He didn't even know her name. But "the Girl," she had willingly stuck out her arm. He could tell the cravings were strong in her. She had stuck out her arm and the Aunt had slowly and expertly inserted the needle into her blue and bulging vein, and then she had laid her head back on his pillow, the small white crisp cotton pillowcase beneath her dark head. She had laid her head back and her eyes had rolled far into her forehead and she had closed them and sighed and just like that she was dead.

The Aunt and Bobby pretended that she had just passed out. The Aunt reached toward her niece and shook her and then said matter-of-factly: "She is just passed out." But he saw fear flick in her eyes. He did not want to see this. But he saw. And then the Aunt said, as she jumped up off the bed, she'd said: "I gotta go take home the kid. Here's some more for ya." And she'd thrown the plastic bag on the bed. And she'd hurried out and she'd left Bobby alone with the passed out/dead niece. The Girl. The niece without a name. The 17 or 18 or 19-year-old niece without a name that would not wake up and still had her head on his pillow.

Bobby sat on the blue plastic chair in his room across from his bed and stared at her for a while. He did not touch the additional drugs the Aunt had left. He just looked at the Girl and willed her to wake up but she did not move. So he went to the bathroom and washed his face and combed his hair. Then he went back out to the living room/bedroom and poked the Girl again. Still she did not move. So he turned his back to her and made a decision.

———

Afterwards, when the deed was done, he methodically re-combed his rumpled hair and changed his shirt – from the blue button-down crisp cotton shirt, to the white button-down crisp cotton shirt with the blue stripes. No wrinkles. He looked nice.

Then he left his apartment, closing the door gently behind him. He heard the quiet "click" of the door as it closed. He inserted his key, methodically, and listened to the click again as he turned the lock. He took the two flights of stairs down to the street and then walked the three blocks to his parents' apartment.

When he arrived, he found his father watching TV and his mother cooking in the kitchen. He inhaled deeply, familiar smells wafting over him and inciting youthful memory. Both his parents were proud of their black and white. A recent acquisition that his father made good use of.

His mother was a good cook. He liked the comfort of his mother. His father nodded as he entered the apartment, his mother's warm eyes greeted him as he entered the kitchen. "You here to eat?" she said.

Ignoring the fact that he was high. Having faith in the fact that he would not always be high. Glad that he was alive. Glad that he came to eat.

"Uh, yeah, Mother, that would be great." And he kissed her on the cheek and went into the living room and sat down in the other easy chair next to the one his father was sitting in. And they silently watched TV together. A preview for *Bonanza* came on – his dad visibly lit up for a moment;

a spark that settled over his brown features and then drifted down and away. Bobby glanced over at him. His father did not look at him again. He only raised his hand to his mouth every now and then to pour more beer down his throat.

Bobby did not care. He was not that close to his father. Had never been, really, come to think of it. It was his mother who moved him. It was his mother who affected him. It was for his mother that he wished to quit. *But, no, I can't think about that now. Can't think about the girl that was lying in my bed at my pad. Just stay here, Bobby,* he thought to himself. *Keep yourself calm, Bobby. You have done nothing wrong. You are helping her. You will let her sleep it off.* But he knew, he knew and he did not want to think about it.

Which is why his father's silence gave him comfort.

And why his mother's cooking would feed and distract him, even though he was not hungry.

It was going to be a simple supper tonight, he could see. A simple supper for a Saturday. Bobby liked putting words together like that. Liked the rhythm of words. The rhythm of the words: *a simple supper for a Saturday.* He mulled them over and over in his brain: *A simple supper for a Saturday.... A simple supper for a Saturday.... A simple supper for a Saturday.* The rhyme of them turning into song. And he felt a small song starting to stir in his brain. Longed to get to his piano. Eyed his mother's piano in the corner, started to get up, but no, didn't. Stayed seated. *Not the time to get up. Just stay put,* he reprimanded himself.

His mother was a good piano player, as was he. Although his mother had learned on her own and he had learned in music school – attended the Greenwich School of Music when he was just 22 – right after he got out of the Army. Qualified using the GI bill, and was so excited when he qualified for music and not just academics. Then on he went to the Manhattan School of music in 1948. Something he was still proud of – and, most importantly, that is when he had first started writing songs – well, when he had written his *first* song.

Yeah, that was after Ruby. Ruby...Ruby...you broke my heart. Bobby chuckled to himself. His dad started and stared at him for a moment, then took another swig of his beer and turned his attention back to the TV. *She really* *messed with my mind...*he thought. *Messed with my mind. Messed with my mind. Messed with my mind.* The rhythm of the words swirling in his head again. His soul stirred. He ached for the piano. He did not get up.

"Dinner!" his mother called. His father lumbered up from the chair. *Louis is getting old,* Bobby thought to himself. And he remembered his father's sprightliness in youth, when his parents would have all those parties up on Sugar Hill. Duke Ellington; the artist Aaron Douglas. He remembered the looks from Aaron to his mother; smoldering looks. And the way she would try to ignore them, to keep the conversation lively; academic; and how she would slightly succumb, the corners of her crimson lips turning up ever so slightly; beyond her control. But control she maintained. And he remembered the women his father had. Right there in their apartment. His mother never seemed to care.

How did his mother do it?

And then when Bobby was thirteen his mother put Louis out of the house — "For good this time!" she exclaimed as she slammed the door behind him. He moved a block away. But she brought him back. Brought him back even though she didn't want to. Brought him back because Bobby had cried for his father, "I want my daddy!" Father and son. *I didn't understand,* Bobby thought now. *We were friends, but I didn't understand back then their relationship.*

He hadn't endured the years of drinking and abuse yet.

Abuse? Bobby never saw it as abuse, why did he think of that word? Term it that way? That was unlike him. He shook his head to himself.

His father was an actor. When he wasn't acting he waited tables, when he wasn't waiting tables he was drinking. And then sometimes he would overdo it and then he would get mean and as Bobby got older, 17, 18, 19, older like the girl that was now lying above his bedroom a few blocks away, they'd drink together and then they would fight and then they'd make up and be pals, friends all over again. Friends. Father and son.

And that was that, Bobby thought, slowly and silently shaking his head again; watching the TV in slow-mo — enjoying the distillation of time — his slow-moving clarity with exaggerated perception.

*Louis, Louis, Louis...*had always been Louis to him. Never thought of him as "dad" or "father." Just Louis. This made things easier. And after a while even their fighting became halfhearted. But his mother kept his father back. A connection, now, that Bobby could not figure out.

Eva...Eva...everyone loved Eva, Bobby thought again to himself, enjoying the delayed clarity descending upon him – a welcome side effect his habit afforded him. He liked seeing his parents' lives this way – with *remove*.

His mother was beautiful, so beautiful that Aaron had painted her. He had snatched a glimpse of that painting in the back of her closet once. The famous Aaron Douglas. Had painted his mother. But she did not put the painting up. She left it in the back of the closet. Bobby supposed it just wasn't her style.

And Eva's cooking was a wonder. People would come from miles around just to have it. Bobby remembered the parties that she would have; the "soirees" as they used to call them. Eva would cook and everybody would come and life was one big party. She would throw a costume ball once a year – His mother, the Belle of the Ball, and his father, with his women. And Eva had a boyfriend too, for a while, said she was going to marry him – Eddie was his name. But he got killed in a car crash. And she just kept on working. She worked first at the World's Fair in '39 – Bobby remembered this clearly. And then she went to work at the New York State Insurance Fund, where she worked now. And she worked hard. And Bobby respected this. Not his dad, though. His dad had few paid acting jobs, even though he had studied with a teacher out in Hollywood. Wanted only to be an actor/concert tenor. But he got paid acting gigs only rarely – not much work for a black man in Harlem in those days, and even now. *But,* Bobby thought, *he never missed a show.* Even when he was dead drunk the night before he always got up and went to act. And he was good too.

Bobby remembered the time his father had invited him to act with him. "You wanna job?" he'd said. "Sure," Bobby had replied eagerly. "When do we go?" Yup, he remembered it now, as he sat next to his dad. The one that now did not know he existed.

He remembered clearly – heading on down to Brooklyn to the Majestic Theatre just after his 13th birthday – just he and his dad, walking together down the street after getting off the bus. It was an Italian theatre; an Italian play and he and his father were going to play Africans. Bobby's crystal mind pictured the little rag they were both handed to wear and being instructed to wear this and nothing else. He remembered sweating under the hot lights in their makeshift African costumes, a big voice speaking above him – "Look fierce." His dad handing a priest a poison. Carefully lifting an amber filled bottle off a glistening silver tray. And Bobby remembered his part clearly: he knocked the poison out of his dad's hand and the priest suddenly raised his cross and cried out in booming singsong Italian: "Thank you for saving me!" Sinking to his knees, supplicating, his father continuing to stand there, feet firmly planted, looking fierce. Then the silly, silly shouts as they ranted and hopped on one foot and then the other – "*Uba! Uba! Uba!*" Bobby hopping and running off the stage his loud "*Uba!*" trailing behind him. The audience screaming and clapping.

His first taste of the stage. He liked it. Liked the adoration; liked the crowd and their cheers. But not the acting part. He had acted only once after that – and even had the lead – a lady that had wanted to put on a play – *Ladies in Retirement*. An English play – played two nights at Carnegie Chambers on 57th Street. He chuckled now to himself at the thought. But after that he had never acted again, never had the urge, with his father or alone. Why? Because you only acted sometime; the work was not steady. But, he liked the warmth between them, then. A kindness that he felt from his father – if only for a moment. Louis seemed proud to be sharing this with his son. To be sharing what he did. Showing Bobby what he did. Yes, he had been proud of his work, and he took it seriously.

And Louis had even played the lead in Orson Wells' all black interpretation of Shakespeare down at the Lafayette during the depression, when Orson was only 20 or 21. But, work was few and far between, yep, and as the roles for blacks in Harlem and New York decreased and his father worked less, he drank more and hit Bobby more. And Bobby had avoided him more. And that moment...that moment...just faded. And they were never close again.

"Dinner!" Eva called again. Bobby liked to call his mother "Eva." He liked the mystery of the name. "Eva...." His strength.

CHAPTER SEVENTEEN

BOBBY OPENED HIS EYES. Lying there on the sofa in his parents' apartment. *What time is it?* The sun streaked through half-closed blinds, but the sunlight was lower – early morning long passed. The apartment quiet. His mother long gone for work, his father was still – no movement. He got up, just in his boxers and t-shirt. Took off his pants before crashing on the couch – stayed up late watching TV – a movie he cannot remember now, something unimportant. Something only to fill the time. Even Louis, usually a night owl, beer in hand staring blankly at the television screen, even after it had gone off and was just a blue, fuzzy flicker, even Louis had groaned, nodded, grabbed his lower back and gotten up to go to bed – leaving Bobby alone to stare at the tube. Bobby nodded back, motioning just enough with his head to *not* show disrespect because through it all, he respected the *notion* of his father, well, at least respected the fact that there was a need to be respectful to your parents. Even if his respect for his father was automatic and without feeling.

"Don't you disrespect me, boy!" Louis had said once as he raised his hand to hit him side the head.

"Don't you disrespect me, boy!" And he had meant it, and Bobby caught a flash of fear in his father's eyes as the words escaped. A fear that was covered by the alcohol and the bravado. A fear that was muted by the women and the tales of the "good old days" and hanging out in their Sugar Hill apartment with the likes of Benny Carter and Duke Ellington.

Yes, Bobby saw the fear — if only for an instant and he understood in that instant his father's need to be respected; recognized. A *need to be a man in front of his son.*

And so, in his own small way, he had acknowledged this and attempted to give his father this respect. In *his own small way.*

But now, he realized, his father was gone and he was alone in the apartment. He padded to the kitchen in his socks and boxers and checked the time by the round, blue clock on the wall with the white dial and large green hands.

10:05 a.m.

10:05 a.m. and he had dragged a girl's cold body up to the sixth floor of his apartment building late yesterday afternoon and left her there.

10:05 a.m. and his parents were both gone.

10:05 a.m. and he needed to *get back* to his apartment, now. Check things out — make sure everything was all right. Maybe do the last of the white powder hidden with his washed needle behind the books and under the window on his bookshelf. The window that overlooked the street.

10:05 a.m. and maybe he would write that song that had been milling itself around his head for the last twelve hours. Swirling. Straining to be freed. Maybe he would sit down at the baby grand in his parents' apartment and clunk it out.

No, he *had to go home.* He felt his nose begin to run. Felt a little ache, not much — just a little. If he could have just the *tiniest bit*....

The little bit of dinner he had eaten last night had revitalized him. Pot roast. Potatoes. Collard greens. His mother was a good cook. He should come over more often — he did not always eat as well as he could.

Just a tiny bit.

He pulled his jeans on.

Pushed his arms through the sleeves of his button-down shirt. Buttoned it up — down the front. Tucked it in — twenty steps to the bathroom. Washed his face; brushed his teeth, combed his hair. Well-groomed. The fact that he was not taking a shower bothered him. But he did not have time. An urgency pushing him back towards the apartment.

The sweating beginning. The *sign.*

Bobby remembered the first time he had tried dope. He had sniffed it in the back of a garage where he was working. That was just after Ruby. Well, two years after Ruby. Ruby had left him – gone and married a Colonel in the Army. Did it while Bobby was out in California playing with Benny Carter's band. "Come out to California if you ever get the chance…" Benny had said during a party at his parents' house. *A Soiree* as Bobby remembered – he'd been sitting at the baby grand in the lively living room – chatter and clamor all around; playing and singing one of his songs.

Ruby, ah sweet Ruby…so plain. Beautiful in her plainness, with ripe hips and a full inviting mouth. But she was a clinger and Bobby did not like clingers – always asking where he'd been, always hangin' around; never givin' him space to *breathe*…. So, Benny's offer to come on over to Cali came at a most opportune time – get himself some breathing room; play his music.

California, warm nights and sea air. Sunshine and freedom. But *all he could think about was her*. Lying in bed at night alone, wet breeze tickling his skin, trying to transport his mind into her mind. To *teleport* himself to her. She'd put her spell on him, she had. And he felt something was wrong. He could *feel* a distance. But why? She loved him. She was attached. She was safe at his mother's house – he had left her there and she by osmosis had stayed there in his bedroom. And she *was waiting for him*. And she was stifling – but he couldn't get her out of his heart or his mind.

He stayed in California two weeks – singing with the band every night – sleeping late into the day – lodged up at the Dunbar Hotel. Heard all the greats had stayed there back in the 20's – Cab Callaway, Duke Ellington, Count Basie. And Benny brought out things in him that had laid dormant. Wet, starry nights seeped into his song; the bright lights of Hollywood. *A glint in my soul*. Bobby thought now, the aching in his arms and back beginning to get stronger.

He had never tried heroin then. He was clean then.

Long bus ride back home. Two aching days. Mother standing at the front door of their apartment building. "Where's *Ruby?*" Anxiety tingeing his voice. Anticipation and longing merged.

"Gone, honey – haven't seen her in a week. Just up and left one day. Poor girl – don't know what's going on with her. She seemed in such a hurry and so flustered and well, she seemed slightly *embarrassed*. Said she was goin' on back home to her mother's."

Bobby didn't even unpack his suitcase, just left it there sitting in the wide hall; leapt back out the front door and down the few steps to the sidewalk and ran, long, sustained strides, the four blocks to her house.

And there she was, standing at the front door in all her glory. Fingernails painted red. Hair coiffed and curled. Slick smile. She had one hand on her hip and she jutted that hip out to the left slightly – resting her weight on that side, left foot planted firmly in front of her.

"Hey, Bobby...." she said, flashing white teeth. *What happened to Ruby?* Bobby thought. *She used to be so plain and now, now she looks like Marilyn Monroe.*

Bobby didn't know if he liked the new Ruby or not. She was so slick – but he was attracted and he felt the passion well between his legs. He wanted to take her right there and then.

He lunged towards her, then pulled back instinctively.

She had an aura of protectiveness around her. A shield that he was not meant to penetrate. *There was someone else present.*

"Ruby, what's goin' on? Why are you dressed like that?"

"Like what? Don't you like it?" She clicked her gum once – a habit Bobby had always disliked, manners being one of his core principles.

"I don't know if I do like it. You look different. Slick." He regretted it the minute the word slipped out of his mouth – what he had really been thinking had been something else, something darker, something like – well he meant to say: "like a slut," but he had stopped himself and "slick" had substituted itself so easily and was said with the same tone and she heard it. And she was mad. But she covered it up because she had a secret to tell. A secret that was only hers and did not include Bobby. A secret that made her special. *Somebody.*

"I'm gettin' married!" Ruby blurted out. Weighing with satisfaction the effect of her words. Watching Bobby's jaw drop involuntarily. Blinking.

Then he closed his mouth, mechanically; his lips tight and his expression set against her and she felt a twinge of sadness; a slight regret that dissolved the instant it appeared.

"To a *Colonel*," she said defiantly. The sting of that remark hung above him. Bobby had been in the military. Bobby had *not* been a Colonel. Ruby knew this.

"Well, I guess we're broken up then." Bobby hoped these words sounded firm; final — not like the question he felt in his heart.

"I guess so," Ruby said, flashing white teeth again.

Bobby just stared at her. Disbelieving the change in her. Doubting his sanity in being with her. Doubting his perceptions. How could he have missed this side of her? This side that had no feelings. That absolutely *did not care.* This side that could trade him so easily — in a matter of weeks — for someone else. This side that faked her emotions for him. *A liar! She was — A BIG FAT LIAR!*

He shook his head in disbelief and disappointment, quickly turned his back to her and walked away, hands thrust deep into his pockets.

"Hey!" Her voice was sharp. It pierced him. He turned around.

"Aren't ya gonna *kiss* me?"

Kiss you?! Kiss you??? You've got to be kidding! You just told me you are marrying someone else. You just showed me you're a liar and that you HAVE NO SOUL. And you want me to kiss *you?*

Stared straight at her; glaring. No words. And turned away again. Never looking back. He didn't have to. He knew she was still standing in the doorway, hand on her hip, smacking her gum. Ruby red lips moving — with no sound. He hoped the Colonel was happy.

CHAPTER EIGHTEEN

Walking back down the street from his parents' house to his apartment that morning, a heaviness weighed his gut. A heaviness that mingled with the aching and crept through his body. An *anticipation* — but was this nagging, turning in his belly, this sinking feeling mixed with anxiety — was it anxiety or the anticipatory excitement of his next fix? He hated that word "fix" — but it did *fix* you — that was all it was — it fixed you and made you right again — not high, just *whole* — like you were before all this began, before the first time, just a little better — or so he told himself.

Just a little better.

He hastened his steps as he neared his apartment, the anticipatory excitement/anxiety churning stronger now.

He noticed a crowd milling about outside the brownstone. How many were there? twenty? thirty? people? Other tenants from his apartment building — some people he didn't know. Joseph the storeowner from Joe's Market on the corner. A couple other shop owners from small shops that lined the street, Jay from the Pawn Shop, Al from Al's Liquor.

Bobby slowed. He was casual. He sauntered up to the eight-story building. Its caramel brick stones glinting flat in the sun. Slow. Measured. Shoulders straight. Head high. Well-groomed. His salvation. Order. His salvation.

"Hey, what's up?" he asked in his carefully modulated tone. Sarah, the 17-year-old daughter of his neighbor, Nina, glanced at him expectantly, admiration and excitement in her eyes.

"They found a dead girl up on the balcony of the sixth floor," Sarah said knowingly, conspiratorially, her voice squeaking with excitement.

Sarah had always loved drama, and *death*, possibly *murder* was drama of the highest order.

Fear sparked Bobby's eyes for a moment. He blinked quickly – film to cover the fear.

"A dead girl?" He repeated only the last half of her sentence as if he had not heard her, could not believe something so heinous could happen in their neighborhood. "Hmmmm...." He hoped wisdom shined through his "hmmmmm." He hoped the fear that flicked his eyes did not show. He hoped Sarah did not see the pounding of his chest against his cotton shirt.

He'd always liked Sarah and had said "hello" often to her in the hallway, or as they had passed in the street, she coming back from the small market on the corner, grocery bag in hand, sometimes alone, sometimes with her mother – for although they were not rich in Harlem – poor by many people's standards – there were families here that held a pride; a striving; a *confidence* in themselves that *this was only temporary*. That although they came from slaves and were reminded of this *every single day*, when they went to ride a bus and were sent to the back, or even tried to use the bathroom in a white establishment and were told to "go out back ya nigga!" which many times meant an outhouse, or worse – just out back. OUTSIDE. No pride. But they had pride and they would never lose it and this pride ran through this community.

And this pride Eva had instilled in Bobby and Bobby saw Sarah's mother instill it in her.

Pride and protectiveness.

And blissful, forced unawareness for girls like Sarah of the true dangers of the street. Of the dangers Bobby had already succumbed to and wanted to protect Sarah from.

He wanted to be an example to her. To help, somehow – to keep protecting her. He wanted to matter. To make a difference. In whatever small way.

"Hmmmm..." he said again. "I better get on up there."

Sarah flashed her large brown eyes; long, brown lashes fluttering imperceptibly, an invisible wind lifting and settling them. Admiration keen.

Bobby set his shoulders back firmly and entered his apartment building. He headed up to the second floor – where his needle waited so patiently. Behind the books. Behind his studying. Behind the wisdom and *information* that he so constantly craved.

Waiting.

Just a little. Just a little to take the edge off. Then I'll quit. This will be the last time. It's not worth it. This was too close – this girl – dying – just dying like that in front of me. So quick. Just like that.

His mind racing circles around itself as he took the steps one by one to his apartment. One at a time; gently placing each soft-soled, leather-clad foot on each worn step. No noise. Quietly. Still. *Don't worry. Don't worry.... Nothing to worry about. It's all going to be okay. Gently. Step gently.* His mind still raced and he spoke to himself quietly, cooing, a slight mumble under his breath.

Don't worry. Don't worry....

His memory flashed again to the Girl – cold memory pushing from the depths. Her cold, cold hands. The slight bluish tinge to her mouth. The eyes that would not close and kept rolling back into her head as he dragged her. *So young! So young!*

How had he allowed this? But he had needed his "fix" and it had all seemed so safe with the Aunt – she was so sure. So, *motherly*. But then she had left and left him alone, alone with the dead girl. The Girl that *wouldn't wake up.*

And he had done just the tiniest bit more – just enough to take the panic away.

And he had calmly, very calmly hooked his arms under the Girl's armpits, dragged her to the elevator, pressed the button, waited, calm; still. No one came down the hall – strangely, he had no fear of that...he knew he was alone.

Dragged her into the elevator, big metal jaws gaping wide to accept them. Balanced her wooden body with one arm while he pressed the button for floor number six. He knew that floor, had been up there before, some nights when he couldn't sleep – he'd found the small balcony at the end of the hall right after he'd first moved in – he'd found it and sat curled up in it, sitting with his arms resting on his knees, head on his arms – balmy summer air caressing him. Dreaming. It was a safe place. High above the streets, invisible to all but the stars; noises far away and muted.

Dragged the Girl down the endless hall, found his way to the small, rectangular, wooden doors with the not-so-see-through frosted rectangular panes. Dropped her for a second as he reached down to flip the latch – opened both doors wide – creak of hinges against still night – nudging those doors open just a little further with the toe of his soft leather shoe – hooked his elbows back under her armpits and dragged her over the threshold. The backs of her calves and heels made a dull thud as they bumped the bottom of the doorframe solidly.

He didn't like the bump. It was heavy. She still had her shoes on. She was dead weight.

He arranged her on that balcony. Just as he had been arranged on many a sleepless night. Watching the city – a city that could not watch him.

He arranged her – just as if she had been sleeping – head resting on her hands in the corner. *Yes, she did some drugs, wandered up here, found this balcony and curled up to go to sleep*, he thought.

And died.

His foot hit the top step of the second floor on that thought. On that word. *Died.*

And as he rounded the corner to his apartment – his stomach dropped to his bowels and the bile from last night's delicious home-cooked meal forced its way up his throat and into his mouth.

His door had been kicked down.

Police were in his apartment. He turned his heel to flee, but could not. Something kept him rooted to the floor. Something would not let him move. He could have walked on past; pretended he was going to another apartment, that this was not his, but he did not do that. He stood in the doorway, and stared.

Stared at the police who had ransacked his apartment. Stared at the blue uniformed policeman who stood with one hand on his baton and the other holding Bobby's well-hidden needle and drugs. Stared at the cops who were staring at him.

"You Bobby Sharp?" the police officer said, through a thick Irish accent. His voice was accusatory. Authoritative. There was no turning away.

"I am," Bobby said. Dignity in place.

"You are under arrest for the murder of Annabelle Brown."

"But I didn't kill her," Bobby said evenly. For this was the truth. *He did not kill her.* And he did not lie.

"We 'ave witnesses that say they saw this girl come into yer apartment yesterday afternoon. No one saw 'er come out. 'Er mother says the girl's lil' boy was up 'ere with you yesterday. Led the girl's mother back 'ere. The girl's mother said she came back down lookin' for 'er daughter," the policeman's thick Irish drawl became thicker in his agitation, he drew a deep breath. "'Er mother said she came back down 'ere lookin' for 'er early evenin' yesterday. Spoke to you, 'bout it when 'er daughter didn't come home. The woman's eight yur old grandson led 'er back 'ere, said he'd been 'ere earlier in the day – *eight yurs old!*" The police officer emphasized the words. Restrained accusatory, disgusted, resigned anger in his voice.

Yes, Bobby remembered the little boy and his grandmother – not much of a grandmother though – couldn't have been a day over forty – more likely thirty-five, Bobby had thought at the time. He remembered them knocking on his door just before he had left for his parents. Asking for her daughter, he remembered the name "Annabelle," remembered the mother saying emphatically: "My daughter was here, my granson says so, where is she? *Where is she?*" Her voice rising at the end. Shrill. Bobby tuned her out. No, he knew no Annabelle. He was polite, yet firm. No, he knew no Annabelle.

And that little boy – Bobby had been amazed at the time that the boy remembered the way back to his apartment – he'd only been there once, earlier in the afternoon with the Aunt and the Girl. The Girl. The mother of the boy.

A small tear flecked the corner of Bobby's eye. *The mother of her son.*
Dead.
But he did not kill her.

"But I did not kill her!" Bobby said again, this time his voice rising. "Sure, she was here," he glanced at the plastic evidence bag dangling seductively from the officer's hand, he glanced expectantly and then uncertainly, his body still craving the drugs. "She was here with her aunt and the boy, she shot up, closed her eyes and *died*. I did not kill her!"

101

The police officer eyed Bobby suspiciously. Really, he did not care. He was tired, it was almost 11:00 a.m., this was his third investigation already today, he had only quickly gulped down one cup of coffee in the squad car on the way over here; a coffee that had scalded his tongue and he was not in a good mood. His Sergeant had an irate and hysterical mother down at the Precinct, with a daughter who was only technically "missing" at this point, witnesses that would testify as to her whereabouts, and now a man who had just confessed to a death in his own apartment; and a cold body found out on the balcony of this very building. Officer O'Malley did not care *how* she had died, he just wanted an *arrest* and resolution of just one homicide in this whole stinkin' dirty city. This *one* of many. *Just one closure.* And he had no patience for drug addicts with their soft whimpering eyes and faux bleeding hearts. *No patience whatsoever!*

"Cuff 'im!" Officer Dan O'Malley said through gritted teeth.

"Cuff 'im and get 'em outta me sight!"

"But I didn't kill her. I just moved a dead body!" Bobby said again, more urgently as the cuffs snapped onto his wrists. He felt the slap of hard metal against his bones; winced as his arms were pinned tightly behind his back. He was beginning to sweat profusely now and he looked wildly around the room – a last ditch effort to procure the salvation he had hidden so succinctly behind the books that bound him to reality. With method. With purpose. Everything was under control.

And now, it had all come undone.

Officer O'Malley jerked his left arm as he grabbed his elbow – "Go now! Nothin' left for ya 'ere!" he barked as he pushed Bobby out of his apartment and down the stairs, to the street.

NICK KENNY'S Disc Derby

Songwriter Vanishes
His Ditty Hit-Bound

TIN PAN ALLEY is filled with Cinderella and Elmer stories. Here's the latest one. A young fellow *named* Bobby Sharpe walked into Bourne Music Publishers *a few* weeks ago. He had a demonstration record of a song called

"Last Night In The Moonlight," which he played for Lester Sims. Lester flipped when he heard it and rushed over to Destiny Records with the dub. At Destiny Recording Studios reaction was the same. To make a long song short they called Bobby Sharpe in and recorded the number. That was two weeks ago. *This* week the song came out and it's breaking a hit. But now with the tune hitting—*Bobby* Sharpe is missing. Even a missing *bulletin* search hasn't turned up the real-gone *song* writer. If you see Bobby Sharpe tell him *the* news. Tell him his Destiny platter of "Last Night in the *Moonlight*" is going big and platter-fans are clamoring for his picture.

NICK KENNY'S DISC DERBY

SONGWRITER VANISHES
HIS DITTY HIT-BOUND

TIN PAN ALLEY is filled with Cinderella and Elmer stories. Here's the latest one. A young fellow named Bobby Sharpe walked into Bourne Music Publishers a few weeks ago. He had a demonstration record of a song called "Last Night In The Moonlight," which he played for Lester Sims. Lester flipped when he heard it and rushed over to Destiny Records with the dub. At Destiny Recording Studios reaction was the same. To make a long song short they called Bobby Sharpe in and recorded the number. That was two weeks ago. This week the song came out and it's breaking a hit. But now with the tune hitting — Bobby Sharpe is missing. Even a missing bulletin search hasn't turned up the real-gone songwriter. If you see Bobby Sharpe tell him the news. Tell him his Destiny platter of "Last Night In The Moonlight" is going big and platter-fans are clamoring for his picture.

CHAPTER NINETEEN

RIKERS ISLAND JAIL – *1959:*

S ULLEN SIPS SLIPPED down his throat. A dribble on his tongue. Surprised they let him have water in here. His head down in his book. Buried. Ten days already he had been here. Ten days and he had gone beyond the aching. Ten days as the water dripped slowly down the cold metal pipe behind his head. Body pressed firmly into the thin, dirty mattress. Coils leaning into him. Ignoring it. Ignoring the hardness. Not thinking about the night.

Robinson Crusoe in his hand. Head bent down reading.

His salvation. A vacation.

This is a vacation.

And there is no smack.

Breathe in. Breathe out. Breathe in. Breathe out. Firm hold – releasing. And although it was technically "jail" and he was not supposed to like it here – Bobby felt a strange sense of peace.

A contentment with life.

A safety.

No drugs. Yes, he was safe.

The adventures before him lead him far away from the mundaneness of his new life. Far away from the gleaming black piano, which waited alone in the corner of his parents' apartment. Friend; confidante; love – the one that knew all of his secrets.

Ruby, once again Ruby snaked her way into his head.

PART II - BOBBY

The catalyst — to everything.

He had written his first song when she left him — chained to the piano for twelve hours a day — pouring his heartache onto the keys. She had emptied him and he emptied her dirtiness onto the gleaming ivory.

She returned three years later, just showed up on his mother's doorstep when he was about to leave town with Lavinnia — oh, lovely Lavinnia, the thought of her still made him stir — 'bout to go to Chicago, finally move in together, maybe get married, and his mother says when he drops by: "Guess who stopped by today?" Glint in her eye.

"Who?" Bobby knew her next words before she spoke them — the cord of Ruby still firmly attached, even though he had long gotten over her, moved way on.

"Ruby!" The excitement rang in his mother's voice — she'd always liked Ruby — why, Bobby now could not figure out, after what she'd done to him — but his mother's warm heart always won out and she'd never turn anyone away. *Should've been a nurse...*Bobby thought to himself once again — a thought he had often.

"Yes, Ruby! Don't be so startled. She still cares for you, you know — says she's been livin' on out in Chicago, had to go back, couldn't wait around to see you this time. Says you should go out and see her sometime." Eva looked at Bobby directly and warmly. If only her son *would let somebody love him* — a thought she had often. Bright, articulate, handsome, so well spoken — all things she had meticulously instilled in him — and he was wasting it on music. Dangerous music. Dangerous arts. She'd seen what acting and music had done to Louis — a concert tenor! ha! Heartbreak and disappointment that's all there was. Negroes had it hard enough as it was.

She'd heard Bobby's songs — snuck into the room and listened when he thought no one was there, and she had to admit they were *good*. Pride filled her heart each time she heard him sing and play. But still, he should be a psychiatrist — it wasn't too late. Being an avid reader she'd discovered that psychiatry was going to be the wave of the future — and Bobby would be *good* at it. He was so good with people, so sincere, so gentle and knowing; so smart. People trusted him. God had certainly smiled on him, even though she and Louis never went to church; never took Bobby. Maybe they should have, maybe the Faith would ease the burdens he carried.

She was raised with the switch and the Bible; a slap and a verse. The Word shoved down her throat early on, and then shoved on Bobby. Bobby sitting quietly on that hard wooden stool, hands folded politely in his lap; made to memorize verse after verse. "Spare the rod, spoil the child!" Grandma Nellie would declare through clenched teeth. A stern taskmaster she was. Grandfather kept most times to himself. Worked hard on the railroad. Let Grandma Nellie run things. Yes, Grandma Nellie was the master of that house.

Eva turned back to her son and spoke: "So, you were once with her? Be friends, son. Don't close yourself down. You were so happy when you were with her. You are not happy now. You do *not seem happy* with *Lavinnia*." Her voice turned down on "Lavinnia." Lavinnia and her controlling mother. Those two were trouble, pure trouble.

Bobby stared for a moment at his mother, looked down at the ground, stared again.

"Hmmmm..." Eva cleared her throat and looked at her son — "so, it seems you're goin' to Chicago to visit Ruby then." She smiled. He smiled back.

"Looks that way." Words with no words; more said than what was said; their unspoken communication holding.

Trip to Chicago; a possible marriage; morphed into a visit with Ruby. Lavinnia beginning to recede. Ruby the Rat.

Ah, life with its wonderful twists and turns, ending strife upon the switch of the blade of a knife. Never knowing if it is going to cut *you; or* protect *you!* He inhaled and whistled under his breath as he made his way up the stairs to pick up some of his stuff.

CHAPTER TWENTY

Cobwebs covered his mind and he wiped them away with his eyes; focusing intently on the words in front of him. Robinson Crusoe fading from view; the *drip, drip, drip,* of the water in the pipe strangely comforting. January now and he knew when his meals would be. Lights out was always at 9:00 p.m. Dinner was always at 6:00 p.m. in the sterile mess hall. He had the same blue coveralls to wear every day. Three changes that all looked alike. One in his small drawer in the makeshift nightstand to the left of his cot, one sent off to launder, and one on his back. Bobby laid low. He did not make trouble, he avoided those who did. *Just doin' my time.* Content. Strangely content.

It was 2:00 in the afternoon and the muddy sun filtered heavily through the gray leaden bars of the window high above his bed. Bobby had no need to go outside. He only did it when he was forced to – during "recreation" when all the inmates were required to go out into the Yard and mill about and attempt something physical. Of course, there were the weight lifters – large, burly men, mostly black, with large tattooed arms that glistened in the cool winter sun; lifting weights two times their size and glaring menacingly at anyone who tried to approach. Bobby did not try to approach. He took a nice stroll around the grounds. He inhaled deeply. He tried not to notice the razor-flecked coils at the top of the chain-link fence. Sometimes he sat on the cold metal bench at the side of the Yard and let the orange rays soak through his skin. He kept to himself.

Yes. He was safe.

Eyes heavy; book falling from his hand; music in the background. Music piped through the place for their listening enjoyment. *A radio, how nice.* Background music. Sleep descending.

You set my soul on fire / Fill me with desire / You made me feel so good /
Just like I knew you would / Last night in the moonlight...

Bobby's head jerked up suddenly, fully awake. *"Last Night in the Moonlight"?* It was *him.* It was him on the radio! What was he doing on the radio? He'd just cut that song back in October! Walked into the tiny publisher's office down at Tin Pan Alley and they'd loved the song and they'd brought him the next day to the studio, they'd laid the tracks, Bobby played piano and sang vocals. And it was done. Bobby got his $150 and walked out. He almost forgot about the song. So many songs he'd sold to publishers and he never heard anything again. Not a word. But here he was on the radio!

"That was Bobby Sharp with 'Last Night in the Moonlight...'" the announcer's voice purred smooth, loud and clear. Here he'd been in here for two months, feeling safe and like he didn't even *need* music anymore and there it was, *in his face. Four more months to go.* He suddenly felt antsy. He suddenly didn't care about safety. He suddenly wanted to get out, *now.* And face his sudden, albeit possibly small and fleeting, fame.

Bobby had had his brushes with fame before. He'd cut that single on the Wing label: "Baby Girl of Mine" – Ruth Brown picked it up a little later, but changed it 'round to say: "Sweet Baby of Mine." He'd been real proud of that, but as usual, the royalties were slow to come. Billie Holiday's people had picked up one of his songs for her next release ... but heroin did her in. Died just last July right there at the Metropolitan Hospital in Harlem. They'd come to arrest her for possession while she lie wasting away in her bed. Let her die there. He pushed the thought from his mind. Mind spinning upon itself.

He'd been on The Dick Clark Show earlier that year, too. He'd sung "Ever Since I Met Lucy," a song he'd penned just a few months before appearing. But his manager and Dick Clark had renamed him Mark Stone.

Seems there was another Bobby Shore, or something of the sort already climbing the charts, and Bobby's name sounded too similar. So right there on the spot, on that day, Bobby was told: "You're now Mark Stone."

Bobby bounced on stage, singing his little song, the girls screaming; bouncing off, the girls gathered around the little table as he signed autographs. He chuckled now at the thought of Dick Clark looking him in the eye and thrusting the large microphone in his face after saying, "Mark, I hear you have a new record out there. What have you been doing with yourself?"

And Bobby's instantaneous reply: "Opening up at a nightclub."

Dick Clark: "What's the name of the nightclub?" Big smile, sideways glance at the audience.

"Oh, no name, it's so new it hasn't been named yet...."

"Well, there you have it folks, Mark Stone and "Ever Since I Met Lucy...."

There was no nightclub. He'd made it up. He wasn't playing anywhere, just thought he should say he was – give himself a little credibility. Felt The Dick Clark Show was a little bit of a fluke, came so fast, outta the blue...like everything.

Yeah, he'd tasted fame. A small drip on his tongue. Not enough to even get it wet. It had to come to you. And then you had to grab it. Yeah, here he is minding his own business, forgetting all about the music industry and it was slapping him in the face!

The constant pounding the pavement, songs recorded and never heard, songs recorded and picked up by publishers and Bobby told he was "going to do great things! great things!" A wink and a handshake, a couple bucks in his pocket. The high of the chase and the conquer, then alone, too much time on his hands, downtown Harlem, walking down to the corner, *just a little, just a little* and it started all over again.

That damned drug! Junk! It was *junk*. Aptly named and it had really gotten' ahold of him. But no more.

Ruby, Ruby, Ruby...yeah, he'd followed her to Chicago. Went over with Lavinnia. Lovely Lavinnia. Lavinnia with the long legs. Sex was always good with Lavinnia, even now he hardened at the thought of it. But

Lavinnia became more and more irritating as they neared Chicago. They'd had a fight about sex of all things — he just wasn't in the mood. Thought to himself: *I'll never marry this girl.* He'd met her mother and her mother was controlling and he was starting to see that Lavinnia was controlling too. Good excuse to leave her. Got out of the car right there when they arrived in Chicago, with nowhere to go and no one to see — but Ruby. So he'd called Ruby, pulled the number his mother had given him from deep inside his coat pocket, gone straight from Lavinnia's car to the pay phone, never looked back and called Ruby.

"C'mon over!" Ruby said, breathlessness in her voice. Bobby wasn't sure which Ruby to expect, or even which one he would see — the sexy Marilyn Ruby, or the nice, plain, good-girl Ruby. But he anticipated her touch again as he walked the twenty-four blocks to her apartment.

"Hey Ruby!" he yelled as he'd rounded the corner. Excitement welling at the thought of seeing her again. Senses honed to her.

"Hey Bobby! My man!" Ruby yelled back leaning out from the front porch of the apartment building. She'd been waiting for him, standing on the step, looking down the street in her short shorts on that hot Chicago day. He quickened his pace. He got nearer. He could see her better.

My, how Ruby has changed. Aged so much in the three years since I've seen her — gotten harder, somehow. More lines around her eyes.

Her mouth had developed deep furrowed wrinkles at the corners, like giant commas and there were tiny lines sprouting from her top lip, little excited exclamation points pointing towards her nose. It gave her entire face an elfin quality she had not previously had. Her deflated lips still wore the same ruby red lipstick from their previous meeting, but it was bleeding slightly into those tiny lines causing her smile to appear more like an exaggerated sneer.

How did this happen? How did this happen so quickly? This transformation. She was neither sweet Ruby, nor vampy Ruby, she just looked like tired, used Ruby and he was not impressed. And there were no feelings left. Nothing. Not a one.

"So, ya here for long?" Ruby said, eyeing him in a strangely suspicious way, as if she were sizing him up somehow, as if she were checking him out to see what he had to offer her, what she could *take* from him.

PART II – BOBBY

"Looks that way..." Bobby said, "just broke up with my girl, not expected, but it happened, looks like I'll be needing to get some work?" He ended that statement with a question, and he had not meant to. He let the word dangle in the space between them.

Ruby smacked her gum emphatically before answering, as if he had asked: Is there a God? or Can you tell me the Theory of Relativity? She stared him up and down and then she spoke: "I can steer you over to my cousin Jack's mechanics shop...it's called *Jack's Mechanics*." She let this tidbit of information settle over him, the powerful network she commanded, the fact that she was helping him, "He might have some work for you...I'll see what I can do. Got a place to stay?" She eyed him like candy. He felt dirty.

"No, you got any recommendations?"

"Ya can stay with me for a day or two, but only a day or two, don't make enough to feed two!" Bobby didn't want to ask what she worked as. "Thanks, Rub, I appreciate it. I'll find a place soon enough, don't you worry." Ruby just kept appraising him, staring him up and down – assessing his meat quality. She did not move, just stood there in her platform shoes and shorts with her hip leaning against the large white column at the top step, as if challenging him to challenge her. He did not.

"Well, ya gonna come in?" she said, no smack of her gum this time.

"I think I will." Bobby picked up his one tan suitcase and brushed past her up the stairs and into the apartment building.

"I think you'll be needin' me to show ya where to go...." Ruby said, hooking her hand into the crook of his arm. "Just like old friends we are...just like old friends...." She smiled for real this time, a smile Bobby liked better, he softened just a bit. Yeah, he'd go upstairs with her, but he wasn't staying.

Funny how someone who affected the course of your life so much can have so little meaning to you when you actually see them again, Bobby thought now as he leaned his head against the cool, rusted pipe of his cell.

Ruby was full of firsts. Ruby was the first one that broke his heart. He wrote his first song about Ruby, and then when he went to Chicago and Ruby had gotten him the job, Ruby had been instrumental in her own strange way in his trying heroin for the first time.

113

He remembered that first time well. Way back in '49 – had ten years passed so quickly? Didn't seem like a big deal at the time. He was makin' batteries out at the car battery factory where Ruby had finally pulled some strings to get him a job – seemed her cousin Jack wasn't hiring. Yeah, there he was at the battery factory six months into his job, happy as a clam and not thinkin' 'bout nothin' when his friend Wilbur said, offhandedly: "You ever tried this?" He handed him over the white powder, real casual like, showed him how to sniff it quickly up into his nostril, bending his head back towards the roof of the battery garage and inhaling again – a quick, short snort. Bobby had copied and sniffed it. Just like that. No thought. He just did it. One, two, three, four, five minutes passed, an initial euphoria, slightly and then – he got sick. After throwing up, the euphoria was cleaner, nice and clean. But he never wanted to try that again. Lucky. He didn't need it. Was only a onetime thing. Stayed in Chicago about a year and a half, happily making batteries and getting to know all the reasons why he did not want to be in Ruby's world.

"Ruby's a liar..." her friends told him. Her *friends*. Some friends. But Ruby *was* a liar, and she would do anything to make her life simpler. She and her Colonel had split, probably fleeced him and he went running. After that, she was always after some man who had money and she made no bones about it. Oh, and did he tell himself that, she lied? Well, Bobby was right about that from the beginning.

Chicago got boring after a while. What was he doing in Chicago anyway? Making batteries? Why? Lavinnia wasn't here. Nothing for him here. Only here to please his mother. He longed to get back to New York – to get back to his music. He missed the people. He missed the nightlife and Smalls Paradise in Harlem and The Savoy Ballroom. He missed a home-cooked meal. So in 1951 he headed on back to his hometown.

Ruby was out of his system. No more Ruby. Ruby with her red, red lips and matching red fingernails had sailed from his heart. He was fixed. He did not need her any longer.

CHAPTER TWENTY-ONE

*H*ARLEM...AH, HARLEM.... *Dirty, gritty, damp, lovely lowdown Harlem.* He had arrived on a drizzly, gray November day, the rain pelting him relentlessly. He stepped off the bus and pulled his collar up over his neck, pulled his hat down low and bent his head against the wind.

Yes, just the thought of it, even now in his cell set Bobby's mouth to water. *I am like Pavlov's dog*, he thought to himself, closing his book carefully and setting it gingerly by his side on the thin and lumpy cot. He wasn't reading anyway, he was daydreaming. Daydreaming about his past.

Yes, he had always been drawn to Harlem. He remembered arriving at twelve years old; face pressed anxiously against the glass of the old Olds his grandparents had driven over from California. The buildings; the gray. The palpitating excitement he felt even then permeating the sidewalks. The squalor; the luxury. His parents were in the middle of a party when he'd arrived. Stepped inside the door of their apartment holding his single suitcase. The look of disapproval on Grandma Nellie's face; Grandfather silent. Eva, beautiful Eva in her green dress, holding a cocktail come to swoop him up in her arms; swoop him up and hold him close to her breast; warm, motherly smells permeating from her to him. Musicians in every corner of the room. Dark suits and cigar smoke. His father holding court with a group of young ladies. A sax player in the corner blowing slowly on his horn. Low, silent moan.

He took to it like a duck to water. One big party; life was one big party.

He watched his mother's face fall when he told her that day he would study music. Declaring it again after high school graduation. The fall. He

115

could not be swayed. No one was going to stop him. Did good, too, going to music school on the G.I. Bill after the Army. So, how did it come to that night he remembered now so desperately?

Heroin, his silent friend. The second time did not make him sick. Snorted it right up and instant euphoria. But that wore off quick; needed something bigger — so he'd started skin-poppin'. Had to beg Joe for the needle that first time before a show. But no go with Joe. He had refused. Straight out refused. Never seen Joe so tight before. Now he knew why, but back then he just thought Joe was being selfish; wanting it all for himself. Bobby wanted their high — the all-encompassed high; the head back against the wall and let all your troubles melt into the peeling paint high; he wanted to play faster to *watch the music* as he heard them describe it. He wanted *more*. So he went outta the club and into the streets, had no problem buying him some and then he'd taken it right back to the back room at Smalls. Got a needle too. Inserted the needle right under his skin; watched the small bump appear as he injected the liquid.

Head back against the wall. Warmth oozing through his pores. Pores big and small. Needed *no thing*. Only himself and this wall and this room. How could he describe it to himself, now, in this cell at Rikers jail? The evocation of the memory of the feeling created a longing Bobby thought was gone forever. *Damned drug!!*

But that first high was the best. It never got better than that.

He knew that now — but even skin-poppin' lost its appeal; high not so good anymore; natural evolution to shoot it straight into your veins. *Straight into your vein.* Directly into the flow of his blood. Life to life. The high was better than he knew could exist and it came immediately. Swiftly swooping him up; erasing any fear that crept in him. Instant relaxation. He was complete. And he was hooked.

*Oh, yeah…*he thought mournfully…*oh yeah, once you start puttin' it in your veins, you're hooked. There's no turning back then.* And that's the way it was. From that day forward the sweats started. The queasiness when he didn't have it — did it at night and in the morning his nose would be running and that peculiar all-encompassing aching need for more. He could not put it into words, even now in his own head, to himself, the description of the aching need — that is the only way he could describe it. *Aching need.*

Yeah, he remembered Harlem. Walking slowly down that gray and dirty street. Trench coat collar pulled up close to his ears; head bent down towards the ground. The night air cold and foreboding, the drizzling rain pelting the exposed skin of his neck; the 1920's street lamps casting an eerie shadow upon the pavement. His contact in front of him, walking briskly around a corner and into the rundown tenement building where he kept his stash. Bobby would stay there sometimes for fifteen minutes; maybe half an hour. Shoot up right there, he wanted so badly. Shoot up and then go home, stashing the rest deep in his pocket. And the walks home, the wind biting and ever-present…what did he feel? Just like he wasn't sick. Just like he got his fix. He felt fixed. That was all.

But he no longer wished to be broken.

How had it come to that? Bobby shook his head back to the present and out of his revelry — the slip had been so easy, so imperceptible — he had hardly noticed. He leaned his head again against the cool metal behind his cot. Listening once again to the *drip, drip, drip* of the tainted water. No feeling of refuge in the repetition of the sound this time. Only an urge, an inescapable urge to *get back out there.* To find "Last Night in the Moonlight" and get his money; get his *shot.* Maybe, now, he would get his "break." He could stay away from the drugs — he'd been in here now for months already without them. Sure the first few couple of weeks were tough — the sweating at night, the aches, the *vomiting* — it began and ended with the vomiting — a *spitting up* of his past. A retching that released him of his demons and the demon of his drug. But he had done it. He was purged. And clean. And he wanted to *get out.* Now.

Only three months to go. A sentence for assault. Three months of sober clarity. Three months to pick out songs in his head. Could he wait that long? Could he do it? What before seemed a safe haven in which ambivalence marked his only major emotion — ambivalence about getting out. Ambivalence about his drugs. Ambivalence about love; his music. All those feelings had flickered and died the moment his voice came over the loudspeaker in this cell. His prison. His haven.

It was evening now. And he had not left his cell since afternoon.

He had missed dinner, feigning a headache. He had closed his eyes wearily when the guard had come to get him after he didn't show with the others to line up for the mess hall supper. The guard had not protested. The guard had let him be. Did he know about the song and Bobby's secret and sudden fame? Could he sense Bobby's complacency turned to anxiousness? — an underlying anxiety that threatened to take over and mute *every other existent emotion?*

No...the guard had said nothing. He had just nodded his head and slammed Bobby's cell door shut.

And now the full moon — its gray, round globe shimmering in the warm night, was shining through his small window. And it spoke silently. And Bobby knew; he *knew* — that this was his last night in the moonlight. His life would change. He would make his mark. A shift and a blink. Imperceptible.

Inexplicable. Forever.

Bobby closed his eyes. His night bathed in silver. And waited. For his release.

CHAPTER TWENTY-TWO

H E SQUINTED INTO THE MERCILESS SUN, looking straight up into the sky, his hand over his brow for shield. *May – 1960.* Christmas and New Years spent alone in that cell on Rikers Island.

May and now there was no snow. No wet cold. The bloom of spring had come and was fading already into the hot New York summer. *Hot early this year...*Bobby thought. He'd only been outside ten minutes and already his shirt was wet in the armpits and down the middle of his back, one small droplet of sweat snaking its way slowly down the arched path between his pointed shoulder blades. He wiped the perspiration forming along his brown and curly hairline. His hair was short – always had been. And his shirt was buttoned up and tucked in expertly and neatly. Two hours spent spit-shining his shoes the night before – anticipatory excitement riding high.

His mother should've already been here to pick him up. He'd called her the afternoon before just to confirm the time and place – he'd waited with the other hopeful inmates in the long line for the pay phone for his once a week; three-minute-per-call allotted phone time. Over that amount and either a guard grabbed the phone out of your hand and slammed the line disconnected, or another inmate hit ya side of the face – backhand or full fisted – either one not pleasant. So Bobby, ever the diligent one to follow the rules and try to avoid trouble whenever possible and especially in his current situation – always kept his eye on the large, metal clock covered with wire hanging high on the wall across the room. He kept his eye on that clock and he began to say his goodbyes at two minutes, thirty seconds. By two minutes, fifty seconds he had hung up – silently nodding to the inmate behind him and making his way purposefully past the single file line of overall-clad men.

Yes, they'd confirmed the time, date and exact place of pickup – both being of somewhat precise nature – and Bobby scanned the horizon and parking lot now for signs of her. Eva had told him that she would be bringing Aaron Douglas' big blue Impala. Eva did not have a car of her own – saw no reason for the expense and enjoyed the four block walk to the bus stop every morning, and the forty-five minute bus ride to work each day. *My readin' time!* she'd exclaimed more than once, amber eyes lighting from within; throwing her trademark white-toothed smile at Bobby. Then there'd she'd go – off to her job at the State Insurance Fund, a job she had kept and steadily worked for the last ten years.

Bobby remembered now fondly her other job in 1939 at the World's Fair. What fun that had been! He'd been about fifteen years old at the time and he'd go on down there with her every now and then. He reveled in the large and unguarded personalities of the multicolored and multisized characters behind the high Fair walls – all cloaked in their individual idio-syncrasies, unaware or uncaring of the world outside. Insulated from it. The large colorful buildings all glowing majestically in the sun. The giant Ferris wheel slowly turning high in the sky – the first he'd ever seen. Named after Mr. Ferris, its inventor. How he had longed to ride that giant wheel; but he never did. He'd walked by and stared as he'd wandered the massive grounds. He'd stared up at the many giant sturdy structures, each with their own theme. Bobby liked the party atmosphere of it all; the living for the moment; it reminded him a little of home – one big party with everyone laughing and carryin' on and having a good time. Yes, a small, segregated, insulated world. Separate.

He couldn't recall what she did, though.... *What did she do?* He searched his mind now to find the answer, but nothing came. They'd go straight to the back of the low-slung square wood building, and she'd sit at the makeshift desk in the corner of the front room; it's four small, rectangular windows letting in little light, dust circling up from the floor unnoticed. And then

PART II - BOBBY

she'd begin her "paperwork" as she would call it, and send Bobby out to "visit the fellows." *She musta done bookkeeping*, Bobby surmised now. It was such a short span in his life — six months; maybe nine months? But it had left its imprint behind. The freedom of it all. A lack of regard for outside mores and rules; an *individual approach to life*. A freedom. Yes, Bobby liked this. But couldn't seem to live it.

Damn! He was half-connected to conventional mores and half led by his creativity; a slight, constant conflict that bashed between his mind and soul. Something he chose to ignore most of the time. He scanned the horizon again for signs of his mother. Two guards watched from the tall tower above, amused at his confusion. They chuckled to themselves, but did not move to help.

"I enjoy my time alone to read my books!" Eva had said many a time most emphatically. She read a book a day and her son admired her for that.

Eva sat alone now in the big blue Impala on the other side of the large, concrete, windowless building, its oblong structure throwing dark, elongated shadows across the parched pavement. She waited patiently. There would be no reading for Eva today. Today she had taken off of work. Today was a special occasion — her boy was coming home and she wanted to pick him up in style. He was going to make a new life, and she was going to help him do it! She knew Bobby had an affinity for nice cars — although he had never actually owned one himself — who needed one in Harlem, really? She *hmmmfd* to herself and readjusted her now widening ass in the sticky leather seat, pulling down the brown wool skirt that had begun to hike up her thigh. She looked in the rearview mirror and expertly adjusted her brown short brimmed hat slightly, smacking her lips together once to smooth her pale red lipstick and then dabbed at the corner of her mouth gingerly with her pinky to remove just the slightest bit that had bled into the corner there. Satisfied with her reflection she scanned the parking lot again for signs of her son.

Eva's mind went back to her thoughts. Yes, everything was walking distance and if you had to go way into the City, there was the subway. She enjoyed the subway. Even though it had first opened way back in '07, Eva still thought of it as new — she loved the smell of the interior and the *clang clang* of the bell as it slowly approached. She liked the dark, stillness of the tunnel; the lack of air; the anticipation of its arrival. No one spoke; all waited. This agreed with her.

Then there were the buses, of course — so many of them, you could always hop on — and she did ride the bus to work each day. But a bus ride lacked the solitariness of the subway — you were more exposed; more confined in a strange way; and there was the ever-present traffic, the sound of which bothered Eva. Then of course there were the cars, which they did not own; no need; and finally the taxis, which were expensive but always available.

But today Eva was going to inspire Bobby with this car. *He has a good heart and is a hard worker when not on that damned stuff!* she thought once again with increasing irritation. He was smart — and *talented* — that she had to give. It was a talent that alternatively made her proud and scared the *hell* out of her. But, if that's what he wanted to do, then bygone-it, she was going to help him. She *hmmmfd* again and sat up straighter in her seat.

She had borrowed this car from dear Aaron — *Ah, Aaron, such a gifted artist*, she thought to herself. He'd painted her once — her eyes flicked closed momentarily at the memory, a soft exhale escaping her lips involuntarily. The painting was beautiful, she had to admit, but it embarrassed her in some strange way — this brash celebration of her beauty — and after hanging it on the wall for about a week, only to not offend Aaron and his generous gesture — she'd taken the frame down one cloudy afternoon, removed the oil canvas, rolled it up quickly, tied it with a thick piece of brown twine and stashed it in the back of her closet — hidden — in her bedroom.

Eva forced her thoughts to the present and again peered through the glare of the sun streaming through the dash window. She'd been here almost an hour already and there'd been no sign of Bobby. She'd been specifically told by him and then corrected by the guard who answered the phone when she'd finally gotten through to the main guards' office — that, no, she absolutely *could not* go inside to meet him — A place she'd been every Saturday for the past six months to visit. She absolutely was to wait in the designated area of the parking lot for her son. She was instructed not to get out of the car – which she found quite odd – but to "wait inside her vehicle." Bobby would find her. Bobby's release needed to be "processed" and the head guard she spoke with couldn't tell her exactly how long this would take, but that she should arrive for his pickup at 2:00 p.m. It was now 3:00.

The first day for Bobby in the sun. In the light. Everything was going to change now. Eva just knew it.

She kept scanning.

The two guards sat and watched from their perch in the high tower and chuckled to themselves. Amused at their little joke. "Damn niggas!" one of them mumbled under his breath, and he lit another cigarette from the butt of the first, throwing the still burning ember upon the ground and grinding it out with the rough heel of his boot.

Bobby still stood, at the other end of the parking lot, scanning the horizon, surprised at his mother's lateness. She was never late. He could always count on her. He looked up at the guard tower – should he? could he? wander around the parking lot to look for her? He was not sure. He signaled to the guard tower, the two guards, stared back down at him mutely, rifles resting neatly on their shoulders. No...he better stay here. This is where he was told to go.

———

Eva *HMMMFFD* again. She was getting irritated. This was ridiculous. She maneuvered her car to a space she found at the corner of the lot, turned off the engine and then proceeded to "get out of her vehicle" as she had oh-so-ceremoniously been instructed *not* to do. Someone was playing with her and she *did not like it.* If she could go inside to visit her son every Saturday, she could go inside and find out where he was. She stepped onto the hot and steaming pavement, her camel suede Savoy-style shoes with the dark brown leather trim softly hit the pavement. A pair she had kept in mint condition since the 30's. Still looked like new. Expensive when she bought them, but worth every penny.

123

UNCHAIN MY HEART

The guards stared down at her from the tower. She ignored them. "Looks like she's on the move, betta get on the horn and tell the front desk she's on 'er way in," one of them said, spitting brown phlegm onto the concrete floor. "Have 'em bring the inmate on over and around to the front desk." He spit again, as if chewing tobacco and not smoking cigarettes, a habit he'd had before but quit, all except for the spitting.

"Inmate's on the wrong side of the building," he heard Chuck, his partner bark into the military green walky-talky, "bring him 'round to the front, his ride's on her way in." *Damn stupid niggas*, he spit again.

Eva stood defiantly at the counter. She looked the man straight in the eyes. She told him she was here to pick up her son. "Bobby Sharp," she said matter-of-factly. She did not mention that she had been waiting. She did not mention that she had a sneaking suspicion, that they had tried to have her had. She did not let her now rising temper show. She felt a trickle of perspiration crawl down from behind her ear and start to make its slow way down her long, caramel neck. She let the feeling cool her; she felt the temptation of it. She adjusted her hat with her right hand deftly. She did not touch her skirt. She did not want to appear fidgety. She stood tall, with her shoulders back; proud...and waited.

"Of course," the man behind the glass window said. "Let's try and find him for you," completely unaware of the security guard's private little joke. Didn't care really. Kinda felt bad for half the inmates here. Some of them seemed like such good fellows. Not all, but some. She seemed nice.

"Bobby!" Eva turned suddenly to the sound of soft footsteps on linoleum and recognized him instantly as he came down the hall. He looked *better*, healthy, good. HAPPY. She was happy. This had been good for him in some strange way.

"Mama...Eva!" he replied automatically correcting himself. He had slipped back into the small boy he once was for a moment. He let his mother enfold him in her large, strong arms. Inhaled her scent momentarily;

pulled away. Slight tear welling in the corner of his eye. He had *missed* her. Eva, so strong. So *there*.

"Thank you, sir, for your help."

"Of course, ma'am. Good day to you."

They walked out of the double metal and glass doors leading to the parking lot, Eva's arm linked through the crook of Bobby's, the small metal wires crisscrossed throughout the glass of those doors glinting off the sunlight. She motioned her head to indicate the Impala. Bobby moved in front of her, the blast of the sun's heat hitting him again. She handed him the keys. He unlocked the door of the passenger's side, the quick "click" of the lock unleashing a tiny pang of excitement in him. Motioned for her to get in. She nodded her head towards him, elegantly positioned herself within the confines of the leather and he shut the door, *bang!* hard and closed her in. He went around to the driver's side, slipped in, started up the engine, slowly backed it out, and drove himself off the confines of his previous home. He looked back once.

Bobby stared through the waves of heat that rose from the hot tar road. A mirage of rippling water before him. He tightened his grip on the steering wheel, blinked twice; cleared his vision, focusing only on the road, and drove back towards his City.

CHAPTER TWENTY-THREE

THE DARK WAS ENVELOPING. The blue of the night cast against the darkness of his skin. He felt the high seep into him. Again. He walked, alone, down that empty back street. The moon following his steps. Accusing him. Feeling flooded his body. Again. Out only two days and he had done it, again. Deep sigh, release. The drug coursing through his veins. Immortal. He breathed.... And let go.

She looked straight at him from the back of the room as she kicked her leg high up in the air – her white skirt flying high in her face – covering it, just a bit and only for a second. Long, black lashes batted furiously; jet black hair straight and streaming down to the square of her shoulders – Bobby could see those lashes even from his seat at his usual small, round table, directly in the center of the room.

Bobby loved Smalls Paradise – had been comin' here for years. And he still loved to watch Tempy, kicking her long legs with abandon and staring straight into his eyes from high on that stage. Ah, Tempy – the fun they'd had together after she would get off from a show back in the days when there was still a Chorus Line. Her nights were long – five and sometimes seven solid hours of dancin' and twirlin' and kickin'. Ed the club owner, his gray and grizzled features covered by sparse facial hair, in theory gave the dancers fifteen minute breaks between shows, but it was more an idea than a reality and he rode them hard while on stage and made sure they worked for their fleeting stardom − each one of them hoping for a shot at the big-time − maybe down at the Apollo, if they were lucky. They gave it everything they had − different shades of bright, eager faces bobbing up and down in time to the movements of their bodies, pearly whites reflecting the strobe on stage. Skin gleaming ebony to tan to milky; Tempy falling somewhere near the end of the spectrum with her toffee-color skin rich, like spun honey glistening under those hot unforgiving lights. He noticed again with admiration her high Indian cheekbones − white lineage mixed deep within her Negro soul.

Tempy started out in '44 and Bobby remembered wistfully the rambunctious nights they would spend together − he waiting at the back door for her at 2:00 a.m. − cigarette in hand, smoothing his hair back with the other, licking his lips in anticipation − and she finally emerging, all smiles and giggles, so young and full of hope. She had changed out of her tap shoes and into some other high heeled number more sensible for the street but still made for dancin', and she always wore a flouncy knee-length skirt and sequined top − even if they were just going back to her place, but always in hopes of a stop at the Savoy.

Bobby was in the Army then, an MP − how he lucked into that one, he had only his mother to thank. He'd just up and joined one day in November '43 and found himself standing outside at Fort Dix, New Jersey, at 4:00 in the morning, freezing, thinking: *This is not what I envisioned....* He figured he was going to get drafted anyway − might as well do his patriotic duty and enlist. Maybe he'd miss the hard fighting that way − be able to choose a bit what he was going to have to do.

He'd just graduated from high school and was having trouble finding a job − had even marched on down to Wall Street after reading the classifieds in the New York Times and stood there in his best suit and tie and polished shoes − didn't even notice he was the only Negro in line, or even in the room for that matter. He, as usual, was dressed well. He took pride in his appearance. He thought a job on Wall Street would be perfect for him.

"What *you* doin' here?" The short, slightly balding gruff man at the oversized maple desk had singled him out of the line before he even got to the front to fill out his application.

"I'm here to apply for a job."

"We don't have anything for you!"

Surprise – hard – like a bullet. He looked around the room for the first time carefully and noticed his color. The white people staring at him. Silence.

He said nothing. Nodded silently, tipped his hat slightly to the clerk at the desk, and then to the room that was staring at him, turned on his heel and walked out of the building.

Eva knew some people down at the Rockefeller Foundation and got him an interview and he worked for a bit as an office boy, sorting and delivering mail. Good old Eva – she had her connections and always came through. People would trip over each other to do favors for her, she with her gentle Midwestern ways and persuasive manners. Bobby chuckled to himself now at the thought of his mother and her mischievous smile.

That job lasted about a year and half and then he had up and enlisted in the Army. Seemed like the thing to do at the time. But then came the 4:00-in-the-morning–raining–and–freezing–standing–outside–epiphany of: *What the hell have I done here??!!* Army not so good as he had imagined.

Yeah, Eva she'd pulled some strings, made some calls to some people she knew in the 372nd infantry stationed in New York, got him transferred right back to Harlem – to 110th Street between Fifth and Lenox Avenue, as an MP, no less.

And there he was back at Smalls Paradise lookin' to round up other soldiers that'd gone "AWOL," the short name for those soldiers absent without leave – most just left to go out drinkin' without a pass – and then there were those who had a pass, but never made it back to the base, got drunk and stayed out way past curfew – and he'd drive around town in his gray jeep, stopping by the Savoy Ballroom and all the bars up and down Harlem with the other MPs and round 'em up, gun and baton fastened to his holster. Round 'em up and take 'em on back to the base, and then, because he was an MP and had special privileges and no one really watched what he did – at 2:00 a.m., after he got off, he would go out again. He'd head on back out to those clubs he'd just raided for soldiers, Smalls being his favorite, and live it up with the chorus girls like Tempy and the lonely wives and girlfriends left home alone by the guys in the 369th Infantry who were over in the Pacific. He'd be out carousing until the morning light and then sneak back into base. Nobody ever was the wiser.

Aahhh, those were the days.... He whistled again silently to himself at the memory, a deep slow intake of breath hissing beneath his teeth.

When the Army decided to send the 369th home they sent his unit, the 372^{nd,} out to Kentucky, so the injured boys wouldn't be mad at them for being with their wives and girlfriends. Bobby shook his head now slightly at the thought of it.

No, he had *not* wanted to go down into the South and possibly get lynched. Not even a soldier's uniform protected blacks down there. He remembered it clearly, they would say: "look at those niggas *tha*...." He remembered getting on a bus to Baltimore to visit his cousin and going into a restaurant and when he sat at the counter was told to go around the corner and sit with the blacks. Big change from Harlem. Harlem was progressive in that way...if you could call it that.

And he remembered being in Kentucky in soldier's uniform going to the theatre and being forced to sit on the top level with the black people; *even in uniform*. No special privileges given there. He was surprised at this.

But what surprised him even more was his next action. Even now it forced a small laugh from him, a laugh that was not heard above the loud din of music coming from the small stage at the front of the room.

He was in a jeep accident and had a small contusion on his head. He was sent to the hospital. While in the hospital he got to thinking, he had had enough of the Army, and especially of Kentucky. He asked to see a psychiatrist. He told the psychiatrist that he had problems and that they had all started with his grandmother. Damned Grandma Nellie and her religious ministrations, hitting him all the time with that switch.... They put Bobby in the psych ward for a while. And then they sent him home. Then he got discharged for psychological disturbances. Free.

But life as an MP had been an easy life; a good life.

Bobby took a small sip of his whiskey and chuckled again to himself at the memory. He, of slight build and tender heart with his MP uniform and guns and holster. Yeah, those *were* good times. A sigh escaped his lips as he watched Tempy. Here he was back at Smalls again – so much time had passed and so much change – all had changed, even Tempy and her dancing legs. She was now in her mid-thirties and aged a bit; the realty of her dream of being a big Broadway star hitting her hard now that she was reaching midlife. And she held onto the last vestiges of her inherent spark with all her might. Teeth still whiter than white and hair still as lustrous, but Bobby could see the wrinkles that had begun to form at the corners of her eyes. Her face; her beautiful face was succumbing to the endless nights at Smalls. But her spark never wavered.

Of course, now, in 1960 there were no more chorus girls – there were straight musical acts and Bobby had gotten up on that stage from time to time to play; looking out over that crowded smoked-filled room; watching the players; the movers and shakers; the fur coats and brandy.

And Tempy had stayed on, never makin' it to the big time like she'd dreamed – her legs kicking away to the tune of the piano. She and Bobby would still sneak on over to the Savoy making their way from Smalls down 7th Avenue from time to time right on up until it closed in 1958, and they'd strut their stuff on that polished floor. Blacks and whites dancin' side by side – the Lindy Hop and things he'd never even heard of; best dancers in the world graced that floor and Tempy and Bobby right alongside. So much action there, so much energy and everyone dancin' off the musicians' energy or the sound comin' over the loudspeaker.

Nope, Tempy's fire never wavered – not once in all those years and she politely hid her disappointment in never quite achieving her dreams.

Bobby licked his lips and waited in anticipation for her set to end so they could get out of there. Tempy, his friend and confidante. Stable; always there. They'd go out after and have a drink or a cup of coffee. They could talk. He watched her make her way down the narrow steps at the front of the stage and move towards him.

"Hey Bobby," as if he was expected, "how ya doing? Haven't seen you in a while."

"Yeah, yeah, been out and about, you know, doing my *thang*."

She smiled at him, noticing the one brown curl looping down towards his forehead, the warm smile of an old friend. And waited. "Let's get out of here," she finally said as she reached down and took his hand, pulling him up. "We don't need to wait around for no *thing*, do we Bobby?"

Bobby stubbed his Pall Mall out in the round glass ashtray, "Nope, nope...nope...we don't, my lady." Her spirit was bright against him and they made their way out of the club and down the darkened Harlem street under a sliver of a moon, shadows dispelled by Tempy's cheery presence.

"Down on over to the corner for a coffee?"

"Yup...."

Bobby woke up and groaned, and laid his arm over Tempy's warm body. Here he was again dropped into Tempy's life – a sporadic figure; transient. But *nice*. This Bobby knew. All saw him as *nice*, and nonthreatening.

When he'd first met Tempy, he'd sneak in at night and sneak back out in the morning before the sun came up – tryin' to get back to Base before all hell broke loose and they discovered he'd been out all night; and more importantly, to get out of Tempy's house before her mother found him. Bess was a hellcat and "wasn't goin' to be puttin' up with no nonsense from Tempy." No hesitation to slap her hard if she was misbehavin'. But no Bess now that Tempy was all grown up.

He was given a lot of leeway back then, being an MP and all, but if they found he'd never come back to base, well that would be pushin' it – definitely. But after a night with Tempy he'd be refreshed and energized and ready for anything – back then he didn't need much sleep and drinkin' was his only bad habit.

But now...now all that had changed, and as he fumbled with his eyes closed for the comfort of Tempy's warm breast; as he caressed the firmness of it, cupping it in the palm of his right hand, pumping it slowly, hearing her moan and stir and then roll towards him – he felt the stirrings of his new desire and the familiar ache began to surge simultaneously through him. He reached with his left hand to wipe the drip that was beginning in his nose. A twin ache growing within him – one for his music and one for his junk – pushing the other, more primal need far to the background. He groaned.

Tempy took this as a groan of submission; a final admission of his never-ending attraction towards her, even after all these years, and she rolled towards him, her lithe body encircled within the fold of his arms, snuggling her nose deep into his hairless chest; taking in the scent of him – the scent of the sex of the previous night and aroused, she reached down for him, to coax him to life.

But Bobby was unresponsive; the craving taking over his body; and he rolled away from her and jumped out of bed awkwardly tripping on the shoes he had left on the floor in their haste for love. "Gotta get going, man; sorry Temp…you *know*…got things to *do*…"

Tempy, not easily stunned and used to covering up hurt emotions, rolled slowly away, her back to him, *"Yeah, yeah, yeah…"* she mumbled under her breath.

He pulled on his pants and fumbled with the zipper, button and belt; then pulled on his white t-shirt and pulled his arms through the sleeves of his previously crisp, starched, off-white, button-down shirt and began to button it up – hands trembling slightly. Trying to hide the tremble. Licking dry lips – clearing his throat, nose running – wipes it again. Ache increasing. Tear to his eye – frustration. "God damn it!" The exclamation is loud and definite, the anger and frustration welling out of him spontaneously. Tempy's intake of breath is short, immediate and hard and she holds it for a moment before she slowly exhales.

She knows what's going on. But she doesn't want to see it with Bobby. Her sweet-souled Bobby.

So she says nothing. Just lies with her back to the wall. With her back to the door. With her back to Bobby as he leaves the room.

Click.

Another one gone.

CHAPTER TWENTY-FOUR

BOBBY WALKED OUT of Tempy's place on 110th street and made his way on over to his parents' place – 409 "H" Avenue, his home since childhood. He pushed his hands deep into his pockets as he walked, head bent low against the chill of the wind; watching the brown leaves swirl at his feet – swirl and scatter away from him and into the wet gutter.

He stepped over an iron grill. The steam from the sewer below misting up around his ankles, a slight stink of warmth that left him empty.

No change. Not even a penny. He had not one dime to his name and nothing in the pipeline. He'd met with that publisher, Teddy Powell a few weeks before – showed him some of his stuff – a few lead sheets he'd had lying around. He caught the excitement in Teddy's eyes as he said, "C'mon back when you have some more – I'll take care of ya, kid, don't ya worry a bit." Chewing on that stubby cigar absently. It wasn't even lit, Bobby remembered. Wide-brimmed hat pushed back on his sweaty head; perspiration trickling from that thick red forehead, even on that cool, autumn day. Beet-red face; bulging eyes.

Bobby had found Teddy's lack of hygiene slightly repulsive; but Teddy had come with good references – some of the other guys down at Smalls had gotten cuts off of him, and at this point – Well, at this point....

Bobby cleared his throat and straightened his shoulders, lifting his face to the wind. "I will not be taken by this!" he exclaimed out loud. No one noticed him talking to himself. No one cared. The wind lifted his words and carried them away.

"I will not be taken by this!" he said again, more loudly this time, not caring if anyone heard, not that it mattered. "Unchain me!" Two words that twirled down and mixed with the leaves at his feet, sailing down the dirty sidewalk into the street.

He put his head down again and quickened his pace, turning the corner to "H" Avenue and taking the steps to the third floor, two at a time.

"Hi, Hon," his mother said as he walked in; warm, emblematic smile on her face, opening her arms to encircle him after wiping her hands hastily on her apron.

Bobby let her hug him, a cursory hug that he could not feel and then walked past her and the kitchen and the wonderful smells of beans and rice and collard greens and chicken. Ah, the miracles Eva performed in that space. But not like the "no space," as he now liked to refer to it – the "no space" being the itty-bitty closet with the hot plate she used to cook on when they lived in that one room place during the Depression. No kitchen there. Not so here on Sugar Hill.

Bobby shrugged the memories off quickly, not important now. He walked purposefully past his father, who sat in his chair, holding his beer and watching *Perry Mason*. Louis acknowledged Bobby with an upward turn of his full, thick mouth, Bobby barely turning in his direction as he strode past – past the family room and the black-and-white and *Perry Mason* in all his stern, integrity-filled admonishments, straight into the living room and the Wurlitzer piano that sat there. Waiting for him.

He sat emphatically, fingers poised over the keys and began to play the words that tugged his heart.

A-minor – his fingers hit the keys. *A-minor, D-minor* – the tone was set. He closed his eyes and let the song pour from long, aching fingers onto worn white and black. Up and down the piano, slow and rhythmic; beating – the tune teasing him sporadically.

He stopped and grabbed a blank lead sheet from under the worn mahogany bench. He grabbed the pencil from the ledge. He wrote the notes in hastily. He began playing again. Words escaping his soul – wisps into the air.

Unchain my heart, baby let me be... Unchain my heart, 'cause you don't care about me..."

He dropped his hands from the keys, picked up his pencil and lead sheet again and hastily scribbled in words. Lead sheet on his lap now, picking out the rest of the tune with his left – *scribbling, scribbling.*

...*I'm under your spell like a man in a trance / But I know darn well, that I don't stand a chance so / Unchain my heart, let me go my way...*
...*Why lead me through a life of misery? / When you don't care a bag of beans for me / So unchain my heart, please, please set me free...*

Half an hour and the song is done. Jumps up from the hard bench, grabs the lead sheet, hurries past his parents, who are now both sitting watching *Perry Mason*; Eva gingerly fingering her tall glass of iced tea with lemon, Louis' beer set on the TV table between them, shoulders slouched, staring straight ahead. Walks straight past both of them, doesn't say a word, and leaves the apartment – slamming the door unintentionally behind him.

Eva winces internally, but says nothing.

Bobby runs the four blocks to the bus stop; jumps the bus at Broadway and lands on Music Row at Teddy Powell's office at 3:00 p.m.; sweat trickling down his back, hands trembling. He feels weak, he knows he looks pale, but at least he is dressed well, and *damn!* he just wants to *sell that song*; get some cash; buy a stash and *move on!*

Teddy Powell looks up as Bobby rushes in. "Back so soon?" he asks. Bemused. Expertly taking in Bobby's agitated state. He knows what's going on, he's seen it a thousand times with these niggas – got hooked on heroin and couldn't think a nothin' else.

Bobby doesn't say anything. He just pushes the onionskin lead sheet across the cluttered desk to Teddy. And waits. Teddy takes the time to put his stubby, half-lit chewed on cigar in the dirty ashtray on his desk. He looks down at the lead sheet and after a moment or two his face lights up. His eyes twinkle, he scrunches up his face as he reads more closely. His beet-red face gets even redder.

He had a hit! Bygone-it he had a hit!! This kid had gold and didn't even *know* it goddam it! And Teddy had just the artist for the song, too – *knew* he would take it – just *knew* it; he'd have to, Teddy would make sure of that.

Teddy could see the dollar signs appearing all over Bobby – he was going to be his little black cash cow – strung out and talented; no, bordering on *genius* – wouldn't ya know?

"When'd ya'all write this song, son?" Teddy asked, carefully modulating his voice; expertly hiding his excitement.

"Just now, at my parents' house."

"How long'd it take ya?" His carefully crafted casual tone dripping from his mouth like maple syrup.

"I dunno, twenty, thirty minutes…I dunno. Do you like it? Do you wanna buy it? I need cash now, though. I need to leave here with *something*…." Bobby's voice trailed at the end, his energy lagging. The word "something" somehow divesting him of the last of his spirits. The chills coming on now. The ache intensifying. The drip of his nose unstoppable.

"That's a tall order, son," Teddy said, assessing his superior position once again. "Well, let's see – if ya want cash right now, it's gonna have to come outta my own *pawket*, you see. But I'm fair and I have a weak spot for ya yung musicians. I wanna give ya somethin' yur gonna feel *proud* of." He cleared his throat for the drama of the pause, for effect, "*tell ya what I'm gonna do….*" Bobby looked around the room anxiously and thrust his hands deep into his pant pockets to keep them from openly trembling.

"I'm gonna give you fifty dollas – cash, right here and now!" He knew it was an amount that was more than Bobby had seen in a long time, these small-minded punks – always in it for the immediate – never lookin' at the big picture, not smart like Teddy.

"And, I'm only gonna take fifty percent of the writer's credit, ya see. And ya understand, me bein' the publisher, the publishin's mine, now, don't you?"

"Yes, yes, of course." Bobby nodded in agreement.

PART II - BOBBY

"Now, let's see, now, where'd I put those damned contracts? Got a standard one 'round here somewa...." He slowly and methodically fished around his dirty desk drawer with his fleshy fingers. He knew exactly where it was, he never misplaced his blank contracts, but he was enjoying the game – watching Bobby squirm a bit gave him the tiniest of thrills, and it had been a long time since he'd felt any thrill at all. The power of it all was intoxicating, intoxicating as the bottle of Bacardi 151 hidden under all this crap, the thought of which set his mouth to watering – *almost*. He refocused and pulled the smudged paper up and out of his drawer.

"Ah, here it is," he exclaimed triumphantly, while simultaneously brushing off a few cracker crumbs that had spilled from the paper to his lap. "Must'v fallin' outta my lunch," he muttered under his breath as he filled in the blanks for advances, writer's splits and royalties.

"You just sign right *thair* – right on the dotted line by the 'x'." He stretched his sweaty hand towards Bobby who was now seated across from him, sitting poised and with a straight back. Teddy fixed an eager grin on his bloated face. "Don't y'mind that-there grease stain..." Bobby carefully attempted to wipe off the small gray grease stain on the signature line, "sometimes those papers are so damned absorbent, never know what they're bound ta soak up!" Teddy laughed nervously, trying to keep it light; casual. Trying to hide his extreme enthusiasm for his sudden good fortune. *He was going to be rich! He was going to be rich!* He just knew it – and this poor slob sitting across from him had no idea the gold he was signing away.

"*Thair we go now*," Teddy cooed, as if talking to a volatile child or a wild animal; exhaling as Bobby signed his name where he had indicated, "and date it, too, if ya don't mind."

"Oh, sorry." Bobby's voice was calm. He felt strangely calm. He cleared his throat to give it presence. He printed the date boldly.

"Uh, thanks," Bobby said, "I really appreciate you taking this song, giving me the advance on such short notice." He was nothing, if not polite.

"Oh, no problem, son!" Teddy exclaimed heartily rising from behind his large desk and moving towards Bobby; moving behind him and slapping him hard on the back unexpectedly, deriving another small pleasure from the forcefulness of the slap. "Yup, fully my pleasure, don't ya worry 'bout a thing, I'll take care of everythin', nope don't ya worry, son."

Bobby sat. And waited. Teddy looked deep into Bobby's watery eyes. Bobby cleared his throat, "*Um, mmmm, the $50?*"

"Oh!" Teddy cleared his throat as well and laughed heartily at the same time – it came out as a deep growling cackle. "Of course, of course, how stupid a me to ferget. Here it is – I thank I might just have that amount in my *pawket*."

He reached deep inside the front pant pocket of his cheap, white linen suit, and fished out a thick wad of bills. Flipping through them seductively he pulled one lone $50 from the pack. "Here ya go, son – come back any-time…anytime, ya hear?"

"Sure," Bobby said, and turned and quickly left the room.

The cool November air hit his skin, a slap to his bones as he escaped Teddy's office. Gray clouds hung low in the muted sky, marking fall's definite descent into winter. The rain held back now, a hesitation against the backdrop of the black sky, behind the soft, swirling gray. Shades of gray that did not look menacing to Bobby, but comforting – a *warmth* ema-nating from them – a warmth in their lack of differentiation. A warmth in the *haziness* of it all. These clouds were not black and this small, simple thought comforted Bobby, gave him hope, as he rounded the corner to-wards his apartment and the streets he knew so well.

One, two, three blocks from his childhood home on "H" street. He saw Gus lingering on the corner, raincoat pulled tight around him. Bobby slowed. He spoke before thinking. "Hey, man, you got some?"

"Only for you, man, only for you…." Bobby slipped Gus the bill and Gus slipped him the dime bag. One swift motion and he had dropped the neat square pouch into his pocket. Two breaths more and Bobby was bounding up the steps. Three more breaths and he was in the door. Slammed tight behind him. Straight to his books. His salvation. He ex-pertly fished the needle and spoon out from behind. Lighter in hand, lighter always kept in the front, left pants pocket. A safety. White pow-der sprinkled onto the cool metal spoon; drops of water. Lighter flicked, once, twice, three times – hiss of flame. Hand trembling; he sighs. Mouth watering; in anticipation. Inhale. Exhale. Needle into the liquid. Suck it up. Tie off the arm. Head back against the wall; slow injection into blue vein. A nod. Sleep with no sleep. Dream with no dreams. Sweet, sweet relief. A stomach that settles. A mouth that loses water. No food. No love. No breath. Just this.

He dreams for a moment.

The sun sets.

The clouds dissipate from the sky with the night. And only an inky blackness is left over the city. No stars to see in Harlem. The lights – are too bright.

CHAPTER TWENTY-FIVE

S HE STOOD ALONE in the kitchen. It was 8:00 in the morning and Louis had not come home again, and at this point she didn't care anymore. She had left him mentally and emotionally years ago, had actually left him physically, kicked him right out of their apartment when Bobby was only thirteen years old, but had taken him back after Bobby had cried and howled for his father. A mistake. But she had to do it. It was the right thing. She wanted her son to have his father. A lot of good that did. But now, she knew, it was only a matter of time before she left him for good.

They hardly spoke anymore. Had they ever really spoken? Could Eva even remember the initial attraction that drew her to Louis? The spark that had kept her attached to him; despite the other opportunities she had had.

Ah Eddie, she had been truly in love with him — was going to marry that man. Leave Louis and his women and partying and carrying on once and for all and marry Eddie.

He had lived next door for three years — tall, slight of build and always dressed in the finest suits. Eva remembered now the way his hat sat perfectly at a slight tilt on his closely-cropped brown curly head. She remembered his impeccable manners and his long, tapered fingers. Used to be a piano player, but went into business for himself and was a fine, upstanding pillar of their community. Kind-hearted and sincere. No troubles. No unexpected surprises.

But he'd gone off to Nantucket one day in his nice big convertible. And never returned. Got in a car crash and died. *Just like that.*

PART II – BOBBY

Eva sighed, and wiped her hands on her apron, then removed it with a swift, sure motion. She picked up her small clutch from the kitchen counter and tucked it gently into her larger bag with her book. Walked purposely to the hall closet and took out her brown, camel hair knee-length coat and put it on, her movements fluid and expert. She smoothed her hair back with her left hand, expertly feeling for any loose strands; her auburn hair tucked neatly into a soft bun that twirled and sat at the nape of her long, soft neck. She walked to the front door and picked up her house keys, which she kept in a small tray in the tiny alcove by the door. Opened the door, stepped through, locked the door, carefully placed the keys deep into her coat pocket and walked downstairs and up the street to catch her bus to work.

Bobby had read Emily Post in high school and he remembered a passage that had always bothered him. Emily suggested that you take your hat off when passing a lady in the street, and he knew the words exactly, an uncanny knack he had to, without much effort, remember entire passages:

> "Lifting the hat is a conventional gesture of politeness shown to strangers only, not to be confused with bow-ing, which is a gesture used to acquaintances and friends. In lifting his hat, a gentleman merely lifts it slightly off his forehead and replaces it; he does not smile nor bow, nor even look at the object of his courtesy. No gentleman ever subjects a lady to his scrutiny or his apparent obser-vation...If he passes a lady in a narrow space, so that he blocks her way or in any manner obtrudes upon her, he lifts his hat as he passes...He lifts his hat if he asks any-one a question, and always, if, when walking on the street with either a lady or a gentleman, his companion bows to another person. In other words, a gentleman lifts his hat

whenever he says 'Excuse me,' 'Thank you,' or speaks to
a stranger, or is spoken to by a lady...."

Yes, he remembered it perfectly – even to this day. But to Bobby it did
not make logical sense.

Especially now, with the cool November breeze blistering his skin –
already unusually cold for November. If he were to *take off his hat* as he
passed a lady, as opposed to simply *tipping* it, his hat would fly away in the
wind. It just wasn't practical. So Bobby had decided long ago to *tip* his
hat as he passed a lady in the street, tip it lightly and bend his head down
slightly, holding on to his hat tightly so the wind would not catch it and
carry it away.

He thought about this now as he made his way 'round Central Park.

He loved Central Park in the late afternoon. 4:00 p.m. and near-
ly dusk – the sun already beginning to set and the last of the lingering light edging its way out of the slate sky. He walked its trails slowly.
Concentrating on each measured step. Breathing in deeply, taking in the
conflicting sights and sounds. A shout, somewhere in the distance – was
it a shout of joy, or fear? Bobby could not tell. No one would care. He
shook it off – not his business. Not a good idea to invite trouble.

The birds, invisible, yet always ever-present in the trees, chirped
away their seduction, lending an air of mystery and exoticism to this oth-
erwise deeply urban city. Yes, a park, set right smack in the middle of the
City. He liked the duality of it.

His escape.

Green grass; tall trees; all so well manicured. No time for release of
pain. No time for anything.

But the sun setting on the drizzle that was beginning.

He pulled the scratchy wool of his coat collar up high around his neck;
tugged his center crease Fedora hat down low on his forehead.

Head to the wind.

His escape.

His time to *think*.

Thinking both his salvation and his torture.

PART II - BOBBY

Thinking is what has made this downward journey so horribly palatable.

His ability to *think through* and justify his actions.

His ability to measure *each tiny step* and not let it get too out of hand.

Never had he been passed out somewhere in some dark and dank alley.

Never had he lost his "cool" and ended down on skid row with the homeless – and, he knew, this would never happen.

Okay, sure, he had to be honest with himself, as he always was – He had ended up in jail for six months – not good, obviously. But, really, it was not his fault – he had only *moved a dead body*. His charges had been reduced to "assault." Hell, he wouldn't have even had to serve that second six months if he hadn't slipped while out on bail and had just the tiniest taste....

Ah, the sweet relief, as always. But Bobby had lost control on that one, and he did not like losing control. And, of course, the judge had found out and sentenced him to Rikers. Bobby remembered the judge's words quite clearly:

"Tell you what, young man, Beethoven and Bach did not need drugs in order to create music and neither do you, so I am going to put you somewhere where you will not be able to get any drugs...."

And, strangely enough, Bobby had felt *relieved*, actually relieved to be put away. He saw it as a vacation – from responsibility – the music – and most of all, from the drugs. He hardly even missed them. And the withdrawals, once they passed were worth the moments of peace he found, in his reading, and his *mind*.

His strength and his weakness.

Until that day "Last Night in the Moonlight" had come blaring over the radio and wrecked his peace.

Until that day he had received the clipping of the newspaper article that his mother had sent him.

Until that day that it had *all come flooding back to him* – the urge for the music; the drugs; the longing; the *aching need to create*.

A slight torture that tickled his soul and propelled him forward.

And into – today.

Walking through Central Park. Listening, intent only to the sound of the birds in the trees; watching the squirrels and other wildlife dash in and out of shadows. Lending an air of exotica to this misplaced patch of trees and grass.

His escape.

Deep sigh. Release.

CHAPTER TWENTY-SIX

B OBBY WALKED OUT of Central Park. The sun had set and he liked the feeling of being alone, in the dark, in the City. He looked up at the sky and counted: one, two, three, four, five, six stars he could see clearly on this moonless night.

He shoved his hands deep into his pockets; no snow in March, it had already melted. The early, cold winter, which had hit hard at the end of November, had dissipated as quickly as it had come, March bringing with it sudden blasts of warmth, and snow that melted before it hit the ground. He remembered walking through the park last November. And in December. And February. Now March. March so similar to November. No snow. Either melting or about to begin. March and November had similarities. Fall and spring – the seasons between the seasons. The seasons leading up to the *real thing* – either winter or summer. Real weather. He liked the in-between.

Bobby knew, that were he to be walking in the day, he would see tiny sprouts of green pushing their hopeful tendrils between the cracks of the sidewalk.

He knew that he would see bursts of white, pink and tangerine-colored buds on the trees placed so strategically in the small, brown patches of dirt squares every half block or so along the grimy sidewalks.

He knew, if he were walking in the day, he would not notice the gray, rounded streetlight; that it would not cast a muted mustard glow on the street.

He would see only the trees. And their buds.

Not the street and its eerie, gray shadows and yellow-gray pools of light cast in small round orbs.

Orbs he stepped through.

Momentary moments of lightness.

Then darkness, as he stepped out and back into the shadows.

His walk back home.

He pushed his hands deeper into his winter coat's pockets, pulling the collar up higher against his neck. He'd lost his hat in the park – that damned wind so unexpectedly picking it up off his head and carrying it away on its twirls – sighing deeply with its acquisition. He finally gave up chasing it and just let it go, took it as a sign, that he should just let it go – and let go of his concept of tipping his hat at the ladies. Hell, he wasn't even going to wear a hat at this point – *too much trouble*. But, he mused and chuckled to himself – He was right. The wind does carry it away, even if it is on your head, so *tipping* is definitely preferable to *lifting* – Not practical.

A lot of the things Emily Post suggests are not practical. He kicked a small white stone that appeared in his path. Kicked it and listened intently as it rolled away. The City was eerily quiet this evening and he relished the silence – it was as if the City was all his. Made just for him. He looked up at the moonless sky again – ink black – with six stars. Three street lamps he could see with glowing orbs on the sidewalk ahead; half illuminating the street; half the sidewalk.

He walked his first step back into Harlem. A decided "thump" in his brain. A step down into his past. The familiar aching returning – an instinctual memory ignited in him by the step into these familiar streets. Five dollars, it was all he had left to his name. Five dollars and no way to pay his rent.

It had been almost six months since he'd sold that song to Teddy, and he hadn't heard a word since then. Well, one call – a message left at his parents' house. A message that Eva had relayed excitedly: that Teddy thought he had a singer for the song, but he'd let him know more when he heard more – then, nothing.

Bobby looked up, abruptly. A feeling to his right – a hit to his shoulder – an unasked question – eyes staring at him from the dark.

Two small beacons hidden in the shadows, furtive yellow eyes shooting their glance his way – corner of Lexington and 112th. Gus's arm shot out, touched the sleeve of Bobby's coat. No words were spoken, just those two eyes and that arm. Just Gus's light, fleeting grip on the outside corner of Bobby's sleeve.

Bobby instinctively broke into a sweat.

"Hey man, you got some?" He heard the words come out of his mouth before he knew he had spoken them. "I need a nickel bag."

"Got it," Gus mumbled as he slipped Bobby the marble sized powder in the plastic bag tied tightly with a red rubber band. Bobby slipped him the $5.

All done in an instant – with hardly a thought. Almost instinctual. And Bobby, on leaden foot and semiautomatic, made the way the rest of the four blocks back to his apartment and shot up.

Midnight. And as usual and as had been happening quite often these days – it wasn't enough. One small sigh of quick relief, not even a "high" anymore and already, only hours later, he was craving *just a little more.* Just a little to take the edge off.

But he was out of money. Nothing left. Absolutely nothing.

He'd gone through all of his drawers, the envelopes he kept stashed in various books as "savings" to hide from himself. Looked under his mattress. All his money hiding places had already been raided. There was nothing left.

He had only one choice.

He put on his heavy, gray wool coat. No hat, of course, because it had been lost. Pulled his black leather gloves over his long tapered fingers; slipped on and laced his black, patent leather wingtip shoes, and headed over to his parents' house.

He knew they would both be asleep. His mother had to get up early for work tomorrow morning and his father would be passed out after coming home from waiting tables. He got off at 10:00 p.m. most nights – drank heavy and solid for a few hours, would stagger in at about 12:30 and be out by 1:00 – perfect timing....

Bobby had a key to the place, his mother had given it to him long ago, just in case he needed anything "or just a place to stay..." she'd said affectionately, the caring ever-present in her voice; a hint of reprimand unsaid and hidden behind her words; her big amber eyes flashing with love and warmth. He pushed this thought forcefully out of his mind and focused only on the mental picture of Louis, passed out in the spare room, slobber dribbling from his mouth, white t-shirt stained and stretching over his large belly.

He kept this picture firmly in his mind. He pushed his mother's face far to the back – this did not concern her. This was between he and his father.

Still no moon to watch him and he stepped lightly up the three wide concrete steps leading to his parents' apartment on Sugar Hill, stopping for a moment to lean against the great concrete post majestically support-ing the porch and its awning.

Then he stepped through the main doors and took the three flights of stairs up. The outside hall was dark and he did not bother to turn on the lights.

He quietly fished the key out of his pocket – a single brass key that he did not keep on his personal ring with his other keys – a key that he kept in an envelope in the copy of Robinson Crusoe sitting so succinctly on the bookshelf, along with his "savings," which at the moment did not exist. So, the key had sat alone in that square, white envelope, a sad reminder of the only stability he had. He gently inserted the key into the lock and turned it quickly. A soft *click*. He pushed the door open and closed it gently again. He did not turn on the lights. He knew his way expertly around this apartment he had once lived in from age thirteen – he could close his eyes and find anything in here. His mother had not changed a thing; not rearranged one piece of furniture in all this time. The only addition was the small TV tray between the two large easy chairs, and of course the television, something added in the mid-fifties. *No matter.* Bobby shook his head to stay focused. He stood next to the front door, near the small alcove where Eva kept her keys, nestled in the round porcelain dish, a gift from her mother. He slipped his shoes off and padded quietly to the spare bedroom.

Even from the center of the family room he could hear his father's snoring, snorting, grumbling and growling in his sweaty sleep. Bobby made his way towards the noises escaping from the spare bedroom, expertly avoiding the two easy chairs and their mutual TV tray. He knew there would be an empty beer bottle sitting atop of that TV tray – his mother refused to clean up after Louis, and in an eternal statement left his empty beer bottle sitting there night after night for Louis to pick up himself.

Yup, he knew the drill, expertly zigzagging his way through the darkened room – avoiding other potential perils, like the umbrella stand and blue umbrella, which sat, not near the front door where it should be, but sitting six full inches away from the wall, just outside the hall closet between the spare bedroom and the coat closet. He pushed the door to the spare room open. He knew it would not be closed all the way, it never was, the knob was broken and the tongue never inserted into the small square hole in the door jam; unless you pulled the door up, then down, then pulled it shut hard after closing it. That is, if you wanted it locked, and Louis never had the motivation nor the need or desire to do this in his inebriated state – which sometimes would include women in the past – but not so much anymore.

Anyway, Bobby knew he would have pulled the door shut, not noticed or cared when it popped back out and went slightly ajar and then, Bobby knew, with certainty, that his father would have stumbled happily to bed. He was right.

He crept silently to the bed and searched the night table with eyes that had adjusted quite nicely to the darkness.

No wallet.

Damn!

Sometimes his father would have the foresight to take his wallet out of his pocket before tumbling into bed, rolling over and snoring. But not tonight. "*Just my luck!*" Bobby mumbled to himself, then admonished himself silently for speaking aloud; then laughed silently under his breath for even worrying that his father would wake up – he was dead to the world.

He crept closer to the bed and bent over Louis – peering intently into his snoring face. No movement. He slowly removed his glove from his right hand, something he'd forgotten to do at the front door when he'd removed his shoes; placed the glove carefully in his right coat pocket, and gingerly reached down towards the bulge he could see in the right, front portion of his father's pants.

He slid the wallet ever so smoothly and gently from that tight, stretched pocket – never taking his eyes off of the slack and passive face. Continuous eye contact, even if Louis's eyes were closed, gave Bobby a sense of control over the situation; a sense of control over the man and his volatile temper and inconsistent moods.

Wallet sliding, slowly, slowly, out.

No movement.

Constant snoring. Reassuring in its consistency. Bobby stood right there, by the bed, streaks of slivered moonlight angling his face; emboldened – and flipped the wallet open with a slight slap.

Louis' tip money should be there, could be as much as $20 – the customers liked him, he was friendly and fun and loved a good party, he laughed readily and heartily, and they could share a joke or a smoke when he was in the mood –

But nope, no such luck! Only ten lousy singles. He took them quickly, folded them and put the small wad in his left coat pocket, the one without the glove. He carefully placed the wallet on the nightstand. He knew his father would have no memory of *not* dropping it there; and he knew he would have no idea what had happened to his money. Could of used it on drinks, or dropped it somewhere on the street, or in a bar; or *gave* it away in a moment of forgotten exuberance. Yup, Bobby knew his father would have absolutely no idea what happened to his tip money – and he knew he wouldn't be blamed.

He carefully left the room, not bothering to try to shut the door properly behind him. He strode through the living room boldly, stopping at the front door to silently slip his shoes back on, his one glove. Gently he closed the door behind him, enjoying the soft *click* it made as it shut.

He took the time to lock the top bolt too from the outside, something that he noticed had not been done when he arrived, a momentary concern for his mother's safety, and strode down the hall, down the steps and back out into the streets to get his fix.

PART II - BOBBY

Junk! he thought quickly and automatically to himself as the cool night air hit him. Then no thought. Just movement.

Eva laid in her bed. Eyes wide open. Staring at the ceiling. She had heard the *click* of the door when Bobby had entered, and heard it again when he left. She listened to the darkness.

She let him go.

She knew why Bobby had come here – she'd heard him come in late before. She willed herself silently to go to sleep.

CHAPTER TWENTY-SEVEN

THE CLOCK TICKED — 1:30 a.m.; 2:00 a.m.; 3:00 a.m.... Eva still lay looking at the ceiling. Sleep eluded her. No thoughts in her mind, really, just this vacant darkness and this inability to fall asleep; the wind whirling and hitting the pane of her window with insistent indulgence. Again and again, the rhythmic tapping of the wind; of the tiny tendrils of the thin branches of the elm tree that stood outside her window. The only one in the neighborhood. *Should have been cut down years ago,* Eva thought to herself, a wonder that it had survived this long, that it even existed in the first place in this tangled jumble of buildings and sidewalk. But that tree soothed her, and finally, finally, her lids became heavy and the sweet release of sleep fell upon her.

A Dream: of Central Park and a giant elm tree looming in the dark.

It is set away, in the corner. And ashes fall from its branches in a glittery, gray dust. The wind whistles through the green and glowing branches — a slight "tinkling" noise, like faraway bells, moving through and gently shaking the dust from the glowing green leaves, onto the barren ground. A small hole begins to open, just under the tree. It is a "sensitive" hole — Eva can feel this most succinctly as she stands and watches from the corner; in her body, but not in her body; an observer, but part of this hole. And this hole has "feelings," and is "tender." It wants only to envelop the glittering, gray dust and keep it warm; safe; in a strange way — from the elements of the wayward motion of the wind.

The tinkling, chime-like sounds continue as the dust falls lightly into that expanding hole in the dark earth; and like arms enfolding a baby — this mouth in the warm, dark earth invites her further in. Yawning open its embrace.

PART II - BOBBY

Allowing the dust to settle in.

But, as quickly as it began, the "tinkling" sound stops. The wind is still; the ground smooth. A great, white light fills the park reflecting its brightness on Eva's face as she watches.

A warmth.

And an emptiness.

Eva wakes with a start. Blinks. Blinks again rapidly — wiping the dampness from her forehead. Had she been sweating? In this chill? The glare of the sun reflected on last night's late snow singed her eyes.

Snow in March? she thought to herself, incredulously — *how odd.* And sweating again, she thought she'd long-passed those night sweats ten years ago when she was at the height of her woman's change. Plenty of yams and collard greens for that — but no, here she was, sweating again. She felt the slight tinge of youth briefly wash over her, her sixty-year-old body responding automatically.

But the dream, the dream — it lingered in her memory. It haunted her.

A sign?

A warning?

Did she even want to wonder about it at this point? She was sure she had overslept after her restless night and she squinted in the semi-haze of the morning darkness at the small, round white alarm clock that sat reliably on her nightstand.

The nondescript black numbers on the white dial stared back at her. *7:30 a.m., right on the dot — woke up the same time I do every morning*, and at that thought the silver chimes began ringing, the little metal hammers beating furiously on the rounded bells on the top of the clock. She reached over mechanically, without thinking and switched it off, pushing the tiny button on top of the clock down with a swift click of her index finger.

She rolled over and gingerly pulled down the pink, silk, knee-length nightgown she had worn to bed, and which had now crept up over her hips. Eva had one in blue, one in white, one in off-white and one in pink; and she was sure to "dress" for bed every evening — an important part of her daily ritual; for beauty, cleanliness and touch were important to Eva.

The small things, like the feel of the silk against her thigh; or the way it rolled so smoothly between her thumb and forefinger.

She pushed herself out of bed.

She knew Louis would still be sleeping in the spare room, she had heard him come in last night, also – tossing and turning with all the goings-on about her home. And it was *her home.*

Louis didn't even bother pretending to contribute for expenses anymore, everything he made, *every thin dime,* went to drink or women, or nights out on the town.

She hardly ever saw him anymore. And she knew it would be a matter of time – only days maybe – before he would just stop coming home, or she moved out and found a place that was *really* her own – without all the memories.

They had been here too long on "H" Street and Eva felt it was time for some changing.

Some big changing.

She walked to the bathroom. Gingerly pinned up her still lustrous chestnut hair, grabbed her towel and placed her shower cap carefully on her head. She turned on the water and waited for it to warm – hopping from foot to foot on the cold tiles; dropped her silk and slipped into the shower, letting the warm, warm water wash over her.

Yes, there were gonna be some changes....

CHAPTER TWENTY-EIGHT

BOBBY WOKE UP WITH A START. It was his last day in his apartment, he knew. The sunlight streamed through his window — what time was it? 8:00? 9:00? He glanced at the medium-sized black clock he kept on the wall, across from his bed, above his bookshelf.

The black plastic frame showed the thick white hands at 9 and 12. 9:00 a.m. – on the dot.

The snow from the previous night had turned to rain and pelted the window, even through the gray sun. He remembered clearly now the light snow pelting him as he entered his apartment; the slush collecting at his feet. He remembered clearly coming up the stairs late after leaving his parents'; he remembered stopping off at Gus — lucky to have tracked him down at 2:00 in the morning – lucky Gus was still standing on that corner, under the awning in the gray and black shadows. Then, rushing upstairs, quiet, so that he would not wake his landlord, whose apartment was on the first floor. Chester was always intent on catching Bobby now as he came into the building, now that Bobby was more than two months late with his rent.

"Yeah, yeah, I'll have the money for you by tomorrow," Bobby had said. "I'll be out by tomorrow, too." Bobby did not like to leave loose ends. Bobby did not shirk his responsibilities, even if he had to borrow, which he knew with certainty he would have to do today.

Borrow from his mother. And then move back in with her and his father temporarily, just until he could get himself back together.

UNCHAIN MY HEART

He remembered tying his arm – he remembered inserting the needle into his vein – he remembered pushing the tiny plunger down slowly – he remembered the warm, warm shot as the clear liquid filled his veins.

He remembered *relaxing*, his head back against the wall.

And now, he was awake.

"This has got to stop!" he said out loud to himself. "Now! Been fight, fighting and yet I always end up back at this place. In the blank stare of a morning where my body is wracked with sickness. Where my head lies somewhere between life and misery. And my consciousness hangs on by a thread." He shook his head, as if to shake the cobwebs out of it; as if to bring his consciousness *back*. As if the act of shaking his head would bring him back to reality; take away the aching sickness that even now was be-ginning to form inside of him.

Panic; anger; for only an instant, and then that quiet, comforting re-solve; an interior will that so instantly and unexpectedly came to save him. The thread that pulled him back to the world and weaved him fully into the fabric of his life.

A dignity that was inherent; a straightening of the shoulders. A need to *use his mind*. That old urge; fully flooding him – urging him to create. A motivation to go *forward*.

Life. Coursing through aching limbs. A brain straining for clarity.

His friend James Baldwin, was doing a play called *Blues For Mr. Charlie* down at the ANTA Theatre on Broadway, and had given him the script to read. He picked it up now, not moving from his sitting position on the bed. Reached out towards the worn bookcase to his right and began to read, taking up where he had left off the afternoon before.

The play was loosely based on the murder of a black boy, Emmett Till, down in Mississippi back in '55 and the white murderer who was acquit-ted for it in a mock trial. James had asked Bobby to write a song by the same name. The play was intense and controversial and some said echoed a hatred for whites, and Bobby read late into the afternoon stirred by its intensity and honesty. And he thought, as the afternoon sun set and he flipped closed the last page and laid it down on the white coverlet that still lay over his legs from the morning; he thought, as he reached for the Pall Mall's and pulled one out of the pack, tamped it expertly against the edge of the bookcase, slipped the soft, white cylinder between his lips and lit up; he thought, as he inhaled deeply, the smoke sitting in his mouth a moment before flooding his lungs, tendrils trickling out of his nostrils. Two, thin wisps curling up to the ceiling.

He thought that *Blues For Mr. Charlie* ended with a cry for unity and desegregation. It was just what he needed.

He stared absently out his window, watching the gray swirls of clouds move slowly through the tepid sky, the murdered boy's father's words still echoing through his head: "The truth cannot be heard in this dreadful place." The words were a voice and stuck with Bobby – reverberating again and again. *The truth cannot be heard in this dreadful place.*

Yes, he wanted to capture the essence of the black man in Harlem – juxtaposed against the white man: Mr. Charlie. A 1950's young man, son of a slave, first generation, born here – throw this against hope, a hope with enumerable odds. Black opposite white; color defined. He wanted to capture a man with hope; but – dejected.

His quick and agile mind quickly clicked his thoughts into place.

And, as he felt a wellspring of hope well up within *him*, he also felt a song coming – one he had been waiting for – as he always did with songs.

He never pushed.

He just *waited*.

And now it was coming.

And he had things to do.

He hurriedly dressed and showered, forgetting for a moment the eternal ache that nagged his gut and had become such a normal part of his life.

He ignored it.

For the moment.

And rushed over to his parents' house.

He knew his mother would already have left for work, she did so each morning, as she had for the last fourteen years, promptly at 8:30 a.m. with her book to the bus stop. But he would wait for her. And ignore his father, hopefully he would have already left for – someplace...

No such luck!

He knew – but; still he rushed.

Almost running up the concrete steps; bounding up the steps to his parents' third floor apartment – tripping on the top of his wingtip shoes – stumbling only momentarily – catching himself – steady – holding the cold and dirty banister – He lands at the top step, rushes down the hall, inserts his key quickly into the lock. Of course, again, the top dead bolt has been left open. Bobby shakes his head to himself, *Tsk tsk!* His mother was *too* trusting! Too naive at times; *too* nice. He enters the house. Walks right by his mother's bedroom. He can hear the shower on – his father up, and singing loud and strong. *Good! He is going somewhere!* Bobby thinks hopefully to himself. Not one more thought to that, he heads straight for the Wurlitzer piano and sits down.

He begins to play – grabbing his pencil and blank onionskin lead sheets from under the bench. The writing coming out of him automatically. The words pouring out of him automatically.

> *Blues for Mr. Charlie is a mournful refrain / Born out of sufferin', misery and pain / They came across oceans to plantation farms / Where mothers' little babies were torn from their arms...*

Deep breath, hands removed from the keys for an instant. Intent scribbling. More words; feelings; *images...*

> *Blues for Mr. Charlie is killing his soul / For the way he betrayed human beings for gold / And now his dreams haunt him wherever he roams / And the harvest he is reaping / Are the seeds he has sown....*
>
> *Mr. Charlie thought that because of his color / No other was equal to him / But he is finding out beyond a shadow of a doubt / Nobody's skin – makes a God out of him....*

His skin crawled. Did he think he was a god because he was writing about another so blatantly? Did he even believe in God? No! Push the thought out of his head. Harlem. Opportunity. Writing. Courage. *Hope...*

PART II - BOBBY

This blues for Mr. Charlie he can't comprehend / All the reasons some boys want to grow into men / And walk with their heads high / In true dignity / In this land of the brave and home of the free....

————

Eva stepped slowly up the stairs of her apartment building. She should have been walking fast, rushing, actually. She should have hurried down the street, clutching her umbrella in her hand tightly, letting it shield her from the wet and the wind; she should have had her plastic rain cap unfolded and tied smartly over her head, a neat clear bow tied under her chin; her head down to the rain – a gray drizzle left over from the downpour that had been pelting the streets all day.

She had watched the rain from her workstation as she juggled calls and shuffled paper. Almost fifteen years now and her job was second nature, something she did as if sleepwalking. She took pride in her work, certainly, and no one did a better job than Eva. But it no longer challenged her. Now it was *automatic* – done by rote, and at this point in her life, well at this point, this was all she needed.

She paused many times during the day to stare out across the vast lobby of the great building that housed the State Insurance Fund, to stare out of the giant glass-paned windows hanging in their brick frames over the tired street. And she watched the big wet drops slip easily down the clear glass with a dreamy fascination. She had a good feeling today. And although it was pouring and cloudy and perhaps gray and dismal to others' eyes, to her the rain was signaling a new beginning, a cleansing of the past. The rain was washing the city clean of the winter's chill – bringing the spring, and one last blast of cold to refresh and energize them for the summer; but first, the blooms of spring. And this rain would feed the flowers in the park, and the sparse, stick-like trees that sat in their small, square patches of brown earth, so sequentially placed along the sidewalk on her walk home, every half block. Like clockwork. Bare arms outstretched, waiting for the rain to feed the tiny buds that would soon pop out. The trees the only color on the gray of the street. Gray buildings, gray sky, gray sidewalk and brown trees with bright white, pink and slightly peach blooms. A tiny reminder of a slight order in the chaotic city of Harlem.

*Ah, but Sugar Hill...*Eva thought now as the rain hit her bare head. *What times we've had on Sugar Hill.* And Eva firmly believed it was named Sugar Hill because of all the sugar that little patch of earth brought to the world. The great works of art and music that had been inspired and born in Harlem. And although she fought the notion of artistry in both her son and her husband; she also knew only a fierce attraction to it. And she knew deep in her heart and soul that this is what had made her fall in love with Louis. This spark in him, that gave him the courage, at least in the beginning, to think that he could affect change with his voice; and his acting. Eva had admired his courage, in the beginning. But, yet, she still held onto a steadfast need to create order in this chaotic world. And this she had done. Brought order to their lives. And she respected the order of the seasons. And of nature.

And Harlem, now, was a city she had grown to love and hate with the same passion. A city, she knew, she would never leave.

And she felt all those possibilities well within her once again as she walked those wet sidewalks home from the bus stop; content, a good day's work done. She walked slowly and methodically along that familiar concrete. Holding her umbrella lightly in her right hand; twirling it ever-so-slightly, devoid of the plastic rain cap she always kept folded neatly and waiting at the bottom of her purse for these rain emergencies.

New York was a wet town. Even when it was not raining, a heavy dampness hung in the air – a heaviness that became quite oppressive in the stifling heat of summer.

And liberating when it would sweat upon the streets in spring, washing away the cold unforgiving snow of winter.

She took each of the three, wide steps one by one. Carefully. Letting the last of the raindrops slip by her umbrella and splash onto her face. She reached the top of the porch. Shook her umbrella quickly and efficiently to remove the last few drops – and closed it. Wrapped it up expertly with the long, cloth tab that hung snapped to its side, and carried it with her pocket book and larger bag upstairs.

Dry and cool the air was. A slight must that assailed her nostrils as she entered the building. A smell she had become accustomed to. A smell that brought her comfort.

Home.

She was finally *home*.

She loved her home and the quiet familiarity it brought her. She turned the key in the lock. Top bolt, bolted. She knew instantly Bobby was there. Bobby, in all his protectiveness. Always locking the top bolt when he left, to protect her from the elements and wildness of the City. And always locking the top bolt when he was inside. To protect himself from what? The City coming into *him*? Harlem creeping into their tidy apartment somehow and shaking his sense of safety. *Well, he's already done that to himself!* she thought angrily as she reached for the worn brass knob. Anger rising quickly; a flush from her gut to her face. Her breath tightened; she held it. Let it out. *Calm down, now, Eva. Calm down, now. The Good Lord has his ways....*

Eva was not overtly religious; had never attended Sunday mass regularly, but statements like these gave her comfort, a deep-seated relic from her past – and she wondered if she had made a mistake in not enforcing religion in Bobby as it had been enforced in her. Personally she had rejected her own mother's strict religious upbringing when she married and went out on her own. Rejected it and threw it out the window as she and Louis made that long freedom ridden drive on out to Hollywood – vowing never again to step inside the cloying, claustrophobic insides of a church – hot and musty, sinners yelling and screaming for redemption; falling to the floor in anguish and ecstasy asking the Lord to save them. Save them? Save them from what? *Only you does your own saving.* That she firmly believed. But yet she prayed at night when falling asleep – her faith in God never wavered – just her belief in the *church* and the *people who ran it*, with all their idiotic human frailties and *sin*. Prayed and thanked the Lord for all the blessings she had been given. *Nope, never got 'round to takin' Bobby to church,* she clucked to herself. *Should I have? Would it have made a difference? Given him a foundation, something to turn to in times of trouble?* Again her temper rose and again she forced herself to quell it. *Deep breath. Calm down.*

She turned the key in the dead bolt now, continued to turn the door-knob, and stepped inside her apartment, shaking off the last of the rain from her wool coat. Didn't own a raincoat, thought they were silly. *What's the use?* Empathy and resolve coloring her thoughts, *you wear your nice, warm, wool coat, and then you let it dry. That's all there is to it.*

She stepped purposefully inside and across the living room to the coat closet, opened the door to grab a hanger, brushing against the soft fur of her sable mink with the back of her hand; memories evoked of silk stockings and high heels; nights out on the town with Louis; hand on her thigh; the high of their love and her fashion. Thrill to her core not erased yet. Grabbed the hanger and hung her coat up on the rack just outside of the telltale closet to dry; untied her umbrella and placed it carefully in the umbrella stand to dry out and headed directly to the family room where she was certain she would find Bobby sitting at the piano. His solace. She could see that clearly.

And funny thing, he was under the impression she didn't have a clue about his "problem." But she knew. Eva saw things clearly. She'd been around and was a no-nonsense woman – she told it like she saw it.

She stopped at the doorway of the family room and leaned her shoulder against it casually, folding her arms across her ample chest. Bobby was deep in concentration, bent over the Wurlitzer, pencil in hand, scribbling away on his lead sheet. Playing intermittently; notes flying from fiery fingers; possessed by the tune consuming him – voice shooting to the ceiling and raining down a hail of words:

> *Blues for Mr. Charlie is a mournful refrain / Born out of sufferin', misery and pain*
> *They came across oceans to plantation farms / Where mother's little babies were torn from their arms....*

Eva became motionless then; a wisp of invisible breeze slipped by her face, she adjusted her hip slightly against the cold door jam. She did not move her arms. Purity poured over her sweet and simple — like the rain still tinkling outside. And she once again acknowledged his talent; and once again cursed his fate and his choice. They had fought about this heartily when he got out of the Army and announced he was going to use his G.I. bill to go to music school. "Music school!" she had spat, without thinking. "You think you's going to *music school???* *You got to be crazy boy!*" He'd said nothing in that quiet way of his. Just looked at her and she'd known then he'd be going. She'd known then his path. The comfort of rote praying slipping in each evening to console her as she lay awake in her bed, "Oh, dear Lord protect him and serve him in his endeavors; oh, Lord bless us all in our struggles; oh, dear Lord let righteousness be his path; let him find peace; let me be strong..." on and on it went, an empty mantra until she finally drifted off to sleep.

And then gone, he had — against her strongest intuitions. All good intentioned and starry-eyed he'd been.

Yes, she'd seen what show business could do. Oh, yes, they'd had their share of fun on Sugar Hill. Duke Ellington, Artie Shaw, Benny Goodman, the artist, Aaron Douglas, Benny Carter — musicians droppin' by to play. They called them "house parties" back then, intellectuals and musicians mixing and mingling. And it was a great way to make a little extra cash too — charge a little fee, everyone would come by and they'd play and talk and dance 'till early morning light. It was a wistful memory, even now.

Duke, always the ladies' man and a talker, hated his music to be termed "jazz," he told her once as they spoke late into the night that he felt the impact of his work would be lessened by the term and he warned the other musicians in the room (in a loud and authoritative voice no less) to not let their music be limited by anyone else's label. He was sassy and confident and sure. And he carried with him an innate wisdom that got him through the harder times.

Even back then in the 30's and 40's there were drugs. But not heroin, heroin didn't hit Harlem until right after WWII, and she saw what it did to those musicians — jazz or not — how some got addicted almost instantly — Jackie McLean, Art Pepper and then others, and then *others*...what did one guy tell her once as they talked late into the night? "It makes me *play* faster – I can *listen* better."

"Yeah, maybe…" Eva had said, eyeing him suspiciously, then covering it up with a chuckle, "but you *look* worse!" They had all laughed, smoking and then disbursing; and Eva had felt the fear in her gut, even then. And she watched one by one each of them try the damned drug and then get hooked. A slave to the white powder.

"It takes the edge off…" one lone trumpet player with red hair trailed as he let the feeling take him, closing his eyes; leaning back languidly against the burgundy cushion of the couch. Head back. No care for the others around him. Just for the drug. "Horse," they'd called it. Like it was a pet! *Stupid!*

Eva hated it at that instant. She hated the slaves it created. And she hated that so many did it. "From slaves to slaves!" she stated ruefully out loud to the din of voices and music. No one responded. No one seemed to hear. The few that had taken it nodded. Sick, silly grin. She had turned away then.

So she yelled at Bobby hard and mean when he said he wanted to be a musician. She yelled at him and told him he should be a psychiatrist. She could see the sensitive side of her son; could see him helping people. Could almost *feel* it, as if it were going to come true. She *knew* this was the best path for him.

But he, of course, refused. "Don't want to," he'd said flatly. Defying her as he never did. Wanted to "try [his] hand at music…" Eva softened, eventually. Didn't have a choice, really. So she quietly attempted to support her son's decision. The fear lingering those first few years as he traveled back and forth to Chicago; came home – looking deeply into his eyes – *okay, Eva, he is okay, Eva. Nothing to worry about, Eva.* Off to L.A., to sing with Benny Carter's band, home he comes again; and that damned Ruby, hurting him like that – but, no, once again, she looked deeply into his eyes – no signs. No signs.

And, of course, home in Harlem, *in her own neighborhood,* HE COMES AND HE GETS DRUGS. Coming over high, thinking she's not gonna notice. *Hmmmff!* Sweating, fidgety. She'd seen it before. But in her *son?* No longer could she bear to watch this nightmare – been going on for too long now. Out of control. He was thin; thinner than usual. The sweats were constant. The fidgeting. The knee that always shook. He was; well, *shifty.* Always looking from side to side; wiping his nose. *And he thinks I don't or won't notice?????*

No longer could she stand quiet; hoping, somehow against hope that it would work itself out. *Perhaps he will get that hit song he so desperately wants,* she would tell herself, *he does work hard pounding the pavement night and day down at Tin Pan Alley; hitting every possible publisher's office. Perhaps he will get that hit song and it will snap him out of it.* But no, that had not happened.

She was kidding herself, had been all along. Her son needed *treatment.* No one just "quit." Even Eva knew that.

"Well, hello, son," she said calmly. Still standing in the doorway, hip against the door jam, arms still folded across her wide bosom. Her smile spread so easily when she saw him. He looked up, jerked his head, really – wiped his nose, smiled, wiped his nose again. Smiled. "What you working on there? I like it...."

"James Baldwin asked me to write a song for his play...am finally writing it.... I think its pretty good...I'm really on a roll."

"Well, when you finish up, we gotta talk," Eva said. Fishing his eyes for some sort of connection. But Bobby had already turned his back to her; hunched over the piano, couldn't see her; tuned her out.

"Okay," he said.

"I'll fix us a little something to eat," she said, turning towards the kitchen – would give her time to think....

CHAPTER TWENTY-NINE

*H*OW DO YOU PROPOSE *to your son that he needs treatment?* Eva wondered as she pulled the pots and bowls out of the cupboard in preparation for dinner. *How do I approach it?*

Strangely, Eva did not feel mad anymore. She did not even feel the well of anguished fear that used to unexpectedly rise up and overtake her. She felt a strange calm. She felt the same calm she had felt all day. The sound of the rain against the glass above the sink pelted her insides; keeping steady rhythm with the beat of her heart. *Thump, thump* against the small kitchen windowpane. *Thump, thump.* Repeatedly. Steady. She liked this.

She pulled the potatoes out from under the cupboard, where they sat in the dark in their round wicker basket. She pulled the greens from the small refrigerator. She remembered the days when they did not even own a refrigerator, the days of the Great Depression and even after, when she cooked on a tiny hotplate in a small closet of a kitchen. *Amazing what you can do with a hotplate!* she thought to herself. But she cooked up some good meals on that little hotplate, with the little food they had had. Potatoes were always a staple. So many things you could do with potatoes. So many ways to cook them. And eggs. *Lucky to have had eggs,* she mused now as she slowly peeled the waxy skins off – long, slow curls she let drop from her knife into the sink.

But today she didn't have those worries. Today she had everything she needed. She was a college graduate, an achievement she took pride in, something she had achieved back in Kansas before coming out to L.A. with Louis. She brought in a decent enough income now to take care of all of their needs, even managing to squirrel a little bit of it away for a rainy day; or to leave for Bobby upon her death.

She had started thinking about this lately...her death. And she thought about it as she thought of most things these days; *calmly.* Death did not scare her. Sometimes she felt it would be a welcome relief. No, she wasn't depressed, nor necessarily sad. Her life had been rich and colorful and full. She had done exactly as she wished and had a freedom most women only dreamt of. Nobody and no one told Eva what to do – she made her own rules. And that was how it was going to stay.... *A life where I made my own choices,* she thought now as she continued to peel the small white round potatoes and drop them into the large bowl of water to soak; her back straightening; her head lifting just a bit higher. Pride deep in her bones extending outward.

Her thoughts turned to Johnny – lost her oldest to whooping cough when he was just four years old. *Bobby and he both gets the cough and Bobby survives and Johnny dies. He'd been the strong one – no reason for it at all, no reason at all. And taken so suddenly. Just like that. Weak little frail Bobby left behind. Survived it. Only God knows his plans. Only God knows....*

Depression was on, she and Louis still livin' out in Topeka with her mama and papa. Grandma Nellie and her "spare the rod, spoil the child" approach – used to grab a switch and beat Bobby with it, if he ever misbehaved, did the same thing to her as a girl. Just the way things were done.... Used to call little Bobby, Robert – make him go to church two or three times on Sunday and several times a week. Taught that boy the Bible front to back. Eva let her. Felt she had to, it was right. Nellie was tough, descended from slaves and Old Grammy – Nellie's Mother – used to tell Eva winding stories of cannonballs raging through their cabin in the old days; being down on her belly, sliding 'cross the dirt floor...wonderin' if they going to live to see the light of the next day. Christian too. "Christian faith and prayin' done *saved* the slaves," she used to say, rocking in her chair smoking her pipe, far far away.

But Nellie's no-nonsense approach had instilled in Eva a certain lack of vulnerability and sturdiness that carried her through many trying times. And although Eva never could woop Bobby; never could bring herself to force him to go to church; she had hoped that Nellie would instill in Bobby the same resilience she had carried through her life. But that hadn't happened. Bobby was still vulnerable. Vulnerable, yet closed. A searing contradiction.

But Johnny, oh little Johnny! Only four years old. Get's the cough....

Used to beat Bobby, Eva thought now randomly, *one time accidentally stabbed him in the leg, thought that boy was gonna really hurt him one day.* Bobby the sensitive one. Eva always feared that *he* would be the one to die. Big wide, honest eyes, even as a kid. But Johnny, he was going to make it in the world. Had all the odds stacked in his favor. Big muscles already developing, naturally, like his Papa. Thick, firm calves, full arms. Strong already, even at four, and tough. Handsome light-skinned face with a big, white-toothed grin. He was going to be a looker, that was for sure.

Then up and died. What a surprise.

Nellie had said: "It be your fault he died on ya, Eva — you don't praise the Lord enough!" Eva had sat quiet. Mute. No words. No need to. She mourned the death of her young son silently. And never spoke of it again after the funeral.

And then she and Louis had moved on out to L.A.

The death of Johnny had discretely broken a part of her — a crack that appeared and slowly widened within. Invisible. *To lose a child* — she thought now, the knife slipping against the silk of the starch beneath her fingers; slipping and cutting her index finger, blood dripping methodically into the sink; watching it — *it is a parting; a tearing away of something; someone that is so engrained. Time does not cause its slip into the distance; it never recedes. It sits with you, always. A hole in your gut. It can be ignored; mutated and swallowed; but it never goes away.*

So why if she was mourning the loss of her son did she up and move to Hollywood. *Don't make no logical sense, Eva!* She dropped collard greens into the wide boiling pot, ham hocks bobbing expectantly in their broth. At the time she thought she was doing the right thing. She justified her move by telling herself that there was more opportunity for them out in California — they'd get settled and send for Bobby. Nothing going on in the vast flatlands of Kansas; endless stretches of nothing reaching dusty fingers towards nothing – under her parents' roof; no independence; *a college degree and no independence! hmmmff!* The depression had left its wide thumbprint upon its empty plains; opportunity was scarce. Louis, a gifted concert tenor, wanted to be a star; to sing; to be in the movies.

And to bathe in the light of his glow in the beginning, Eva thought now characteristically, reminding herself *why* she had gone; why she had left their child behind. *Why* she let those lights call her too. Louis was charming and charismatic and their nights together were intimate and sensual and when he touched her leg, *when he touched her leg,* running his long fingers up the outside of her thigh…she felt the chills again even now at the memory. Her mother never liked Louis. But his voice was like low satin and he'd sing out into the night and it seemed he called the stars with that voice and that voice promised her everything and *how could he fail?* They were young and they were beautiful and full of hope and they would send for Bobby later. And Louis was going to make it and Louis was going to take care of her. And he flashed his smile at her and ran his hand further up her thigh in the night and she could think of nothing other than their future together away from there; away from those flat plains and their endless nothingness.

Yes, California was calling with its twinkling lights and limitless opportunity. Movies had hit – Louis slipped it in her ear one night after quietly making love in their tiny bed in their tiny bedroom right next to her mother and father's room – that there was work on out there for the black man. The glitter attracted Eva, and she could find work too; which she always found solace in. Work; and get lost in the lights of Hollywood.

And, she had to admit now, though she had never allowed herself to think this thought before: She could leave motherhood behind for a moment. Painful motherhood. Was she being honest with herself with this thought? Yes. She had wanted to be free, if only for a moment. She had wanted to *erase* the pain of losing little Johnny. And Bobby had been a reminder of him.

Bobby would be fine with her parents for a while. She had been fine. Bobby would be fine. It wasn't forever.

And, of course, she had missed him terribly all the while she was gone
— six long years. Finally sent for him to come out to New York when he
was twelve years old. They were settled on Sugar Hill by then and they
lived a good life and she took pride in dressing well and owning a fur; a
beautiful chestnut sable. They were surrounded by music and art; they
were going places.

No, not so much opportunity for the negro out in Hollywood after
all — all the work went to whites. It was Broadway that had the opportunity; Broadway and the big city lights; Broadway calling Louis. And
Eva's mother's instinct had won out, the hole had receded; imperceptibly shrinking, just a dot that only opened up with thought. No thought.
There was no more need to escape. Yes, by then they were somewhat
established. By then she had a good job as a guide at the World's Fair. And
her heart longed for her son. *A mother is nothing without her children.* She
thought to herself now. A thought she had often.

And, yet, and *yet* — she felt a strange trepidation at his coming out. An
inner knowing that warned her with its small voice. But how do you stop
these thoughts? She began to cut the potatoes into quarters and drop them
into boiling water. *You don't. You just go forward and make the best decision for
the time. You does the best with what you've been given. That's all you can do. And
this is what I must do now.*

She coated the chicken legs in seasoned flour and dropped them one
by one in the hot, sizzling oil; liking the sound of the hiss as they hit. She
covered the pan with a lid and let them be. Checked the greens simmer-
ing in the pot. Pulled the potatoes in the boiling water off the stove and
dumped them into the colander sitting in the sink. Brought the colander
to the large bowl, tipped the potatoes inside. Added the buttermilk, the
butter, the salt, the pepper; smashed them hard and good with the potato
smasher. Put her nose over the steam that rose from the big, yellow bowl.
Inhaled deeply.

Mmmmmmm. She loved the smell of smashed potatoes. One of her favorite foods. And Bobby's. She hoped he was hungry. She hoped he would eat.

It had not always been easy; but when was life easy? She could not
think of one person she knew; not even the white ones who had had an

"easy" life. *Everyone gets their tragedies in some way or another.* She lifted the lid off the chicken to take a peek – then set it down again tight. *Yes, everyone gets their tragedies.... It's all relative, of course, the degree of tragedy and the depth of its effect.*

Duke Ellington for example, had *everything* now. Successful, did what he wanted, had led the life, met so many rich and famous people; worked with all the jazz greats. Eva remembered clearly the early 40's when the white bands of Artie Shaw and Benny Goodman were pulling in up to $20,000 per week – but Duke and his band, with all his talent and all his rich and privileged upbringing with parents who worked in the White House, didn't get paid as much as Benny Goodman. White Benny, who came from the Chicago ghetto.

Duke never said a word, though, never complained, just went right on doin' what he did. He lived and breathed his music, never talked a nothin' else. She remembered the headlines now as if it were yesterday: "Are Colored Bands Doomed as Big Money Makers?" *Downbeat* cried. And there was no room for the black bands – though it was their sound, their background involvement that the others were drawin' on. And although Duke was an innovator, refusing to let his music be typecast as "jazz" – one who always seemed to do well no matter what, one who always put a positive spin on things, refusing to get caught in the muck; and although Benny publicly adored Duke, Eva wondered now how he deflected so easily the latent animosity towards negroes at that time. But he did. "The time it takes to pout I used to write a blues song," he'd once said with his characteristic grin. Eva liked that.

And his son, Mercer – she remembered quite clearly Bobby and Mercer going to Robert F. Wagner Jr. High School together. Just the other day that horrible shooting took place there, the one in which that policeman shot and killed that poor negro boy. So sad, and the three hundred teenagers, mostly colored kids, that had hurled bottles and cans at that force of police wearing those strange metal helmets...looked like little metal bugs in the news clipping. She remembered that article in the local paper, everyone all abuzz *because a white officer was hit in the head with a can and had to be hospitalized.* Eva's mind had wandered.

She pushed her thoughts back to Mercer — always hanging out at the house back then. Loved to play the trumpet. Eager and wide-eyed, jumpin' up and down like a little jackrabbit, all he ever wanted was to play in Duke's band. Admired his dad to no end. But Duke had put his foot down with his son right from the beginning; no hesitation there, business as usual, "No, you cannot play with the band."

Poor Mercer, just wasn't good enough. Ended up travelin' with the band tho', playing only occasionally, for the most part a roadie; just helping out where things needed to be helped, lifting gear, helping to get things set up. As a matter of fact, I think right now he's down working as a D.J. at station WDIV, I think Bobby said — good for him — always was a go-getter! She reached out absently to the tiny radio sitting on the kitchen counter and switched on the dial; twirled the knob to the station, pressed her ear a little closer to the speaker, *Ah! he's on!* The passion for music was clearly evident in his voice. He had a passion, but not a talent. Eva could see what that did to the poor fellow. But Duke always put his band first, always put his *work* first, and he was not going to let his band be second rate — even for his own flesh and blood. No, not while he was alive.

So, Duke had to live with that, Eva thought to herself. *Did he care?* It was hard to tell with Duke, he was serious and good-humored at the same time; and wise and closed and sometimes a contradiction. But he'd had his tragedies, in his own way he'd had his tragedies. *Like when his mother died back in '34. He was so close to his mother — died of cancer, so quickly, was diagnosed and within the year was gone. Duke took it hard. Lost his will to live; to compose. Said he lost his strength. Said he used to feel he could do anything and with her gone — well — he just stopped.* Eva was surprised at the time. Strong Duke. Enigmatic Duke. Duke who could do anything, fell into a depression, didn't even come out of his apartment for a while. He drank heavily. Something that surprised Eva. Duke drank, but never heavily.

Finally wrote a tribute to his mother called "Reminiscing in Tempo," a composition that Eva loved — started out with hope, she felt it dip down, become dark, then move up again. It was truly something special, *but was given a terrible review by that John Hammond,* she thought now with disdain. John had always had something against Duke, Eva could tell that, and his review was scathing, saying his music was superficial and that he purpose-ly was out of contact with the troubles of his people. How did he handle it? Well, once he wrote that song and pulled out of that depression he was back to his old self. Stronger even, still never showing his disappointment in things, always turned it 'round to something he could use. That was the good thing about Duke.

And then there was Benny Goodman, she clucked to herself at the thought. *Musicians had a love/hate relationship with that fellow, always had. Called him "cheap," and hated it when he gave them the eye when they did something wrong in their playin'.* But his childhood was hard – came from the toughest part of Chicago, Russian immigrants of Jewish descent, come over to escape perse-cution. And although he was white, he had it harder than most blacks. *Always fightin' and such a perfectionist!* Eva scoffed now to herself as she remembered him discussing the faults in his work and his band and not the strengths. He was tough sometimes. But what fun they had when he let go! A great band leader no doubt. But his life was a hard one from the beginning and though he became successful, he never seemed happy, just driven to perfection. Just fightin' for his share. Eva sighed as she remembered how nothing seemed to shake his sense of awkward entitlement fueled by an underlying fear of loss. *Ah, "Good Time Benny" that's what we used to call him,* she recalled now with a smile. *Leader of the band – was gonna succeed at any cost – never let up, never let up....* She shook her head at the memory, *gonna make himself sick some day with all his strivin' and perfectionism!*

Things were changing now. Eva knew. Everyone knew. The swing era was over, jazz was fallin' to the background. The house parties were gone. Duke was in his early sixties; still touring the world in that damned stupid bus of his; writing prolifically, even though his concerts were not all full. She remembered one of his favorite sayings: "Fate has been kind to me. Fate doesn't want me to be too famous too young."

Rock-n-roll had hit, music was changing, and Bobby, Bobby was part of that change. Part of the generation that was changing with it. Could he do it? The fear flicked momentarily again and then subsided.

He is part of something, yes, her thoughts moved again. *He is combining influences. Taking what he soaked up while young and applying it to the now.* He was part of the new generation and Duke and Benny and Artie had influenced him and for this she was grateful. And nervous. As always.

The streets were rougher now. The sense of hope had diminished and in its place was anger. Racism was no longer tolerated, the streets were bubbling. She felt it every day as her feet hit the pavement and she made her way to the bus stop. She felt it seeping from the pores of the sidewalks. She felt it hit her. And she ignored it. She stayed in her circle of friends — Molly Moon, her cousin Virginia. They drank wine on Friday nights and talked about the old times. They ignored the anger on the streets.

But she could not ignore it in Bobby. It had touched Bobby. All the gray. Had touched him. And she saw it in the photographs he snapped. Black and white grainy images that captured mutely the desolation that permeated the darkened corners and doorways of Harlem. She saw it in his face each time he came through that front door and locked it so securely behind him.

Her decision was cemented at that moment. A decision she realized now, she had made long ago. She would feed her son. And while she was feeding him she would speak to him directly. Directness had served her so far and it would serve her now. Bobby was going to go in for treatment at the Metropolitan Hospital. He was going in tomorrow. It was what he needed.

It was a bad drug; a horrible drug. He needed her. He had lost control.

CHAPTER THIRTY

H E EMERGED INTO THE STARK SUNLIGHT and it was quiet. The traffic streaming by in silent buzz. Clarity a strong fix against the backdrop of his night. No chains to bind him – no clouds over his head.

Thirty days in a locked ward at the Metropolitan Hospital – thirty days weaning him off the smack. The first two weeks were rough, his gut ached and he wretched and sweated and tossed and turned; the drug, a monster – crawling to get out of him – but first trying to destroy him; wrack his body with its spasms, force him to take it back into his skin; his bones; his soul. Be he could not.

He had come here willingly. His mother had dropped him off out front and he had walked in of his own admission. Opened the two glass and metal doors that led to the hospital, taken the gray, steel stairs to the third floor and checked himself into the locked ward.

Eva made the call, made all the arrangements, but it was Bobby who had to step inside.

And he had made it through those first two terrible weeks; and then the second two weeks, and then, as he regained his strength and began to walk and wander the long shiny corridors, he had come upon his old faithful friend at the end of one long lone hallway; shining black against the yellow-gray of the worn linoleum. They struck up a conversation, he and the old black-and-white; his fingers striking the keys in sympathy of its worn rhythm and the stories it had heard. Others gathered around and listened to them sing. They sang along. A peace he had forgotten or perhaps never known melted through him.

Music. Laughter; the entertainment of others.

And by the time he emerged he was clean, and healthy. And he looked and felt *great*. Couldn't remember feeling this good in a long time. How long had it been since he tried it that innocent first time in Chicago? Nine years? How those nine years crept by. How the drug seeped into him so slowly. Insidiously snaking its way into his soul. Until it was all he could think about. All he wanted.

But not anymore. He had beat it. And he was clean. And he had money in his pocket and he was going to treat himself; take his mother to a nice supper.

A new beginning.

"Mama, I'm home!" he shouted jubilantly as he entered the apartment.

"Fresh-faced and youthful you look Bobby!" Eva exclaimed as she swung her arms wide to encircle him. "And fattened up too! My boy is back to his old self!" She let her arms go; gave him a big kiss on the cheek. She'd been cooking and the aromas from the kitchen wafted past him and mixed with her musty perfume, the warm Saturday afternoon familiar – and he was grateful – and *hungry*.

It seemed it had been *so* long, *so* long since he felt the normal pangs of *living*: Hunger, thirst, sleepiness. And these pangs; this physicality overjoyed him.

He could *feel* again!

He felt great. And he smiled big. Ear to ear. Happy to be home. Happy with the simple things.

It was May and spring was long past and moving into summer; warm, balmy air bathed Bobby's face as his feet hit the street, well fed and happy; feeling great. Healthy, good – well – *healthy* really, and *so* much energy. Clean.

Good time for a little walk, he thought happily to himself. *Enjoy the neighborhood and the last of the day's sunshine.* His step was light on the warm pavement and he inhaled deeply, the smells of the City folding into him. He looked slowly around him, enjoying the familiarity of his surroundings.

Joe's Market was just around the corner and he headed there now to pick up a soda. A nice, cool can of pop. He anticipated the taste as he walked. And he would get one for his mother as well, who he had left, cleaning up the dishes, warm smile on her face as he got up to leave after tooling around on the piano for a bit.

Bobby knew Eva liked to hear him play. Even though she had resisted his musicianship at first, she had grown to accept it, and then to love it – he could see this now clearly. And he enjoyed playing a little tune for her now and then. It seemed to relax her.

So he had played the Wurlitzer, his old friend and then gotten up to leave, kissing Eva on the cheek quickly.

"Be back in a few..." he'd said breezily. Light. Lighter than he'd been in years.

And out he'd stepped into the light of the last of the day – and down that worn sidewalk he'd gone.

Stepping lightly.

Towards the store.

Alone.

Gus.

On the corner.

Strange queasiness in his stomach – just on seeing him – shady eyes – head bent down as if against an invisible wind. Bobby's knees buckled unexpectedly as he passed. Had to steady himself; suck his breath in hard. Felt weak; immediately broke out into a sweat. Instantly. A craving. *Just by walking down the street and seeing Gus.* An innocent stroll. A grip. That was overpowering. Crippling.

He ignored it.

He walked by.

He was strong.

He didn't need it; didn't *want* it.

He was *too strong.*

He only wanted a soda.

That was all.

He slid into Joe's – the sounds of the streets muted behind him as the door swung closed. Sharp jangle of the bell attached to the door knob. Silent fan swirling above his head, long lazy twirls that moved the air gently above him. "Hey Joseph! How ya doin'?" he shouted a little too loudly from the doorway. Forced casualness and cheeriness apparent.

Joe looked up from his paper. He was sitting behind the counter at the cash register and he stubbed the last of his cigarette out in the small round olive-green ashtray next to him. "How *you* doin' Bobby? Haven't seen you 'round here in a while..." he replied, wide gap-toothed grin fixed in place on his dark, round face. Requisite coveralls over light blue work shirt, sleeves rolled up to the elbows.

"Yeah, I've been outta town for a while," Bobby lied and knew Joe knew he lied but continued, "just got back – workin' some things out. Good to be home, tho...good to be home...." He whistled under his breath. A sharp intake of air that was moderated and made long and slow. He headed for the red, square refrigerated box that sat waist high next to the cashier's counter, slid the top glass door back; reached into the soda case and pulled himself out a Fanta. He flipped the cap off with the bottle opener that was attached with a string to the side and took a long, cool swig. He let the bubbly orange liquid sit on his tongue for a moment before swallowing loudly, relishing the slight burn as it slid down his throat. Then he grabbed another for his mother.

"How much I owe you for these, Joseph?" Bobby asked, bringing the bottle down from his lips and setting it smoothly on the counter. Licking lips still ripe with fizz.

"Ah, its on the house, Bobby...good to have you back...you take care now, you hear? No more gettin' into trouble..." Joseph winked at Bobby. Bobby smiled back. He knew Joseph knew where he had been this past month – even if his mother hadn't told him. He'd known Joseph since he'd first moved here. And Joseph had watched him go through his changes, had always been there; always knew what was going on with whom.

A fixture. A constant in Bobby's sometimes-chaotic life. Bobby liked constants.

PART II - BOBBY

He turned and walked out of the store. And back out into the street. The sun was setting and dark was descending on the gray. Casting large orange and blue shadows across him. He stepped through them. Back. Home.

CHAPTER THIRTY-ONE

THERE WAS A CRY from the back of his throat as he felt the needle pierce his skin. A cry of remorse; of physical pain; of relief; of terror. And he pushed the plunger down and pressed hard. Emphatic. It was over. Done. No turning back now. Clarity descending in a new way. No fight left within him. Body relaxing. Again.

CHAPTER THIRTY-TWO

SMALLS PARADISE, HARLEM – *1964*:

COLD AIR HITS his face as he steps from the cab to the icy sidewalk; adjusts the lapels of his dark suit, aligns his fedora hat; nods at the doorman, dressed in his red uniform, the gold braided tassels gleaming in the steel moonlight. No need to censure Bobby; he knows him – he lifts the heavy golden rope and waives him through, almost imperceptibly. The long line of expectant hopefuls waits impatiently; some gazing longingly at the heavy rope as it settles back into place.

A limo pulls up. Dark-skinned man, pumpkin tinged suit impeccable; wingtip shoes shining. Gorgeous woman of mixed heritage at his side. Red scarlet lipstick. Smacks it once seductively. Silver fox fur stole caressing bare shoulders. Sequined dress beneath. Silver beneath silver. They are waved in. A flash bulb pops. Bobby is inside.

Hot blast of sweaty air hits his skin. Wishes he could take off his jacket. Nods to the bouncer. Bouncer pats his pocket. Nods again, towards his table. Round, small – made for two – could seat four. Red and white checked tablecloth on top.

Sits, pulls out a cigarette. Waitress slides up. Dressed like a chorus girl, light-skinned black. Flirty lashes.

"What you havin' Bobby?"

"Brandy, Mabel, thanks sweet thang."

Slight curtsy.

Snifter placed in front of him. He picks it up, leans back in his chair, long drag on his cigarette. Swirls his drink, takes a small sip.

Smalls is jumpin' — lotta action. Tony and Jake'll be here soon.

Looks 'cross the room — nods at Bill again — Billy holds up a finger slightly — "You want *one* — *one hour*?...yeah, got it, no problem...." Silent exchange. The dancers stop. Momentary quiet. A quick breath and the dull roar of anxiety and excitement mixed. An *edge*.

The women have slipped off their furs. Some sit in the laps of the men in the front rows; *the* place to be. In the back; up high — the outskirts of the room — you are no one there. Everyone knows you are no one there. Important; but not important. You are in. Music starts up again. Bobby'll go on soon. Billy knows this. He'll slip him the stuff just in time. Billy keeps everything in order; everyone supplied. Everyone on their toes. Everyone in line.

Another sip of brandy. A wink at Tempy on the stage. Just the intermission act now. Legs that propel fantasies. Warm breast hits hard memory. Hot sweat mixed with musk — mimicking sex — lusty heat.

Nod to Billy. Get up. Almost time to go on. Heads to the backroom. Just enough time.

Insulated from outside — racial tension; riots; the shooting of the fifteen-year-old black boy by the white cop. WWII long over, now the war raged right in the middle of Harlem. The poverty deeper. The streets meaner. The drugs more rampant. But the music still beat upon the pulse of the city, and it was changing to reflect this new bloodline. Bobby steps up and onto the stage.

Gonna do his same old set — what he knew; what he *felt*. Doo-wop stuff just wasn't his bag, just kept on doing what he did. Hittin' the street; hittin' the stage. Some majors — but so far not much money. Needed more money last year — so sold the rest of "Unchain" to Teddy for $1,000. *Went quick, but hell, gotta make some livin'* — Teddy still sayin' he gonna make him a star. "Ray Charles gonna make it a hit!"

Just give it time, Bobby.... Just give it time.

Slide onto the worn bench; a nod to the drummer and he begins to play:

PART II – BOBBY

*Blues for Mr. Charlie is a mournful refrain / ...Born out of sufferin', misery
and pain...*

Words coursing through his bones as he pounds out the song he wrote
for James. But it was no longer a song he wrote for another. No longer a
song that represented the black man's suffering only. No longer a song he
wrote for hire. It was *his* song. It was *his* story. It was *his* soul that dangled
at the edge of each word and dropped like a thud from his mouth.

*Blues for Mr. Charlie is killing his soul... / For the way he betrayed human be-
ings for gold... / And now his dreams haunt him wherever he roams...*

Well-dressed man stands at the back of the club. Separate from the rest;
arms folded neatly across his dark suit. Watching. Words dumped onto
the crowd; most do not hear; most do not see. A heavy palpitation in
the air; an anticipation; that does not include Bobby. Bobby Sharp. He'd
checked his name already with the doorman. "Been comin' quite regularly," he'd been told. "Good songwriter; got some majors." He notices
the sweat trickling slowly down his forehead – even from his spot at the
door he sees it clearly; glistening under the lone spotlight; curls dripping
onto his forehead. Quincy watches.

He does not see that Bobby's leg is shaking uncontrollably under the
piano. He only sees the sweat. One single shining line steadily rolling
down, over his eye, onto his chin, dripping onto the keys.

Everyone does it. Quincy ignored it. Chet Baker, Art Blakey, John
Coltraine, Sonny Rollins, Tadd Dameron, Dexter Gordon and eight of
the sixteen guys in Woody Herman's band. Even Stan Getz had held
up a drugstore to try to support his habit and wound up spending six
months in jail. *Why?* Quincy could not figure it out. Called it "horse,"
then succumbed. All they could think about. Well, *he* hadn't succumbed. Never had the urge.

Billie, he thought to himself as Bobby belted out the last of his mournful
song...*Billie Holiday...now that was a sorry sight* – after her jail stint she stopped
playing out – had her New York cabaret card revoked. Quincy himself hardly

185

ever played at the Apollo anymore. Things had changed. But that beautiful voice, the soulful of the soulful – it was that crazy Joe Guy brought her down. A trumpet player; good lookin' fellow; charming as hell! – had once been in Minton's band. Addicted to heroin, brought it to Billie and she started using. Low-class guy. *Never should of hooked up with him....*

His thoughts moved back to the stage. He watched Bobby, yes, Sammy Davis, Jr. would be perfect for that song.

He did not introduce himself. He did not need to. He turned and left the small dank club and stepped up into the balmy summer night. Shiny patent leather shoes reflecting the moonlight's cool stare. Head held high. The kid was good. He slowly whistled to himself.

———

Bobby's set ended and he grabbed his sheet music from the ledge of the worn walnut and mahogany Baldwin piano, slipped Jake the drummer a couple of bills (the last of his money) and sauntered off stage. He made his way to the bathroom. Rusted pipes under dirty porcelain sink. Turned on the cold, waited for it to run clear, splashed his face, reached for a towel, nothing, wiped his hands on his jeans; lifted his shirt up, patted his face gingerly, careful not to spot it in places where it would show; hands trembling; turned around –

"Need a little something?" The man pushed a small plastic bag toward Bobby. Bobby turned away, sighed, turned back, accepted. The man watched passively as Bobby inserted the needle into his arm, head languid against the wall. Bobby nods. The man smiles.

CHAPTER THIRTY-THREE

H E SAT ACROSS from the boy and he knew! He was fluid and didn't feel it. Fluid like water on a slow, hot melting day.

Fluid like the liquid coursing through his veins. Fluid like the fuel used to fuel him.

Yes, Bobby saw this, now. In this young man before him. Saw his calling. Saw what he had to do. Saw why he had to *give up the music business* and only concentrate on *this*. This *saving* of another – for he could not save himself. And he saw, *he saw* – the desperation in the eyes of the other.

The pleading for help from a substance that had chained him.

And he knew *this* was his calling. And music was gone forever.

He could only save his life by leaving what he loved most.

He could only save his life by *saving another*. So he looked deeply into the boy's eyes and said: "I know what you goin' through, man – I *been there* – don't bullshit me now...."

Bobby Sharp and Ann Wedgworth (who was in the production); Dressing Room, *Blues for Mr. Charlie*, ANTA Theater, New York, 1964.

Bobby Sharp, Stairwell, *Blues for Mr. Charlie*, ANTA Theatre, New York, 1964. (Bobby is holding 45rpm of the song he wrote – "Blues for Mr. Charlie.")

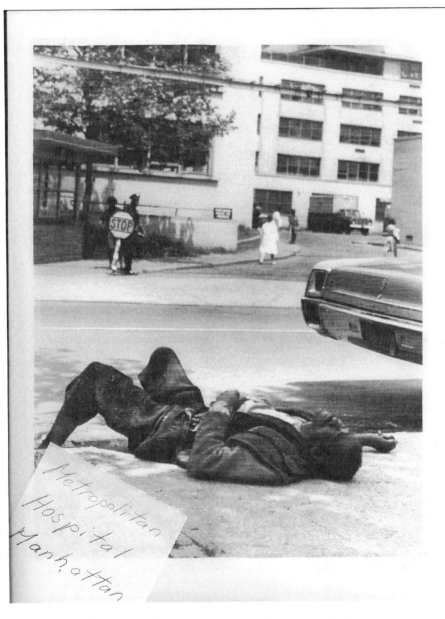

Picture taken by Bobby Sharp - Harlem
©Bobby Sharp

Picture taken by Bobby Sharp - Harlem
©Bobby Sharp

Picture taken by Bobby Sharp - Harlem
©Bobby Sharp

Picture taken by Bobby Sharp - Harlem
©Bobby Sharp

Picture taken by Bobby Sharp – Spanish Harlem
©Bobby Sharp

Picture taken by Bobby Sharp – Tangey the Cat
©Bobby Sharp

©Bobby Sharp

Mr. Bobby Sharp

Lisa
Here is painting
of my mother
Eva, painted by.
Aaron Douglas in
NYC in the early
30's I think
Bobby

Bobby's mother, Eva, as painted by Aaron
Douglas – circa 1930's

Bobby & Natasha – Yoshi's, 2006
Photo credit: Amy Tolbert

Bobby Sharp – Fillmore Jazz Festival, 2005
Photo credit: Amy Tolbert

PART III – *Bobby & Natasha*

I sent my soul into the invisible, some sing of that, after life through spells, and soon my soul returned to me, and said I myself am heaven and hell.

Omar Khayyam

CHAPTER THIRTY-FOUR

ALAMEDA, CALIFORNIA – *2003*:

B OBBY DROVE SLOWLY down the tree-lined street in his Cadillac Seville, savoring the monotony of the drive. He took a long, deep breath and inhaled the scents of the impending Northern California spring – intoxicating; spinning – all around him.

Slowly, the smile spread across his face. A secret smile sparked by the memory of that last performance down at Smalls so many years ago, so much had happened since then, so much time had gone by. Seasons that lingered upon him still.

The lack of weather in Alameda had startled him at first. No change of seasons like New York. No gray and dirty sidewalks flecked by white snow like Harlem. No blinding snow in the dead of winter.

Yes, there was rain here, sometimes. Rain and sometimes a cold sleet. He remembered his first visit to Fisherman's Wharf when he had arrived so long ago. The train ride into San Francisco; the cold, gray air hitting his face as he walked its wooden docks, sinking through his t-shirt and light jacket. A chill that went straight to his bones. A wet, unexpected chill that woke him up; slapped him hard and let him hang dry, alone at the edge of that creaking dock. The smell of bread wafting through the fog, the deep sourdough mixed with the lingering hanging shades of fish. The calls of the fisherman as they unloaded their giant russet nets onto that dock; wriggling forms that glistened and jumped and slapped against each other before hitting the deck through misty fog.

So much time had gone by — and here he was seventy-nine years old and feeling younger and freer than he did at forty.

He'd finally gotten himself out of old New York, out of Harlem, a city he was beginning to detest more and more as the 60's rolled on. *Ah, but the Harlem Renaissance,* he thought, *that's what they'd called it way back when — so many of its ideas had seeped into the 60's....* He chuckled to himself. And chuckled that he'd even been a part of it, and that so many greats had recorded his humble music. He made a mental list now, as he meandered down Oak Street and made a leisurely left on Maple, taking time to notice the fresh white, peach and pink blossoms on the ample trees:

Sarah Vaughan

Sammy Davis, Jr.

Ruth Brown

He remembered the single he'd cut on the Wing label back in '56 — "Baby Girl of Mine." Ruth Brown sang it later that year, but called it "Sweet Baby of Mine." *Cool ice...*he thought now, whistling between his teeth. And Sarah Vaughan had cut his song "Hot and Cold Running Tears" later that same year.

He'd worked with Dan and Marvin Fisher whose father, Fred, had wrote "Peg o' My Heart." He'd had cuts with major artists, worked with others who had cuts with major artists. And still he had been flat broke and hanging out at Smalls.

Sarah's version of "Hot and Cold Running Tears" never became a hit. *Just wasn't her style...*he thought now. No, her style was entrenched; sultry, blue and deep. But back then, in '56, she was still experimenting, or rather, the record company was experimenting for her and they'd picked up his song. And he still had that 45 record back in a box in his apartment. But never made any money on that one either.

He'd hooked up with Charlie Singleton for co-writes — he'd pen a pop song and put Charlie's name on it; Charlie'd put down an R&B song and put Bobby's name on it...double their odds of a hit — cool deal for both of them. But then Charlie hit with "Strangers in the Night" — wrote the damned thing and didn't put his name on it as they agreed. Hit big in '66. Bobby wondered at the time if the whole world was full of liars and cheats. Just wrote Charlie off – let him fall away, life was too short, no point in working with a liar. They'd never spoken again.

And then, of course, there was Ray Charles and "Unchain"; and even in the '80's Joe Cocker had re-recorded "Unchain," made it more modern – gave Bobby a slight amusement now to think about it –

"And the way 'Unchain' saved my life," he said out loud now to no one. He'd made this statement before. He'd made it to the Alameda Sun when they'd interviewed him back in the late 70's when he'd first come out and someone had gotten his number and said "hey we've got a local celebrity right here in town!" He was noticed for a moment. And then forgotten – obscurely fading again into the background. *As it should be.* He was through with music.

It'd been a long legal battle – that Teddy Powell, didn't want to give up a thing, and even weaseled the other fifty percent of Bobby's writer's credit out of him. Bobby, of course, had been out of money, a regular thing with him at that time – out of money, strung out and needin' a fix. He didn't want to go to his mother again, lie and say it was for treatment. At that point his mother was so disappointed and fed up she'd just throw the money on the floor.

"Here you go! Here's your damned money!" He remembered the rage and disappointment in her strong, clear eyes. Rage and helplessness and disappointment all mixed into one. She always gave in. She always gave him his money. She never denied him.

Bobby would just bend down slowly and deliberately and pick it up. And then leave the apartment quietly and go buy drugs.

No fightin' the Dragon.

So when the song started to hit with Ray and he'd heard it come on the radio while driving that Gypsy Cab in the worst parts of Harlem – sections people, even of Harlem, were afraid to go into – when he heard that song and the announcer breaking the hit, *"And now our new number one...."* he thought he'd finally hit the big time. Well, he went to Teddy and asked for an advance. He remembered it clearly.

"No money come in yet, son. Got the airplay, but ya know how those record companies are – take forever to pay ya...but *tell ya what I'm gonna do*, 'cuz I like ya, see.... If you've got anotha song, I'll give ya an advance outta my *own pawket*...how much y'all need? How 'bout a thousand dollars?...just sign here — right here on the dotted line. I'll take care of ya, *don't ya worry....*"

So, Bobby in his frantic attempt to get "well," as he had still liked to refer to it to himself at the time, signed away the other fifty percent of his writer's credit to "Unchain," plus all the rights to another song: "Don't Set Me Free," that Ray Charles also recorded. Bobby took the money and only later found out through his friend Solly Loft that Teddy had paid him the "advance" with money he'd already collected. Money he'd been collecting all along, without telling Bobby a thing about it. Been braggin' about it to Solly after they tossed back a few. Bragged to him how smart he was in cheatin' Bobby out of his own money. Laughed and laughed about how he had gotten Bobby.

Bobby remembered that laugh now — big and hollow and *loud,* usually accompanied by a hard slap on the back. Some sort of communal camaraderie that Bobby never understood at the time. But he did now.

He hit you hard when he was hurtin' you. Hit you hard on the back as if it was a gesture of affection, but yet it was only what it was — he was hitting you hard on the back. Bobby now fully understood the saying: *Watch your back....*

He chuckled silently again to himself now as he drove; and he inhaled another long, slow whistle, a habit he'd kept from his younger years.

Well, Solly liked Bobby, was friends with Bobby, and he said something to Teddy about how it wasn't right. And what did Teddy say to Solly? He slurred out the words: "*You dirty Pol....*" Oooh, that got Solly going. Solly didn't like racial slurs and especially when they were directed at *him.* So Solly told Bobby just what Teddy had done.

"I'll send you to an attorney," Solly said conspiratorially, "and if you win" and he had winked then, "give me fifteen percent." Well Bobby ended up getting $25,000 and promptly paid Solly. Sure as hell he did. First thing. Because he was an upfront guy of his word and had a strange and twisted belief in some sort of karma in life. Hell, it was only recently that he even *allowed* himself to revisit his successes – or semi-successes he should say, he really never got much money from any of them – except for "Unchain." But that was down the road. Way down the road.

Seven years of legal battles – Seven years of negotiation. Funny how people will do the stupidest things in their greed and arrogance. Teddy had made that mistake of calling Solly "a dirty Pol." And all of Solly's gory details to Bobby helped him get his song back. He gave Bobby the name of his attorney, Richard Aaronstein and Richard won the case for him. Bobby still had the same attorney today and he'd helped him with many things. A trustworthy guy. Someone that had helped Bobby when he most needed it. Hard to find in the music business. Bobby was glad that he was out of it.

Yeah, seven years of legal battles, seven years of negotiations; almost a *trial*, for God's sake and Bobby had finally won the rights back to his song – fifty percent of the writer's credit and half the publishing and that lump sum of $25,000 with all the copyright reverting back to him after twenty-five years. This last judgment had not given him much pause, twenty-five years was a long time, and at the rate he was going at the time, he didn't expect to be around that long, really.

Richard took the case around '64 or '65 and whatever happened, it was going to hit calendar in '70, that's when Teddy got scared and settled. The lawyers had their lawyerly discussions and on their merry way they went. He did keep ASCAP rights to "Unchain" and "Don't Set Me Free." *Teddy Powell's heirs still get fifty percent of the performance royalties – even to this day – will forever,* Bobby thought now to himself, but he was okay with that. No problems there. Teddy did place the song after all. Karma…it was all karma. And Bobby still got one hundred percent of everything else, mechanicals, movies, all the publishing, etc. *'Till the day I die….* He let out another slow whistle. That song had brought him in more than a million dollars so far.

Yup, here he was – *seventy-nine and doing fine*. He still made those little rhymes in his head automatically, even though he hadn't written a song in years. Engrained in him, really.

Seventy-nine and doin' fine.

He whistled a little tune along with the jazz coming out of the radio and let his mind wander. And it meandered to his mother, as it often still did, even after all these years. *Poor Eva,* Bobby thought as he shook his head silently to himself. *She went through so much, was so strong....*

She had finally kicked Louis out — well, actually, Eva was the one that up and moved, apparently she'd been saving for quite a while; then one day, she just told Louis: "Louis, I'm leavin' you. You do what you want to do, but I gotta be out on my own." She said this straight faced, without much emotion, in that quiet, resolute way that she had.

Louis had not said a word, just sat in his easy chair, staring at the television set. Bobby wondered if Eva had wondered if Louis even cared at that point — or if he was just *expecting* it — accepting silently to himself that Eva had put up with him as long as she did.

Eva had then methodically packed her things, taken a few pieces of furniture, given the piano to Bobby, packed up all of her dishes and pots and pans and left Louis everything else. She took the umbrella stand. For some reason she was attached to it.

She lived a fine life for a while, Bobby thought again. *A fine life. Finally had the freedom she deserved — only wished she'd done it earlier....*

By the time Eva left Louis she was already close to seventy and Aaron Douglas and Eddie were long gone. Aaron, back to Kansas were he was from — *funny how he and Eva had that connection, both from Topeka.* Bobby wondered if they'd known each other way back in the 20's before they headed out to New York. But, no, Bobby didn't remember him around, although Bobby was *small,* probably wouldn't have even noticed.

And Eddie, yes, so sad that he had died so unexpectedly like that. Eva was going to marry him for sure, that Bobby was certain of, certain because Eva had declared: "I'm going to marry that man — soon!" Joy in her eyes, Louis and his women forgotten.

But he had died — Eva's fate.

And Louis had stayed until Eva moved away.

Bobby shook his head slowly to himself as he carefully cruised his baby blue car. Brand new and blue, he'd just bought it this year. And he liked driving slowly, very slowly, down the tree-lined streets of Alameda, just cruising along, listening to the jazz radio station. Remembering –

Poor Louis, even Bobby had felt bad for him at the end – finally died of cancer in '76. Eva had passed a year after that. *Here she tried to get away from him and they ended their lives so close together...*he thought sadly. She'd let Louis live with her after the cancer hit, felt sorry for him, Louis couldn't work and Eva got soft and let him come back.

The memory was clear in his mind even today. His father standing up one day after he got sick, pulling back his cheek to expose black, decaying gum, the empty hole gaping where his tooth had been. "It just came out." He had said it blankly; matter-of-factly.

"Does it hurt?" Bobby responded, staring at the decay dispassionately; surreal.

"No, it doesn't hurt," his father's voice was flat, musing sardonically at the slow rot of his body, slight wonder tingeing his voice. That cancer had eaten right through his jaw – just ate right through it. Yeah, just a part of the illness before he went to the hospital. They had all taken it so calmly.

Then one sunny day, just like the sunny day before it, his father had gotten up to change the channel on the television set – and fell and broke his hip. Bobby still lived in Harlem at the time, back in his own place, just six blocks from his mother's (which once again included his father) apartment.

Yup, just got up to change that channel, broke his hip and off to the hospital he'd gone. Bobby blinked rapidly now at the slant rays of the 4:00 p.m. sun as they beamed through the front window of his shiny Cadillac; blinked rapidly at the memory that moved over him –

Louis had gone into the hospital on the weekend – they'd said he'd have to have an operation on his hip on Monday. On Monday, Bobby and his mother went back to the hospital to see how it'd gone, checked in at the reception desk and the receptionist said, just as straight-faced as could be: "Oh, Louis Sharp, he's dead." That's how they found out.

Just like that.

They had him cremated and a few days later Bobby took his father's ashes out to Central Park with a couple of guys, dug a hole under a big, wide oak tree and buried him there. He watched the dirt settle over his father and then he walked away. And never returned to that tree.

The amber rays were stronger now and they dappled and danced against the dashboard and glared through the windshield burning and sparking Bobby's eyes momentarily so he had to squint harder to see through them.

That momentary blindness the sun gives off just before sunset.

Well, they say the most dangerous time to drive is sunset, not night, as most people assume. Too many blind spots. His thoughts tickled him; reminiscing gave him pleasure. He loved the fact that he *could* reminisce, so easily, with no torment, nor complaint about his past. He'd made his peace.

He felt good.

Eva, dear, dear, Eva – Bobby had been hoping at the time that she'd have a few years of peace and freedom herself after Louis passed…but no, not meant to be. He remembered sadly, how her hand had shook when she placed the phone carefully back into its cradle after talking with her friend Molly Moon, still wearing the same startled, stark look that had descended during the doctor's call jut a few minutes earlier.

"Bobby, I'm going to go to the hospital and have this surgery," she'd said. Looking him flat in the eye. He thought he saw momentary fear behind her eyes, then peace, calm, courage. Resolution.

Bobby was not worried. His mother was strong. His mother always made it through.

But she had died in that hospital, just as Bobby later came to find out, she had suspected. Died just three days later.

He remembered clearly the letter he'd found in her belongings after bringing them home from the hospital; folded neatly into fours and tucked into the outside pocket of her gray, wool coat. He chuckled to himself. Here he'd made plans to cremate her, just like they'd done with Louis and the letter he found specifically asked for a burial. So, he traipsed back down to Sunny Valley Mortuary, changed it to Fernquest and redid all the plans he'd made – picked out a casket – made all the arrangements for a burial.

Bobby patted his shirt pocket and felt the neatly folded paper sitting there. A reminder of her last wishes. Of her love. Of her strength.

On impulse he slowly maneuvered his large car to the side of the road, letting the round, shiny wheels lightly touch the curb – for balance. He put the car in park and left the engine running. He pulled the worn, folded piece of paper out of his pocket and in the last of the day's light he read the letter quietly out loud to himself:

Dear Bobby,

I have been meaning to write this letter for a long, long time. Please do not feel bad if I do not survive this operation. I guess I'm a little tired. All necessary information is in the deposit box and all bank statements and checking are in your name. Please leave the small diamond ring to Molly to be passed on to Little Molly. White wool coat and collar to Terri. Aquamarine ring to Lorena and the large diamond ring to Debbie. Mink coat to Virginia. Everything else at your discretion. You will be surprised at the amount in the deposit box. Perhaps it will help you find dreams you have missed. I love you deeply and want you to remember to not feel too much sorrow.

Love, Mother

P.S. I want a nice wooden casket. Lot's of flowers and to be buried at Fernquest Cemetery up in New York.

He studied the gentle curve of her cursive and then folded the paper neatly back into fourths, carefully put it back in his right upper shirt pocket, and eased back out onto the pavement. The sun was setting far on the horizon, casting warm orange and red streaks across ice blue sky. 5:30 p.m., on a Tuesday.

He took a deep breath and remembered cousin Virginia – his mother always treated her so well, but Bobby never quite trusted her. And sure as the day was bright there was cousin Virginia going through his mother's things when he got home from the hospital that day; looking through her drawers for papers – see what she had – what she could *take*.

"What you doin' Ginia?! Bobby had yelled at her when he'd found her, her hands still in his mother's lingerie drawer. She shut the drawer quickly. Looked up. She'd been staying with them while Eva was in the hospital. Supposedly to *help*.

"Nothing, Bobby…why you so *jumpy*?"

"You're goin' through Eva's stuff; her things *and she hasn't even been gone two hours*! What are you looking for?"

"She said she gonna leave the mink coat for me, I's just lookin' for the papers; set it all straight. That's all. Just lookin' for what she said she was givin' me."

Mad…mad…mad…he was at that. Doesn't even wait for the funeral. No manners; no manners AT ALL. "Get out! Ginny! You only wanted Mother for what she could give you; you've *always been that way!*"

"I don't want *nuthin'* from you or your *mother!* Never *have*, never *will!*" And with that she turned and left the apartment and slammed the door behind her and *didn't even show up for the funeral.* Supposed she was embarrassed at being caught. Bobby never did give her that mink coat…. Gave everything else as he was supposed to, though, fair is fair…and he wanted to honor his mother's wishes.

Suppose it is time to put that away now, he thought to himself, smiling slightly. *Time to put it away.*

He turned up the music on the jazz station and began the slow drive back home.

CHAPTER THIRTY-FIVE

N ATASHA SAT QUIETLY in the waiting room of jazz station KCSM-FM. She was lucky to get this interview, she hadn't wanted to miss it, nor to be late. Her back was killing her though, and sitting, for just the hour it took to get here and then this fifteen minute wait for her interview, was bordering on excruciating. The band of pain across the lower half of her extended belly was almost constant now, and still, she had been reassured that she would be fine. *Absolutely fine...*Dr. Simpkin had said. But she did not feel fine. She felt *wrong*. She knew something was wrong. But everyone around her assured her – she was *fine*.

So, I am fine, then, she said to herself.

I am just fine. Her frustration was almost constant now.

A general annoyance at life. A general irritation at everyone, but Fontana. Her little love.

She looked forward to sitting quietly alone on her drive back home, in her new little used Volvo station wagon, contemplating life and trying to take her mind off of her searing pain. *Searing pain....* Was she exaggerating it? Was she just more fragile this time?

Did she even care about anything at all? She was utterly exhausted.

Normally a chance at an interview like the one she had today, at a major jazz station in San Francisco – a *major city* – would have left her jumping with anticipation and excitement. But it had taken all of her will just to get out of bed, get dressed and get *over* here, *on time* – well, early, actually.

Promptness was one of her virtues, and despite the effort, Natasha refused to be late. So, she had arrived fifteen minutes early, as was her habit and waited patiently in the lobby for the secretary to give her the okay to go back into the studio.

"You ready, honey?" Midge's voice slid through her thoughts.

"Yes, of course," Natasha replied, noticing again Midge's gray-haired and decidedly unhip countenance.

"Okay then dear, you can go back on into the Studio now. Dan is waiting for you. Just through this one door to my left, down the hall and it's the third window on your left," she said, absently pushing the silver rims of her pointed 50's-style eyeglasses further up her long, thin nose with her index finger.

"Thank you Midge, I appreciate it." Natasha heaved herself up from the hard plastic chair with effort, glancing in Midge's direction as she did so. She knew Midge from the multiple quick conversations they'd had confirming her scheduled interview time and verifying directions and address. Midge's voice had been young and sincere, very different from the picture she now presented. She glanced again at the petite elderly lady in the baby pink sweater with the white lace ruffle settled against her creped neck. She had instantly felt a connection with Midge when they spoke on the phone. A feeling that was made stronger now by the fact that she was not some cool chick in her mid-twenties. Natasha liked the fact that Midge was old.

She nodded politely and made her way across the lobby and through the single dark brown door, closing it gently behind her; stepping onto the orangey/brown of the worn carpet with a thud (she thought) and walked, no *lumbered, ugghhhh!* down the hall, between walls that looked to have been once white, but were now a decidedly tanner version of that original color and badly in need of a paint job. *A decidedly 70's feel...how retro...* smiling to herself at her little joke, she turned the corner into the glass paneled office labeled "Studio B" and was instantly met with Dan the DJ's look of total surprise at her markedly un-slim state (very different from the picture she had sent with her bio). She returned his look with an even stare. A stare that said: "Just don't go there buddy, I've had a hard day, my back hurts, I'm tired and I want to go home." Coupled with a firm fixed smile and her haunting, endless brown eyes. The effect was devastating.

"Well, hello, Natasha," Dan extended his hand, she took it and they shook. He cleared his throat into his fist, lust shooting into the small hole created between his thumb and forefinger. "So glad to have you here," he lowered his hand then raised it again and slicked back the piece of brown hair which had fallen haphazardly over his eye and threatened to poke him. "Let me get you a chair. Can I get you some water? Coffee? Oh, uh, no, not coffee…herbal tea? Anything?" He shifted nervously from foot to foot. *How unlike me,* he thought, *to get nervous like this…I'm acting like a teenage kid….* But her affect was unbalancing him.

Natasha continued to return Dan's stare evenly. Even in her very pregnant state she had Dan the DJ falling all over himself to please her, and she, of course, hardly noticed. "No, thank you. Just water, please." Half-smile firmly in place.

"Thank you," she carefully reached for the plastic cup he offered her minutes later and gingerly took a sip, "I needed that." Her lips felt dry, her mouth parched, a seemingly constant state these days. She licked her full bottom lip slowly with her tongue – wetting it with the tiny drops of water still lingering there in an attempt to relieve the never-ending dryness.

Dan noticed of course. And was surprised at his intense attraction to this pregnant girl; no *woman*. Shook his head. *You sicko!* he thought chuckling to himself.

Natasha looked up sharply from her cup of water, startled by his quiet laughter. "Did I miss something?" she asked. Dark lashes flitting towards him, right eyebrow arched up in question.

"No…no…." Once again Dan felt flustered, "Just thought of something – nothing to do with you – you have to excuse me, I've had a long day."

"Me too," Natasha said with relief, inhaling deeply, feeling the band of pain increase sharply; small foot kicking out; stretching; letting out her breath quickly; hand instinctively flying to her belly to massage the little foot back in; to soothe it; comfort the child within. Protect it from the pain.

"Kicking?" Dan asked. Surprised at his interest in the unborn kid, given that he was a bachelor, with no children of his own, no *intention* of children in the near future, or ever for that matter, and a sordid history of fleeing if marriage or children were ever mentioned or he felt *might* be mentioned sometime in the future.

Their eyes locked for an instant. An intense gaze that sparked them both, then simultaneously they pulled away. Instinctive. Having crossed some imaginary moral boundary.

What the hell is wrong with me?? Natasha thought to herself. *Again having these feelings – sensuality – is the only word she could use to describe it – and I am eight months pregnant.*

"Oh God," Natasha said out loud.

"What?" Dan said, turning back towards her, feigning indifference to their recent eye encounter.

"Nothing." Natasha took another tiny sip of her water.

"Looks like we're on in five..." Dan said hurriedly, quickly back in business mode, "four, three, two, one.... And here we are on jazz station KCSM-FM in beautiful downtown San Francisco, and we have a very special guest today. Today we have an up-and-comer who is one to watch. She has a new album out entitled *Talk To Me Nice* and even our own Melanie Berzon, the program director here at KCSM refers to her as: '...a woman who understands the importance of the human voice and its impact on humanity. She sings from the heart and gives us music for the soul.' And Jerry Dean, Producer of Dean Broadcast Services says: 'Natasha is blessed with deep musical knowledge not only as a vocalist but as an accomplished instrumentalist. This professionalism is clearly evident in her recent musical endeavors and is a delight to experience.' And Andy Gilbert of the Contra Costa Times describes her as a 'rich, supple voice...a first-class production all the way....' Wow, that says a lot." He nodded at Natasha, catching her eye fleetingly, "Natasha I also know that you began your musical career as a classical violinist, serving as concertmaster for a symphony in the Midwest and you founded your own string ensemble, *The Sapphire String Quartet*. And you also play piano and guitar. Wow! That's quite a resume," he was gushing and he knew it. "You're quite diversified. Natasha...."

Natasha smiled silently to herself. She liked hearing positive praise of her work.

"Can you tell us a little bit about what went into making this album, what inspired you?"

"Well," Natasha took a deep breath before speaking, gathering confidence and poise around her – a cloak to her thoughts; measuring her words as she spoke, careful to modulate each one. *Never let 'em see you sweat…*her father had told her more than once, and she took these words to heart.

"I went to college and as you said, studied violin – actually had a scholarship for violin. Strange, I know for a jazz singer to play violin," she laughed huskily at the thought, her voice a little lower, a little more sultry than usual, a combination of her extreme exhaustion and whatever dynamic was currently going on between she and Dan the DJ. A dynamic she did not even want to think about. "But I really started out wanting to be a musician. Playing my violin has always been my first love. My dad is a pianist, you know jazz, blues, etcetera. I have such a clear memory of him teaching me to play in early childhood. Me sitting at the piano bench in diapers, reaching with my stubby little fingers towards the keys to play…." She paused here, looking around the room. Blinking at the memory, "then at a fourth grade school assembly, my teacher said: 'Does anyone want to try violin?' I drew the bow across the strings, I remember clearly that first stretch as the bow hit the taught strings…."

The description made Dan wince, he felt himself begin to stir; harden; he readjusted himself in his chair. Continued to stare at her. Fiddled with a few dials in front of him. Looked away.

"Well, anyway, my teacher said: 'You're a natural…' so I started violin lessons. Classical violin then. I played in orchestras…actually I was the youngest member of the high school orchestra at age eleven. The first piece I ever played was 'Beethoven's 5th Symphony.' Like I said, I actually received scholarships to college by playing violin. I loved to sing all through this time, but I wasn't getting a scholarship for singing, just violin, so I wasn't really able to hone that skill." She took a breath. "Anyway, I moved from the Midwest to San Francisco and broke free from the title of violinist. I still played, but I decided: *Here I am in the big city, I'm going to make a go of it.* And jazz was just sort of a natural projection from that. I had my daughter right about that time,

Dan raised an eyebrow at this. She had a *kid, already?* She didn't look past twenty-four...

"and singing jazz paid the bills at private functions and parties. So, I started honing my skills in that genre. And besides," A pregnant pause sat between them. Natasha thought, hard, intensely, "Well, besides writing and singing, there was something, *something* else..." She paused again, took a small sip of her water, turned again to the microphone. Put her mouth close to it, the words spilled from her forcefully — a sound both intense and quiet; a strange purring from her gut. "It's hard to describe.... It was a feeling in my *soul.*" She pulled back from herself at this description. She hated any reference to "spirituality" or "soul" or any other mumbo jumbo sort of thing. Had enough of that growing up with her (albeit wonderful, but sometimes a little quirky) dad. She was surprised she had made this statement. On national radio. The pregnancy had made her too sensitive. She reached down. Rubbed her swollen belly again. Cleared her throat, tried to erase the huskiness of it, wouldn't go away, began to speak again. More focused. *Stick to business.*

"Anyway," she emphasized the word, "I've rambled. What we're really here to talk about is my upcoming show with the Oakland East Bay Symphony. It's to be my debut, really. I am very excited about it, over two thousand people are expected to attend. And I would love for anyone, *anyone,* who has a love for this kind of music to come and support us in our endeavor. A portion of the proceeds will be donated to help homeless shelters and abused children. It really is a project of my heart." She stopped then. Said all she needed to, more really, than she had intended to. More, than she had said to anyone this past month, especially Brett. And here she was, so very chatty on the radio. And *how in the hell,* she wondered, was she going to be able to do a show in less than a week? A show of that caliber. Well, it was going to happen, and she would be *fine.* A word she seemed to use often these days. And in some deep part of her, she wanted to share this with little Aiden. She was looking forward to being on stage with him. Singing *for him.* Sharing that moment with him. She was excited. As if in response, his little slow foot kicked out again and she absently reached down, as she had done a hundred

times before and massaged it back in. Settled him. Silent communication between mother and son. *It's going to be okay. Everything is going to be okay.*

Dan noticed the gesture, but said nothing. There was a moment of dead air, just a split second; but something Dan never allowed. He silently chastised himself for his mistake and tore his eyes from Natasha, hoping she hadn't noticed him staring; noticed the dead air; noticed his lack of professionalism. But, no, she was still looking down, slowly rubbing her belly in a somewhat dreamy way.

Dan sensed there was something wrong and was silently alarmed. Then ignored it. What was wrong with him? His concern for Natasha was bothering him. He didn't even know her.

Natasha suddenly looked up, realizing she had stopped speaking. "Anyway,"

"Well," they both spoke at the same time. Laughed, started over, Dan nodded to her, indicating she should go first.

"Anyway, to get back to my story, one thing led to another, and well, here I am...."

———

Bobby turned up the dial on his car radio and slowed down even more leaning into the dash to hear better....

———

"Well, we're going to get some more music on now – you've already heard one track from her recent CD, *Talk To Me Nice* entitled: 'Good Morning Heartache'; well here's another one. I wanna show you what else Natasha's got to *give*." He growled on "give," slow and low; Natasha flashed him a look. Dan ignored it and reached for the dial to play "Peel Me A Grape...."

"Here's a nice song interlude by..."

UNCHAIN MY HEART

————

The soft, smooth voice filled the car – sultry – easy. A longing for life hidden beneath the texture of the notes. Up and then down the voice went – like silk on his soul. Smooth and *inviting*.

He drove very slowly all the way home as the sun set on Alameda and listened intently to the radio. He listened as the DJ interviewed Natasha. He listened intently to her voice.

He was mesmerized by that voice. And by the inherent quick wit and intellect he detected from that voice.

This had not happened in a long time.

Astute! he thought to himself. *She is genuinely astute.*

Bobby was drawn to strong, smart women. And he detected that Natasha was both of these things.

Like his mother.

He pulled into the driveway of his small cottage, got out of the car, locked it carefully from the outside. Walked the three shallow steps to his front door, turned the key and slipped inside.

CHAPTER THIRTY-SIX

I T WAS RAINING OUTSIDE when she returned from the hospital. Raining and gray. And she knew that her life would never be the same.

Her child was dead. Her heart was dead. Her feelings were – dead.

All she had was Fontana, and Fontana had been so sweet and silent in her own little way. Watching Natasha carefully. Natasha would catch her peering intently at her from around a corner. Just those two little amber-flecked eyes, and the edge of a face – poking hesitantly around the white edge of the wall. Waiting.

Natasha always made sure she smiled quietly to Fontana, sent her spasms of love through the air, but the sorrow engulfed her like a slow flame and she had no urge to speak – even to her daughter.

The funeral had been hard, everything had been *hard* – Natasha going through the motions by rote. Leaden; wooden. No aspiration for *anything.*

And still, here she sat exactly one month later, at the edge of her bed, staring at the wall and past it to the window – and again, it is raining.

Natasha watched the drops hit the top of the pane and slowly ride down the glass. She watched the drops make their way from top to bottom for one full hour. She knew she had done this because she looked at the clock on her bedside table and it had said: *10:00 a.m.* – digitized numbers unblinking. She had slowly turned her head away from the clock and watched those tiny drops slip down. Unblinking. Unflinching.

Not breathing.

Did she even remember to breathe? Did she *have to??* *Oh, yes, breathing is automatic. I do not have to* remind *myself to do it. I do not have to* make *myself do it.*

She liked this.

And with that thought she had turned back to the clock and saw that it was 11:00 a.m.

Fontana was at school.

Safe — away from her.

Natasha could clearly see that her daughter was worried about her, the little worrywart in Fontana standing at full command at the new duties being offered her, the biggest duty of all, in the biggest way — the duty of *caring fully* for her mother.

But she doesn't have to worry about me.... She thinks she does, but she doesn't. All I ever wanted was to let her be a kid; to not have to worry about anything.... Free; easy; childhood.... The haze of the room swam around her and she watched the colors of the flowered curtains blur against the white of the wall, enjoying the slow motion of it all. Not lifting her hand. Not wanting to. The thought being all. The thought being *all she could do.*

She wished sometimes that Fontana would let herself relax into the little girl she was, tomboy and all, and not try so hard to be grown up; in charge. *But,* Natasha thought with a sigh, and she lifted her wrist slightly from the white eyelet coverlet on the bed and let it drop again, *that is her way, and this is just the thing I admire most about her — her maturity....*

Taking another long, deep sigh she heaved herself up and off the edge of the bed. She had been sitting there quite serenely and the clock had turned again to eleven-thirty.

Fontana would need to be picked up from school at two-thirty, which was no problem since Natasha had broken down and bought the Volvo — *in anticipation of Aiden,* she thought drearily; once again the thought of her stillborn child sucking the life from her. The little energy she had mustered to get up off the edge of the bed dissipated immediately. And she panted, silently to herself. Quick, shallow breaths. A leftover effect of the toxemia. She was still upset with her doctor, the hospital and everyone and everything that had to do with that tragic labor and delivery five weeks ago.

She'd had the pains – searing pains; called her doctor, panicked. "This is *not right!*" she practically screamed into the phone. "Something is not right!"

"You're going into labor, Natasha, nothing to worry about," Dr. Simpkin's voice was calm and reassuring over the phone line. "Get into the hospital, Natasha. As calmly as you can, get into the hospital. Do you have your bags packed? Have Brett put them in the car and drive you to the hospital. Tell him to drive *carefully*, now...."

Natasha did not bother to respond. Just slammed down the receiver, annoyed at Dr. Simpkin's patronizing tone. Slammed the receiver down, picked up her one small packed overnight bag that had been sitting near the front door for the past week, ready for just that event, called to Brett, "Come, *on....* We're going, *now!*" Waddled down the stairs on her own to the gray Volvo, fitted carefully with the infant seat in the back. Brand new. A splurge they'd found well worthwhile, given their safety consciousness and their love of their little guy, almost on his way.

She had grasped the metal handrail for support on the way down the gray concrete steps; she remembered the way she had watched as Brett had taken the car seat out of the shiny new box just the week before, carefully placing it into the backseat and how they both had struggled to adjust the seatbelt securely; knocking against each other, Natasha's big belly getting in the way, Brett supporting her as she bent over to lock it around the bottom; familiarizing themselves with the tiny strap that would secure their newborn; anticipation and excitement made all the more real.

She remembered marveling at the advances in baby car seats, even since Fontana's baby days. She read out in delight from the instruction manual of the one they had finally chosen, the *Graco Super Safari Snug Rider2* infant car seat, "You know, it has an ergonomic carrying handle and easily snaps into the accompanying stroller?'" They had both laughed. Light. Excited. A nice relief from the tension they had been feeling.

Trish had been standing by, as always. Watching Brett suspiciously from afar. "WoooWeee! That's quite a contraption ya got there, Tasha!" she'd said, snapping her ever-present gum emphatically.

"Yeah, yeah, really different from Fontana's car seat," Tasha replied, wondering as ever, why in the world Trish still had such a heavy southern accent, when she had been in Northern California, as far as Tasha could tell, for most of her adult life. She wondered if a lot of it wasn't put on for show — something she reinforced for attention...to be different. She shrugged it off and continued, lifting her head out of the back seat for a moment as she spoke.

"I remember I used to just roll a towel up and squish it up over her head to steady it, when she was a tiny baby and then when she got older, well I removed the towel and *Voila!* — bigger car seat. That's all there was to it. And, I used to be able to put Fontana into the front passenger seat — they don't let you do that anymore...." Sweat had started to form on Natasha's upper lip as she spoke.

Sweat and a slight dizziness from the exertion of figuring out and getting to know this new contraption. She pulled her head out of the back seat of the car again, tried to take a deep breath to steady herself but began to see those familiar black dots forming behind her eyes — reached out to the car; held on lightly; waited for it to pass.

"You all right?" Trish asked, concern clearly clouding her watery blue eyes.

"Yeah, yeah..." Natasha said breathily, "doctor said some women just get light headed during pregnancy — said its nothing to worry about. But I have to say, it's starting to get to me. I just don't remember feeling this tired, this *exhausted* with Fontana."

"Maybe it's because it's a boy," Trish said wryly. "You know how those males are — start suckin' you dry right from the start!" She laughed. A half snort, half giggle at her remark. She really did crack herself up sometimes! She glanced over at Brett. He stood, hovered partially over Natasha, glanced at her; steadied Natasha. Said nothing.

"That man don't speak much, now do he?" Trish muttered under her breath.

Natasha just looked at her, sight returning slowly. Breathing slowly becoming steady. And at that moment, she had been sure.

Something was wrong.

And just one week later she was again making her way down those steep concrete steps to her car and then to the hospital.

PART III – BOBBY & NATASHA

Yeah, I made it into the hospital all right.... Made it in, they offered me a shot of morphine, a shot of morphine, no less and sent me home. Didn't even see a medical doctor. Didn't even offer one. No one came to see me.

She was still bemused by this occurrence. *No one came to see me.* She remembered sitting alone in that hospital room, then the offer of the morphine. Which she declined. And then being sent home.

"Do you have someone to drive you home, Natasha?" the helpful blonde nurse had inquired, patiently; faux-earnestly, a hundred other patients that night to see.

"Yes, yes, Brett is here. Brett will drive me home..." Natasha had responded, semi-automatic. She had been in a fog then, and hadn't even known or noticed. And she had gone home.

She had felt the baby kicking on the way to the hospital.

Felt it kicking.

And then it had stopped.

By the time they got back to the house there was *absolutely no movement.*

And the pain had been excruciating, she now remembered clearly. And she could not move off the couch. She remembered how she had rolled off the couch and crawled, knees scraping on the too-rough carpet, finally making it to the kitchen for water. How *thirsty* she was. She drank over a gallon of water that long weekend. No food. Could not eat food. *No eating.* The words had reverberated in her mind at the time. *No eating; just water. Water...water.... And Brett? Working, yes working, he had to work.... Said to call him if I needed him; call him and he'd cut his class short and come right home. No need for both of us to be off...no need at all; no....*

Of course, the second time in the hospital is when they discovered, as she lay dying while trying to give birth that she had preeclampsia; also know as "toxemia." She found out later that the baby had definitely died at home and that her own liver and kidneys were failing; something she had instinctively known at the time, but could not comprehend or respond to. A defense mechanism. She had acquired a lot of these.

She was told sometime during her hospital stay by someone...who??? she thought now, *which doctor??* Was it the Indian doctor who had held the stethoscope to her belly when she had returned to the hospital and said in

that soothing and melodic voice "no heartbeat; so sorry no heartbeat...."
Just like in a dream. *Yes....* He was the one that told her that when major organs fail, the body goes into shock and you do not think clearly.
Everything just shuts off.... Is that why she did not call emergency when she
could not walk? When she had to *crawl on the floor* to get water? Is that why
she didn't call *anyone??* *But why did they send me home??*

Even in her near death and drug-induced fog she thought she remembered Brett wrapping little Aiden up in the hospital blanket – but it could
have been a dream; a hallucination. The way he tenderly caressed the still
baby's small cheek with his large forefinger. Stroking it so slowly. Like he
had all the time in the world. This memory was embedded in her brain
and would not go away.

And then she was wheeled away and there were doctor's shouts and
comments like "vitals dropping!" and requests for various medications
"stat!" She knew she was given Magnesium to stop her from having a
stroke and Pitocin to speed up her labor, but the rest of the names of the
medications Natasha no longer remembered. She didn't care to. It was
over. *Over.*

She had blacked out then.

And here she was today, four weeks after the funeral. Still no energy.
Still no drive.

Still no voice.

No *life*.

She had attempted to sing one evening late – attempted to sing when
her father flew in from New Mexico, where he'd been for the past ten
years, holed up, writing. Flew in, now and then, to see her and Fontana
and he made a special trip this time to cheer her up. Talking, talking like
nothing was wrong; filled with love but not giving her *peace*. Reaching
for the memory of them singing together; her childhood with him, she
sitting at the piano reaching with tiny stubby fingers; her lifeline; but no,
no voice; just a slow croak and then nothing. It was gone. *Recurring. A
recurring dream. Is that what this is?* This latent memory that would not let
her go? He laughing and encouraging her. Excited at her natural musical
talent.

She shook her head again slowly; felt the softness of her hair as it fell into her eyes. Did not move to brush it away. Mute.

And she had just accepted it all.

As she had accepted the death of her child; her boy; her *son*.

A given.

Her *fate*.

No resistance.

It just was.

Brett had gone every week to the gravesite to visit Aiden. Quietly and on his own – not asking Natasha to come along. Somehow he sensed she did not want to go, although he never asked.

She preferred to honor and remember her baby in her own mind.

She was fine with that.

Going to the gravesite seemed to her like some undo strain. Some self-inflicted punishment.

An opening of a fresh and fierce wound.

No, she would keep him safe in her memory. And thank him silently every day for giving his little life to save hers.

Thank him.

Silently.

Bobby was no longer wondering what he should do, nor feeling bored.

He'd had his successes, in many small ways. He'd had what he wanted in life; albeit in a strange, sometimes fascinating and roundabout way.

That year back in '62 when "Unchain" hit the charts he was in and out of rehab at the Metropolitan Hospital in New York City three or four times – in for three weeks, out for a couple of weeks – back in again; sitting alone, playing piano in that locked ward, he had *truly wanted to quit*. He remembered the solace the keys had given him; the momentary peace.

Then back in '67, going on out to Synonon House in Santa Monica, California – friends talking about it, how good it was, beautiful too, right there on the beach – how they got clean and stayed clean. So he went in, four months in, four months out – but back to New York and he's back on smack. Just couldn't break that Harlem tie. Back admitted to the Met Hospital. The doctors and staff knew him well by then, like an old friend. "Hey Bobby, how's it going there?!" they'd call cheerfully as he passed them in the hall, as if he wasn't a patient, as if he *belonged there.*

"Hey there, doc, how're you doing?" he'd call back. Cheerful; affable; charming; easygoing. He was friends with all.

One day the dialogue changed, "How'd you like to work here, Bobby?"

Walked in a patient came out an employee, the thought amused him now. *Eva always wanted me to go into psychiatry, and here I did it in such a roundabout way!* The irony hit him and once again he found it funny, and chuckled, slowly sipping and savoring his weak, hot coffee and flipping to page four of the *Currents* section in the *Alameda Sun.*

He liked to read the obituaries; liked to read the little blurbs of the various unknown lives that had crept by and around him. See their life's accomplishments condensed to a single paragraph. One in particular caught his eye now. It was smaller than most, only three lines:

Sylo Hanson, age 76, died Tuesday of a massive stroke.
He was predeceased by his wife of 40 years,
Martha Eugene Hanson. He has no known descendants.

Hmmmm…three years younger than me. NO KNOWN DESCENDANTS. The line screamed out at him. He flipped another page. Went back to his thoughts.

Yup, ended up working at the Metropolitan Hospital in the biological psychology department; and after a while was even assigned his own patient – acted as his doctor. Patient was a failure, though. *They were* all *failures…*he thought, *no one got off the horse. NO ONE. Some got on Meth and stayed.* He had gotten on Methadone and stayed – instinctively put himself on a low dose, 10mg., when the norm was 50. Had to do it; couldn't counsel addicts if he was an addict. Then weaned himself off. *It was a miracle.* He had thought this many times. *A miracle.* Some got from heroin to Meth – would put them on the standard 50mg. That was the success.

Four years he worked there. Seemed like a long time. Long enough to get stable. But he had to leave New York. Had to *get out* of New York. He remembered now the day he finally quit that job and moved back out to California. California, *where it was safe.*

Landed in Lafayette, near Oakland. *Brought that girl with me – a good girl that worked with autistic children. Lucy...Lucy...Lucy...with her dark hair and giving nature. Lived together for a year. Lived on love and the little money I got from my case.* He shook his head to himself. 1970 – a new decade; a new life and a new car. The first new car he ever owned. Worked out at the Pittsburgh Community Hospital for a year and then got bored with it. Living out in the woods – in the boondocks, really, no city; no lights; no *action.*

A demon got in me, he thought as he flipped to page five, ignoring the fact that he easily accepted the concept of a demon and not the concept of a God. Ignored it. Not rational.

"A demon got in me and I drove down to Oakland," he'd told this story a hundred times to a hundred rehab patients. *An example. I am like you. I* know *you. Don't try to pull any shit with me. I know all the tricks. Just tell it like it is. Tell it like I'm tellin' it. That's all you gotta do.* And he'd look straight into their eyes, deep solitary holes into the blackness. "I drove into Oakland, and I thought, I'll go where they sell drugs and I started using drugs again. It had been five years without drugs. I started to go to Oakland every day from Lafayette, taking money out of the bank. The bank tellers are lookin' at me like I'm crazy. Taking money out every day. Then things got so bad I took my new Monte Carlo and sold the car to a dealer on Broadway – it was a used car dealer so it was quick money. I took the money, went back to Harlem; got back into heroin, lost my license and started driving a Gypsy cab – yellow cabs wouldn't go into Harlem; so people would get their own cars and put a sign on it that said: 'Gypsy' cab – had an old '63 Chevy Bel Air by then, was in bad shape; dented. Dead cold of winter; went to the front of the house to start it up; early morning gray sky beating down. Car froze. Everything *frozen.* Air frozen. Asked the junkyard: 'how much can I get for this car?'

'Ten dollars, man, that's all we can give ya.'

'Come on over and get it then....'

That was the end of my cab driving." Staring, staring, two solitary holes. Patient staring back. Waiting. Dead eyes. Needing a fix.

It was his spiel. And it was honest and true. And it was *all he had to reach them.*

He flipped to page six of the *Sun,* studied it intently; checked the weather. Had *all the time in the world now.* All the time in the world.

Or did he?

He felt somewhere in the back of his mind; his soul — if indeed he had a soul — he had his doubts on that, having been a full and complete atheist since his early twenties.

There was no God. *And you is what you is. So you better make the most of what you've got here on earth before it's gone. It is all there is.*

This is why Natasha's practical nature had attracted him. Practicality mixed with a vague sensuality. Practical passion. He liked that. Her matter-of-fact approach to life. And when they had finally met up at that little coffee shop/diner in Alameda — how surprised he still felt that here she'd been all this time — living and working in the city he had lived in so peacefully for the last twenty years. "How long have you lived here?" he'd blurted out feverishly, as he sat across from her in the tiny coffee shop. The emotion had risen unexpectedly in his throat; his throat constricting and almost choking the words from him.

"Oh, about five years," she'd replied casually, absently, even — not thinking about it. Only thinking: *Five years out of music school — five years of singing jazz and leaving my beloved violin, five years of* waitressing *at this damned coffee shop and playing gigs at night. Oh God, my back hurts!* Firm half-smile slipping so easily back in place, corners of her mouth turned up just a little more than usual. Hand to her lower back to massage it. Random thoughts, while Bobby gazed intently at her.

Bobby was not easily moved. He had seen too much; been through too much to be deeply affected by people. He had learned to keep a slight distance. And he had gotten used to existing alone. He was quite peaceful with it, actually. And happy. Or so he thought.

But this person, woman, girl, child, soul? was flicking his emotions to life, and somehow fears he did not know existed were popping to the surface now randomly. A knowing that his life was coming to an end. And he didn't want it to.

"There is no God," he had said suddenly as he sat across from her. Natasha said nothing. Just returned his stare. Accepting.

Looking at her, at those large brown eyes flecked with pain and longing, just a hint, visible when the sunlight caught them just the right way, Bobby felt a feeling he had not experienced before. He wanted to pour his soul out to her. Tell her all of his secrets.

Unburden.

He wanted *life*.

"I am not religious," he continued. She leaned in closer to him. Intrigued.

"This I do believe: when you die you are dead and you will never return again. I figure when you are gone. You are gone."

Natasha smiled at him. She liked the way he compartmentalized things. Liked the way he was so *sure*. She was not so sure.

Bobby continued, lowering his voice slightly, "I used to read *The Rubaiyat of Omar Khayyam*. He said: 'I sent my soul into the invisible, some sing of that, after life through spells, and soon my soul returned to me, and said I myself am heaven and hell.' He was a Persian poet from centuries ago." Bobby looked down. Looked up again at Natasha. Natasha stared back, the words reverberating in her mind, *and said I myself am heaven and hell.*

"A complete and total responsibility for self," she said flatly; matter-of-factly. "There is no God. There is only us.... Wow! Takes all the responsibility off of the shoulders of some unknown third person," she took a sip of her chocolate. Set the cup down carefully. Her anger dissipated just a bit. Frankly, she didn't know *who* she was angry at anymore. Had lost the will to even *be* angry. She admired Bobby's complete and total responsibility for himself. Left no one to blame; but *himself*. And this blame he had accepted and sat squarely on his shoulders. She could see this. In this responsibility he had found peace. An acceptance. Heaven and Hell of our own making. Life on earth as heaven and hell? They could have a *long discussion* on that one. *Well, we'll have time for that.* Bobby saw the silent statement in her eyes.

Yes, he found himself instantly in love with the spirit of her, yet had no need to touch her. He did not analyze it much. Just accepted, as he had accepted the other events of his life; and moved forward with the knowledge that it would always be.

He gently placed the bone china cup in its delicate saucer, and carefully folded his copy of the *Alameda Sun*, setting it neatly alongside his plate, admiring the lightly etched and faded pattern around the rim of the delicate cup — this china set being the only thing he had taken from his mother's apartment, well, this and the painting he had found in the back of her bedroom closet. Rolled up and faded, with deep creases where it had been folded. It was a portrait of his mother, painted by Aaron Douglas, looked like, many years ago to him — in the 30's, in the heyday of his parents' soirées in their Sugar Hill apartment. He'd pulled that painting out of that darkened closet and stared at it intently; instantly memorizing every line; every angle; every color. The vision of it etched eternally in his mind: The smooth contours of her face; the hands neatly folded in her lap, one placed gently over the other; protecting; the auburn hair crimped and parted down the middle and gently dusting her feminine shoulders; glamour echoing her stare. She was looking out and to the side — *at what?* It looked as if someone or something other than the artist had caught her eye; or as if she were saying: Yes, you are *there*, but *I've* got things to do." Or "hey *that* looks interesting...." Always curious. Bobby remembered that about her. Curious and serene at the same time; as if nothing in the world was bothering her; but there was still so much to *do; to discover.* And her beauty was staggering in its quiet; questioning way. The colors of her dress faded from years of being rolled up in the closet. *Or did Aaron paint them that way?* The blues, whites and pinks fusing together; a muted palette to her beauty.

He sighed. Took another sip of his now cool coffee. Set the cup back down. He had things to do.

CHAPTER THIRTY-SEVEN

H ER HEAD WAS BENT DOWN over the sheet music, which was worn and slightly tattered, a brown hue to the onionskin edges. Trish had offered to pick Fontana up from school today and take her to dinner and a movie. What a godsend Trish had been. And a good friend. Unexpected. It had all been so unexpected.

Had it been three months already since Bobby had handed her this stuff so unceremoniously at Jake's when she was almost nine months pregnant? And still she had no voice. Nothing...nothing....

The songs struck her again, as they had the first time she'd seen them. *Lightning in a bottle!* she'd thought. *Simply amazing!* – *A treasure trove.* Those two words kept coming to mind – a *treasure trove....*

She remembered his simple telephone call. Yup, he'd called right after her radio interview at KCSM-FM. Still slightly dazed from her strange encounter with Dan the DJ, she'd driven back from San Francisco, waddled up the stairs, made it inside – only 3:00 in the afternoon, Fontana not home from school yet – glad to have the place to herself. A little quiet to rest in. She remembered her overwhelming urge to bake cookies and the way the knife had just slipped off the shiny plastic of the pre-made cookie dough; she remembered vividly the sweet, salty taste of blood tickling her tongue as she sucked her index finger; the blaring, startling ring of the phone....

She usually wouldn't have picked it up, she was good at monitoring her calls if she didn't want to talk, but Fontana wasn't feeling well that morning and Tasha had said: "Call me, Hon, if your throat still hurts after lunch and I'll come pick you up early, 'kay?" She, of course, as usual and for the *millionth* time felt guilty for sending Fontana off to school with a sore throat, but she *had* to get over to San Francisco for that radio interview, *absolutely* couldn't miss it and didn't want to ask Brett, who had already left to teach aerobics at 6:00 that morning, to cut his classes short, get a sub and come home.

No, Fontana was her responsibility.

Natasha remembered thinking at first that it may be a crank caller, then waiting, finding out no – O*kay, a fan,* she thought to herself. She could handle a fan, just hoped he wasn't crazy.

She kept her number listed, a bold move, she knew in this day and age. But what you saw is what you got with Natasha and she was not going to hide away in some remote corner of Alameda afraid of the public. She refused to live her life in fear. If someone wanted to find her – well, they could find her – just look her up.

And then the little bombshell: "Well...I heard you on the radio today and well, I'd like to send you some of my music. I'm a songwriter, you may know some of my work...." Bobby had been surprised at himself he'd later told her. He'd known he wanted to call, to say "hello" to introduce himself perhaps, let her know he enjoyed her interview, but he wasn't expecting to offer his music to her. He had not done anything music-related in over thirty years.

"Of course," Natasha had said, automatically slipping into business mode. Polished veneer sliding into place – voice smooth as silk over skin – slight guard up. She tried to muster some of that authenticity in herself now, but it was gone. And she was nothing. Just empty. He had sounded like a nice enough guy, though, so she had let him go on; she remembered hoping he was not a crackpot. Although she had received some weird calls in the past and some pretty terrible songs sent her way.... Her mind had wandered....

"Well, anyway," the gentle voice had continued, pulling Natasha back toward him, "my name is Bobby Sharp and you may be familiar with some of my work."

No...Natasha thought to herself, but continued to listen politely.

"I wrote the song "Unchain My Heart" for Ray Charles, *um...hmmm....*" Bobby cleared his throat again then, still clearly surprised at himself, silently questioning what was compelling him to do this. "I'd like to send you some of my songs, perhaps you'd like to sing them." There it was. Done. He took a deep breath then and waited.

Natasha's mouth opened to speak, but she said nothing. Her jaw just hung, halfway open, moving – sort-of – digesting this new bit of information. Part of her very logical self slightly questioning the authenticity of the caller; but another, deeper part of herself knowing – *there was something there.*

"Would you like to meet someday?" Bobby continued, hopefully.

"Sure, sure, excuse me, Bobby," Natasha said the name emphatically, engraving it in her brain. *Bobby.* "I'm almost nine months pregnant and a little distracted, I think. Excuse my pause. Of course we can meet. Do you know Jake's Diner on Encinal and Park Street near Jackson Park? It's in a big, old gray building near the corner; large floor to ceiling windows, you can't miss it. We can meet there tomorrow, if you'd like – say 2:00?"

2:00 is a good time, Tasha thought characteristically to herself, *give myself an out in case the guy's crazy – Have to leave at 2:45 to pick my daughter up,* she'd say, and that wouldn't be a lie. Fontana would be thrilled to see her mother there unexpectedly (or so she hoped) and if the meeting went well – well, then she could stay. And she thought it best to keep the place neutral, which is why she directed Bobby to her now (former) place of employment.

Quitting on impulse had been the best thing she'd done so far. At the time she had pushed the nagging negative thoughts from her mind, tried to quell that stupid instant anxiety. And luckily she'd secured herself a little part-time work at a design firm. Sort of an entry-level traffic manager – waitress of jobs in the advertising world. Take the proof reading to the art director; to the creative director, move it down through the pipeline. Yes, she was a "traffic management assistant."

At least Agustus had taken her leaving well. And his little revelation had been a bit shocking. Not what she had expected *at all.* But not the reason she had quit. The way he'd looked intensely into her eyes as he spoke and opened up to her that night late at the diner. She felt the longing; the desire welling from him; but knew instinctively he would never act on it. She was a fantasy to him in some strange way. An "inspiration" he'd said. How she could be an inspiration to *anyone,* especially in her current state, she had no idea, but she thought his words sweet. And it did solve one little mystery for her. She had been sure he was gay. So secretive about his clubs in San Fran almost every night. She didn't say anything; didn't matter to her, really. He just seemed, well, *frustrated,* and she wanted to see him have a little peace. His dropped one-liners about the "guys last night," escaping his mouth before he could stop it. It was just a natural conclusion on her part.

But he had revealed it all that stormy night over a cup of coffee. He seemed to appreciate her coffee. She liked this. She listened....

As he told her of his love for the trumpet. How he had always been ridiculed for playing it as a kid; so had done it in secret; never seeing it as something that could be "real" in his life. How he admired her. These words said quickly and straight-faced and directly and not repeated.

It was "their little secret." Agustus never did let Trish go. He had to admit she was a good waitress, and he got a small, simple pleasure from torturing her silently with his stares and gruff glances and silence. Her stupidity amused him. And after Tasha told him with a laugh what he already knew — of Trish's misgivings and suspicions and wild ideas of who he was and what he did with his time — they had both decided to have a little fun with her; intensifying the mystery. *Their little secret.*

He had been there for Natasha. He was family in a way. Family from such strange places. She had never wanted to leave at that moment. It felt so safe....

So safe that she quit. On the spot. *Always have to shake things up, don't you Tasha?* She felt sure of the decision. Sure and easy. Even though at the time she had no future prospects. And then she had instantly felt sad. And strangely nostalgic. And like somehow she had betrayed Agustus. But he had taken it in stride; as if he had been expecting it. At the time she thought she'd take a couple of months off after the baby was born, through maternity leave — she and Brett had discussed it. And then go back to work. Her mind had ticked loudly at the time, *what will happen? What will happen?* But her gigs had picked up, she was being slightly paid. Her fundraising work was paying off a bit. She had a stupid, blind, unexplained trust that everything was going to be okay. *WHERE DID THAT COME FROM????* her mind screamed now. Stupid! Stupid!

Anyway, Agustus, she knew he would keep his eye on her. He always did.

So she'd set the meeting at the coffee shop, throwing her normally cautious nature aside and taking a meeting with that sincere sounding stranger. She remembered him walking into the coffee shop, sprite, thin and glowing — somewhat in a strange way she could not put her finger on. She remembered the instant connection they both had, as if they'd known each other forever. As if this was not their first meeting, but their hundredth. She remembered relaxing.

She remembered looking intently at him then and noticing Bobby studying her; staring into her *soul*. She inwardly flinched at her own uncharacteristic spiritual inflection to his staring. But she let him do it. It did not bother her. She sat up straight and absorbed Bobby. Looked directly at him. Let him look directly at her. It felt — *natural*. Natasha did not usually let people look straight into her soul. It just wasn't done. By *anybody*.

Except Fontana, of course, but that was different, Natasha thought now with a laugh, as she laid the onionskin lead sheet back down on the kitchen table carefully; *and Fontana, for now at least, I can control*. But Bobby's gaze had bored into her steadily and it gave her — comfort. She liked it. She welcomed it. She wanted him to do it again. And she had opened up to him, in a way she had never opened up to anyone.

Yes, that gentle older man. She had gazed into his eyes and seen a wisdom learned through hardship. A gentleness. A being above the rest. She knew the moment she sat down across from him. The songs were secondary. But he *had* brought lead sheets and cassette tapes for her to listen to and as she flipped through the pages she had known instantly the inherent value of those songs — and at that moment the words *treasure trove* popped into her head.

"We've got to get these songs out into the world," she'd blurted out unexpectedly. All guard and reserve down, excited by the material she was beholding; excited to get home and listen to what was on the tapes — wondering aloud if she even had a cassette player.

"I've got one you can borrow, if you need it," Bobby had said, hopefully. He beamed. He had not beamed in a long time. Had he ever beamed?
He did not think so.

He was seventy-nine years old – and he had fallen in love....

Natasha picked up the brown, yellowed and worn onionskin lead sheet.
Bringing her focus to the present. Wondering where that ebullient, pregnant woman had gone. Disappeared. Passion. Disappeared. She really
didn't care. No. Not really. Anymore.

She gently rubbed the tawny edge of the paper with the top of her index
finger, running it down it's side again: liking the feel of the silky, worn paper
on the tender skin of her fingertips. She breathed in slowly. Exhaled.

She had a *duty* to these songs, somehow. A *duty* to get them out into
the world. A duty to Bobby.

She headed toward the kitchen and the old blue telephone mounted
on the wall, a remnant from the last tenant – *probably been there since at
least the mid-eighties,* she thought as she walked. A thought she had repeatedly, along with the corresponding thought that she should just get a new
phone, a portable one, something without a cord, and put it in the living
room. That way she could walk around when having a conversation, not
have to drag and stretch the extra-long teal blue cord when she was talking and had to grab something – a pen and paper, perhaps, or Fontana's
lunch, or dinner – not get caught up and encircled within it's coils, having
to untwist herself as she spoke.

But, no, she never did, because she was kind of attached to the retro
feel of it and she in fact, and she always came back to this thought – she
liked having her little old-fashioned answering machine screen her calls.
She liked being able to listen to who was calling before she picked it up
if she didn't make it to the phone on time. And it saved her from talking
to numerous telemarketers. Her own personal telephone hell. Idiots who
somehow got her number (could it be because she was listed? well...she
refused to hide, so *there!*) and insisted on calling repeatedly to offer her
new credit cards and ask if she needed to refinance her home. Her *home?*

So, once again, she was back to basics and happy to be there. Her one blue phone, in the kitchen, with the curly, extra-long teal blue cord, and the little answering machine sitting next to it that she'd had for the past seven years. They worked. She was fine. She was always *fine*.

She picked up the receiver and began to dial Bobby's number: *(510) 555-4762.* One of the few things that still lingered in her brain. She punched the buttons emphatically.

"Hello?" Bobby's voice hummed through the line. His gentle expecting manner took her aback.

"Hello, Bobby, this is Natasha...how have you bee...."

"Oh, Natasha," Bobby said, cutting through her words; voice rising just a little at the inflection of her name, "Natasha, Natasha, so good to hear from you. How are you doing?" Concern genuinely tinged his voice. Natasha had called him once, quickly when out of the hospital,

"It's dead," she'd blurted out. "I'm tired, so tired, I just need to take a little time off, get my bearings...you understand, yes?"

"Yes, yes, of course, of course...give me a call anytime, anytime, now. Take care of yourself, now."

"Thank you, thank you, Bobby, I appreciate it." And then she'd hung up. And not called for three months. She'd been surprised at herself for her candor, but accepting, even at that point, that this would be the basis of their relationship. Candor. And an openness to each other. Even while just off her deathbed, she felt a *duty* to Bobby. A *pull.* A duty to call him and let him know that it was only something tragic that kept her from contacting him.

She was no longer surprised.

She had no emotions left, she thought.

She just – *accepted.*

And this was why she was now standing in the kitchen, holding the phone receiver mutely.

"Natasha?" Bobby interrupted her; a knife to her thoughts.

"Oh...oh...I'm sorry, Bobby. I'm sorry." Bobby could clearly hear the distress in her voice – mixed with what? apathy? exhaustion? He only knew he felt an overwhelming desire to hold her; go to her, *mend* her somehow. But how?

"May I come over?" Bobby asked, waiting patiently for her response.

"Sure," Natasha said flatly; matter-of-factly. Then she gently placed the receiver back in it's worn cradle and slowly walked back into the living room. She sat herself down on her favorite flowered overstuffed sofa near the window, noticing the soft beige and green patterns of the leaves and petals around her; placed her elbows on her knees, feet planted firmly on the ground and rested her chin on her two balled fists. Waiting. Patiently. As if she had all the time in the world.

It was all she could do.

To wait.

CHAPTER THIRTY-EIGHT

T HE SUN SLIPPED DOWN an orange sky and Bobby slowly reached towards Natasha's hands. He gently placed his old and wrinkled fingers around the softness of her own and drew her hands towards his heart and cupping them gently, as if they were glass, he placed them over the little spot above and to the left of his chest, and let them lie there – the warmth of her long soft fingers pressing through the cloth of his checkered-print, button-down shirt with the one empty pocket on the upper left side. He wore short sleeves, as usual, and because on this spring day it was unusually warm, he did not have on his wool button-down sweater. He laid his hand over her own, and just let it rest there on his chest.

Natasha did not resist. She felt no need. She only felt the *thump, thump, thump,* of his heart – slow and steady. So unlike her own, which, as if in opposition to his, thumped erratically and fast – zigzagging around her chest.

"I remember my mother used to tell me: 'Let somebody love you, Bobby...you *gotta let somebody love you!*'" Bobby let her fingers go as he spoke and she dropped her hand and folded it over the other in her own lap; staring down at them; examining them – silent.

"That's why I married Barbara. She was white, *oh so white,*" a secret smile played his lips at the memory, "white, red-haired, 5-foot-9 inches tall and outrageous. She had a boisterous laugh."

Natasha looked up from her hands, intrigued.

"We met right here in Alameda at a club. She was a little taller than me, of course," Bobby said this shyly, a quick acknowledgment of his shorter stature, "and I'd been clean by then – only had one little slip up – and I'd heard my mother's words clear as a bell in my head as I was driving down the freeway one day, took it as a sign, and married her after only dating six months. *Wooooooo,"* Bobby's long, slow inhale whistled through his teeth.

"*Big mistake!* Oh, yeah, that was a *big* mistake. But I got the little place, you know – you should come over some time.... I kept the cottage and the cat, Tangey, we used to call him. Barbara, well, she moved out. She said: 'we're going to split.' I said, 'since you know California better than I do, why don't you leave and I'll stay in the house.' So, she left and I stayed. Worked out kinda nice." Another long slow intake of air.

"At first it was good, of course, sex was great and she was *so* fair." Bobby's agile mind took him back there instantly as he spoke, and the pictures played behind his open eyes. And he rolled the sight of her very light and pink skin against the caramel darkness of his own around his brain, and he had liked this – this contrast to his darkness.

Natasha looked up again from her folded hands, surprised at his frankness. Looked at his face to see if he was kidding, no, just reciting memory and far away.

He continued,

"People always stared when we went out and I asked Barbara once, I said: 'Barbara, do you mind that I'm black? Does it bother you at all? Does it bother you that people stare?'

'*Heeell* no!' she'd told me in her heavy Texas accent. Her family was from Texas, all of them, and she'd never lost the drawl. And well, it didn't bother me either, really. Why should it? Never had in the past, why then? But I think Barbara put more into it than I did – was with me as some sort of defiance of her people. Part of me always wondered if that was the reason she was with me, and *others,"* he emphasized the word revealing, Natasha thought, *a slight annoyance? Something he hadn't yet gotten over?* She nodded for him to go on.

"Yeah, Barbara said it didn't bother her, and we were happy for a while. Her parents and two brothers lived out in Texas and her mother would call over almost every day after we got married and we'd have the nicest chats. Of course, she'd never *seen* me. We didn't invite anyone to the wedding, just went on down to City Hall one day and did it there. Neither one of us wanted a big tadoo.

"I remember her mother's voice so clearly: 'Oh, Bobby, we yar *sooooo* anxious ta meet ya,' she would drawl." Bobby mimicked her perfectly and Natasha smiled despite herself, "...meet the *fiiiine* yung gentlemin done stole our Bawrbrawa's hawrt."

'Why, of course, ma'am,' I'd respond," he deadpanned the perfect manners of his gentlemanly self and Natasha smiled once again.

"Bobby, you're funny, I didn't know you had such a sense of humor." She reached over to him and touched his hand.

"'And ya seem liiiiike such a well spoken yung man – and *eduuuucated* tooooo,'" Bobby continued to coo his Southern mimick, "graduated from music schoowel in New Yawrk – isn't that *sumthin'*?" His eyes danced toward Natasha and she laughed out loud despite herself.

"Go on," she said, happy to be taken away from her own morbid thoughts for a moment.

"'Yes, Ma'am,' I replied." Bobby ever the consummate storyteller continued, "'I'm looking forward to meeting you too.'" He sat up straight in his chair and tipped an invisible hat towards Natasha.

"But you know, I told her early on, 'Don't go telling you're people that I'm black...you know, they might not take it so well....' For a while she kept quiet – didn't say a word. But finally she just couldn't hold it in anymore and one rainy night when we'd gotten back from a club she spit it out over the phone to her mother and all hell broke loose. My, oh my Nellie! She marched right on over to the yellow banana phone in our place, picked it up and dialed Texas. 'Hi, Mom, I just wanna tell y'all that Bobby's black.' No preamble; no lead-up. Smile spread ear to ear across her face, flushed red with excitement and all the liquor she'd drank.

"There was a high-pitched scream through the phone line, I could hear it even from where I was standing, 'A *nigga*! Ya married a goddam *nigga*! What the *heeell* is wrong with ya Barbara? Are ya *insaaane*? Ya make me sick! Ya both make me *siiieck*.' There was more, of course, loud rants coming through the phone, I could hear from where I was standing, and Barbara laughing like crazy; clutching her sides; laughing so hard she doubled over and rolled to the ground; almost peed her pants. But then after a while she got real mad.

"Things went downhill from there. The phone rang constantly – Barbara refused to answer it and when *I* finally did, my mother-in-law really tore into me," he looked at Natasha then, mischief fading from his eyes. "I could imagine twin Barbara hair flaming on the other end of *that* line. She said: 'we gotta gun, more than one, and y'all step one fut in Texas and my son will shoooot you on *siiite*.' I took that threat very seriously. I avoided Texas from then on. Put it up there on the list with the other places like Mississippi and Kentucky.

"After that, every little noise we heard we thought was one of her brothers creeping up the concrete to shoot us. Barbara was mad as heck, but I was cool about it. Yep, things went downhill with her from there." He had been looking dreamily into space, focusing on the small square space on the wall just above Natasha's head, and he shook himself out of his memory and back to present. He looked at her upturned face, so sad and quiet and stated simply, "The thrill wore off."

He laughed, more to himself, then to Natasha. "I don't know why I'm telling you all this, I feel I've known you all my life." Natasha stared, back, still quiet, *yes, she felt the same way,* but she only nodded, telling him silently it was okay. He nodded back, continued spilling the story into the air between them, one of many stories buried within him. "Anyway, to make a long story short, one day she came home from a club after staying out all night and she had some other guy's afro comb in her hair – I knew it was over right then. She moved out shortly thereafter. I had a quote from Confucius up on my wall in my bedroom for the longest time. It said:

'Marriage is an agreement between two fools...'

I've always thought it rang true. I knew right then I would never marry again."

Natasha nodded again, silently concurring, lost in her own thoughts. The death of Aiden had brought she and Brett back together again. Renewed their love in a way she had not expected. Made her so grateful for the little *simple* things.

But, she knew, with certainty as Bobby spoke, that she and Brett would never marry.

That this respite was only temporary. He had healed her in the most benign of ways. With his steady presence. And calm assurance. He had rehabilitated her in a sense and for this she was grateful.

But she also knew and it was confirmed to her, how precious life could be. Moments...that ticked by...imperceptibly....

She reached over and laid her hand over Bobby's, silently consoling him for his ancient loss. She patted the top of his hand, as if the gesture could erase her pain somehow.

At just that instant the front door slammed hard, jolting them both out of their shared moment, and tearing their locked eyes away from each other, they simultaneously looked in the direction of the slam.

Brett sauntered in forced-casually and headed straight for the living room wondering whose car was in the driveway, and what the *hell* Natasha was up to. Always slightly removed she had been even more so after the death of their baby and he was worried. He didn't know how to reach her; what to do. He felt at a loss; helpless. A feeling he didn't like. Jealousy, an emotion unfamiliar to him, reared its ugly head once again and he pushed it back down; feeling it in his gut – *what is going on?? something is going on....* Bobby's head jerked up and he looked at him, directly, questioning, silently. *Who are you??* Natasha quickly removed her hand from on top of Bobby's. Bobby smiled only. And continued to stare.

"Who is *this?*" Brett asked, confused, feeling the intensity in the air, but unable to comprehend the situation. He felt he should feel jealous. His male ego and instinct immediately kicking into gear; should feel jealous, but jealous of an *old man? An* older *man, that's for sure.* He laughed internally at the thought, the laugh forcing a bright smile to his face, he extended his hand out automatically, a manly gesture of goodwill. "Hi, I'm Brett, and *you* are?"

"Bobby, Bobby Sharp," Bobby said quickly, slightly annoyed at the intrusion, but knowing it was not his place to be, he the newcomer to the situation, that felt he knew Natasha so well.

"Ah, Bobby!" Brett's enthusiasm and surprise startled Bobby. "Natasha's told me *so much* about you," one thing Brett was, was extremely supportive of Natasha's career and this guy was *good* for Natasha's career, "glad to finally meet you." Brett pulled his large hand from Bobby's slender one, noticing the length of his fingers and the caramel color of his skin. He thought he glimpsed a certain femininity about Bobby, an ethereal quality emanating from that skin. Something *otherworldly,* then discounted the thought — *no, no, just slight; kinda frail... No threat here.* All moments and thoughts flashing across his face as he attempted to make mental peace with the intimacy he had just interrupted.

"Get ya a beer?" Brett asked cheerfully, slapping Bobby on the back hard in a gesture of manly camaraderie. "Tasha doesn't drink much, but maybe you could use a brewsky on a warm day like today?"

"No, thank you, I don't drink either. But thank you for the offer. I appreciate it." Bobby began to rise from his chair, having slipped back into himself and away from Natasha. "I suppose I should be on my way, it's getting late, I'm sure you two have some catching up to do."

"Oh, no — Tasha and I are fine, stay...stay for dinner." Natasha's silence in the months since Aiden's death had been taking its toll on Brett. And though he felt a closeness to her that he had never felt before; a bond forged of loss and need; the last thing, really, he wanted, was another long, silent, strung out dinner where Tasha ate slowly, if at all, and stared at the wall, not acknowledging him. His anger was flaring and he knew he had no right. But, *God damn it! Just snap out of it!!* He'd gone to the cemetery every week, maybe twice, Natasha refused to go. *Living in some sort of mute denial.* No, another dinner alone with Natasha, was not his idea of a good time right now. Maybe this guy could help cheer her up.

Natasha glanced at Brett, questioning; they locked eyes for a moment, she arching her left eyebrow up; surprised at his hospitality — he wasn't usually so friendly to the opposite sex, even if this one was fifty years older than her. And she was sure he had felt the electricity in the air when he had entered so suddenly. Had he done that on purpose? That grand, sudden, entrance? Had he had one of his male instinctual premonitions that she was not alone at home? Or was she just reading into it, once again, adding more to Brett's actions than were really there. *Oh stop it, Natasha!* she silently reprimanded herself. *You're being ridiculous.* She laughed out loud – both men turned and looked at her, startled by her sudden emotion. *She* was startled by her sudden emotion.

Brett smiled.

Bobby smiled.

Natasha smiled.

It was the first time Brett had heard Natasha laugh in eight weeks.

"So, what's for dinner Tash?" She glanced at him, he put his arm around her and he felt so solid. She let herself lean deeply into him – for a moment. And then she moved toward the kitchen, thoughts ripe within her. Pushing them deep down, not wanting to feel them, but at the same time happy at least that she had some feeling. "I don't know, thought I'd make pasta." *Yes, pasta, some garlic, a little basil, maybe a little tomato. Something quick. Something simple.* She pulled the vegetables and herbs out of the fridge, turned toward the counter and began to chop the tomatoes; rolled the basil into a cigar shape and chopped the bright green leaves into thin slivers. Grabbed some garlic; pounded it open; chopped it quickly. Grabbed a pot from the cupboard and began to fill it with water. Glanced over at Bobby; smiled....

Bobby stepped lightly down the concrete steps after dinner. He felt – *light*; easy, younger than he had felt in years.

He remembered the way he'd touched Natasha's hand before Brett had arrived – an urge he'd had and indulged; the way she'd placed it so tenderly over his heart. And held it there, still and steady. As if her hand were healing him; healing his heart and pushing him forward. And in his step he felt this new vigor; this energy that she had infused in him.

And he no longer felt like his life was over; slowly rolling to a nonclimactic end.

He felt – inspired – and *surprised* at himself for allowing such intimacy, an intimacy he had not felt since his failed marriage twenty years ago. And even then, had he let Barbara hold her hand over his heart? Had he

UNCHAIN MY HEART

allowed Barbara to look into his soul? Had he let down all of his defenses so easily; so readily, as he had just done with Natasha? A young woman more than fifty years his junior. *Could be my granddaughter,* he thought, and chuckled as he fished the car keys out of his pocket and expertly turned the lock. His car key had an automatic button to lock and unlock the car doors, but Bobby never used it, he preferred to open the doors manually; something about just *pressing a button* felt too easy to him. He liked the comfort of the flick of his wrist – the "click" of the lock. A feeling of safety as he walked away from the car; a feeling of pride of ownership as he unlocked the door to get in.

He slipped into the cool leather of the driver's seat, inhaled deeply and let his mother's words ring in his ears: "Let somebody love you, Bobby...*you gotta let somebody love you!*" Said so long ago, and so lovingly and urgently, an unshed tear in the corner of her eye.

He pulled away from the curb, her words ripe and reverberating.

CHAPTER THIRTY-NINE

FONTANA WAS ALONE on the playground. She felt the hot sun on her neck as she bent down, frustrated with herself for taking too long to pull her sock up. *That same sock...always have to pull it up....* She huffed, looked around; stared at the tortured little sock, stretched out around the edges because of the way her mother folded them, rolling them into little balls and then pulling the neck of the sock around itself; so Fontana had a drawer full of neat little balls with one stretched out sock and one that fit. *Irritating!* She huffed again, silently vowing to just fold her socks in half when she could do wash.

She stood up defiantly and wiped the tiny bead of sweat that had formed above her left eyebrow. She placed her hand over her eyes and squinted into the sun. She liked looking into the sun, even if her mother said it was bad for her eyes, actually said it could "blind" her. Well, Fontana had not been blinded yet.

She liked the way she lost her vision for a moment and everything went black and then to white. She liked how she had to blink a bit after turning away from the sun to bring back her vision. She liked to watch the tiny black spots form in front of her eyes as her sight returned.

She liked being momentarily blinded and then slowly blinking her vision back.

It was a silent risk. A strange defiance. One she relished in her quiet contemplative way. For as single-minded and strong-willed as Fontana was, she had absolutely no urge to defy her mother. She didn't have to, her mother never gave her reason to. Fontana always felt that what she did was *her* choice. So, there was no need for defiance.

But, the sun, the sun, with its ability to blind was tantalizing. Fontana wiped her forehead again.

Just then Claire came skipping across the playground. Sweet, sweet Claire.... Fontana shook the rest of her vision back as she watched her come closer. Smile soft and bright at the same time. Earnest and sincere in her friendship. Hand already extended towards Fontana.

Too open...Fontana thought to herself. And, of course, as soon as Claire approached it was out of her mouth: "You're too open, Claire."

Claire's face crashed – smile descended. Eyes momentarily hurt. Fontana's instant regret. *Gotta check that...gotta check that,* Fontana silently reprimanded herself, and reached out and grabbed Claire's hand hastily. "C'mon, let's go play on the monkey bars!" Pulling Claire along, Claire's slight unwillingness evident, but the smile returning, blonde hair flying behind her as she ran behind Fontana, arm stretched before her as Fontana pulled her.

"C'mon Claire!" And Claire's smile returned full force, as she followed Fontana out across the playground – towards the tanbark, pink dress flying in the wind behind her. Unaffected by the sun. And glowing. And she held onto Fontana's hand lightly as Fontana led her.

So sweet and delicate. Claire affected an attitude of ease, which sat heavy against Fontana's commanding presence. Fontana would place one hand on her hip and cock her head to the side when she was about to say something; whereas, in seeming opposition to this, Claire would only stand, silently. And wait for what she wanted to come to *her.* Yet she was not waiting. She was only *being*, as Claire had not mastered the art of womanly seduction. She had only partially mastered the art of safety. Quiet. No talking.

A silence.

That made Fontana protective.

For although Claire had never come right out and said: "Someone has hurt me," Fontana could *feel* it. Feel that a small part of Claire was always afraid – in all her childlike banal beauty.

And Fontana saw.

The fear that flicked in Claire's eyes. Her beautiful solitude. The way her long, brown lashes flicked down and then up; her blue eyes suddenly glazing over; feeling gone.

So Fontana let Claire cling to her. She let her grab her hand lightly; and Fontana *always* grabbed Claire's hand firmly. As if by her firm grasp she could instill in Claire a *solidness*. A strength. Some sort of back bone; or house, to protect her.

Claire ran to the tanbark with Fontana and watched with a big smile as Fontana jumped up and grabbed a monkey bar with one hand. Blue skirt hiked high, revealing white shorts underneath. Right, white miserable sock, scrunched down near her ankle; reaching for it. Trying to pull it up. Exasperation; letting go of the sock – right hand to monkey bar; left hand to monkey bar – swinging across; free. Claire admired Fontana's freedom, the way she swung from bar to bar with such abandon. She wished for such abandon in life herself. But even now, in her tiny soul, she knew she would never have it.

And as she thought that thought, Fontana's hand slipped off the ring and she fell with a loud *thump!* straight onto her butt and onto the tanbark. Fontana sat for a moment, stunned. Color drained from her face. And then she got up, brushed off her butt, turned around to check the brown/ orange colored stain left on the back of her skirt, turned and walked quickly to the classroom, ignoring the pointed stares in her direction. And headed back to class. Ahead of everyone else. In anticipation of the bell.

Leaving Claire to stand alone at the edge of the box. Staring at the monkey bars, still swinging slightly, though no one was there.

School was over and she trudged up the concrete steps – took the bus home again today. The Man was at the bus stop, as he had been several times a week for the past eight months. She did not know his name, but she liked him – fear and remove dissipated. Many times they would only sit quietly next to each other; did he sense her loneliness? Did he sense what was going on at home? That she just *needed someone to talk to* – But could not speak.

Sometimes he would tell her a story, like the one he had told today:

"There was bird in a tree," he said, hands folded neatly in his lap, small smile playing the corners of his lips, "and this bird sat and tweeted quietly yet no other birds heard him, nor the people passing down below. It was a blue, beautiful bird with a red spot on its chest that puffed up when he breathed in the dirty air of the earth and strong wings that could take him to fly anywhere in the world he wanted to go."

Fontana watched intently the neat, tiny gray-brown curls bob slightly against his forehead as he spoke; liking the warmth emanating from his soft, brown eyes.

"Well, this bird tweeted lightly, for he did not want to complain, of his loneliness, and the fact that he was so small, so much smaller than the big powerful black birds that crowed loudly above him. He did not notice the beauty of his colors; he took for granted his power to fly anywhere in the world – for this small area, that one tree was all he had ever known and he had no desire to leave, for this was safe and perhaps, he thought, if he waited here and tweeted quietly, he would attract others like him. He did not see that although he was different, this is what made him special; he wished only to hide from the black birds.

"He did not see:

That his colors gave him beauty;

His size gave him speed in flight;

His agile and inquiring mind knew more than the lumbering black birds above him would ever know.

And that – that one tree, although a base to him, was only the *tree of his foundation* – something that he could come back to. But something that did not own him.

One day he was to see that he had choices...."

Just then the bus drew up, long and lumbering and loud and a cloud of exhaust puffed between them and Fontana got up reluctantly and waved goodbye and stepped up the sharp metal steps and took her seat inside by the window sill closest to the Man and pressed her nose lightly against the glass and watched the two round fog circles appear and fade under her nostrils and waved again – faintly and let the bus take her away from the bench, under the tree where the birds' tweeting receded and Bobby sat, mutely and waved back.

And here she was home, trudging up the concrete steps, on her way to her room; taking off her soiled dirt-stained shorts, gathering up the rest of her clothes – a load that especially included socks. She grabbed a wad of coins from the change bowl in the kitchen, which she stuffed deep into her pocket and made her way outside, downstairs and around the corner to the laundry room. Her mom left the laundry soap and dryer sheets in the washroom, never bothering to take them back to the apartment; another thing that bugged her.

"Where are you going, honey?" Natasha called from the kitchen, blue teal phone on her ear; every ounce of maternal energy forced into her nonexistent voice,

"Outside, to do wash," Fontana replied over her shoulder as the screen door slammed against the last of her words.

Natasha just shook her head, went back to her conversation, she knew better than to try to stop her strong-willed daughter. If she wanted to do wash, let her do wash. Actually would be good for her to learn. Just hoped she wouldn't ruin all her clothes. But something in Tasha knew that Fontana would be fine. And she didn't want to have the laundry supply conversation again, something Fontana, for some reason seemed to take very seriously.

Fontana trudged down the stairs remembering the last conversation she and her mother had had about the laundry supplies,

"Why?" Tasha had asked, when she had inquired as to her need to supply the entire building with washing materials and truly stupefied by Fontana's question, "I'd just have to carry the stupid things back and forth every day."

"But then *someone else* will use them," Fontana had protested, ever in her wisdom, wondering why on earth, in their current financial state, her mother would want to provide laundry detergent and dryer sheets for the entire building.

"If they need it that bad, they can have it," Natasha had replied, exasperated. "I don't have time to worry about little things like that, honey." As always, Natasha's eyes were filled with love as she answered her daughters incessant questioning, but her voice was clearly vexed. Noticing

Fontana's continued pointed stare she repeated: "If they *need* it, they can *have* it," eyes rolling heavenward, "it's only *laundry soap* for heaven's sake — If I need laundry soap one day, perhaps I can borrow from *them*."

Life doesn't work that way...Fontana's thoughts screamed. But she kept her mouth shut. Sometimes she and her mother had diametrically opposed viewpoints and Fontana had realized long ago that trying to understand or even argue with her mother was pointless at some point.

There was a slight drizzle in the air, and she walked quickly with her little load bundled up in her arms. All her whites. White t-shirts, white ankle socks. Two white button-up blouses and that white pair of cotton shorts — badly stained from her fall off the monkey bars earlier that day. The fall was hard and definite and she'd hit her butt with a *thump!* on the ground. It had hurt — *bad*. And her spine had jarred deep into her head. She'd had a headache all throughout the rest of the day, and her tailbone was still *killing* her, but she hadn't let it show at the time, she'd just gotten up, brushed the tanbark and dirt off of her butt, fully aware of the few stares her way, and the fact that she was going to have ground in dirt on her shorts for the rest of the day. And she had resolved there and then to begin that day to do her own wash.

Sometimes when you sit alone you wonder, where the blue went and why the world has stopped on a gray and cloudy day. This is the thought that Bobby had as he made his way up the stairs that fateful second day. He did not bother going in. Natasha did not ask him inside. They both sat on those concrete steps, silently for a moment, hands entwined, before he began to speak.

"I've told you so much, *so much*. I have so much more to tell. I feel, well I feel as if you are my *repository* in a sense. Do you understand this? He had slipped into "Fontana" mode and did not know why. This woman reminded him of that little girl at the bus stop somehow. She'd told him her name a few months ago — said hesitantly at first, then he watched as she gained confidence and sat up straight. He had watched as she had started to trust him. But this is not who he was with Natasha. With Natasha, he was different. Honest; raw; *she* had something to give to *him*, somehow. He just couldn't put his finger on exactly what it was.

And within his words he found freedom. And from his words she derived a strange peace, and a will to live. And they both knew at the same moment, that they each had something to give that far superseded the rain that had preceded their meeting the previous day.

"You are my soul mate," Natasha said simply. Knowing instantly as the words left her lips that Bobby did not believe in such things. Bobby blinked back. His beliefs challenged for an instant. Then accepting. Just accepting. *Stranger things have happened*, he thought as he resigned himself to this friendship of the soul. This intertwined love that blossomed so easily. This easy trust and confidence in another.

So it was now alone at the edge of this new dawn that they still sat. Hand in hand on the cool concrete of the sidewalk. "I don't know why I'm telling you all this," Bobby said again, sincerely. Looking straight into Natasha's eyes. Small tear on the inside corner of his eye, threatening to roll down, but it never does. He blinks it back. Swallows it down the back of his throat, feels it roll slowly down his insides. Inhales. Decides it is his turn to speak. To tell her, not of the years of his addiction; no – that was too ordinary a tale for him. Nor of the ordeal with "Unchain," his Savior.

"'Unchain' saved my life," he said simply. Plainly stating the truth. Natasha knows and understands his meaning. She needs to hear no more. She nods for him to go on.

He tells her about the years when he has "recovered." When he is better. His one lapse – the way he drove slowly down the street that hazy morning, bored. "I had too much time on my hands...don't know why I did it, to tell you the truth, Natasha."

He told her again his old story – *started doing drugs again – every day would go to the bank and withdraw money – every day they thought he was kind of odd – how he'd drive to Oakland, get the drugs – drive back home, do them.*

And then how he finally quit. What a miracle it was that he quit. What a miracle it was that he was *alive*. "Finally quit the Methadone, but I drank every day. I was edgy." He patted his shirt pocket in reassurance, no letter; no cigarettes; no safety; no need; pulled back towards Natasha, remembering his cigarettes were in his jacket pocket; *good; relief;* he continued: "It took the edge off, and I drank kinda heavy," again he is far away; again he is deep in the past, "get off from workin' at the hospital go on home drink a bit and then one day I stopped. Just didn't need it anymore. I see now I was trying to cope. Lucky...so lucky to have gotten off the Meth – most don't y'know."

No, she didn't know, but now she did. She understood. She saw none of the darkness that he described as she looked back through him, noticed the moisture at the corner of his eye; wondered how this slight man could have been through the things he had described to her. She saw only light. *Do you have to go through the darkness to reach the light?* The dark night of the soul as she had once heard it described. *Do you have to endure incredible pain; incredible suffering in order to reach others? To make music? To appreciate life. To live.* Her mind twisted upon itself and turned the memory of Aiden over in her stomach a physical flip that jolted her. Flushed; instantly, she turned away, momentarily, and turned back.

His words continued. Finally and simply he spoke of the time he tried to buy drugs and got taken – the way he got home and found out it was Alka Seltzer. A simple story. A simple save. Apparent relief as he exclaims: "I was beat in the street!" smile perking his angelic face. "That's what we used to say back then, *'beat in the street.'* Happened to me twice, once in Oakland in '88 and once back in Harlem. Got home and found out it was bogus. I was kinda glad – why would I do that after all those years? I guess I was just bored. Never tried *that* again...." Voice trailing off at the word *again;* sigh escaping, as if thanking some imagined force of circumstance that had stepped in to help him; the fate of these circumstances unquestioned; the concept of no God unquestioned. Life being only life. As it is and real.

Here and now, she thought. *HEAR! and NOW.* She listened. Holding his hand – the thought wrapped itself around her. *Why has he been hiding himself?* She was compelled and she felt herself relax into his stories; as if they were *hers,* as well. A gift – to belie her youth with wisdom.

Youth! Ha! She felt ancient. As if she had heard these things before but in the past heard *nothing;* as if she knew *each word* before he said it; knew what to expect; what would come next. Her stomach opened up. And she could not get his music out of her head, circling as it was through her. Hell, she had given up being mainstream long ago. And these songs were breathing life into her. She had to sing them to *live*.

She had woken up this morning, to an amber sky filled with gray streaks etched upon hope. And for the first time in *months*, she actually felt an anticipation to her day. When he had arrived, she had been standing, waiting for him on the porch, coffee cup in hand; chocolate steam swirling into cloud-compressed air. Leaning against a post. No makeup. Brown hair down, long and streaming.

And Bobby saw: youth in her as he had walked up those stairs. Youth. And simplicity. A presence devoid of his long and tattered past.

She was clean. And wise. And strong. And he had moved towards her.

And as she had listened to him. She had decided. It was time to face her past.

CHAPTER FORTY

S HE STARED AT HIM from across the table; this slight, older man with gray curls and fine build. She stared at him and she sipped her chocolate and she waited for the waitress to leave. Remembering an earlier time when this had been her fate. Relieved it was no longer. She looked at him, and then she continued:

"Because she abused and neglected me as a kid. Because she made the choice to *go into the darkness* instead of *protecting* me. I believe that as she got older, she was without the ability to speak to me; to see me; to *deal with me*. And I had to make peace with that...." She could talk about it now. Talk about it without feeling that swirling sinking feeling pulling her completely down.

"And I have to admit, that when she got sick, when she got cancer, I did not feel empathy for her. At all. I wanted her to die. And I wanted to feel *guilty* about it. But I couldn't. It was my true feeling. I felt she deserved it. And then I felt she deserved more than death – she deserved to suffer.

But then, when I got sick, something broke in me. She came to me – only time she's come to see me in fifteen years – she thought she was losing me; and she let her guard down and she told me how *sorry* she was for the way she treated me. She did not explain *why*. I was among the dead when she did this – I think she was panicking because she thought I was going to die. But I saw, for a moment, *something* in her eyes. Something behind the darkness and the fear and the hatred I had always seen. *Something....*" Her voice trailed off. Bobby just looked at her. Blinked, she continued,

"And in that moment I let it all go. I just accepted it. And accepted her for the way she was. Who she was. Her limitations. And accepted the fact that perhaps she could not control it. She was mentally ill and needed treatment. It was something *beyond* her. And she was sorry, in her own way. And, well then, I just *accepted* the situation; the past; what had been. I accepted it and then I let go.

I wish I could say…wish I could tell you that I "forgave" her, but I can't say that I have…that I did. I think forgiving will take a long time; if forever. But I don't hate her anymore. I understand in a way. And I accept."

She said all of this straight-faced. Unblinking. Looking at him. Directly. Her brown hair falling gently to her shoulders. Her brown eyes smooth; even.

Her memory moved backward; going so swiftly; so easily into the past. A past it seemed of another life…a life she had fought so hard to forget. Unwilling; drifting…without her wanting it to.

Sixteen and in her own apartment…. Sixteen and on her own…. Sitting, alone at the edge of the bed as a kid. Trying to make sense of it all. She could not fathom the possibilities that lay before her, so subtly. The feel of the wind in her hair; a hand, placed gently upon her thigh.

Slowly; methodically, she brushed the hair from her face. Put everything back in place. Together again. Not lost within the confines of time, any longer. But placed; gently; sewn together.

And where was the world now? Now that she was lost and alone and no longer bleeding at the edge of a crevice; that craggy hill that used to be her salvation?

NO. She was only here. Alone. Sitting, at the edge of the bed; in this basement; with the dripping water. Slowly, dripping…drip, drip, drip…. Alone at 16.

And did she make the right choice? Coming out here like this? Is it better to be alone and afraid; then with someone and afraid?

Yes.

UNCHAIN MY HEART

And strangely…strangely…she had a strong *faith* in what was to be. A strong faith in that which was to come to her. A faith.

She did not know where it came from. She did not know why it was there. But it lingered; deep within her breast. Alone and tainted. Yet beating; subtly.

Subtly…subtly…a word she felt; heard; said, often.

Subtly.

For what had it been before she left? Before this time when she felt ancient and somewhat wise and scared and isolated, yet protected, somehow. What had it been? And why?

The face flashed before her again; and she cringed at its memory. Mother…mother…protector of all. *But why was she so filled with* hate *for me? I do not understand it.*

Tasha shook her head, slowly. Shook it and let her brown bangs fall slowly, again onto her face. Shook it and shook herself back to reality.

What to do? What to do? She looked around her new room slowly. She let the light shine down on her; slightly from the high window above. She tried to feel *pride* in all she had done so far. Removing herself from that environment. She had done the right thing.

And school…school…something she should be doing. But she felt so different from all the other kids. So different. She did not want to go. She did not have to go. So she stayed home.

Violin, sitting, against the wall; her savior. The one thing *pulling her forward.* What was this yearning that she did not yet understand? What was the *one thing* that would make her mother understand? – That she was *not a bad person!!* No!

Tasha took another deep breath. She reached for the cookies that lay under her sparse bed. She took one out; nibbled it slowly. Reached up and pulled down the top that had become too tight. Too much. She ignored it. Continued to eat slowly.

One, then another, then another. Three. Three cookies were enough. She opened a Coke; flipped the top; took a sip; lightly. Refreshing. Longed for chocolate; hot and warm – of the type her father would take her to have; when she and her mother had been fighting. Come home from work; smooth it out; smooth it out – "Tasha, let's go get an ice cream!" he'd say, so lightly, as if nothing in the world had been happening. As if the day had all just been a horrible dream. Something of *another* reality. Something that did not include him.

Can't think about that! Tasha thought now, reaching for her fourth cookie. *Can't think about that! That is not my reality. This is my reality. Must move forward.*

She picked up the backpack that was heavy with her books; picked it up, heaved it over her shoulder and made her way up the stairs, through the happy family's house, waving lightly; slight smile; permanent smile. Slightly far away. Impassive. Reserved. Carefully. She walked outside and to school.

A place she did not fit in. A place she did not want to go to. So she went sporadically. She did *just enough* to get by.

Why, why, why?????

She would make it through the day; make it through her classes. She was smart. She knew the ropes. She just didn't; it just didn't – *interest* her enough. It didn't hold her attention.

But violin did – violin she could do – violin she waited for after school. And to play together with her teacher; and the love and support she gave her. Encouraging her. Quietly; patiently.

This got her through her day (when she made it over to the large, brick structured building; which was not always....)

She shook her head and brought herself back to reality. A reality that *she* could control. *Well, that's what set me up for my eating habits now...*she thought as she purposefully and with a slight indulgent guilt took another long swig from her chocolate. She shook her head again, memory fog dissipating; she continued,

"You've told me so much about yourself, Bobby. Listening to you, what you've been through and then looking at you, what you have become because of it...well it's taken me away from my own problems. My own patterns. Thought patterns, I guess you'd call them. Brett's been great about it – solid as a rock...but...but..." she paused for a moment, looked down at her hands, "my mind has just sort of been rolling over around itself. An endless circle. Numb...." she drifted off.

Bobby nodded in indication for her to continue and she did, still surprised at her response to him. She looked up at him then, all guard down. Blunt. Direct. The way she had always chosen to deal with things. She was unable to soften the blow. To another. To herself. She did not have that ability.

"My mother threatened to kill me. Many times, growing up. It started as a young child – maybe four or five and it escalated. She would threaten me and would hit and scratch me and she would take a butcher knife and follow me around the house and push me. It was pretty consistent. She would say: 'I would rather kill you and go to jail then have to live with you....'" Natasha's voice drifted off....

"I know why people drink and do drugs, but for some reason, that wasn't what I turned to. I guess I'm comfortable suffering without softening the blow. I just have to stand there and take it.... But as a kid you're turned upside down. I have this weird recurring dream. Someone chasing, chasing me, with a knife, it slips deep into my side. I wake up. Covered in sweat...." Another deep breath...something she rarely would talk about, if ever, but feeling a strange and welcoming release. Not something she wanted to relive.... She was done. And why was it coming out now? Again? Why was she exposing herself this way to Bobby? – a man she had just met, really. She cleared her throat.

"I had a lot of fighting for myself and my own self-respect. I moved out when I was sixteen. Emancipated myself. Just couldn't take it anymore...." Her voice trailed off. She had said enough. For today. Enough. She breathed in deep again. A slight peace in her inhale. And she let it drift down into her.

And Bobby just accepted. As with all things. Accepted. And he reached over and he patted her hand. Again. That slight smile playing his lips. And he was silent. And they let it go. Drift away and dissipate into the air between them.

CHAPTER FORTY-ONE

ANOTHER DAY AND THE SUN is beginning to set. *It has been a good day,* Bobby thought as he glanced at the amber rays sliding through the small slits in the blinds, casting angular shadows across the carpeted living room floor. Natasha had just left, her light footsteps still echoing in his ears, the light *slam!* of the screen door behind her; dusk descending. They had spent the afternoon together in this living room of his. Sharing. He did not tell her he was sick. He did not need to.

"You have cancer, Bobby. Prostate cancer," the doctor had said not two hours before her arrival. "You *are* older. Treatment may be difficult."

"What are my chances?" Bobby had asked; blankly; matter-of-factly. No feeling really in the question.

"We don't like to give such 'set in stone' prognosis's," the doctor said, "but let's just say it's *serious*. There are a few dietary and other changes you can make to prolong your life, *hummummm"* the doctor cleared his throat conspicuously, "and quitting smoking would be helpful." Obviously, Bobby noted, the doctor clearly emphasized those words. "And aside from that, you have the option of radiation treatment, there is a pill...but it will make you very sick. We need to weigh the consequences of this course of action against its possible benefits. We need to take some blood today, check your CEA count – we'll need to check that regularly, keep tabs on it if you will, along with CAT scans at regular intervals, make sure the cancer's not spreading. We may be able to get it under control; I'm not making any promises, mind you, but we'll need *your* cooperation." The doctor paused here, looked up from his notes, he'd been speaking without looking at Bobby and this bothered Bobby, this impersonal approach, the way the doctor did not look at him as he spoke these seemingly routine words. Words, he had presumably said hundreds, maybe thousands of times before.

Words that had no meaning for him.

Empty words. Bobby hated that.

"It may be prudent at this time to choose *that* course of treatment," the doctor concluded, as he neatly steepled his fingers, cleared his throat again matter-of-factly; and now, finally, looked clearly and intently into Bobby's eyes.

"Well, thank you then," Bobby said, clearing his own throat conspicuously and hopping up off the table. He shook the doctor's hand in his most formal professional manner and then purposefully walked out of the drab treatment room, and made his way down the long hospital corridor to the exit.

"Make sure you check in with Cindy at the front desk and make your follow-up appointments," the doctor called after him. "It is most imperative that we treat this *sooner* rather than later..." his voice trailed behind Bobby. Bobby did not turn around, just waved his hand behind his back slowly as if swatting a lazy fly on a hot New York day.

"*Stubborn little man,*" the doctor muttered to himself under his breath, as he prepared to see his next client, patiently waiting in the next room. "*Damned cancer....*"

Bobby walked out of the hospital and did not look back but drove straight home, went directly to the small closet in his bedroom and pulled out the little packet of pictures he kept there next to the iron vase and brass sculpture of the horse.

Natasha had arrived shortly thereafter to the quiet stillness of his little cottage. She had knocked timidly at first, then louder, afraid to wake him should he be sleeping. But, no, he was not sleeping. Just sitting silently in his one easy chair, staring at the half-closed slates of the beige blinds, folded packet in his lap, waiting. Not thinking. Mind clear. And he went to the door and let her in. Feeling happy. Content; peaceful.

He took her to his bedroom. Sat her down on the edge of the low-slung double bed, and pulled out the contents of that worn and neat packet. 8x10 photographs. One after the other he slid them by her. Black-and-white still life's of Harlem in the 1960's – "The Boy Behind the Bars" stopped him, he paused, "I like this one," he said, eyes belying his casual tone.

"It's haunting." Natasha stared at the picture, unable to tear her eyes from the bleak image. The youth gazing back at her; never wavering; round, warm, brown eyes absorbing. Intently.

Young black boy, maybe twelve or thirteen years old – staring out past the camera. Vacant. Yet intense. Face partially in shadow and captured behind a series of slashed, steel bars. He is between the bars and the concrete of the building behind him and he seems to say: "I will inherit all this: This turmoil; this change; the weight of your revolution is upon my shoulders. And I accept it. I am young. I am weary already. And I accept my fate." A slight heaviness and intensity hangs upon the captured image – magnified by the absence of color; and it springs towards her. *Black against white.* She pulls away.

He pulls more photos out of the packet, one after another, slowly. This capturing of images his part-time hobby – something he used to do in his spare time in the 60's and early 70's. Shots from Harlem and then from California: the homeless man laying in the gutter in front of the Metropolitan Hospital – unnoticed; people walking by without looking. The lone cat in a small garden somewhere away from here fixed its stare upon Natasha; then another; it has turned away.

And now Bobby is safe here in this little cottage, and there are no more pictures. He is done. Left with his reminders and mementos. The Steinway piano with the simple black wood bench. The piano bench that held his music for so many years. Music that just sat there, waiting. Music he had forgotten he'd written.

Later he and Natasha are sitting side by side on that piano bench, thumbing through sheet after sheet of music. He pulls out his little shoebox of cassette tapes, a glory to his past. Natasha looks at them blankly for a moment.

"Remember? I don't have a cassette player, Bobby," matter-of-factly said, for it is the truth.

A smile. Bobby reminded, once again how things change so quickly it seems. Change, yet stay the same. He had only recently purchased a CD player and it had taken him months to get used to the mini records he would play. Tiny little disks in their tiny little boxes.

He preferred cassettes. And he had three cassette players in his place.

"Remember, I told you, I have one you can borrow," he replied immediately, almost too quickly, as he reached toward the window and grabbed his newest purchase with a spitfire agility that belied his current diagnosed condition: a combo cassette deck with CD player; a bulky contraption that he'd instantly fallen in love with a year earlier.

"You'll never use the cassette deck," the young male salesclerk had said authoritatively after he'd hunted down Bobby's seemingly odd request, "I'm surprised Audiovox even makes them anymore – I don't even know if it will record...."

Bobby looked at the box. Excited. A new cassette deck. He had two small units at home, those rectangular flat models with the large flat buttons at the front. But this one – this one – would be perfect.

"Ah, here it is, yes, you *can* record – wadda y'know..." the youth had said, whistling under his breath, clearly fascinated by the ancient contraption. "Ever checked out an iPod? If you're into music, well; you *definitely* need one of *those*...." But by that time the sales boy had lost Bobby's attention and he was quickly heading towards the cash register tenderly carrying his bulky box.

And there he was, less than a year later giving his prize to Natasha.

"Take the cassettes home, play around with them, *listen*...." Bobby was still clearly and silently surprised at himself for just continually handing those cassettes over to Natasha. Cassettes that had been sitting in his closet and on dusty shelves for years – how many? Twenty, twenty-five, thirty? He hadn't written a song; hadn't had an urge to. Piano just sat there, a memorial to his past.

Photos upon it. Bobby with Duke; Bobby with Ruth Brown; "Unchain My Heart" words and music, picture of Ray Charles on the cover of that sheet music; brown and worn. No urge to sit at that piano bench and write. No urge whatsoever. Until Natasha.

And the *giving* of his music to her.

Her voice had returned. Bigger. Deeper. *More soulful*, Bobby thought now.

Loss and tragedy having a way of *commanding* and then *transforming* you. Bobby knew this more than anyone.

And how long had it been, now since he first met Natasha? Since *she* transformed *him* with her light and her love? There was no time when he was with her.

But the day had slipped by too quickly and Natasha was gone. He glanced now out the one window set low to the right of his bed and noticed the orange streak etching its way across the blue-gray sky, signaling sunset. Slowly, methodically he removed one shoe and then the other, leaving his still clean white socks on. Content again with the hours he had spent with her, he lay down in this small room. Not bothering to remove his jacket. Not bothering to turn down the covers. He set his head gently back on the white cotton pillowcase; felt the pillow deflate slowly as he sank deep within the crisp folds; feathers spread like a fan beneath his weight – hair reminiscent of the small fro he wore in the mid-seventies. Fingers entwined across his gut, one leg crossed over the other. Eyes closed.

Sweet, sweet relief. He is at peace.

———

Natasha grabbed Fontana and hugged her, "This is our big night, Honey," she said, smile spreading wide across her face. Beaming. She looked at her lovely daughter.

"Ah, Mom, I think it's *boring...*" Fontana said. Suppressed smile of her own making its way across her flushed cheeks. She fingered the small, gold heart-shaped locket which hung around her neck. The one Claire had given her earlier today, sitting on the outskirts of the lunch area, balancing their butts precariously on the edge of the metal cafeteria-style tables. Holding hands, while Claire spilled out her secrets, then slowly took off the gold chain that hung around her neck, small heart dangling by its rounded arched top at the bottom of the chain; balled it up in her fist and handed it to Fontana.

"Here, this is for you," Claire had said, a forcefulness in her voice that Fontana had never heard before, "I want you to have it, my mother gave it to me before she died — I, I hardly remember her, but I do remember her blue eyes. And the way they watered before she closed them that night while she was lying in bed." She looked away, blinked twice and then looked back at Fontana and continued, as if striking up a conversation they had started years ago, as if Fontana had *asked* her to tell this story, *asked* her about her mother, though she hadn't. But this time, for some reason, Fontana kept her tongue silent. She stared back, an indication for Claire to continue, but Claire was not looking at her, she was looking way *past* her, into the distance of her childhood.

"It was raining," she continued, "that's all I remember.... And my dad, standing there in the corner — even then he scared me, and I was only four or five. He left me alone, sitting by mother. She had a blue nightgown on — she'd just handed me the necklace," Claire wiped her eye with the back of her hand, though there was no tear there, and smudged a small smear of dirt above her brow, the first dirt Fontana had ever seen on her.

"Made my dad get it out of her dresser drawer, which he did, and then he just went back to the corner of the room, and stood their quietly, in the shadows with his arms crossed — and he leaned back into those shadows, kinda like he was trying to get *lost* in them; disappear. And he still didn't s-say anything and my mom bunched the n-necklace up in her fist and she handed it to me and s-said…" Fontana looked deeply into Claire's eyes. Claire had all the mannerisms of someone who was crying, the shaking, hunched shoulders, the stuttered speech, but there were no tears. Her eyes were dry.

"She s-said," Claire sniffed, "'This is 'cuz I love you, hunny…wear it and think of me — I'll always be with you, even if things get rough, re-member *you are strong*. Not weak. Your beauty is a seducer to men, like mine was; protect it. But learn to love. *Oh...'*" Claire coughed slightly, inhaling sharply.

"She'd coughed then, on '*Oh...*' I remember that so clearly. And she closed her eyes and I thought she'd died – she was *so* pale, and she hardly moved.

"But then she finished – and she s-said: 'You will always have my love. Hopefully you will find love in the world. It is the greatest of gifts. If you find it – treasure it. It is rare....'

"And then she died. With my heart necklace still in her hand. Her fingers still curled around it. And I pried it from her fingers and turned to my dad," Fontana arched her eyebrow at this description, inquiring, and Claire responded acknowledging: "I know I 'pried' it because my dad used to tell the story at dinner parties – how I 'pried' the necklace from my dead mother's hand. And he would laugh. Like it was a *funny* story." Fontana gazed steadily at Claire, not wanting to move, watching intently the silent pain move deep behind those porcelain eyes. Claire blinked again, once.

"After I had the necklace I turned to my dad, but he did not move. He just stood there. And I couldn't tell if he was crying, his face was so hidden in those shadows. And I wasn't crying. I didn't feel anything. Nothing. I have never cried. I don't want to.

"But I think you are the love my mother told me about. And I want you to have this...." And with that Claire had handed the necklace to Fontana. And Fontana had put it on automatically without thinking; without hesitation. And she had said nothing. But only thought silently to herself how much she hated Claire's dad – and how mean he was to her. And she mused; bewildered – she had mistaken Claire's continuous silence for stupidity. And in that moment felt so grateful for her poor, albeit *loved* and sheltered life.

She saw her mother in a different way as the sun beat down upon their backs and heads that afternoon. She recognized, momentarily the love and shelter Natasha had given her. The protection. *A lioness with her cub.* She'd read that today during reading time at the library. *A lioness with her cub.* She turned again and looked deeply into the eyes of her new friend.

Yes, she'd seen something new in Claire today, her keen intelligence; an agile mind. *A lot to digest*, she thought as she looked forward to her walk home later that day, to her mother who sheltered and loved and protected her.

Anyone ever looked wrong at Fontana and Natasha was all over them. And Fontana had not even noticed.

So, how happy she was now, in her mother's arms, letting her smile spread slowly across her face, eyes lit up. Feeling it with her *whole* being, she hugged her mother back. "Okay!" Fontana said, grin spreading even wider. "I *will* go, Mom..." and with that she threw her arms even wider around her mother's neck and hugged her boldly; momentarily surprising Natasha.

Natasha pulled back slightly then hugged her daughter harder. She wasn't used to such covert shows of affection from Queen Bee, Fontana usually saved these physical displays for something extremely special; or when she was feeling especially vulnerable after a tantrum or escapade and momentarily reverted to the small child still lingering somewhere in her ageless soul. This hug was an unexpected surprise and seemingly for no reason.

*Everything is going to be okay...*Natasha thought to herself.

Everything is going to be okay.

———

Somewhere in the distance a dog barked. And Bobby rolled over in his bed. Once. And groaned. Once.

No thoughts as he fell into sleep.

CHAPTER FORTY-TWO

THE MIRROR REFLECTED Natasha's nakedness. Face devoid of makeup she reached for a pot and sponge and began to apply a neutral shade of foundation. She stopped for a moment, feeling she had all the time in the world, though she was due to go on in less than an hour, and patted her flat belly and smiled silently to herself.

Loss, she still felt the loss – but the dull, constant ache had receded. It no longer bothered her in a strange and ethereal way.

And her voice, had returned, soulful and resonate; it came from her gut now; some deep welling within her that grew stronger with each song.

She and Bobby had been working on his songs and tonight was the first night she would perform them live. She was going to perform "My Magic Tower," a song Bobby had written long ago and that she had fallen in love with.

She'd had a sold-out show at Yoshi's in Oakland just a month earlier – a jazz club that many of the greats had recently performed at – Diana Krall, Herbie Hancock, John Lee Hooker (*well, he wasn't jazz*, she thought ever in her logical and attention to detail way, *but great blues all the same, and definitely a legend*) Oscar Peterson, Nancy Wilson, Bruce Hornsby, Charlie Hunter, Billy Higgins; the list went on and on.... She was nervous, yet calm and a high anticipation colored her cheeks. Slightly flushed, her eyes sparkled.

She lifted the auburn lip liner from her green makeup case and with one smooth motion lined her lips; first the underside of her full, bottom lip, accenting the center to enhance its fullness, then the bow of her top lip, lifting the liner up as she applied the line; *only enhance not overly define,* the reprimanding voice ringing as ever in her head. She lifted her lip brush and dabbed it lightly into the mauve, caramel lipstick, applying it deftly, then pulled her wand of gloss from the top shelf and applied a light layer, smashing her lips together twice to spread the effect.

Her eyes were nicely rimmed in kohl liner and her lashes fringed with dark mascara. Her hair was down and straight. Hanging halfway down her back. No bangs. She had let it grow.

Rummaging the bottom of her case, searching for the brush, her fingers brushed against the corner of a small, soft piece of shiny blue silk – silk that had been lodged behind the bottom rack of makeup trays, stuck there for how long? She gently tugged the corner and out came a single long blue ribbon, slightly tattered from age and the pull. It was the ribbon Fontana had given her that Christmas seemingly so long ago – another lifetime; the ribbon she thought she had lost that dark night. She was surprised to see it; had almost forgotten about it really. Memory flashed to that makeshift dressing room at The Stagecoach. Fontana so small and silent, asleep on the floor. That strange but somewhat kindly-seeming janitor that had held his hand up to wave goodbye as she had stormed out.

All these things she saw now through the fabric gauze of hazy misinterpretations. And she smiled to herself. And picked up the ribbon. And tied it gently around her small wrist. Blue and forgiving. It begged for formality. Sensuality. A softness she had never felt; yet was forced upon her.

She looked straight at herself in the mirror and blinked her chocolate brown eyes. Then blinked again, watching her thick black lashes bump up against each other. She shook herself to the present. She smiled again.

A spray of perfume under each arm and onto her navel, a routine she had long ago concocted before a show – at least if she should sweat, which she knew she would under those lights, well, at least she'd smell good – though who was going to bother smelling her up on stage she had no idea. But, really, the perfume was for after the show when she was greeting fans and possibly still perspiring – well, at least if she should feel the need to perspire, which she was sure she would, it would not stink. *"God. . .my mind is rambling. . .!"* she spoke aloud to no one and stopped the circle of her thoughts cold.

PART III - BOBBY & NATASHA

The band was onstage warming up, she could hear the *eek eek* of the violin, an occasional crash of a symbol, abstract guitar riffs drifting under her closed door. Fontana was out in the audience with Brett. *Brett...* *Brett...*she thought to herself for the umpteenth time. A love that had been renewed had faded again. The baby had died and brought them back together. Taught her to love; to *let go* and let another care for her completely. And again, after a year and half, they had drifted apart, the same things that had come between them before — just a lack of common ground, common thinking. They'd had some good times together; *nice* times. But nice times just weren't enough. She needed more. And that lack of mental connection; *not being in the same place*, well to be with someone *forever* in that place, well that could be just as painful as other forms of pain.

But at least this time, the friendship would stay, in a sense, she knew. The friendship would stay. And perhaps that was the reason for all of this. To not part in anger. And they would always have the shared memory of Aiden. She had rolled these thoughts over and over again in her mind these past few months. Rolled them over and put them away — in a tiny crevice carved into her brain.

So many unspoken words had lingered in the air between them. Dead air. Muted.

Yes, he too, had wished to move on.

So he'd packed his things and moved out and left her and Fontana sweetly and sublimely alone in their little apartment.

They'd hugged, and vowed to stay friends. And even Fontana had hugged Brett goodbye, and in his departure had finally offered the poor guy some warmth.

And still she felt badly, why? He had tried to be what he thought she needed and yet, he would never be enough. Something had stepped in and saved them. Her child had saved them. Aiden had saved them.

And Natasha had immediately found the cutest little Victorian apartment across town for she and Fontana and their new life, with lots of corners and a beautiful yard. A place she could stay for a long time. A place she could get lost in. Oh, her soul was so ready to be free. She was tired of tying herself in chains of restraint. She wanted to *live*. And *experience*. She wanted to lose herself in the corners of that small Victorian house with its angles and expectations and secrets....

"Five minutes, Tasha," Eddie, the dark, curly-haired backstage hand called out casually from behind the half-open dressing room door –

"Shit, I didn't even hear the door!" Natasha jumped, startled. She was so deep in her revelry she had missed the knock.

"Sorry, Tasha, didn't mean to scare you, but you should probably get backstage – you've got five before you're on. Bobby's already back there."

"Okay, right – be right there. Thanks, Eddie. T-Thanks."

Was she stammering?? How ridiculous. She stood up and smoothed her black, stretch flared pants and pulled her black knit top down to accent the line of her waist. Her breasts, ripe and full, strained against the stretchy cotton of her top. Fuller, after this pregnancy – a change she liked and accepted, her womanhood accentuated, the secrets of her womb exposed. Not afraid of her sexuality. She felt a new power surge through her; one she had not felt fully before; one she had pulled back, she now realized. She simply had not had the time.

She had been too busy *surviving*. Now she wanted to *live*.

She made her way out of her dressing room, down the hall and towards the back of the stage.

"The show went well, didn't you think?" Natasha looked straight at Bobby as he sat across from her at his small kitchen table.

Bobby looked back, blankly. His mind had not been clear lately and while Natasha was living off the high from last night's show, he was still feeling its effects.

He'd been losing weight recently, and although already thin, his doctor had suggested cutting out all sugar – "just in case...." Bobby knew what this alluded to, "just in case" he was heading for diabetes, a national epidemic, as he saw it, but something that had never run in his family. But, he had followed doctor's orders and cut out sugar and white bread, which only seemed to increase his weight loss. He replaced the apple pie he used to enjoy occasionally for dessert, with fruit. He made the most of his fruit, usually an apple, peeling it slowly with his sharp paring knife, watching the small, red and white curls drop from his knife to his round plate; savoring each slice as he cut it away from the core, attempting to extrapolate the memory of his cherished apple pie; the aroma of which used to induce the Pavlovian memory of his mother's apple pie, which was pure *heaven*. It was unsatisfying. But he wanted to live.

"Bobby?" Natasha was looking at him with concern. "Bobby, did you hear what I just said? You were great up there, really *great*," she gushed. "The audience *loved* you. You got a *standing ovation*. How great is *that*?" Natasha silently and momentarily rebuked herself for saying "great" three times in the same sentence, but *hell*, she was excited. She wanted to let her guard down. He *was* great. Although he had not performed in over thirty years, when he got up there on stage and sat at that piano, it was as if he were alone up there; alone in a solitary light made only for him. Even if he didn't believe in God – she knew, without a doubt that the heavens shined their light upon Bobby Sharp.

Bobby blinked. And tried to clear his head. He looked straight at Natasha, flushed in her exuberance. And felt happy for her. Him – he'd done this before. It was nice. The attention. And although he had left his music behind years ago, he had felt a part of him flick to life as he sat on stage at that piano. So natural; as if he had never been away; memories of Harlem tickling him as his fingers hit those keys, and in the dim lights he thought he saw familiar faces haunted and staring back; the glare of the amber strobe stroking velvet fingers upon his cheek. But then his eyes had adjusted and he had seen only the quiet, well-heeled white crowd waiting in anticipation; expecting; not knowing what to expect; his hands to the keys. Playing. Croaking out his songs in an unsteady voice. No one seemed to notice this limitation. He didn't fight it. He had never "fought" his fame. Nor doubted his small success. Only accepted it. And then thrown it away.

He looked now straight and intently into Natasha's deep eyes; at her flushed face. At her earnestness and excitement. Saw her *hunger* for life. He knew *she* would never throw it away. And he made a decision at that moment. A decision known only to him. A decision that would color the landscape of Natasha's life forever.

Natasha reached over and took Bobby's hand, concern in her voice.

"Bobby, you all right?"

"Oh, yes," he said, smiling warmly at her. "I'm fine. Just fine." He took a long sip of his now lukewarm coffee, something his doctor said he should not be having – *damned doctor!* He purposefully took another long swig.

He patted the bulge of cigarettes in his pocket. Safety.

"Just thinking about the past." Blinking again. Clearing the haze in his head. "Just thinking about so many things, how much time has gone by. It goes so quickly, you know…so quickly. My time is going so quickly."

Natasha saw the sadness in his eyes. No fear. Just a sadness; tinged with wisdom – and a recognition.

He brightened.

"The show *was* good last night, wasn't it?" A small, secret smile played the corners of his lips and his brown eyes sprang to present, the words escaping his mouth more quickly than he had intended, "but don't know if I want to do *that* again."

Natasha just looked at him, knowing Bobby too well to take him seriously. He loved the stage, she could see that. He'd perform again. But first, they needed to get into the studio and record some of those songs. "Show me some more of your stuff, Bobby…."

And before the words were out of her mouth he was up, with an agility he had not shown just moments before, and heading towards the piano. He carefully lifted the solid lid to the square, black piano bench, stroked the worn, black wood momentarily, memory in his touch; and then pulled a stack of lead sheets from the top of a large pile. "I have more in there," he said, motioning towards the closet in his small bedroom, "and cassettes over there," he said again, pointing towards a small white bookshelf to the right of the piano.

Natasha knew this, they'd gone through this routine last time she was over. It was getting to be a habit. She smiled; encouraging. Couldn't wait to see what other treasures he was going to pull out and had probably, in her best guesstimation, already gone through the stuff he was showing her last evening after coming home from the show....

"But, we'll start with these." His voice was firm; final. Resolved. Authoritative. Natasha continued to watch him; amused, and then moved towards the piano, sitting cross-legged on the floor at his feet; staring up at him like a teenage girl in the 50's. He tenderly placed the worn and yellowed lead sheets on the piano ledge and positioned himself to play, easily slipping into his seat. This was the second time he had sat at this piano bench. The second time in the last thirty years. He ignored this. It felt natural; as if he had never left. His old friend.

Time passed unnoticed as each song rang from his fingertips and out into the still afternoon air. Perfectly concise. Transported, she listened without speaking and worked out arrangements in her head, humming along as he played, feeling as if she already knew the songs, though she was certain he had not played them for her before. And she knew, because Bobby had told her, that this was the first time that *anyone* had heard many of these songs – little tunes he had cooked up years ago while sitting alone at this same piano and then shoved and forgotten into shoeboxes and drawers. She mentally began compiling a list of musicians to contact, her practical, business side clicking to life. This deserved the full production. It needed horns, piano; *the works*. But she said nothing. She listened.

Afternoon descended imperceptibly, tamarind sun sliding through pale half-closed blinds, casting awkward shadows about the now gloomy room. Her legs ached and she glanced at her watch nonchalantly, a subconscious habit of checking time, *almost 3:00 p.m.!* – they'd skipped lunch and today was the day she picked Fontana up from school. *Shit!*

Though Fontana had begged, she was *not* going to walk home every day, no matter her age – "Twice a week. That's it," Natasha had told her firmly. Especially since her walking involved a short bus ride. She knew Fontana enjoyed the independence of walking home alone, but Natasha just couldn't let her do it every day – she was too young. There were too many variables.

"I've gotta go, Bobby," Natasha said suddenly, jumping up, running to the kitchen, hastily grabbing her purse and keys from the kitchen table where she had thrown them earlier that morning and heading for the door.

Bobby looked up startled. He was right in the middle of a song he'd forgotten he'd written. Lost in hazy memories, happy to have company. "Oh, okay, then," he said, mid-note, as he got up, with decidedly more effort this time.

"Sorry to run out like this, don't bother to walk me to the door, really," she called behind her, glancing momentarily at him as he struggled to get up off the piano bench. Felt bad for making him get up like that, shook it off. "I have to get Fontana from school. You understand...? I don't want to be late. She hate's it when I'm late. I try not to be." Voice urgent; *consistency in the little things*, if she could give Fontana consistency in the little things it would counterbalance all else. She firmly believed this. She moved hastily through the front door that somehow Bobby was already standing next to, and gave him a quick peck on the cheek – a silent sprite, holding the door open for her. His agility constantly surprised her. Almost seemed as if he floated from place to place....

"Thanks, Bobby!" she yelled behind her as the weathered screen slammed and she bounded down the two military-green concrete steps of the tiny square porch. "Thanks! I'll call you! I've got lot's of ideas...we'll talk...." By this time she was at her car. She hoped Bobby had heard her. She'd call. And explain again. She wasn't so sure about his hearing.

Bobby just stood on the small walkway leading to the sidewalk, and waved. He'd heard her perfectly. But he liked to keep her guessing.

Fontana has been unusually loving, Natasha thought as she drove quickly along the streets of Alameda. A slight drizzle had begun and she maneuvered her little car towards her daughter's school, determined to get there before Fontana emerged and had the urge to begin her walk home alone, something she seemed to love to do. To tell the truth, part of her hesitation in letting Fontana walk home was in the *letting go* of her. She knew she was growing up, would no longer curl up in her lap on impulse now and then and let Natasha wrap her warmly up in her arms.

She was halfway through twelve; gangly and ever-aware of her changing body. Soon thirteen and then what?

Natasha had already heard and read horror stories of perfectly normal adolescent girls turning into unrecognizable monsters – with erratic mood swings and intense hormonal changes, and endless battles about what to wear.... *But Fontana's going to be different, right?* Natasha thought to herself with a smile. Still, her daughter's uniqueness brought a smile to her, and still it surprised her. She had stopped asking questions long ago; wondering what was "normal" – *What I see as normal; that is it.* She blinked rapidly. Feeling a confidence in her decisions, something that cemented itself within her gut. A swallow over a throat whose words had been strangled out of her once; but no more. A slight insecurity that had disintegrated more and more with each black and blue setting of the hazy sun over the distant lights of San Francisco. A sturdiness that engulfed them both now entirely.

No, to tell the truth, she had a certain calm resignation about her daughter.... *An Indigo child*, her father had once said. *A child sent to this Earth to help change the world.* Well, Tasha thought her dad had gone just a little too far with that one, and she still firmly rejected all that spiritual mumbo jumbo, but she felt, and perhaps it was only foolish mother's pride, but she felt that Fontana had something special to offer this world. Fontana had a *strength*; a *calmness* Natasha had never possessed in her youth.

Natasha was removed, yes. And used to easily covering up her feelings. And she did not feel she was easily hurt. But she was sensitive. Deep down inside, Tasha had to admit that she had a *sensitivity*. Perhaps it was her artistry that cursed her with this weakness. She had long ago stopped trying to figure it out; or fight it. If she felt it, she felt it – she just tried not to show it.

But Fontana, ah, she wished she could have been more like her daughter when she was young. Decisive. She had a clear view of who she was. And Natasha knew that in the long run Fontana would be okay. Natasha's heart was clear; there were no worries for her daughter imbedded there. No thump of regret. She pushed her high-heeled foot on the gas peddle decisively; as if the speed of the car on the slick black tar road would bring her farther from her past. No, there were no worries deep down in *her* heart.

But damn anyone who should try to hurt my daughter! Natasha thought suddenly, anger flashing hard in her heart. An anger that came from nowhere and was not provoked. Her fierceness surprised her now, as always. She lifted her foot off the gas and willed the hammer of her heart to slow to the rhythm of the ballad playing on the oldies radio, slowly sucking cool wet air deep into her lungs. She knew her eyes were dark and almost black, as they always were when anger ensued. She relaxed her grip on the steering wheel and pulled carefully around the corner at a reasonable speed and slid to a stop in front of the school to wait in line with the rest of the parents and carpool moms eagerly scanning the horizon for their offsprings' arrival...but until then...a moment of peace. The rain had dampened the red trim of the gray building and she watched its shimmer in the silver-clouded afternoon light.

"Aahhhhh...." a sigh that was audible and loud, she leaned her head against the high back of her seat and closed her eyes for just a moment before glancing at the clock: 2:59 p.m. She had just one minute before the bell rang. One minute to calm completely down. One minute to realize that she was really hungry and had forgotten to eat that day – *again*. Maybe she and Fontana would go over to the Pasta Pelican on the Marina, a favorite little Italian restaurant of theirs right on the water. Fontana loved it, because she could look at the boats for hours.... *Something about Fontana and boats, fascinated her since she was a little thing, would ask questions for hours; ask when they could go on one....* Yes they'd go for an early dinner, just the two of them, like they used to do. Yes, that would be fun....

CHAPTER FORTY-THREE

B OBBY LAY ALONE on his bed in his small cottage. Sock covered feet crossed one over the other. Hands folded together, fingers entwined, lying neatly over his firm abdomen.

He closed his eyes. And breathed deep. Pain in his lungs; tiny needles that dazzled his intake. Felt like glass, really. *Not entirely an unpleasant experience,* Bobby thought. *Yes, I am a twisted soul...*he thought again, and laughed to himself, the laugh getting caught in his throat, a slight scratchiness that had been with him for twenty years.

Had the cancer spread?

From his prostate to his lungs?

"It is only a matter of time," the doctor had said, matter-of-factly. "You are, after all, a *smoker....*" The doctor had emphasized that word: "smoker" distastefully, as if it were Bobby's fault. Bobby resented this, but did not say anything. He was eighty-two. If he was going to die, he was going to die. No need to feel bad about it. And he didn't need to be judged.

Only a matter of time....

Bobby lay on the bed and rolled the pea of this thought slowly over in his mind; let it tickle the crevices of his brain. Strangely, after all his recent will to live and heart-wrenching outpouring of confessions to Natasha, he felt – Resigned.

Not afraid.

Yet, still clinging to the youth of her.

And of Fontana.

He remembered how surprised he was to see her walk in one day, backpack hanging heavy on her back; books loading her down; slightly sweaty and having trudged home from school. Opened the door to he and Natasha sitting together at the dining room table. He remembered the love that had instantly sprang to Natasha's eyes the moment Fontana had stepped through that door. The way she had quickly gotten up, forgetting everything else and moved urgently towards her daughter; the way her arms automatically opened, then pulled back; giving Fontana her space; the warmth that emanated back from Fontana – and the *trust*. He noticed this the most – the trust. A secure caring she had always been treated with that shined back from her to her mother.

All this Bobby took in instantly, and Natasha turned to him to introduce him and Fontana registered her instant recognition and surprise and ran to him and threw herself into his arms – and Natasha had stood there, dumbfounded and they had explained.

He could still hear Fontana's little voice ringing out in the still air – "*He's* the one I *told* you about Mom! He's the Wise Man at the bus stop."

Natasha just looked at her and then Bobby. Truly she thought Fontana had been making him up, he sounded so, well – *mythical* with his stories of birds and trees and personal power. And Fontana was so good with stories herself.

But, no, he was *real*. To both of them he was real.

Bobby watched all this, too, flick across Natasha's surprised face; watched her eyes widen and then narrow. Watched her watch them hug – and then release.

Really, it was not his place to hug her daughter. They had never hugged before. Fontana's warmth had surprised him.

Yes she had accepted him fully into she and her mother's lives.

Such a spark, that Fontana, Bobby thought now – *A real firecracker. She's really going to be something, give her mama a real run for her money.* "Well, she already *does* that!" He said these last words out loud, laughing again to himself, and coughing at the end, tasting the blood in his mouth; moving to get up to spit it out and then swallowing it instead.

He still had not mentioned anything about this to Natasha. He didn't want her to know. She was already so covetous of him and the last thing he wanted or needed was for her to favor him or act differently towards him because she thought his life was ending. Or that he "didn't have much time...."

He didn't want her telling anyone.

It was private.

His secret.

Something he would hold close to spur him through this final chapter of his life.

This chapter of recording.

And he was writing again.

Through all of his music ups and downs and hanging around, the failures and small triumphs, the one thing he had *never* done was to record and release his own album – *well CD now*, he reminded himself, slow smile descending. He'd recently composed a new song while tooling around on the piano last week and called it "New Horizon." He was excited about it. He'd shown it to Natasha and she'd been beside herself with enthusiasm in her own calm, even way. She'd confessed to him her nervousness at times; he'd been surprised to find she'd felt that, or more so, admitted to feeling this. She seemed so – well, *stoic* most of the time and he was beginning to wonder if anything truly rattled her.

She'd been working like a bee getting their recording sessions ready, one for him and one for her; all with songs he had written, most of which had not seen the light of day for forty years. Gotten together a group of great jazz musicians – been performing all over town and up in L.A. Had press at every event, all the major newspapers and the local ones too, more press than he ever got in his heyday when he was working with the greats.

He smiled at the irony of this.

The irony of life.

The sharp rap of knuckles on the door jarred him to the present and Natasha's smooth voice slivered through the mushroom of his thoughts. "Bobby?" She wiggled and then turned the front door knob, pulling it open and reaching for the screen. "Bobby? Are you in there? Are you ready?" she called in warning, afraid of walking in on him while he was getting dressed. His apartment was *so* small, the rectangular living room opening to the small square bedroom or vice versa and divided by an opening that looked as if it might have a sliding door between the two rooms – something hidden in the recesses of the old wall – but she'd never seen it, or more precisely, had never seen it *used*.

"Bobby?"

"In here," Bobby said, heaving himself forcefully up and off the bed, trying to hide the effort it took to perform this small and ordinary task.

"You okay?"

"Yes, yes, I'm fine. Just taking a little rest. Getting old, you know... bones don't work like they used to."

Natasha smiled at him knowingly. Bobby was nothing if not the *youngest* old person she'd ever come across. "Old" was definitely not a word she would use to describe him. She peered at him intently. "You okay?" she asked again rhetorically, raising her right eyebrow and squinting in his general direction. She thought she glimpsed a glimmer of pain in his eyes as he lifted his thin body from the bed; a slight clenching of his teeth; a wariness that had not been there before. She tensed; watching him closely. But then his eyes cleared, his mouth relaxed...easing into normal. He smiled at her. Auburn lips closed; firm. Taste of blood receding.

Natasha sighed. *Just my imagination...*she reassured herself. "Well, I've got everything set for today. Musicians are already setting up at the studio. We're recording at Fantasy Studios in Berkeley, one of the best in town. It has a rich jazz recording history; I thought it would be *perfect*. And Stephen Hart is going to be engineering and I'm going to be producing you! I'm *so* excited, Bobby, I can't tell you. And I feel so privileged to be able to be a part of this – you know that, right? These songs...these songs...they've just got to get out into the world." Bobby nodded imperceptibly, Natasha took a quick breath and continued,

"You remember Josh Hartnet, did all the arranging for the live shows? Well we'll use his arrangement on your one track, the one you just did. He's really young – well – twenty-seven, but an amazing arranger and piano player. He was great at the show didn't you think?" Bobby nodded again, walked toward the living room.

"We really lucked out. Everyone was available. I liked the song you composed last week – let's include that one too. Let's try to get that one down today if we can, while its still fresh...." Natasha continued to talk as she helped Bobby with his sweater and ushered him out the door, waiting patiently as he meticulously locked the door from the outside with his small, brass key.

She had begun to notice that he had kind of a thing with locks.

"C'mon Bobby, I'm driving, of course – Brought my car."

Bobby could clearly tell she was immensely proud of her used blue Volvo station wagon and made a mental note to buy her a new car for Christmas. Christmas was six months away, but in his mind the car was bought and the season over. She opened the passenger's side door and ushered him into the car as if she were ushering him into a stretch limo – with a grand flourish of her hand. *Ah, Natasha has a silly side,* Bobby thought, liking these daily Natasha discoveries. She never ceased to surprise him.

She jumped into the driver's side, kicked off her teal colored flip-flops, jammed her key into the worn ignition, started up, pushed the car into "drive," hitting and breaking one freshly manicured nail on the round black knob. "Damn!" she muttered under her breath and then quickly pulled away from the curb. "We're off!" She turned and smiled broadly at Bobby and glanced into her rearview mirror after the fact.

Bobby just sat quietly. And, as discreetly as he could, reached for the small bar hanging above the passenger's side window.

And held on....

The studio was dark and Bobby blinked. It had been a long time since he had been in a studio.

His bones ached.

He hated that.

Natasha had gone on in ahead of him and was already speaking animatedly with the musicians. Jon the engineer/co-producer sat at the large dark engineering board, its lighted dials and levels glowing in the dim room behind a clear-paned glass window. Dan the DJ sat behind the control board, earphones on, listening; waiting intently. His gaze followed Natasha discretely as she spoke and moved about the room.

"Ah, here he is," Natasha said, smiling profusely, as Bobby entered after her. "Bobby, I want you to hear what we recorded recently. Dan, hit "I Had A Feeling" on all speakers, let's give him the full treatment." Natasha was in her element now moving from the soundboard room towards Bobby. "It's just vocal and piano right now – You know Josh, right? Remember him? He was at the show. He arranged everything."

Bobby glanced up at her, he hated it when she told him things twice.

She continued, not noticing, "anyway, like I said its just a scratch: vocal and piano, but it will give you an idea. I *like it*, but tell me what *you* think...." She beamed at Bobby. She wanted his input, wanted him to feel comfortable with it – with these songs of his that she was singing, it felt so *right* when she sang this one, so *right*...she *knew* it was *damned good*. And she was excited. "Okay, Jon, go ahead. Hit it..."

I had a feelin' when you walked through that door / A lovin' feeling like I never had before.

Her voice wafted through the room and over him; he stood still; unable to move; mesmerized; once again.

That's why I ran to you right from the start / Offered you everything, including my heart...

Pure. Sweet. Cotton candy to his ears, bouncing off soft pillow walls and back to him.

I had a feeling that I couldn't control / A crazy feeling from deep down in my soul / To taste your candy kisses all life through / And share this love of mine with no one else but you...

286

He stood there in the middle of the room; stopped where he had entered, camel colored sweater dangling absently from his left hand. Listening.

It was magical.

Her voice. It had a *quality*; but more than that its pure resonance and feeling rang through him completely. *She has captured what I was feeling when I wrote that song....* He was unwittingly transported once again to Harlem; his apartment; the memories that had laid dormant for so many years floating up; round, wide smoke rings surrounding and seeping into him.

It is truly amazing.... With that thought he shook his head "no" to himself slowly, disbelieving what he was hearing; and then, without warning: SILENCE; loud, demanding and immediate. He blinked his vision hard – back to present and turned towards Natasha, imploring her with his gaze to break the stillness again with her song. For it was *her* song...now.

"You didn't like it?" Natasha asked, distress clearly evident in her tone; smile faded and concern crinkling the corners of her eyes, which were now morphing to deep dark chocolate, furrowing the smooth space between her arched brows.

Stillness.

Bobby cleared his throat.

"I like it. I like it. Just sort of took me by surprise. It's been so long since I've been in a studio. I'm a little rusty." He glanced furtively around the room, bringing himself back into himself. "It was wonderful, Natasha, just *wonderful*...." His voice trailed off.

"Really? You're not just saying that now are you? You know, *you're* part of this process too. We're doing this *together*. Anything you have to say, anything at all...any changes in arrangements," she glanced at Josh quickly and then quickly turned back to Bobby, "any vocal inflections you would suggest. I'm *completely* open. This is for *both* of us, Bobby. I just want to get these songs out into the world. I just want to do them justice. Tell me if I'm not, promise?" Bobby was silent. How could he articulate what he felt?

"Promise?" Natasha said again. Staring straight at him.

Wow, she can be intense. He brought the word straight from his Harlem past and let a hiss of satisfaction escape through the long, slow, cool whistle of pursed lips. A whistle that vibrated against him and sprang to life.

He liked that. He nodded. "Sure, Natasha, I'll be sure to do that," and smiled, half to himself; half to her.

Natasha came from behind the tempered glass of the control room and moved towards him, reaching out to gently squeeze his elbow. She nudged him towards the folding plastic chair along the back edge of the wall and in the corner of the room and discretely took his sweater from his hands…"I'll hang this here, Bobby," she said, as she reached up and hung the sweater on the sparse gray metal coat rack, its skinny mutilated arms pointing desperately towards a nonexistent sky. "Sometimes it gets cold in here, gotta keep the equipment from getting overheated, you know. If you need it, grab it. But you sit down now. It's going to be a long day, and I don't want to wear you out before we have to!"

She laughed quickly at these words. A little nervous, but her excitement returning. "To tell the truth, I can't wait to get started! Enough of this playing around. Bobby, I want to record "Turning Point," I liked that one and I think it is apropos for the situation, don't you? Josh can help with the arranging – that is if you want it…." Bobby gave her a glance, *what was it with her and repeating that Josh was arranging? he knew that.* He conveyed this silently to her, *no I am not stupid, and yes, I heard you the other two times you mentioned it.* She acknowledged, ignored, went on,

"Anyway, I liked it just the way it was for the show…hate to get you up again, but, come back here, you're going to have to come into the booth where the piano is – let's get it down while you're fresh. We'll just check levels quickly and then we'll lay your composition. Sometimes the first one's the best. But don't think about that. Just do what you do and play the piano."

She had him again by the elbow and was leading him to the other side of the studio where the piano was located, slightly enclosed behind a partial wall and also separated by glass.

"This piano bench comfy for you?" she asked solicitously. "Everything all right? Can I get you some water?" Her chattiness surprised her now as always. But at this point the project had a life of its own and it was propelling forward at a rate that left behind her outmoded insecurities and self-criticism.

"I'd like a little water if you don't mind," Bobby said. Patting his upper shirt pocket, looking for his cigarettes, and then remembering he had purposely left them in his sweater pocket and that he was no longer supposed to smoke.

"Sure, sure, I'll go get it. Josh, Jon – you want to make sure the levels are right so we can get Bobby down relatively quickly?" Natasha asked as she left the room and headed over to the small adjoining makeshift kitchen/lunch room to grab a cup of water from the cooler.

"Hey, I thought *I* was the producer here," Dan said, playfully. Natasha turned abruptly towards him, said nothing, turned away.

Frankly, there were already three producers on this project, she, Jon and Bobby, who she already knew she was giving "Executive Producer" credit to. They were *his songs,* ultimately *his* arrangements; *his* style – he was the main guy in her mind. But Dan was doing this project basically on spec. They'd kept in touch after her interview and she'd come to find out that he'd done a little producing of his own. Natasha had shown him some of Bobby's songs; what they were working on and he had been immediately taken, and the fact that Bobby had written "Unchain" for Ray Charles hadn't hurt either. They both agreed that the songs had a timeless quality; that they needed to be released – *somehow*; they were both on the same page basically. Frankly, Natasha could see that the songs moved him and she needed and wanted this guy on the project, call it a hunch; intuition. It just felt right. He had told her that he was doing this for "love," of the music that is; told her "any way he could help...." So she'd brought him on in and set him behind the board. He had a good ear; good ideas so far. *Producer...hmmmm.* Natasha turned back around and gave him a second instinctual glance but did not respond. She walked out of the room and to the cooler to get Bobby's water.

Natasha is definitely green, Dan thought as he watched her, *But God, that voice, she has* something *– a sad, clear, soulful quality to her vocals that belies her youth and compliments Bobby's songs in the most natural way.* He continued to stare at the little doorway she had just exited and realized with a start as she made her way back through it that he was still staring and he quickly bent his head to stare down the board as she returned and moved towards Bobby.

"Whoops," she said as she headed towards the piano and spilled a little of the water on the floor. She found Bobby with his fingers already poised over the keys – playing lightly, head cocked to the left, as if he were listening to something invisible and far away.

But, no, he was only testing the piano's tune. Making sure all was right with his notes, fingering the keys, tapping out the song he had instantly memorized while composing. "I brought sheet music for everyone," he said, authority tingeing his voice. Down to business. Then the quick smile and shyness.

This sudden change in Bobby momentarily surprised Natasha, she had only seen the shy, humble man who had offered her his songs. This new guy was quite an interesting fellow – *never ceases to surprise me…*she thought and sat down next to Dan behind the board.

Dan fidgeted with a dial and adjusted himself in his seat.

"Should we start?" Bobby asked, looking around the room.

Everyone jumped to attention.

"Sure," Natasha said. "Hit it boys…."

CHAPTER FORTY-FOUR

I T WAS RAINING OUTSIDE and Fontana pressed her nose against the warm glass of the school library window. She stared intently into the gloom hovering over the wet, abandoned lunch tables.

Despite the warm summer storm there was a definite chill in the air.

Claire had not come to school that day, nor the previous day. And Fontana was worried. And, she realized now, as she absently wiped her nose with the back of her hand, slightly lonely. After three years as best friends, she had gotten used to having Claire around. She *liked* it. Her still, quiet presence was comforting.

She fingered her locket absently.

Thunder clapped loudly in the background and lightning echoed off the metal angles of the benches and she remembered fondly the round of her beloved rings swinging forcefully in the wind of another storm; the way they'd met that day over the tanbark. Fontana watched the water spatter on the gray-black of the asphalt that now replaced the playground of another time; watched it soak partially into the black and disappear. This weather was not normal for Alameda.

She didn't like it.

———

Natasha returned home earlier than she had expected. She had a headache. Rare for her, she almost *never* got headaches. *Perhaps it is the pressure of the storm — some sort of atmospheric imbalance.* Her rational mind was quick to try to find a scientific explanation for this unexplainable event.

She wiped her brow slowly with dry fingertips. Her head was *throbbing*.

Perhaps she'd just take a little nap. It was gray and stormy outside, she wasn't due to pick Fontana up for a few hours. They'd finished up in the studio and the CD had gone to press.

Yes, she'd lie down – just for a moment.

Claire slowly packed her things. One at a time she put them in her big blue suitcase. It was time to leave, her father had told her. He'd been called to work in London. School year almost over and she doesn't get to finish *again*. School year over and she was going to have to start at a new school, *in another country*, where they do not know her *again*. She thought of Fontana. One small tear rolled down her cheek. The first tear that had actually come from her eye since, *since*.... She blinked it back. Choked back the sob that welled from her heart. Her father waited for her impatiently in the car. She didn't want to go. For the first time in her life, she had felt *happy*. And satisfied. And slightly content in her own way. She wanted to call Fontana, to say goodbye. But she couldn't bring herself to do it. What was she to say? *I am being taken away again. I have no roots again. I am losing a friend, my only friend*, again. It was too hard. It was not possible.

She clicked her suitcase shut, dragged it to the door and made her way down the curling staircase to Nanny, the one that had been through all this with her from the beginning it seemed, the only real steady thing in her life, who waited patiently for her at the bottom of those stairs. The tread was long; each step thumping beneath her foot. Each step heavy and recently unknown to her; this heaviness that seeped again into her being.

Hilga waited. Silver hair pinned tightly behind her head; neat bun. No slight curls like Fontana. Little waves of "dishwater blonde" hair that seemed to bother her so much; the description making Claire wince; but no, no self-consciousness there – only a matter-of-factness, an *accepting* of her limitations as well as her strengths. One of their many girl-talks, first on the playground and then later on those lunch benches; huddled together, nose to nose almost; their own little world.

And her mother…her mother…Fontana was *so lucky* to have her. So warm and free and loving and affectionate. How she yearned for that affection herself. Well, Fontana had given it in her own way and Claire had given her the only thing she had to give, really: her necklace. And she hoped Fontana would continue to wear it and remember her, always.

Her foot hit the bottom step. She swept her blonde hair behind her. Her dark dark lashes now fringed lightly with mascara, closed momentarily, then opened. She nodded for Hilga to let the driver know her bag was ready and he could put it in the car. No words. They never needed many words. Hilga knew.

The rain hit the large pane windows as she stared at the front door. Silently saying goodbye to this momentary life. The thunder and lightning now echoing off the sky, her goodbyes. She nodded to herself and stepped through that door. She let the rain hit her head as she made her way to the waiting car, alone, not wishing someone to cover her with an umbrella. Wet she was; the rain sliding down her face. Yes, these were her tears. This was her goodbye. This was her life. She stepped inside the car; to her father, who waited. And did not smile.

———

Thunder clapped in the distance, echoing off the walls around him and bouncing back to him its reverberation. Bobby lay on his bed alone. Cocooned in sound. Breathing in the rain. His window was open and he glimpsed steel lightning flashing in the corner of the sky; jagged knife-edge reflecting silver against the coasting blue-gray clouds.

He did not move.

He breathed in.

And released.

He had made a decision. He had one call to make. He got up from the bed went to the phone and dialed. He was old. He did not need much. It was done. Now, in his mind. Sweet, sweet peace.

PART IV – *The End of the Beginning...*

Somewhere in the past — a melody plays — long and lovely — a gentle etch upon the time that lingers, just above, and to the right, of our souls.
And it sings — soothing, continuously. And it molds our lives — with its song.

CHAPTER FORTY-FIVE

NATASHA STARED INTENTLY into the mirror. She noticed the few wispy lines faintly snaking their way from the outer corners of her eyes; accentuated by the loose powder she had just applied. She was aging and it did not bother her. She liked herself better, in fact. Gave her character, somehow. Proof of living. An imprint of past emotion and experience etched upon her skin. She ignored the television and magazine ads that tried to hammer into her brain that she must be flawless to be beautiful. Not for her — she was what she was. No panic about it; actually looked forward to aging somewhat wistfully...the letting go of the naiveté of youth; the marks of time and hopefully wisdom etched upon the contours of her youthful face. The duality of it gave her pleasure.

She was going to sing "God Bless America" tonight in front of a sold-out crowd. Over 50,000 agitated fans anticipating the Oakland Raiders football game at what was now called the O.co Coliseum in Oakland. She had to admit, though, she liked the old name better: *The Oakland-Alameda County Coliseum.* It had a certain ring to it, sounded more formal somehow; more imposing; more *proper*. Why every stadium had to be renamed after a major, boring corporation, she had no idea.

Her thoughts turned to Bobby — his presence tonight was something she looked forward to. He had quietly and without fanfare told her about his illness, and it was all still such a shock; something she could not fathom; nor believe to be true. The car he had given her had been too much, but she had accepted it. And then, after he had told her, right before that other show, he had quickly run next-door to the 7-Eleven and bought one

hundred lottery tickets and begun to hand them out to friends and strangers with a grin. *Just like Bobby,* she thought with a smile. *Probably out there
right now, handing out lottery tickets, one by one, giving the random chance to win,
the one in a million chance he got. Funny guy. Funny, funny guy.*

Yes, so she had accepted the SUV, but the cancer, no, she would not
accept that. He had told her the doctor had said it was serious, but that
he didn't think it was…he thought doctors were overrated and overcau-
tious and overly pessimistic. *He had told her he was fine.* The treatment
had worked. He was cured. He had become an integral part of she and
Fontana's life, *and it is going to stay that way, god dammit!* She shook her
head to herself – Bobby there to witness her rise, silently pushing her
on. Bobby there to watch her change and grow these past few years, the
twinkle in his eye ever-present; his silent nudging, the strength he con-
ferred in her just by his presence.

He saw his CD of original material only begin to sell well. This
seemed to be enough….

And her music career was taking off. Strangely enough, and she still
couldn't get used to it, though she had dreamed and felt it for so long:
She was making it. In her own right. Yet she still felt small in the face of
it all. Her pop/jazz vocals had found a niche and she was booked solid for
shows for the next year and a half. She and Bobby had even been featured
on the front page of the Calendar section of the L.A. Times, an article
by Don Heckman for a show they did out at The Vic in Santa Monica.
Great show; she had so much fun with him there. Her voice came out
easy; light; Bobby glowing as ever. She had watched the twinkling lights
reflect off the golden beach that warm L.A. evening; bare feet sunk deep
into cool sand; the sound of the surf crashing against the shore; round full
moon shining down the possibilities…. She consciously squeezed joy out
of every moment of it. She did not know how long it would last; if it was
a fluke; if she could count on it forever; much less *forever* – if she could
count on it next *year.* She only knew what was *now.*

Her thoughts turned to Fontana. *She's grown up so fast…*Natasha thought
for the umpteenth time. *So fast….* Now at fourteen, Fontana's inherent
wisdom gave her beauty. And her cocky unabashed self-assuredness had

melted into calm assurance. A clever quiet she carried with her and into all things. She was writing. Beautiful half-finished stories that she left lying around her bedroom. She had a knack. Natasha felt at times that she, as a mother, was groping blindly through these teenage years. Teaching by intuition, only. Hoping she was doing it "right." She wanted Fontana to make the most of her talent. Knew in her heart of souls that she would do everything in her power to help make it come true. *But is that always the best thing?* she thought now to herself. *To "help" someone achieve their dream? Does that dissipate it somehow?* Had anyone "helped" her? Her mother? Certainly not. Her father, by his presence, but he had a good knack of staying removed at just the right times. A presence she knew she could count on. She knew he knew he could have done better. She knew that he carried the burden of his perceived failures. But what he didn't see, *and perhaps,* Natasha thought to herself, *perhaps that is my fault too. My silence allowed him his self-flagellation.* No, what he didn't see was that to Natasha there was nothing to "forgive," though he begged forgiveness at times, it showed in his eyes. Quickly covered up by his words of support. But what he didn't see was that she loved him wholeheartedly. She forgave him his humanness. For she had the same human tribulation with her own daughter. Had she done the best job she could? Would Fontana someday ultimately forgive her for her selfish career motivations? Had she even noticed? Or was she like all children, silently accepting; because they knew no other reality? *The forgiveness of children likening to the amnesia of giving birth. Nature's defense mechanism.*

She dabbed some lipstick onto the inner part of her bottom lip and smacked her lips together twice.

Natasha was silently amused to watch Fontana do what she did best. Take the role of silent protector. As she had done for Claire. *Poor Claire.* Natasha always felt protective of her; concerned. And then she just disappeared like that and no one ever heard from her. Used to come over to their house to play, and then, later as the girls got a little older they would sit in Fontana's room giggling and supposedly doing homework.

*Yes, Claire was a quiet girl, shy, unassuming...*Natasha thought as she applied another light coat of mascara. Sweetly beautiful when she was younger and then as she hit twelve and then thirteen her beauty morphed into a stunning visual. Her gold hair a halo around those haunted blue eyes – Something she seemed unaware of; or uncertain of; or unable to control; somehow. Natasha could not quite put her finger on it. Not allowed to go out much, Natasha thought her only overprotected.

But then when she disappeared, *just disappeared without even calling to say goodbye*. Well, Natasha found it strange; and to see Fontana so silent and sad...it was heartbreaking. She realized how much Claire had helped Fontana through those trying times. Three long years had passed, but it had been a slow-heal, and she had been so *tired*; just so tired – and *empty*. Claire had been there for Fontana. Claire had helped Fontana. Claire had been a little golden haired angel.... So, fueled by a silent, gnawing guilt she had asked Fontana to go with her to Claire's house to check things out. Her home was about three blocks and around a few corners from them, a nice walk on an early summer evening; dusk just settling over the sky; not dark yet, days longer, but not as long as they soon would be. They both strolled, arm in arm that dusky evening, the purple shadows settling around them, Fontana silent and placing her head gently, yet only momentarily against her mother's shoulder from time to time.

Fontana had been so quiet as they had walked, and when she did finally speak, mentioned, almost absently; that Claire had never asked her inside when they'd get to her house after school; made Fontana wait on the porch while she knocked, *on her own front door no less*, and waited for the formally dressed maid to open it and let her in. Fontana described how she would stand on the porch and stare at the closed door long after it had quietly clicked shut.

And then, as they turned up that wide-flecked flagstone porch and stepped gingerly between the neat rows of cheerful flowers, she told her of the bruises she sometimes would see on Claire's arms...probably nothing she said. She'd never asked, she said. Claire had never said anything about it.

They had reached the landing then, and Natasha knocked firmly on the large and imposing forest green double door. No answer, just the hollow echo of her knock. So she rang the bell, twice, but still no answer.

All was still and strangely silent. So, giving Fontana a sidelong glance she tiptoed onto the perfect grass and tried to peek into one of the large, high windows, but the heavy crimson curtains were drawn. She felt the desertion. No movement. No life.

She remembered that day as if it were yesterday; as she squinted through the glare of the bulbs – The way they had marched right into the principle's office first thing in the morning. Told him how she thought it was very odd that after three years in a town, a little girl and her family would just disappear. That Claire's arms often had bruises. Never even called Fontana, her *best friend* (and only friend as far as she could tell) to let her know that she was leaving. It just wasn't normal. Natasha had had a bad feeling about the whole thing. Just a bad feeling.

The principal was cordial, but indifferent and disobliging. Told her they needed "proof" that something was amiss and no proof had been given.

"Claire's father was a well-respected man, *Ms*. Miller," he emphasized "Ms." as if it were a crime to be single. Natasha had stared back at him defiantly, unblinking. "He has been of great help to the school and took Claire out only because his business was taking him out of the country sooner than expected. He was quite distraught about it. And very sincere."

Natasha clenched her fists tight and squeezed her lips shut so that she would not scream at this idiot. He continued to speak, plaintively, as if placating a small child. "Mr. Simone left a generous donation for the school library, *one that is greatly appreciated,*" had he been referring to the fact that she did not donate enough time to the school functions and fundraisers? Things that she was constantly being bombarded with but never seemed to have enough time to fit in? He continued, "and one that is going to be used partially to improve the library, since Mr. Simone, pointed out, his daughter Claire was quite shy and loved to read and would miss the library and all her teachers." He waited for Natasha to respond and then stated vaguely that Mr. Simone had mentioned finding a lovely private all girls boarding school overseas, where she would get all the *nurturing and special attention* (he emphasized these words heavily) she needed – and then the whiny, sniveling principal had purposefully folded his hands together on his desk and stared, pointedly, at Natasha, silently willing her to leave. Natasha did not move. She bunched her fists tighter together and composed her rising temper.

He had then placed his hands, palms up, on his desk and stared at Natasha plaintively. Pleading silently: *Can't we just let this go? He was a nice man; you are a flustered woman. JUST LET IT GO.*

Natasha still said nothing; continued to stare him down, and then seeing that her staring was doing *absolutely no good* – she turned to leave, stating clearly, "Money solves *everything* doesn't it, sir?"

No response, of course. She motioned to Fontana, who had been sitting quietly in the chair across from the principal's desk, that it was time to leave. They made their way to the door. Natasha did not say goodbye. They left his office and then the building; Fontana walking silently behind her.

What Natasha did not know; what she did not see was that as Fontana walked behind her she had simultaneously experienced two conflicting emotions/reactions to her mother's behavior. The first had been *worried...worried...was her mother's behavior going to affect her grades?* Then she looked up at her mother, so protective and concerned over someone else, *who wasn't even her own daughter,* and she remembered the coldness that used to greet Claire when she returned home; and how Claire had been so warm and almost bubbly when she was at their house and how she had longingly looked after Natasha when she had left the room; and how she had told Fontana once: "You're *so* lucky! Your mom is *so* nice." Something Fontana had taken for granted. Something she had accepted as a given all her life. She had her mother. Her mother had protected her, always. Her mother had been there for her, always. Yes, she *was* lucky.

A gust of wind slammed the heavy school door hard behind them as they hit fresh air.

"Hmmmfff!!!" It was all Natasha needed to say. Fontana kept quiet.

They then drove directly from the school, northeast down Sandcreek Way toward Otis Drive, made a quick right; took Otis to Park Street, where they made a left, headed down to Encinal Avenue, took that to

Oak street made another right and landed in front of the Alameda Police Station at 1555 Oak, screeching to a halt. Natasha walked purposefully into the station with Fontana and filed a police report, and *finally, finally* felt that she had reached a concerned human. She gave all the information she had: which was just a name and address, really. Fontana supplied the detailed description of Claire.

It was all she could do. She felt only slightly better.

"Let's hit McDonald's, Hon!" Natasha said impulsively while a mischievous smile played the corners of her mouth. Normally, Fontana would object. It was a school day, it was almost lunchtime, and she had already missed most of her morning classes. But this new appreciation of her mother was welling over her, and she let it seep into her and wash her and she sat back in her seat and simply said: "Okay." Natasha gunned the car and made her way to the fast food chain. They smiled at each other. They both relaxed.

During and after this episode, Natasha reflected now as she sat applying her makeup; she had, as usual, felt fiercely protective of her daughter. But, somehow, and this was the strange thing, the whole experience had markedly changed Fontana – and not in the negative as Natasha would have expected. She had more of an *appreciation* for life now, if Natasha could call it that. A subtleness that had seeped into her. She was less demanding. More grateful, in her own little "Fontana" way. Natasha chuckled to herself. *We are all born with our inherent spirits aren't we? From the moment we take our first breaths. Experiences shape our lives; but our spirits, our "essence" is there from the beginning.* She had seen it in her own child. That small spark that had now grown into the young woman that stood before her today.

And the *wise young woman* that she was had suggested that they ask Bobby to come up on stage with her tonight. And Natasha had agreed, thinking it a beautiful idea! Bobby there, to share with them their success. She listened to the faint bump and scrape and *toot* and *eek* from behind the wall and the one lone piano tone that ran out into the air as the roadies loaded the last of the equipment on stage, and the techs got the lighting set up and perfect, waiting for the sound check. Then the song.

Fontana walked into the dressing room then, requisite skinny jeans hugging her slim figure; long dark blonde hair hanging past her shoulders; startling Natasha out of her revelry.

"You okay, Mom??"

Natasha smiled, half to herself, half to Fontana, "I'm good, Hon, how 'bout you?"

"I'm good. Just wanted to check in on you, see how things were going."

Always thinking of someone else...she'll never change, Natasha shook her head to herself, "I was actually just thinking about your friend Claire...I miss her a little."

"Yeah, me too," Fontana paused, reflectively, for a moment, and then continued, a firmness in her voice, "but I think she's okay...I think she's going to be okay."

"Strange you never heard from her."

"I know...." Fontana paused again, looked down at her shoes "I think she had a hard time with 'goodbyes'." She fingered her locket.

"Remember when we went to talk to the principal at the school?"

"Yeah...." Fontana's voice trailed off as she stared at Natasha's face through the hazy glass of the lighted mirror; the round, glowing bulbs exaggerating every flaw and line on her mother's face; yet at the same time washing it out. The duality was fascinating and she kept staring as she continued, "Yeah...I never liked him...."

"Me neither." Natasha scrunched up her nose and then relaxed as she applied powdered blush to her powdered face.

"So, here we are...." Natasha said with a sigh.

"Yep," Fontana replied. Short hesitation and then a breath; "I love you, Mom."

"I love you too, Sweetheart." Natasha closed her eyes for a moment, then opened them; one strong tear lodging in her throat. "You better go out and get your seat, we're going to start soon." She looked clearly and intently at Fontana. And then Fontana turned around and quietly left the dressing room.

Natasha bowed her head then. She did not pray, it was not her style. But she silently thanked God or whoever it was that watched over them for the privileges she had been given. And she thanked Bobby. For being. That was all.

CHAPTER FORTY-SIX

S HE DIED STANDING UP THAT DAY. The pools of light like blood around her feet. Illuminating the edges. The crowd a dull roar in her ears. A thud to the brain. Her heart beating out the last bits of her tattered past.

She closed her eyes. She opened them again. She looked out from her perch on the stage. A small figure. Dark brown hair cascading down her back. Pale skin reflecting the strobe that surrounded her. She looked to her left. Her knees still weak and slightly wobbly. And there he sat, behind his piano. The light reflecting amber against his dark skin. Gray curls neatly combed upon his head. Slight smile on his lips. Peace. Reassurance. He winked at her. A wink only the two of them can see. And with that wink he pushes her on – and she steps forward, towards the crowd. She leans into them and moves the microphone she has been holding towards her lips and places them gently over it, almost touching it. She opens her eyes. And begins to sing.

God...

A soft, gentle note fills the crowded arena. Softer at first and then growing louder; fuller, filling the stadium with that one note, filling it and feeding it.

bless...

The Coliseum is silent. As if all are afraid to take a breath; afraid to break the spell of that single note, which hangs on the air and then cascades down upon them.

America...

Unintentionally they are roaring and clapping.

Land that I love; Stand beside her, and guide her, through the night with a light from above...

The silence is broken. The song has begun.

Bobby Sharp – Yoshi's, 2006
Photo credit: Amy Tolbert

EPILOGUE

Silence.
Is all she heard.
And she turned
    to look behind
    her.
But no one was
    there
No sweet smile.
No blank stare.

No angel
    abiding
To care for
    her.

And she hadn't
    even realized
    he had been
    doing it!

She thought
    she had been
    caring for

UNCHAIN MY HEART

him.

In his elderly
   frailty.

But no,
He was a
   tricky and
   wise one

That Bobby.

He had been
   caring for her.

And he had
bestowed his
gifts upon
her

Leaving her
all he had
In the last
lingering breaths
of his soul

And he had shared
   his dreams
With his songs.

And he had
   given back
   to her —
   Her *dreams*

Dreams she had
    not known
    She'd lost.

A lust for
    life.

Inserted into
    her

So carefully.

Without her
    even noticing.

How funny

She laughed
    to herself.

And looked at
    her teenage
    daughter

Now fifteen.

And beautiful.

And completely
Unaware
of her beauty.

Natasha
    smiled.

UNCHAIN MY HEART

And silently
    thanked
    Bobby.

For the life
    he had lived

For the life
    he had
    given

And for the
    beautiful
    songs

He had written.

EPILOGUE

Hang down your head boy
    and pray for forgiveness.
Your humbleness lays upon
    the tilt of your hat.

Central Park looms – waiting
quietly in the distance.
The ashes of a past lying
    silently
    under a tree.
Never to disagree
With your decisions

Hang down your head, boy
    and pray for
    peace.
You are down on your knees,
I see
And aching with resistance.

Mother's words
    sharp
    in the distance.
A rock
Stern and never-moving

New York only a misty
    memory, now.
A past to be recounted
    in calm, cool glory.

Leaden heart lifted
with deadened finger.
Memory
    tinged with regret

UNCHAIN MY HEART

Woman
The strength
    of the World
Within the *palm of her hand*

She looks down now,
And flicks her eyes to the left
Banal beauty.
Calling to you, "Bobby!"
Smile lights beatific face
Features content
Eva
Eva
"Everybody loved Eva."

The memories are still;
    haunting.
Shifting within your soul
Even now
Turning over, like a baby in
    a womb.
Content, but *moving*.

A soul that sits *through* you.
Soft soul *compels* you
In all your compulsion
And even truth.

*She is what moved you
    to write.*
Words into songs
The darkness only
    temporary.
A response to the
    inadequacies

of hate
and disappointment.

Forlorn father —
died long before
You buried him under
    that tree
In Central Park.

Expiration with the
    hit
    across your face
Drink stinking.

And here you stand
    age 83.
Heritage; pride
    tucked beneath
    fine gray
Mother;
gone so long ago
peacefully.

She left
you

Your:
    Warmth;
    Generosity
    of spirit
    And your Honesty

Integrity that weaves
    the fabric of your
    existence.
Humor flashing behind

golden eyes.
Cleanliness
Nobleness
Humbleness
Knowledge
Wisdom
Life.

These things she
    left behind
With the note
    you found
    in her pocket

Picture painted
hung on the wall
Hands folded in soft
    lap —
Glance to the left —
Serendipitously
Caramel colored skin
    oozing forth from
    black canvas

Beauty —
Beauty —
Banal beauty...

You have unchained my heart
She says to you —
And I have set you free —

AUTHOR'S NOTE

This novel is based on a true story. After reading an article by Don Heckman in the Calendar section of the Los Angeles Times in 2004, I was compelled to contact Bobby Sharp and Natasha Miller and interviewed them at length. This is what makes up the basis of the novel. Some characters and situations have been fictionalized.

Many hours of research were done on the burgeoning jazz and music movement in Harlem and in California from the 1930's to present. The letter from Bobby's mother was the actual letter Eva left for Bobby as he read it to me. The *Disc Derby* piece is the article that appeared in 1959. The snapshots of Harlem and the cover photo were taken by Bobby and are from his private collection. The attached notes of description are his original notes as he sent them to me.

Sadly, on January 29, 2013, Bobby Sharp passed from this earth. He was a great gift and light to this world and I feel privileged to have had the chance to get to know him. He had a great generosity of spirit and an openness to life that belied all he had been through. He shared with me his belief that life itself was all there was, and that what we did here on earth was what mattered. I know he will be missed by many.

I want to thank Natasha Miller and Bobby Sharp for sharing their wonderful story with me. Thank you. You have been a blessing.

Following is a short Bibliography of some of my sources:

BIBLIOGRAPHY

Ward, Geoffrey C. and Burns, Ken. *Jazz a History of America's Music*. Alfred A Knopf, 2000

Tanner Paul O.W. and Gerow Maurice. *A Study of Jazz*. Wm. C. Brown Company, 1973

Brown, Ruth with Yule, Andrew. *Miss Rhythm The Autobiography of Ruth Brown, Rhythm and Blues Legend*. Penguin, 1996

Various. *Seeing Jazz Artists and Writers on Jazz*. Chronicle Books, 1997

Anderson, Jervis. *This Was Harlem*. Farrar Straus Giroux, 1981

Gawande, Atul. *The Score*. Annals of Medicine, The New Yorker, October 9, 2006

Selvin, Joel. *Bobby's Forsaken Catalog of Songs Became "Unchained" by Twist of Fate*. The Chronicle, April 19, 2004

Various. *Savoy Ballroom 1926-1958*. www.savoyplaque.org

Various. *Aaron Douglas*. Wikipedia, http://en.wikipeida.org/wiki/Aaoro_Douglas

> References:
> "Douglas, Aaron". *American National Biography*. New York: Oxford University Press, 1999 6:789-790.

Kirschke, Amy Hellene. *Aaron Douglas Art, Race, and the Harlem Renaissance.* Jackson, Miss.: University Press of Mississippi, 1995

Myers, Aaron. "Douglas, Aaron." *Microsoft Encarta Reference Library 2002.* CD-ROM. 2002 ed.

Schoener, Allon. *Harlem on My Mind, Cultural Capital of Black America 1900-1968*, Random House, 1968

Gold, Scott. *Singing a Sadder Song in South L.A.; The Landmark Dunbar Hotel, Once a Spot for Jazz Greats, Has Fallen Into Debt and Disrepair.* Los Angeles Times, October 10, 2008

Watson, Steven. *The Harlem Renaissance.* Excerpts: pages 124-144, http://xroads.virginia.edu/~UG97/blues/watson.html

Wadhams, Nick, Associated Press Writer. *Architectural Historian Fights for Harlem's Treasures — Tryi.* Wired New York.com August 8, 2003, http://www.wirednewyorl.com/forum/archive/index.php/t-3363.html

Avent, Nicole; Jones, Quincy. *Q and Me.* Los Angeles Times Magazine, April 5, 2009

Baldwin, James. *Go Tell It on the Mountain.* Bantam Dell, 1958

Baldwin, James. *Blues for Mr. Charlie.* Dial Press — 1964

Heckman, Don. *Two Lives, Reclaimed.* Los Angeles Times, September 11, 2004

ACKNOWLEDGMENTS

I wish to thank my husband for his love, caring and support; my son for being the wonderful light that he is; Elaine Trebek-Kares for her words of wisdom and encouragement; and Tony Gumina for his courage and inspiration.

And lastly, thank you God.